The Golden Road

GREAT TALES OF
FANTASY AND THE
SUPERNATURAL

Edited by Damon Knight

SIMON AND SCHUSTER NEW YORK

ACKNOWLEDGMENTS

The author wishes to thank the following for permission to reprint previously published materials. Every effort has been made to locate all persons having any rights or interests in the stories appearing in this book. If any appropriate acknowledgments have been inadvertently omitted, they will be included in all future printings of the book upon written notification to the publisher.

"Are You Too Late or Was I Too Early" by John Collier, copyright 1951 by John Collier. Reprinted from *The New Yorker* by permission of Harold Matson Company, Inc.

"Entire and Perfect Chrysolite" by R. A. Lafferty, copyright © 1970 by Damon Knight. Reprinted from *Orbit 6* by permission of Virginia Kidd.

"Jenny with Wings" by Kate Wilhelm, copyright © 1963 by Kate Wilhelm. Reprinted from *The Mile-Long Spaceship* by permission of the author.

"The Words of Guru" by C. M. Kornbluth, copyright 1941 by Albing Publications. Reprinted from *Stirring Science Stories* by permission of Robert P. Mills, Ltd.

"Postpaid to Paradise" by Robert Arthur, copyright 1940 by the Frank A. Munsey Company. Reprinted from *Argosy* by permission of the author's estate.

"Will You Wait?" by Alfred Bester, copyright © 1959 by Mercury Press, Inc. Reprinted from *Fantasy & Science Fiction* by permission of the author.

"The King of the Cats" by Stephen Vincent Benét, from *The Selected Works of Stephen Vincent Benét,* published by Holt, Rinehart & Winston, Inc.; copyright 1938 by Stephen Vincent Benét, renewed © 1963 Thomas C. Benét, Stephanie B. Mahin and Rachel Benét Lewis. Reprinted by permission of Brandt & Brandt.

"The Word of Unbinding" by Ursula K. Le Guin, copyright © 1963 by Ziff-Davis Publishing Company, Inc. Reprinted from *Fantastic* by permission of Virginia Kidd.

"Magic, Inc." by Robert A. Heinlein, copyright 1940, 1950 by Robert A. Heinlein. Reprinted from *Unknown* (where it appeared as "The Devil Makes the Law") by permission of Lurton Blassingame.

"Anything Box" by Zenna Henderson, copyright © 1956 by Mercury Press, Inc. Reprinted from *Fantasy & Science Fiction* by permission of Collins-Knowlton-Wing, Inc.

"Artist Unknown" by Heywood Broun, copyright 1941 by Heywood Broun. Reprinted from *Collected Edition of Heywood Broun* by permission of Heywood Hale Broun.

"The Silence" by Venard McLaughlin, copyright 1941 by Albing Publications. Reprinted from *Stirring Science Stories.*

"The Dream Quest of Unknown Kadath" by H. P. Lovecraft, copyright 1939, 1943 by August Derleth and Donald Wandrei, © 1965 by August Derleth. Reprinted from *At the Mountains of Madness and Other Novels by H. P. Lovecraft* by permission of Arkham House.

"The Weeblies" by Algis Budrys, copyright 1953 by Future Publications. Reprinted from *Fantasy Fiction* by permission of the author.

"Not Long Before the End" by Larry Niven, copyright © 1969 by Mercury Press, Inc. Reprinted from *Fantasy & Science Fiction* by permission of the author.

 Published by Simon and Schuster, Rockefeller Center, 630 Fifth Avenue, New York, New York 10020.

First printing
SBN 671-21554-X
Library of Congress Catalog Card Number: 73-11541
Designed by Jack Jaget
Manufactured in the United States of America

Contents

We travel not for trafficking alone;
  By hotter winds our hearts are fanned:
For lust of knowing what should not be known
  We take the Golden Road to Samarkand.

JAMES ELROY FLECKER, *Hassan,*
ACT V, SCENE 2

Introduction

FANTASY in the modern sense had no existence until realistic fiction came into being in the nineteenth century. Before that, what we call fantasy was just the kind of thing that happened in stories and poems: I mean, of course, the doings of gods and demons, witches, goblins, enchanted princesses, ghosts and monsters. These were the kinds of things stories were *about*, and if you had tried to distinguish them from the topics of "straight" or "mainstream" stories as we do now, people would have given you funny looks. Even after the invention of realism, fantasy only suffered a loss of respectability; it didn't disappear—far from it. When I was a child, the first things my mother read to me and the first things I read to myself were stories about talking animals by Thornton W. Burgess and Kate Greenaway. Then, in the library, I discovered Andrew Lang's and the Grimm brothers' books of fairy tales, in well-thumbed editions that must have been printed around the turn of the century. They had blurry black-and-white illustrations that I loved much more than the bright drawings of H. J. Ford and Howard Pyle: the very darkness of them gave them an ambiguity and a touch of horror (epitomized, much later, by an illustration I found in a book of C. G. Jung's—a king sitting on his throne with his mouth incredibly agape, about to swallow the young man who stands before him). The tales of people who ventured into underground passages, or fell down wells, and found another world there with its own skies and people seemed to me to have a peculiar and unaccountable rightness.

I kept on looking for such stories after I had run out of fairy tales (but not outgrown them—I read them still). The notion that there are other places, not to be reached in ordinary ways, is extraordinarily persistent. I found it in Poe and Ambrose Bierce, and in Wells and Kipling.

I'm trying to remember when I first read about ghosts. It must have been early, because I remember an interminable Halloween tale I told in the second grade (it really was going on forever, because I had no idea of plot and was just making up one thing after another; the teacher had to suggest that I stop now, please). My first monster must have been the one in "Beauty and the Beast." There were spooky stories in the magazine *Weird Tales,* but I got at best a cloudy idea of what they were about, and concluded I was not old enough yet; it was not until years later that I realized the stories were dull and badly written. As for the afterlife, and the devil, and miracles, I was a religious child up until the age of seven or eight, and must have found these first of all in the Bible.

I believed absolutely in all these things at one time or another; for example, I once asked my father to bring me home a book about magic from the library, intending to learn spells that would enable me to turn flowerpots into bicycles, etc. What he brought me was a book about magic tricks, but that was so fascinating in its own way that I got over my disappointment almost immediately. As another example of my credulity let me mention that I was convinced I could fly if I could only get properly started: I used to jump as high as I could and then try to jump again before I came down, but never succeeded in being quick enough. (When I revealed this recently to my youngest child, who is six, he collapsed with laughter.)

In fact, I still believe in most of these things, with certain qualifications. I have given up hoping to fly by an act of will (or to get to Mars by yearning toward it, as John Carter did); I no longer believe in heaven or hell; but I remain convinced that there are realms beyond our knowledge, and that to explore them would be the most fascinating and dangerous thing in the world.

The stories in this book have been chosen because they gave me delicious glimpses into certain of these realms—the kingdom of pure evil, for example, in Arthur Machen's "The White People," or the land beyond the veil of sleep, in H. P. Lovecraft's "The Dream Quest of Unknown Kadath." There are ghosts here, and monsters (although if you are expecting a conventional monster when you read Kate Wilhelm's "Jenny With Wings," you will be pleasantly surprised), and magic, both white and black, and witchcraft, and several interviews with the devil. Some of these stories are meant to be taken with absolute seriousness, others to make you laugh—but to wonder while you laugh.

DAMON KNIGHT

Madeira Beach, Florida
February 13, 1973

Are You Too Late or Was I Too Early

BY JOHN COLLIER

IN THE country I accept the normal and traditional routine, doing what every man does: rising early, eating when I should, turning up my coat collar when it rains. I see the reason for it, and shave at the same hour every morning.

Not so in town. When I live in town I feel no impulse in the starling migrations of the rush hours. There is no tide, in any submarine cave, anywhere, that is not more to me than the inflow and outflow at the cold mouths of offices or the hot mouths of restaurants. I find no growth in time, no need for rain, no sense in sobriety, no joy in drinking, no point in paying, no plan in living. I exist, in this alien labyrinth, like an insect among men, or a man in a city of the ants.

I despise the inconsiderable superiority of the glum day over the starless night. My curtains are always drawn; I sleep when my eyes close, eat when I remember to, and read and smoke without ceasing, allowing my soul to leave my wastrel and untended carcass, and seldom do I question it when it returns.

My chambers are in the stoniest of the Inns of Court. I keep no servant here, for I mean always to go back to the country within the week, though sometimes I stay for months, or . . . I don't know how long. I supply myself with immense stocks of cigarettes, and such food as I happen to remember, so that I shall have no reason to return from the landscapes of Saturn or the undescribed gardens of Turgenev in order to go out into the streets.

My fingers are horribly blistered by the cigarettes that burn down between them while still I walk in the company of women with the heads of cats. Nothing seems strange to me when I wake from such reveries unless I part the curtains and look out into the Square. Sometimes I have to press my hands under my heart to resume the breathing that I have entirely forgotten.

I was constantly ambushed and defeated in I forget what journeys, or what loves, or where, by the fullness of a saucer in which a hand of mine failed to find room to crush out its cigarettes. Habit, which arranges these things, demanded some other receptacle. I rose, holding my thoughts as one holds a brimming glass, and was moved into the bathroom, drawn by the vague memory of a soap dish, which lay stranded like an empty shell on the empty beaches of a blank mind. But, swallowed by God knows what high-reaching wave, that shell was gone, and my reviving eyes, straying at first aimlessly, soon called me all back again, poor Crusoe! to regard on the cork mat a new, wet, glistening imprint of a naked foot.

It was not long before I assured myself that I was dry, dressed in my pajamas and slippers, and that I was not clean. Moreover, this foot, the prints of whose toes were as round as graded pearls, was neither long, like that of a man, nor hideous, like that of a bear; it was not my own. It was that of a woman, a nymph, a new-risen Venus. I conceived that my wandering spirit had brought me back a companion from some diviner sea's edge, and some more fortunate shell.

I drank up this moist footprint with my hot eyes; it dried as I looked upon it. It was not the air took it, but I; I had it for my own. I examined it for days and nights, building, upon its graceful rotundities, arched insteps, ankles equally graceful, and calves proportionately round. I deduced knees, haunches, breasts, shoulders, arms, plump hands and pointed fingers, full neck, small head, and the long curl, like the curve when the wave breaks, of the green-gold hair.

Where there falls one footprint there must fall the next; I had no doubt I should soon be vouchsafed the dull gleam of her hair. For this, I at once became ravenous, and slunk restlessly from room to room.

I noticed, with half-unconscious approval, that even the neglected furnishings seemed responsive to the goddess, and stood clean and tidy as onlookers at a holiday. The carpet, as if she were Persephone instead of Venus, bloomed with new flowers beneath her invisible feet. The sun shone through the open window, and warm airs entered. At what moment had I swept back the curtains and extended this invitation to sun and air? Perhaps she had done so herself. It was, however, impossible to attend to such lovely trifles. I desired the gleam of her hair.

"Forgive me for having rejoiced in the pallor of the dead! Forgive me for having conversed with women who smelled like lions! Show me your hair!"

I was devoured by a cruel nostalgia for this being who was always with me. "Supposing," I thought, waking in my strangely fresh bed, "supposing she appeared terrifyingly in the darkness, white as marble, and as cold!" At that moment I felt an intermittent warmth on my cheek, and knew that she breathed beside me.

There was nothing to clasp but the empty air. For days I moved to and fro, my blood howling in me like a dog that bays the moon. "There is nothing but the empty air."

I persuaded myself that this was nonsense. I had seen the trace of beauty, and felt the warmth of life. Gradually one sense after another would be refracted on this divine invisibility, till she stood outlined like a creature of crystal, and then as one of flesh and blood. As soon as I was well persuaded, I saw her breath dimming upon a mirror.

I saw some flowers, which had appeared, part their petals as she bent her face to them. Hurrying there, I smelled, not the flowers, but her hair.

I threw myself down, and lay like a dog across the threshold, where, once or twice in the day, I might feel the light breeze of her passing. I was aware of the movement of her body, or an eddy in the light where she moved; I was aware of the beating of her heart.

Sometimes, as if out of the corner of my eye, I saw, or

thought I saw, not her bright flesh, but the light on her flesh, which vanished as I widened my eyes upon it.

I knew where she moved, and how she moved, but I was destroyed by a doubt, for she did not move toward me. Could there be some other existence, to which she was more responsive, some existence less tangible than her own? Or was she my unwilling prisoner here? Were those movements, of which I was not the object, the movements of one who longed only to escape?

It was impossible to tell. I thought I might know everything if only I could hear her voice. Perhaps she could hear mine.

I said to her, day and night, "Speak to me. Let me hear you. Tell me you have forgiven me. Tell me you are here forever. Tell me you are mine." Day and night I listened for her answer.

I waited in that unutterable silence, as one who, in a darkness equally profound, might await the arrival of a gleam of light from a star in whose existence he had good reason to believe. In the end, when I had ceased to hope or believe, I became aware of a sound—or something as near to a sound as the light on her cheek was near to the flesh of her cheek.

Now, living only in my eardrum, not moving, not breathing, I waited. This ghost of a sound increased: it passed through infinite gradations of rarity. It was like the sound in the second before the rain; it was like the fluttering of wings, the confused words of water; it was like words blown away in the wind; like words in a foreign tongue; it grew more distinct, closer.

Sometimes my hearing failed me, exactly as one's sight fails, dimmed suddenly by tears, when one is about to see the face one has always loved, after an ineffable absence. Or she would fall silent, and then I was like one who follows the sound of a brook, and loses it under the muffling trees, or under the ground. But I found it again, and each time it was clearer and stronger. I was able to distinguish words; I heard the word "love," I heard the word "happy."

I heard, in a full opening of the sense, the delicate intake of her breath, the very sound of the parting of her lips. She was about to speak again.

Each syllable was as clear as a bell. She said, "Oh, it's perfect. It's so quiet for Harry's work. Guess how we were lucky enough to get it! The previous tenant was found dead in his chair, and they actually say it's haunted."

Entire and Perfect Chrysolite

BY R. A. LAFFERTY

Having achieved perfection, we feel a slight unease. From our height we feel impelled to look down. We make our own place and there is nothing below us; but in our imagination there are depths and animals below us. To look down breeds cultishness.

There are the cults of the further lands and the further people. The Irish and Americans and Africans are respectable philosophical and industrial parties, but the cultishness is something beyond. Any addition to the world would mar the perfect world which is the perfect thought of the Maker. Were there an Africa indeed, were there an Ireland, were there an America or an Atlantis, were there Indies, then we would be other than we are. The tripartite unity that is the ecumene would be broken; the habitable world-island, the single eye in the head that is the world-globe would be voided.

There are those who say that our rational and perfect world should steep itself in this great unconscious geography of the under-mind, in the outré fauna and the incredible continents of the tortured imagination and of black legends. They pretend that this would give us depth.

We do not want depth. We want height. Let us seal off the under things of the under-mind, and exalt ourselves! And our unease will pass.

—AUDIFAX O'HANLON, *Exaltation Philosophy*

THE *True Believer* was sailing offshore in an easterly direction in the latitude of fifteen degrees north and the longitude of twenty-four degrees east. To the north of the coasting ship was the beautiful Cinnamon Coast of Libya with its wonderful beaches and remarkable hotels tawny in the distance. To the east and south and west were the white-topped waves that went on forever and ever. The *True Believer* sailed along the southernmost edge of the ecumene, the habitable and inhabited world.

August Shackleton was drinking Roman Bomb out of a pot-bellied bottle and yelping happily as he handled the "wheel" of the *True Believer*.

"It's a kids' thing to do," he yipped, "but there were never such beautiful waters to do it in. We try to call in outer spirits. We try to call up inner spirits and lands. It's a children's antic. Why do we do it, Boyle, other than for the fun of it?"

"Should there be another reason, Shackleton? Well, there is, but we go about it awkwardly and without knowing what we're doing. The thing about humans (which nobody apparently wishes to notice) is that we're a species which has never had an adult culture. We feel that lack more and more as we become truly adult in other ways. It grows tedious to stretch out a childhood forever. The easy enjoyments, the easy rationality, the easy governments and sciences are really childish things. We master them while we are yet children, and we look beyond. There isn't anything beyond the childishness, Shackleton. We must find a deeper view somehow. We are looking for that something deeper here."

"What? By going on a lark that is childish even to children, Boyle? I was ashamed before my sons when I confessed on what sort of diversion I was going. First there were the séances that we indulged in. If we raised any spirits there, they were certainly childish ones. And now we're on this voyage on the *True Believer*. We're looking for the geographical home of certain collective unconscious images! Why shouldn't the children hoot at us? Ah well, let us not be too ashamed. It's colorful and stimulating fun, but it isn't adult."

The other four members of the party, Sebastian Linter and the three wives, Justina Shackleton, Luna Boyle, and Mint-green Linter, were swimming in the blue ocean. The *True*

Believer was coasting very slowly and the four swimmers were clipped to outrigger towlines.

"There's something wrong with the water!" Justina Shackleton suddenly called up to her husband. "There's weeds in it, and there shouldn't be. There's reeds in it, and swamp grasses. There's mud. And there's green slime!"

"You're out of your lovely head, lovely," Shackleton called back. "It's all clear blue water off a sand coast. I can see fish twenty meters down. It's clear."

"I tell you it's full of green slime!" Justina called back. "It's so thick and heavy that it almost tears me away from the line. And the insects are so fierce that I have to stay submerged."

But they were off the Cinnamon Coast of Libya. They could smell the warm sand and the watered gardens ashore. There was no mud, there was no slime, there were no insects off the Cinnamon Coast ever. It was all clear and bright as living, moving glass.

Sebastian Linter had been swimming on the seaward side of the ship. Now he came up ropes to the open deck of the ship, and he was bleeding.

"It *is* thick, Shackleton," he panted. "It's full of snags and it's dangerous. And that fanged hog could have killed me. Get the rest of them out of the water!"

"Linter, you can see for yourself that it is clear everywhere. Clear, and of sufficient depth, and serene."

"Sure, I see that it is, Shackleton. Only it isn't. What we are looking for has already begun. The illusion has already happened to all senses except sight. Stuff it, Shackleton! Get them out of the water! The snakes or the crocs will get them; the animals threshing around in the mud will get them; and if they try to climb up onto the shore, the beasts there will break them up and tear them to pieces."

"Linter, we're two thousand meters offshore and everything is clear. But you are disturbed. So am I. The ship just grounded, and it's fifty meters deep here. All right, everyone! I order everybody except my wife to come out of the water! I request that she come out. I am unable to order her to do anything."

The other two women, Luna Boyle and Mintgreen Linter, came out of the water. And Justina Shackleton did not.

"In a while, August, in a while I'll come," Justina called up to the ship. "I'm in the middle of a puzzle here and I want to study it some more. August, can a hallucination snap you in two? He sure is making the motions."

"I don't know, lovely," August Shackleton called back to her doubtfully.

Luna Boyle and Mintgreen Linter had come out of the ocean up the ropes. Luna was covered with green slime and was bleeding variously. Mintgreen was covered with weeds and mud, and her feet and hands were torn. And she hobbled with pain.

"Is your foot broken, darling?" Sebastian Linter asked her with almost concern. "But of course it is all illusion."

"I have the illusion that my foot is broken," Mintgreen sniffled, "and I have the illusion that I am in very great pain. Bleeding blubberfish, I wish it were real! It couldn't really hurt this much."

"Oh elephant hokey!" Boyle stormed. "These illusions are nonsense. There can't be such an ambient creeping around us. We're not experiencing anything."

"Yes, we are, Boyle," Shackleton said nervously. "And your expression is an odd one at this moment. For the elephant was historical in the India that is, was fantastic in the further India that is fantastic, and is still more fanciful in its African contingency. In a moment we will try to conjure up the African elephant which is twice the mass of the historical Indian elephant. The ship is dragging badly now and might even break up if this continues, but the faro shows no physical contact. All right, the five of us on deck will put our heads together for this. You lend us a head too, Justina!"

"Take it, take my head. I'm about to let that jawful snapper have my body anyhow. August, this stuff is real! Don't tell me I imagine that smell."

"We will all try to imagine that smell, and other things," August Shackleton stated as he uncorked another bottle of Roman Bomb. In the visible world there was still the Cinnamon Coast of Libya, and the blue oceans going on forever. But in another visible world, completely unrelated to the first and occupying absolutely different space (but both occupying total space), were the green swamps of Africa, the sedgy shores going sometimes back into rain forests and sometimes into savannas, the moon mountains rising behind them, the air sometimes heavy with mist and sometimes clear with scalding light, the fifty levels of noises, the hundred levels of colors.

"The ambient is forming nicely even before we start," Shackleton purred. Some of them drank Roman Bomb and some of them Green Canary as they readied themselves for the psychic adventure.

"We begin the conjure," Shackleton said, "and the conjure begins with words. Our little group has been involved with several sorts of investigations, foolish ones perhaps, to discover whether there are (or more importantly, to be sure that there are not) physical areas and creatures beyond those of the closed ecumene. We have gone on knobknockers, we have held séances. The séances in particular were grotesque, and I believe we were all uneasy and guilty about them. Our Faith forbids us to evoke spirits. But where does it forbid us to evoke geographies?"

"Ease up a little on the evoking!" Justina shrilled up to them. "The snapper just took me off at the left ankle. I pray he doesn't like my taste."

"It has been a mystery for centuries," said August (somewhat disturbed by his wife's vulgar outburst from the ocean), "that out of the folk unconscious there should well ideas of continents that are not in the world, continents with a highly imaginary flora and fauna, continents with highly imaginary people. It is a further mystery that these psychic continents and islands should be given bearings, and that apparently sane persons have claimed to visit them. The deepest mystery of all is Africa. Africa, in Roman days, was a subdivision of Mauritania, which was a subdivision of Libya, one of the three parts of the world. And yet the entire coast of Libya has been mapped correctly for three thousand years, and there is no Africa beyond, either appended or separate. We prove the nonsense of it by sailing in clear ocean through the middle of that pretended continent."

"We prove the nonsense further by getting our ship mired in a swamp in the middle of that imaginary continent and seeing that continent begin to form about it," said Boyle. And his Green Canary tasted funny to him. There was a squalling pungency in the air and something hair-raisingly foreign in the taste of the drink.

"This is all like something out of Carlo Forte," Linter laughed unsteadily.

"The continental ambient forms about us," said Shackleton. "Now we will evoke the creatures. First let us conjure the great animals, the rhinoceros, the lion, the leopard, the elephant, which all have Asian counterparts; but these of the contingent Africa are to be half again or twice the size, and incomparably fierce."

"We conjure them, we conjure them," they all chanted, and the conjured creatures appeared mistily.

"We conjure the hippopotamus, the water behemoth, with its great comical bulk, its muzzle like a scoop-shovel, and its eyes standing up like big balls—"

"Stop it, August!" Justina Shackleton shrieked from the water. "I don't know whether hippo is playful or not, but he's going to crush me in a minute."

"Come out of the water, Justina!" August ordered sternly.

"I will not. There isn't any ship left to come out to. You're all sitting on a big slippery broken tree out over the water, and the snappers and boas are coming very near your legs and necks."

"Yes, I suppose so, one way of looking at it," August said. "Now everybody conjure the animals that are compounded out of grisly humor—the giraffe with a neck alone that is longer than a horse, and the zebra which is a horse in a clown suit."

"We conjure them, we conjure them," they all chanted.

"The zebra isn't as funny as I thought it would be," Boyle complained. "Nothing is as funny as I thought it would be."

"Conjure the great snake that is a thousand times heavier than other snakes, that can swallow a wild ass," Shackleton gave them the lead.

"We conjure it, we conjure it," they all chanted.

"August, it's over your head, reaching down out of the giant mimosa tree," Justina screamed warning from the swamp. "There's ten meters of it reaching down for you."

"Conjure the crocodile," Shackleton intoned. "Not the little crocodile of the River of Egypt, but the big crocodile of deeper Africa that is able to swallow a cow."

"We conjure it, we imagine it, we evoke it, and the swamps and estuaries in which it lives," they all chanted.

"Easy on that one," Justina shrilled. "He's been taking me by little pieces. Now he's taking me by big pieces."

"Conjure the ostrich," Shackleton intoned, "the bird that is a thousand times as heavy as other birds, that stands a meter taller than man, that kicks like a mule, the bird that is too heavy to fly. I wonder what delirium first invented such a wildlife as Africa's anyhow?"

"We conjure it, we conjure it," they chanted.

"Conjure the great walking monkey that is three times as heavy as a man," August intoned. "Conjure a somewhat smaller one, two thirds the size of man, that grins and gibbers and understands speech, that could speak if he wished."

"We conjure them, we conjure them."

"Conjure the third of the large monkeys that is dog-faced and purple of arse."

"We conjure it, we conjure it, but it belongs in a comic strip."

"Conjure the gentle monster, the okapi, that is made out of pieces of the antelope and camel and contingent giraffe and which likewise wears a striped clown suit."

"We conjure it, we conjure it."

"Conjure the multitudinous antelopes, koodoo, nyala, hartebeest, oryx, bongo, klipspringer, gemsbok, all so out of keeping with a warm country, all such grotesque takeoffs of the little alpine antelope."

"We conjure them, we conjure them."

"Conjure the buffalo that is greater than all other buffalo or cattle, that has horns as wide as a shield. Conjure the quagga. I forget its pretended appearance, but it cannot be ordinary."

"We conjure them, we conjure them."

"We come to the top of it all! Conjure the most anthropomorphic group in the entire unconscious: men indeed, who are black as midnight in a hazel grove, who are long of ankle and metatarsus and lower limb so they can run and leap uncommonly, who have crumpled hair and are massive of feature. Conjure another variety that are only half as tall as men. Conjure a third sort that are short of stature and prodigious of hips."

"We conjure them, we conjure them," they all chanted. "They are the caricatures from the beginning."

"But can all these animals appear at one time?" Boyle protested. "Even on a contingent continent dredged out of the folk unconscious there would be varieties of climates and land-forms. All would not be together."

"This is rhapsody, this is panorama, this is Africa," said Luna Boyle.

And they were all totally in the middle of Africa, on a slippery bole of a broken tree that teetered over a green swamp. And the animals were around them in the rain forests and the savannas, on the shore, and in the green swamp. And a man black as midnight was there, his face broken with emotion.

Justina Shackleton screamed horribly as the crocodile sliced her in two. She still screamed from inside the gulping beast as one might scream underwater.

The ecumene, the world island, has the shape of an egg 110° from East to West and 45° from North to South. It is scored into three parts, Europa, Asia, and Libya. It is scored by the incursing sea, Europa from Asia by the Pontus and the Hyrcanum Seas, Asia from Libya by the Persian Sea, and Libya from Europa by the Tyrrhenian and Ionian Seas (the Mediterranean Complex). The most westerly place in the world is Coruna in Iberia or Spain, the most northerly is Kharkovsk in Scythia or Russia, the most easterly is Sining in Han or China, and the most southerly is the Cinnamon Coast of Libya.

The first chart of the world, that of Eratosthenes, was thus, and it was perfect. Whether he had it from primitive revelation or from early exploration, it was correct except in minor detail. Though Britain seems to have been charted as an island rather than a peninsula, this may be the error of an early copyist. A Britain unjoined to the Main would shrivel, as a branch hewed from a tree will shrivel and die. There are no viable islands.

All islands fade and drift and disappear. Sometimes they

reappear briefly, but there is no life in them. The juice of life flows through the continent only. It is the ONE LAND, THE LIVING AND HOLY LAND, THE ENTIRE AND PERFECT JEWEL.

Thus, Ireland is seen sometimes, or Hy-Brasil, or the American rock-lands; but they are not always seen in the same places, and they do not always have the same appearances. They have not life nor reality.

The secret geographies and histories of the American Society and the Atlantis Society and such are esoteric lodge-group things, symbolic and murky, forms for the initiated; they contain analogs, and not realities.

The ecumene must grow, of course, but it grows inwardly in intensity and meaning; its form cannot change. The form is determined from the beginning, just as the form of a man is determined before he is born. A man does not grow by adding more limbs or heads. That the ecumene should grow appendages would be as grotesque as a man growing a tail.

—Diogenes Pontifex, *World as Perfection*

August Shackleton guffawed nervously when his wife was sliced in two, and the half of her swallowed by the crocodile; and his hand that held the Roman Bomb trembled. Indeed, there was something unnerving about the whole thing. That cut-off screaming of Justina Shackleton had something shocking and unpleasant about it.

Justina had once gone hysterical at a séance when the ghosts and appearances had been more or less conventional, but August was never sure just how sincere her hysteria was. Another time she had disappeared for several days after a séance, from a locked room, and had come back with a roguish story about being in spiritland. She was a high-strung clown with a sense of the outrageous, and this present business of being chomped in two was typical of her creations.

And suddenly they were all explosively creative, each one's subjective patterns intermingling with those of the others to produce howling chaos. What had been the ship the *True Believer*, what had been the slippery overhanging bole, had now come dangerously down into the swamp. They all wanted a closer look.

There was screaming and trumpeting, there was color and surge and threshing mass. The crocodile bellowed as a bull might, not at all as Shackleton believed that a croc should sound. But someone there had the idea that a crocodile should bellow like that, and that someone had imposed his ideate on the others. Unhorselike creatures whinnied, and vivid animals sobbed and gurgled.

"Go back up, go back up!" the black man was bleating. "You will all be killed here." His face was a true Mummers Night black-man mask; one of the party was imagining strongly in that stereotyped form. But the incongruous thing about the black man was that he was gibbering at them in French, in bad French as though it were his weak second language. Which one of them was linguist enough to invent such a black French on the edge of the moment? Luna Boyle, of course, but why had she put grotesque French into the mouth of a black man in contingent Africa?

"Go back up, go back up," the black man cried. He had an old rifle from the last century and he was shooting the crocodile with it.

"Hey, he's shooting Justina too," Mintgreen giggled too gaily. "Half of her is in the dragon thing. Oh, she will have some stories about this! She has the best imagination of all of us."

"Let's get her out and together again," Linter suggested. They were all shouting too loudly and too nervously. "She's missing the best part of it."

"Here, here, black man," Shackleton called. "Can you get the half of my wife out of that thing and put her together again!"

"Oh, white people, white people, this is real and this is death," the black man moaned in agony. "This is a closed wild area. You should not be here at all. However you have come here, whatever is the real form of that balk or tree on which you stand so dangerously, be gone from here if you can do it. You do not know how to live in this. White people, be gone! It is your lives!"

"One can command a fantasy," said August Shackleton. "Black man fantasy, I command you to get the half of my wife out of that dying creature and put her together again."

"Oh, white people on dope, I cannot do this," the black man moaned. "She is dead, and you joke and drink Green Bird and Bomb and hoot like demented children in a dream."

"We *are* in a dream, and you are *of* the dream," Shackleton said easily. "And we may experiment with our dream creatures. That is our purpose here. Here, catch a bottle of Roman Bomb!" and he threw it to the black man who caught it. "Drink it. I am interested in seeing whether a dream figure can make incursion on physical substance."

"Oh, white people on dope," the black man moaned. "The watering place is no place for you to be. You excite the animals and then they kill. When they are excited it is danger to me also who usually moves among them easily. I have had to kill the crocodile who is my friend. I do not want to kill others. I do not want more of you to be killed."

The black man was booted and jacketed quite in the manner of a hunting store outfitting, this possibly by the careful imagining of Boyle who loved hunting rig. The black Mummers Night mask was contorted in agony and apprehension, but the black man did drink the Roman Bomb nervously the while he begged them to be gone from that place.

"You will notice that the skull form is quite human and the bearing completely erect," Linter said. "You will notice also that he is less hairy than we are and is thick of lip, while the great ape to the left is more hairy and thin of lip. I had imagined them to be the same creature differently interpreted."

"No, you imagine them to be as they appear," Shackleton said. "It is your imagining of these two creatures that we are all watching."

"But notice the configuration of the tempora and the mandible," Linter protested. "Not what I expected."

"You are the only one of us who knows about tempora and mandible shape," said Shackleton. "I tell you that it is your own imagery. He is structured by you, given the conventional Mummers Night black mask by all of us, clothed by Boyle, and speeched by Luna Boyle. His production is our joint effort. Watch it, everyone! It becomes dangerous now, even explosive! Man, I'm getting as hysterical as my wife! The dream is so vivid that it has its hooks in me. Ah, it's a great investigative experience, but I doubt if I'll want to return to this particular experience again. Green perdition! But it does become dangerous! Watch out, everyone!"

Ah, it *had* become wild: a hooting and screaming and bawling wild Africa bedlam, a green and tawny dazzle of fast-moving color, pungent animal stench of fear and murder, acrid smell of human fear.

A lion defiled the watering place, striking down a horned buck in the muddy shallows and going muzzle-deep into the hot-colored gore. A hippo erupted out of the water, a behemoth from the depths. Giraffes erected like crazily articulated derricks and galloped ungainly through the boscage.

"Enough of this!" Mintgreen Linter, frightened, took the lead out of it, incanting: "That the noon-time nightmare pass! The crocodile-dragon and the behemoth."

"We abjure them, we abjure them," they all chanted in various voices.

"That the black man and the black ape pass, and all black things of the black-green land."

"We abjure them, we abjure them," they chanted. But the black man was already down under the feet and horns of a buffalo creature, dead, and his last rifle shot still echoing; he had tried to prevent the buffalo from upsetting the teetering bole and dumping all the white people into the murder swamp. The great ape was also gone, terrified, back to his high-grass savanna. Many of the other creatures had disappeared or become faint, and there was again the tang of salt water and of distant hot-sand beaches in the air.

"That the lion be gone who roars by day," Luna Boyle took up the incantation, "and the leopard who is Panther, the all-animal of grisly mythology. That the crushing snakes be gone, and the giant ostrich, and the horse in the clown suit."

"We abjure them all, we abjure them all," everyone chanted.

"That the *True Believer* form again beneath our feet in the structure we can see and know," August Shackleton incanted.

"We conjure it up, we conjure it up," they chanted, and the

True Believer rose again barely above the threshold of the senses.

"That the illicit continents fade, and all the baleful islands of our writhing under-minds!" Boyle blurted in some trepidation.

"We abjure them, we abjure them," they all chanted contritely. And the illicit Africa had now become quite fragile, while the Cinnamon Coast of South Libya began to form as behind green glass.

"Let us finish it! It lingers unhealthily!" Shackleton spoke loudly with resolve. "Let us drop our reservations! That we dabble no more in this particular illicitness! That we go no more hungering after strange geographies that are not of proper world! That we seal off the unsettling things inside us!"

"We seal them off, we seal them off," they chanted.

And it was finished.

They were on the *True Believer* sailing in an easterly direction off the Cinnamon Coast of Libya. To the north was that lovely coast with its wonderful beaches and remarkable hotels; to the south and east and west were the white-topped waves that went on forever and ever.

It was over with, but the incantation had shaken them all with the sheer psychic power of it.

"Justina isn't with us," Luna Boyle said nervously. "She isn't on the *True Believer* anywhere. Do you think something has happened to her? Will she come back?"

"Of course she'll come back," August Shackleton purred. "She was truant from a séance for two days once. Oh, she'll have some good ones when she does come back, and I'll rather enjoy the vacation from her. I love her, but a man married to an outré wife needs a rest from it sometimes."

"But look, look!" Luna Boyle cried. "Oh, she's impossible! She always did carry an antic too far. That's in bad taste."

The severed lower half of Justina Shackleton floated in the clear blue water beside the *True Believer*. It was bloodied and gruesome and was being attacked by slashing fishes.

"Oh, stop it, Justina!" August Shackleton called angrily. "What a woman! Ah, I see it now! We turn to land."

It was the opening to the Yacht Basin, the channel through the beach shallows to the fine harbor behind. They tacked, they turned, they nosed in toward the Cinnamon Coast of Libya.

The world was intact again, one whole and perfect jewel, lying wonderful to the north of them. And south was only great ocean and great equator and empty places of the undermind. The *True Believer* came to port passage with the perfect bright noon-time on all things.

Jenny with Wings

BY KATE WILHELM

"I AM sorry, Miss," the nurse said, "but the doctor sees patients only by appointment. I explained that when you called."

"You said he couldn't take me for three weeks," Jenny said. "I can't wait three weeks. This is an emergency."

There was disapproval in the eyes of the haughty nurse as she examined Jenny with a woman's unabashed appraisal. Jenny knew her hair was too long for this year's style, and her too-long stand-away coat might have passed several years ago, but was now hopelessly outdated. Also her face was hot and red from windburn. She met the nurse's eyes with impervious pride. The nurse's eyes flicked away first.

"If you'll leave your name and number," she suggested, "I'll try to work you in sooner. Today is out of the question; it's past hours now."

Jenny sniffed. "I aim to see the doctor now," she stated calmly.

The intercom buzzed and when the nurse depressed a button to answer it, Jenny darted past her to the door beyond her desk. "Dr. Lindquist," Jenny shouted at the startled man seated behind a desk. "You have to stay ten more minutes! I have to see you!" At her first movement the nurse had risen to follow her, and now she was advancing ominously. The doctor rose, signaled the nurse to halt, and walked around his desk. Jenny ran forward to clutch at his arm.

"I'm sorry, Doctor. I tried to stop her," the nurse said.

Jenny clung to him. "I called first. Honest I did, but she put me off for three weeks, and I can't wait. Please . . ."

"Young lady, I have an appointment in one hour." He started to disengage her hand. "If you can be here at eleven in the morning . . ."

Jenny glanced at the nurse; she drew herself to her tiptoes and whispered, "Doctor, I have wings!"

The doctor became immobile; even his breathing seemingly stopped for a second while his eyes searched her face. Before she knew what he was doing he put one hand on her back and ran it up and down. It all happened in less time than it took for the nurse to cross the room and take Jenny's arm.

"Never mind, never mind," the doctor said hastily. He half pushed the nurse out of his office, closing the door behind her. He turned to Jenny and reached for her coat, but she quickly backed away.

"Send the nurse home," she said. She backed toward the desk, prepared to dart through the other door into the hallway if he did not comply with her demands.

Dr. Lindquist hesitated only a moment and then walked carefully to the other side of the desk, keeping his eyes on her all the time. He pushed the intercom button and spoke into it. "It's all right, Rose. Go on home now." Without waiting for an answer he leaned over the desk and said, "Now, please take off the coat."

Jenny removed the coat and he couldn't repress his sigh of disappointment. She was wearing a cotton dress, fitted in the front, but fully draped in the back. Jenny watched his face closely; he looked strained, as if being forced to fight a tremendous battle. She fumbled with her belt buckle, lowering her eyes as she did so. "I—I have trouble with clothes," she mumbled. "I have to make them, and it's hard to find underthings . . ."

Impatiently he snorted and started to approach her. She backed away. "I am a medical doctor," he said deliberately, coming to a stop.

Slowly Jenny took off the belt and unbuttoned the dress, finally stepping out of it altogether. There was a wide rubber band just under her armpits and another at her waist. She removed them. Then she opened her wings.

"Ah!" The doctor gasped once and became silent. There was

an awed, unbelieving look on his face that rapidly gave way to delight. He walked around her slowly as she stretched first one wing and then the other. They were six feet long and after being confined, they always felt sore and tired. After stretching out the kinks she allowed them to settle and they stood out softly flared behind her.

"Ah," the doctor exclaimed again. "I didn't believe it. Even feeling them under the coat, I didn't believe it. Beautiful! Beautiful! Golden, tawny, like your hair. So soft . . ." She shuddered violently when she felt his hand.

"Are you hurt?" the doctor asked quickly, anxiously. "Have you injured them?"

She shook her head, feeling herself flushing under his scrutiny. "It's not that," she said in confusion.

"Oh," he said. Then, "Oh! Of course, a sheet. Here, let me. . . ."

Primly she took it from him and passed it under the wings, bringing the ends together in front. "A pin?" she asked. He supplied it.

"Here, sit down," he said, placing a straight chair by the desk. Jenny looked up quickly, but he was behind her again looking at the wings. Tentatively he reached out his hand, then looked at her. "May I?" She nodded and braced herself for the shock of his hands.

"What is your name?" he asked abruptly. "How have you kept it secret? Who sent you to me?" He passed his hand over his face and pulled a second chair opposite her. He straddled the chair with his arms crossed over the back, his chin resting on his arms.

Jenny felt more comfortable now, clothed in the sheet, with him facing her. She studied the doctor before answering. He was younger than she had expected. He was thick and solid looking with a certain stiffness in his posture, probably due to suppressed excitement, but even in his excitement he had realized a straight chair would be the only kind she could really sit in. She had seen excitement before when she opened her wings, but usually it overlay greed, or fear. With him there was no sign of either. She said, "Doctor, I really don't want to take up your time. You said you had an appointment."

"Oh, damn the appointment!" Impatiently he pulled the

phone to him and dialed a number, keeping his eyes on her all the while. He spoke into it crisply in a manner permitting no argument, and then broke the connection and laid the phone down by the receiver. "So much for my appointment," he said.

"But this really won't take long," Jenny started again. "I just want some advice. I'm going to be married—I think. . . ."

He jumped up knocking over his chair which he quickly caught. "Oh, no!" he exclaimed. "I'll lock the door and bar the window. . . ." She felt a sickening rise of fear and knew it was reflected in her face. He sat down again and said soberly, "I'm sorry. That was inexcusable. Someone did that to you, didn't he?"

She nodded.

"What can I call you?"

"Jenny. Jenny Alton."

"Very well, Jenny. I promise you I won't try to detain you. Now will you please stay and talk a bit before we get to the reason for this call?"

"I'd like to talk," she said softly and her wings settled once more. She hadn't been aware until then that they had opened, poised, as alert as a bird, ready to spring into the air and fly away. "I've never been able to talk to anyone except Pap about—about it."

"Fine," Lindquist murmured. "I won't interrupt. Just start anywhere."

"I never knew I was different until I started school," she said after a moment's hesitation. "My father was killed in the war, and Mother left us, Pap and me, when I was two. I can't really remember her. Pap is my grandfather. He wouldn't let Mother and the doctor operate on my—on me when I was first born, and after she left he took care of me. He used to stand on the ground watching me and he'd yell, 'Fly, Jenny! Fly girl! Fly!' He was really proud of my wings. Every night he'd kiss me goodnight and say, 'Goodnight, my Jenny with wings!" She looked at the doctor shyly and his eyes were bright and burning with excitement and understanding. "I was so happy," she said and he nodded. "Then I started school." She remembered clearly the second or third day at play period. She said, "I couldn't understand why they were still playing their silly games instead of flying. I thought I couldn't stand to jump rope any more, so I took off my dress and began to fly." She glanced at the doctor in time to catch the slight twitching of his lips. She nodded. "It started an uproar all right." She grinned, remembering it.

"What did you do?" the doctor asked gravely.

"I flew home, naturally," she answered simply. "We moved that day."

She met his eyes and together they laughed. "I try not to find it funny," she said presently. "It shouldn't have been funny, but the look on their faces, and the way they screamed . . ."

"But did you think it was funny then? Weren't you frightened or lonely?"

"You don't understand," she said and stretched out both wings and looked at them. "When you fly you don't need anyone else, and then I had Pap and we traveled a lot, of course, but he didn't mind, and neither did I. We always stayed in the south so I wouldn't get too cold. In one day I could travel hundreds of miles, and I could soar or loop or dive, or just glide with the trade winds. I didn't understand the other girls and they didn't understand me. I couldn't do a lot of the things they did, slumber parties, swimming, trying on each other's clothes, but that didn't matter. I could fly!"

"But people did find out once in a while, didn't they?" he prodded gently.

She looked at him sharply. How could he know that?

"It was inevitable that every boy who put his arm around you was in for a surprise," he said. "And also that boys would want to put their arms about you."

"I found out about boys," she admitted ruefully. "I was twelve, almost thirteen, and I went to my first boy-girl party." Sighing, she remembered the party. "Someone turned out the lights and there was this little boy, Johnny Roland. I'll never forget him. He was fourteen. He sat down next to me and pretty soon his hands began exploring. I was scared, but—" she stopped short, feeling her face grow hot. "Anyway," she continued hurriedly, "he got around to the wings and quit dead. I wiggled one wing a little and he let out a yell that brought the parents of the girl up from the porch. After that the lights stayed on and we played ping-pong. Every once in a while I looked at him and his eyes were big and scared." Jenny stopped and stared at the floor.

The doctor rose and switched on a light on the far side of the office. He busied himself about a cabinet, saying, "I could use some coffee about now. I've been thinking while you talked, you've been lucky. Most people with any sort of difference are generally shunned and made to feel like pariahs. Apparently you managed to have a fairly normal childhood and adolescence."

"Not really," she said, joining him to sniff the aroma of the coffee that was just starting to perk. "I had to quit school in the eighth grade because I couldn't take gym. Showers, you know. It takes a doctor's certificate to get out of it. We moved again and after that Pap told people that I was seventeen. It worked. But he made me study at home. We didn't go about it with any order at all; when we read up the library, we moved on, always choosing small towns and living out in the country."

The doctor poured coffee into two heavy mugs and carried them back to the desk. Jenny wondered about his stiffness. Maybe an old war wound. His face had the look of suffering remembered, a kind look of understanding not present in a face that hasn't known pain.

She followed him across the office, her wings spread, her feet barely touching the floor. His eyes were fastened almost hungrily on the wings. She drew them in tight and took one of the mugs. He closed his eyes and after a moment asked, "Who was it locked you in?"

"He was a doctor," she said faintly. "I was out one day and I landed on a rocky slope. I don't know if I did it, or if it just happened, but rocks started to slide and one hit my shoulder before I could get out. I managed to get home, but then I fainted and scared Pap half to death. When I woke up I was in a hospital. My shoulder was bandaged and I was wearing a gown that tied in the back out of reach. I couldn't get free and I could see bars on the window. I was terrified. A doctor tried to get me to sign a paper of some kind, so he could operate on me, and when I wouldn't do it, they gave me a hypo. The next thing I knew Pap was there with a shotgun and he was cutting the gown off me. We got out, and believe me, we really ran that time."

Dr. Lindquist stood up and came to her side. Puzzledly he asked, "Why would he want to operate like that? What good would you do him with your wings gone?"

"He wasn't going to take them off," she answered bitterly. "He was going to sever some muscles so I couldn't fly. He told Pap it had to be done or I'd die, but Pap wouldn't sign either. He was going ahead anyway. Then he was going to exhibit me to some of his colleagues, and write articles, and after he was famous, he was going to operate and make me normal."

Dr. Lindquist swore once and turned away to pour them more coffee. "Why are you here now? And how did you know about me?"

Jenny rose with her coffee and went over to the window. With her back to him she said in a low voice, "I said I found out about boys, but I didn't, not really. You see, after the operation attempt, I really was sick and I couldn't fly. I got to know some of our new neighbors. There was one boy—I was really seventeen by then, and he was eighteen, or nineteen. He would come over and sit and look at me and be tongue-tied, and I began to dream about him. We had a hammock, we always took it with us," she paused, but the doctor nodded his understanding and she continued without explaining, "and one night I was sitting on it and he came over with a box of candy. He sat down on the ground and began pulling out grass, one blade at a time, and altogether it took him almost an hour to get around to proposing to me. I knew it was coming, and I was afraid, but I didn't know how to head him off. I just sat there and remembered Johnny Roland and his yell when he felt . . . Anyway, I couldn't say anything because I also remembered how Johnny's hands felt and made me feel before he . . ." Shakily she laughed and sat down demurely, her hands resting in her lap. "You must think I'm just a promiscuous woman."

"Not at all, Jenny. I think— Never mind. What happened?"

"I told him to come back in an hour. Then I sent Pap to the store for something or other and I undressed and put on a robe. When Johnny came back, he came into the living room, and I took off the robe." She caught a look of amusement on the doctor's face and quickly she exclaimed, "Oh, it was awful! You should have seen him! All I wanted was for him to make love to me and he fell on his knees and started to pray. That was too much. I was furious with him and suddenly I saw him as a childish, ignorant, superstitious idiot. In my most menacing voice I told him I'd have my eyes on him for the rest of his life and he'd better repent his sins. Then I flew away."

The doctor laughed a long time. "Jenny, Jenny," he said. "And then, no doubt fighting mad, you tried to prove to yourself that you could get a man."

"Exactly," she snapped. "But I couldn't. One ran away and came back with hedge shears. Another fainted dead away. A third one began muttering chants he had picked up somewhere down in New Orleans. The last one asked if I was born or hatched. I gave him a ride he'll never forget! But by then I was tired of it all and gave up. Until now."

"Jenny," the doctor asked seriously, "have you ever been kissed by a man who knew about the wings?"

She turned to him and nodded. "That's why this is an emergency, Dr. Lindquist. I'm really in love this time, and he loves me."

The doctor turned and walked to his desk, seating himself behind it professionally. A subtle change had come over him that puzzled Jenny. This must be how he appeared to his other patients, and the smiling, understanding man he had been before was reserved for unofficial visits. She wished he hadn't gone to his desk. "And now you want to know if I can take them off for you, is that it?" he asked.

Jenny felt her wings rise up in sudden reaction. "No! Never!" More quietly she sat down again. "Don't you see, I can't! I've thought about it, but I can't. What if, in all the world, you were the only one who could see blue, would you give it up just because no one else could appreciate it?" She studied her fingernails minutely. "I said I read a lot, didn't I? Oh, darn it!" she wailed suddenly. "That's all I know! Just what I read."

Dr. Lindquist leaned forward and said. "You mean you just want me to tell you the facts of life?"

She swallowed convulsively and drew back from his incredulous gaze. "Not exactly," she mumbled. "I read the biology books— It's just that I want to know if I can have children, and are they going to be like me— And how—" Her voice was nearly inaudible when she finished. "And how can I do it? The damned wings keep getting in the way."

His shout of laughter was explosive and it was a long time before he spoke. Jenny looked at him angrily until he finished. "I don't think it's very funny," she fumed. "This is a very serious problem for me."

"Oh, Jenny," he gasped. "I'm sorry. Wait a minute." He moved stiffly across the room and ran his finger across the backs of books in a glass-doored case. "Ah, here we are. And here." He went on and extracted a third one. He placed the books before her with a courtly bow. "These should solve the second problem. As for the first—I'll have to examine you, you know."

She bit her lip and lowered her eyes. He led her to the examining room and looked baffled as she shook her head at the table. "I can't," she muttered. "Can't you get it through your head that *I cannot lie down on my back!*"

"Don't get excited," he growled. "I didn't say on your back. On your side. And may the Lord have pity on your doctor if you do get pregnant!"

She eyed the table doubtfully and turned to look at the doctor, but he was bent over the sink washing his hands. In a small voice she asked, "Should I finish undressing?"

"That is the usual procedure," he replied coldly.

Moving slowly, she stepped out of her panties and undid the pin that held the sheet about her. She was approaching the table when he neared her and held out his hand. "I'll help you," he said. She shuddered noticeably at his touch and felt the blood flooding her face and neck as his eyes passed over her body. Abruptly he turned away. "Put the sheet back on," he said hoarsely. "I'll fluoroscope you."

He positioned her behind the machine and closed the door. "It'll take several minutes for my eyes to adjust," he said in a very professional voice. After a moment of silence he asked, "What makes you think you're in love this time?"

Jenny felt the coldness of the machine pressing against her and she sighed. "I've followed spring all the way up from Mississippi," she said. "When the trees start blooming, first the farmers come out, then little boys with kites, and then lovers." She sighed again. "I was over in the mountains watching spring, so to speak. There was a peach tree in bloom and I was sitting in a pin oak looking at the pink blossoms against the blue sky. Suddenly there was a crash of a car, and it was Steve. I went down to see if he was hurt, and he was so handsome— Naturally I couldn't leave him alone to freeze, and he would have frozen. So I held him all night and wrapped my wings around both of us. He hurt his ankle in the crash, that's all, but he couldn't walk all the way to the road for help until morning."

She stopped and the doctor's voice sounded very close and very unbelieving as he asked, "And just like that you fell in love?"

"Not just like that," she retorted. "He was fainting and I had to help him, didn't I?"

"Was he fainting before or after he got a glimpse of you flying around in the altogether?" the doctor put in sarcastically. "And while I'm thinking of it, do you always fly like that? Your bottom is wind-burned."

"Oh," she cried. "See, that's what made him so different! He'd never say a thing like that! He couldn't even believe in me most of the night. He thought he was delirious and that I was an angel. He talked so—so pretty to me. No one ever talked like that before, not after seeing the wings."

The doctor's laugh was short and mocking. He did something to the machine and it glowed. His voice sounded muffled when he spoke again. "And you're in love with him."

"Yes," she said shortly. "I fell in love with him. I felt exactly the way the books describe it, shivery and funny in the middle. And he did too. I stayed with him until morning and we heard a car coming. Then he kissed me and I promised to come to his cabin tonight. We're going to be married."

"Oh, good Lord," the doctor exclaimed and turned off the machine. "You're O.K. Everything's there that should be there. Come on." He held the door open and followed her into the office. "If he loves you so much, why the delay of a week? Why didn't you go to him right away, or better still, why didn't you go with him?"

"He had to come to the city about his job, and he had to

see a doctor about his ankle, and then he was going back to his cabin in the mountains and wait for me. Isn't that romantic? A cabin in the mountains. And then I had some things I had to do."

"Like barging into my office?"

"I didn't want to do it like that," she shot back. "That stupid nurse of yours thinks she's God. You must lose a lot of business because of her." She took a deep breath. "I'm sorry about tonight. Really I am. I ruined your evening. Probably your wife is worrying . . ."

"I'm not married," he interrupted.

"Oh?" She gave him a quick look and unconsciously almost shook her head. "Anyway," she said after considering him and leaving it, "I had to have some answers. After Steve left, I flew back home and made Pap tell me the name of the doctor who delivered me. Then I went to Tennessee and looked him up. He remembered all right, but I couldn't talk to him. He's so old. I told him I needed a doctor I could trust and he gave me your name. He said you specialized in abnormalities, that you devoted your whole life to helping people, that you went out and looked them up in order to help them even. Then I came here."

The doctor sat down on the edge of his chair and looked at her quietly. "Are you sure about this man, Jenny? Do you know the difference between love and infatuation? Do you have any idea of what spring can do to a beautiful, lonely girl?"

She nodded and felt herself blushing again as her hand involuntarily closed over the books he had put on the desk.

"Take your things in there and dress," he said brusquely. "Or are you going to fly?"

Her eyes were on the window, and again she nodded.

"Wait a minute," he ordered. He went into the small adjoining room and returned with a large jar of cream. "Rub this all over yourself. It goes right in and will keep you from wind-burning or getting cold." She looked at him, startled, and he shrugged. "I have a patient who spends most of his time under water," he explained. "Seems he has gills and lungs, and prefers to use the gills. That keeps him warm."

Silently she took the jar into the dressing room and rubbed

in the cream. It vanished without a trace in a few moments. Hesitantly she paused at the window. "Doctor," she said, "thank you. If I hadn't met Steve first—I mean, you've been awfully nice. . . ." She dropped the sheet and, clutching the books to her, she was in the air; feeling the warm updraft from the city fill her wings, she climbed and banked. She looked at the window, but already he was gone and she headed west, climbing.

She flew to the cabin unerringly and slowed only as she reached the clearing. Her heart was beating wildly and she found herself shivering, although she didn't feel any cold through the ointment the doctor had given her. Her stomach felt funny with an ache that wasn't really an ache. Drawing her wings up close to her, she skimmed through the trees and landed on one at the edge of the clearing. She sat on a massive branch waiting for the wild beating of her heart to subside, trying to rid herself of a sudden weakness. Gradually she became aware of smoke, cigarette smoke, and of movement. She pressed back against the tree-trunk and listened and looked.

Finally she sighted the figures, a man and a woman. The woman was stubbing out a cigarette on the side of a tree. Jenny flattened herself on the branch and draped her wings over her body; they were coming near.

"Steve, if this is a gag—" the woman was saying in a low, menacing voice.

"You won't think it's a gag when you see her," he whispered back. "Just keep your eyes on that clearing. She—it—whatever the hell it was will show. Did you have any trouble getting that mask?"

"No. I don't like any part of it, though. You can't kidnap a girl and put her in a circus merely because she has wings. She can talk and yell, can't she?"

"She won't be able to when I get through," he muttered. "God, those wings! Must have over a twelve-foot wing span! With that bird's mask on, and her mouth taped shut— All we need is to keep her doped up real good, and baby, we're in the money! Shh!" They became silent and Jenny listened too. "Thought I heard wings," Steve grunted. "Look, you stay here and watch. I'd better get by the door where she can see me when she gets near. Remember what you're to do?"

"I remember," her voice came back. "You get her inside and I follow and close and bar the door. Are you sure you can handle her?"

He laughed. Jenny watched him walk toward the cabin; everything was forgotten as an icy rage filled her. She waited until he stopped in the doorway and lit a match. Carefully she placed her books in the crook of the tree. Then silently as an owl she swooped down on the woman and without a sound grasped her about the waist with one arm, clamping her hand over her mouth, and swinging upward at the same moment. The woman struggled briefly until they were fifteen feet or so off the ground, and then she went limp. Swiftly Jenny flew with her to the road a mile away and deposited her in the top of a tree, slapping her rudely several times to make sure she was fully conscious before she left her clinging there. She returned to the cabin. Steve was leaning against the doorframe.

Jenny circled around in full view and slowly came in to land thirty feet away from him. She stopped and held out her arms. For a moment Steve hesitated, but then he ran toward her.

"Darling," he murmured into her hair. "I was afraid you wouldn't come." His breath was warm against her neck and she put her arms around him and holding him very tight spread her wings and lifted. Steve cried out hoarsely and tried to squeeze her. She laughed.

"Look down, Steve," she said calmly. "Do you really want me to let go?"

"Jenny," he cried. "I can't breathe. Let's go back down. This isn't funny."

"Soon," she said softly. "Soon." She flew with him into the valley and past a dude ranch and its corral. She had seen a posted area nearby and she thought she remembered exactly where it was, if she didn't tire too soon. Grimly she flew on. Then she recognized the land below. A military area, posted and guarded with men and dogs. She flew in low to avoid the radar, and skimming twenty feet over the ground she sought a lake she knew to be on the other side of the hill. She slowed her flight and said regretfully, "Steve, I do believe I am tiring. Talk your way out of this, Steve, honey." He clutched at her, trying to hold on, but she shook him off and circled him as he fell, screaming all the way. The splash he made was immediately answered by shouting and barking. Silently she flew away only inches above the tops of the trees.

Then, her anger spent, she glided effortlessly, aimlessly. What now, Jenny? she asked herself sadly. Perhaps she would return to Dr. Lindquist and request the surgery that would make her normal. He had been so nice. Besides, she'd have to return the books and explain that she wouldn't need them after all. He had said she was beautiful . . . Perhaps . . . She squealed in fright suddenly and did a quick maneuver, turning over completely and hovering on her back, looking about wildly. Something had touched her! Then arms were about her waist, and a warm body pressing against her back.

She twisted her head about and gasped, "Dr. Lindquist!"

"Call me Tor," he murmured in her ear. This time it was his body twist that righted them both, and another slight motion that headed them up into the sky. They flew in perfect unison.

"Why didn't you tell me?" she demanded, and found that she was shivering. That was why he had been so stiff. His wings had been wrapped around him.

"I wanted to tell you. I couldn't believe it until I saw and touched your wings, and then you said you were in love and I had to let you find out that you weren't. I knew you would find out. You were in love with a peach blossom against a blue sky." His arms didn't have to hold her up any longer, and his hands moved over her unhurriedly.

"Oh," she breathed and his laugh was low in her ear.

"There's the current," he said softly. "Just glide. We'll stay up for hours. There's so much to talk about. So much to do."

To her surprise she found that she wasn't shivering at all.

The Truth About Pyecraft

BY H. G. WELLS

HE SITS not a dozen yards away. If I glance over my shoulder I can see him. And if I catch his eye—and usually I catch his eye—it meets me with an expression. . . .

It is mainly an imploring look—and yet with suspicion in it.

Confound his suspicion! If I wanted to tell on him I should have told long ago. I don't tell and I don't tell, and he ought to feel at his ease. As if anything so gross and fat as he could feel at ease! Who would believe me if I did tell?

Poor old Pyecraft! Great, uneasy jelly of substance! The fattest clubman in London.

He sits at one of the little club tables in the huge bay by the fire, stuffing. What is he stuffing? I glance judiciously, and catch him biting at a round of hot buttered teacake, with his eyes on me. Confound him!—with his eyes on me!

That settles it, Pyecraft! Since you *will* be abject, since you *will* behave as though I was not a man of honor, here, right under your embedded eyes, I write the thing down—the plain truth about Pyecraft. The man I helped, the man I shielded, and who has requited me by making my club unendurable, absolutely unendurable, with his liquid appeal, with the perpetual "don't tell" of his looks.

And, besides, why does he keep on eternally eating?

Well, here goes for the truth, the whole truth, and nothing but the truth!

Pyecraft . . . I made the acquaintance of Pyecraft in this very smoking room. I was a young, nervous new member, and he saw it. I was sitting all alone, wishing I knew more of the members, and suddenly he came, a great rolling front of chins and abdomina, toward me, and grunted and sat down in a chair close by me and wheezed for a space, and scraped for a space with a match and lit a cigar, and then addressed me. I forget what he said—something about the matches not lighting properly, and afterward as he talked he kept stopping the waiters one by one as they went by, and telling them about the matches in that thin, fluty voice he has. But, anyhow, it was in some such way we began our talking.

He talked about various things and came round to games. And thence to my figure and complexion. "*You* ought to be a good cricketer," he said. I suppose I am slender, slender to what some people would call lean, and I suppose I am rather dark, still— I am not ashamed of having a Hindu great-grandmother, but, for all that, I don't want casual strangers to see through me at a glance to *her*. So that I was set against Pyecraft from the beginning.

But he only talked about me in order to get to himself.

"I expect," he said, "you take no more exercise than I do, and probably you eat no less." (Like all excessively obese people he fancied he ate nothing.) "Yet"—and he smiled an oblique smile—"we differ."

And then he began to talk about his fatness and his fatness; all he did for his fatness and all he was going to do for his fatness: what people had advised him to do for his fatness and what he had heard of people doing for fatness similar to his. "*A priori,*" he said, "one would think a question of nutrition could be answered by dietary and a question of assimilation by drugs." It was stifling. It was dumpling talk. It made me feel swelled to hear him.

One stands that sort of thing once in a way at a club, but a time came when I fancied I was standing too much. He took to me altogether too conspicuously. I could never go into the smoking room but he would come wallowing toward me, and sometimes he came and gormandized round and about me while I had my lunch. He seemed at times almost to be clinging to me. He was a bore, but not so fearful a bore as to be limited to me; and from the first there was something in his manner—almost as though he knew, almost as though he penetrated to the fact that I *might*—that there was a remote, exceptional chance in me that no one else presented.

"I'd give anything to get it down," he would say—"anything," and peer at me over his vast cheeks and pant. Poor old Pyecraft! He has just gonged; no doubt to order another buttered teacake!

He came to the actual thing one day. "Our Pharmacopœia," he said, "our Western Pharmacopœia, is anything but the last word of medical science. In the East, I've been told—"

He stopped and stared at me. It was like being at an aquarium.

I was quite suddenly angry with him. "Look here," I said, "who told you about my great-grandmother's recipes?"

"Well," he fenced.

"Every time we've met for a week," I said—"and we've met pretty often—you've given me a broad hint or so about that little secret of mine."

"Well," he said, "now the cat's out of the bag, I'll admit, yes, it is so. I had it—"

"From Pattison?"

"Indirectly," he said, which I believe was lying, "yes."

"Pattison," I said, "took that stuff at his own risk."

He pursed his mouth and bowed.

"My great-grandmother's recipes," I said, "are queer things to handle. My father was near making me promise—"

"He didn't?"

"No. But he warned me. He himself used one—once."

"Ah! . . . But do you think—? Suppose—suppose there did happen to be one."

"The things are curious documents," I said. "Even the smell of 'em— No!"

But after going so far Pyecraft was resolved I should go farther. I was always a little afraid if I tried his patience too much he would fall on me suddenly and smother me. I own I was weak. But I was also annoyed with Pyecraft. I had got to that state of feeling for him that disposed me to say, "Well, *take* the risk!" The little affair of Pattison to which I have alluded was a different matter altogether. What it was doesn't concern us now, but I knew, anyhow, that the particular recipe I used then was safe. The rest I didn't know so much about, and, on the whole, I was inclined to doubt their safety pretty completely.

Yet even if Pyecraft got poisoned—

I must confess the poisoning of Pyecraft struck me as an immense undertaking.

That evening I took that queer, odd-scented sandalwood box out of my safe, and turned the rustling skins over. The gentleman who wrote the recipes for my great-grandmother evidently had a weakness for skins of a miscellaneous origin, and his handwriting was cramped to the last degree. Some of the things are quite unreadable to me—though my family, with its Indian Civil Service associations, has kept up a knowledge of Hindustani from generation to generation—and none are absolutely plain sailing. But I found the one that I knew was there soon enough, and sat on the floor by my safe for some time looking at it.

"Look here," said I to Pyecraft next day, and snatched the slip away from his eager grasp.

"So far as I can make it out, this is a recipe for Loss of Weight. ('Ah!' said Pyecraft.) I'm not absolutely sure, but I think it's that. And if you take my advice you'll leave it alone. Because, you know— I blacken my blood in your interest, Pyecraft—my ancestors on that side were, so far as I can gather, a jolly queer lot. See?"

"Let me try it," said Pyecraft.

I leaned back in my chair. My imagination made one mighty effort and fell flat within me. "What in Heaven's name, Pyecraft," I asked, "do you think you'll look like when you get thin?"

He was impervious to reason. I made him promise never to say a word to me about his disgusting fatness again whatever happened—never, and then I handed him that little piece of skin.

"It's nasty stuff," I said.

"No matter," he said, and took it.

He goggled at it. "But—but—" he said.

He had just discovered that it wasn't English.

"To the best of my ability," I said, "I will do you a translation."

I did my best. After that we didn't speak for a fortnight. Whenever he approached me I frowned and motioned him away, and he respected our compact, but at the end of the fortnight he was as fat as ever. And then he got a word in.

"I must speak," he said. "It isn't fair. There's something wrong. It's done me no good. You're not doing your great-grandmother justice."

"Where's the recipe?"

He produced it gingerly from his pocketbook.

I ran my eye over the items. "Was the egg addled?" I asked.

"No. Ought it to have been?"

"That," I said, "goes without saying in all my poor dear great-grandmother's recipes. When condition or quality is not specified you must get the worst. She was drastic or nothing. . . . And there's one or two possible alternatives to some of these other things. You got *fresh* rattlesnake venom?"

"I got a rattlesnake from Jamrach's. It cost—it cost—"

"That's your affair anyhow. This last item—"

"I know a man who—"

"Yes. H'm. Well, I'll write the alternatives down. So far as I know the language, the spelling of this recipe is particularly atrocious. By the by, dog here probably means pariah dog."

For a month after that I saw Pyecraft constantly at the club and as fat and anxious as ever. He kept our treaty, but at times he broke the spirit of it by shaking his head despondently. Then one day in the cloakroom he said, "Your great-grandmother—"

"Not a word against her," I said; and he held his peace.

I could have fancied he had desisted, and I saw him one day talking to three new members about his fatness as though he was in search of other recipes. And then, quite unexpectedly, his telegram came.

"Mr. Formalyn!" bawled a page boy under my nose, and I took the telegram and opened it at once.

"For Heaven's sake come.—Pyecraft."

"H'm," said I, and to tell the truth I was so pleased at the rehabilitation of my great-grandmother's reputation this evidently promised that I made a most excellent lunch.

I got Pyecraft's address from the hall porter. Pyecraft inhabited the upper half of a house in Bloomsbury, and I went there as soon as I had done my coffee and Trappistine. I did not wait to finish my cigar.

"Mr. Pyecraft?" said I, at the front door.

They believed he was ill; he hadn't been out for two days.

"He expects me," said I, and they sent me up.

I rang the bell at the lattice door upon the landing.

"He shouldn't have tried it, anyhow," I said to myself. "A man who eats like a pig ought to look like a pig."

An obviously worthy woman, with an anxious face and a carelessly placed cap, came and surveyed me through the lattice.

I gave my name and she let me in in a dubious fashion.

"Well?" said I, as we stood together inside Pyecraft's piece of the landing.

" 'E said you was to come in if you came," she said, and regarded me, making no motion to show me anywhere. And then, confidentially, " 'E's locked in, sir."

"Locked in?"

"Locked 'imself in yesterday morning and 'asn't let anyone in since, sir. And ever and again *swearing*. Oh, my!"

I stared at the door she indicated by her glances. "In there?" I said.

"Yes, sir."

"What's up?"

She shook her head sadly. " 'E keeps on calling for vittles, sir. *'Eavy* vittles 'e wants. I get 'im what I can. Pork 'e's had, sooit puddin', sossiges, noo bread. Everythink like that. Left outside, if you please, and me go away. 'E's eatin', sir, somethink *awful*."

There came a piping bawl from inside the door: "That Formalyn?"

"That you, Pyecraft?" I shouted, and went and banged the door.

"Tell her to go away."

I did.

Then I could hear a curious pattering upon the door, almost like someone feeling for the handle in the dark, and Pyecraft's familiar grunts.

"It's all right," I said, "she's gone."

But for a long time the door didn't open.

I heard the key turn. Then Pyecraft's voice said, "Come in."

I turned the handle and opened the door. Naturally I expected to see Pyecraft.

Well, you know, he wasn't there!

I never had such a shock in my life. There was his sitting room in a state of untidy disorder, plates and dishes among the books and writing things, and several chairs overturned, but Pyecraft. . . .

"It's all right, old man; shut the door," he said, and then I discovered him.

There he was, right up close to the cornice in the corner by the door, as though some one had glued him to the ceiling. His face was anxious and angry. He panted and gesticulated. "Shut the door," he said. "If that woman gets hold of it—"

I shut the door, and went and stood away from him and stared.

"If anything gives way and you tumble down," I said, "you'll break your neck, Pyecraft."

"I wish I could," he wheezed.

"A man of your age and weight getting up to kiddish gymnastics—"

"Don't," he said, and looked agonized.

"I'll tell you," he said, and gesticulated.

"How the deuce," said I, "are you holding on up there?"

And then abruptly I realized that he was not holding on at all, that he was floating up there—just as a gas-filled bladder might have floated in the same position. He began a struggle to thrust himself away from the ceiling and to clamber down the wall to me. "It's that prescription," he panted, as he did so. "Your great-gran—"

He took hold of a framed engraving rather carelessly as he spoke and it gave way, and he flew back to the ceiling again, while the picture smashed on to the sofa. Bump he went against the ceiling, and I knew then why he was all over white on the more salient curves and angles of his person. He tried again more carefully, coming down by way of the mantel.

It was really a most extraordinary spectacle, that great, fat, apoplectic-looking man upside down and trying to get from the ceiling to the floor. "That prescription," he said. "Too successful."

"How?"

"Loss of weight—almost complete."

And then, of course, I understood.

"By Jove, Pyecraft," said I, "what you wanted was a cure for fatness! But you always called it weight. You would call it weight."

Somehow I was extremely delighted. I quite liked Pyecraft for the time. "Let me help you!" I said, and took his hand and pulled him down. He kicked about, trying to get foothold somewhere. It was very like holding a flag on a windy day.

"That table," he said, pointing, "is solid mahogany and very heavy. If you can put me under that—"

I did, and there he wallowed about like a captive balloon, while I stood on his hearthrug and talked to him.

I lit a cigar. "Tell me," I said, "what happened?"

"I took it," he said.

"How did it taste?"

"Oh, *beastly!*"

I should fancy they all did. Whether one regards the ingredients or the probable compound or the possible results, almost all my great-grandmother's remedies appear to me at least to be extraordinarily uninviting. For my own part—

"I took a little sip first."

"Yes?"

"And as I felt lighter and better after an hour, I decided to take the draught."

"My dear Pyecraft!"

"I held my nose," he explained. "And then I kept on getting lighter and lighter—and helpless, you know."

He gave way suddenly to a burst of passion. "What the goodness am I to *do?*" he said.

"There's one thing pretty evident," I said, "that you mustn't do. If you go out of doors you'll go up and up." I waved an arm upward. "They'd have to send Santos-Dumont after you to bring you down again."

"I suppose it will wear off?"

I shook my head. "I don't think you can count on that," I said.

And then there was another burst of passion, and he kicked out at adjacent chairs and banged the floor. He behaved just as I should have expected a great, fat, self-indulgent man to behave under trying circumstances—that is to say, very badly. He spoke of me and of my great-grandmother with an utter want of discretion.

"I never asked you to take the stuff," I said.

And generously disregarding the insults he was putting upon me, I sat down in his armchair and began to talk to him in a sober, friendly fashion.

I pointed out to him that this was a trouble he had brought upon himself, and that it had almost an air of poetical justice. He had eaten too much. This he disputed, and for a time we argued the point.

He became noisy and violent, so I desisted from this aspect of his lesson. "And then," said I, "you committed the sin of euphuism. You called it, not Fat, which is just and inglorious, but Weight. You—"

He interrupted to say that he recognized all that. What was he to *do?*

I suggested he should adapt himself to his new conditions. So we came to the really sensible part of the business. I suggested that it would not be difficult for him to learn to walk about on the ceiling with his hands—

"I can't sleep," he said.

But that was no great difficulty. It was quite possible, I pointed out, to make a shake-up under a wire mattress, fasten the under things on with tapes, and have a blanket, sheet, and coverlet to button at the side. He would have to confide in his housekeeper, I said; and after some squabbling he agreed to that. (Afterwards it was quite delightful to see the beautifully matter-of-fact way with which the good lady took all these amazing inversions.) He could have a library ladder in his room, and all his meals could be laid on the top of his bookcase. We also hit on an ingenious device by which he could get to the floor whenever he wanted, which was simply to put the *British Encyclopaedia* (tenth edition) on the top of his open shelves. He just pulled out a couple of volumes and held on, and down he came. And we agreed there must be iron staples along the skirting, so that he could cling to those whenever he wanted to get about the room on the lower level.

As we got on with the thing I found myself almost keenly interested. It was I who called in the housekeeper and broke matters to her, and it was I chiefly who fixed up the inverted bed. In fact, I spent two whole days at his flat. I am a handy, interfering sort of man with a screwdriver, and I made all sorts of ingenious adaptations for him—ran a wire to bring his bells within reach, turned all his electric lights up instead of down, and so on. The whole affair was extremely curious and interesting to me, and it was delightful to think of Pyecraft, like some great, fat blow-fly, crawling about on his ceiling and clambering round the lintel of his doors from one room to another, and never, never, never coming to the club anymore. . . .

Then, you know, my fatal ingenuity got the better of me. I was sitting by his fire drinking his whiskey, and he was up in his favorite corner by the cornice, tacking a Turkey carpet to the ceiling, when the idea struck me. "By Jove, Pyecraft!" I said, "all this is totally unnecessary."

And before I could calculate the complete consequences of my notion I blurted it out. "Lead underclothing," said I, and the mischief was done.

Pyecraft received the thing almost in tears. "To be right way up again—" he said.

I gave him the whole secret before I saw where it would take me. "Buy sheet lead," I said, "stamp it into discs. Sew 'em all over your underclothes until you have enough. Have lead-soled boots, carry a bag of solid lead, and the thing is done! Instead of being a prisoner here you may go abroad again, Pyecraft; you may travel—"

A still happier idea came to me. "You need never fear a shipwreck. All you need do is just slip off some or all of your clothes, take the necessary amount of luggage in your hand, and float up in the air—"

In his emotion he dropped the tack-hammer within an ace of my head. "By Jove!" he said, "I shall be able to come back to the club again."

The thing pulled me up short. "By Jove!" I said, faintly. "Yes. Of course—you will."

He did. He does. There he sits behind me now, stuffing—as I live!—a third go of buttered teacake. And no one in the whole world knows—except his housekeeper and me—that he weighs practically nothing; that he is a mere boring mass of assimilatory matter, mere clouds in clothing, *niente, nefas,* the most inconsiderable of men. There he sits watching until I have done this writing. Then, if he can, he will waylay me. He will come billowing up to me. . . .

He will tell me over again all about it, how it feels, how it doesn't feel, how he sometimes hopes it is passing off a little. And always somewhere in that fat, abundant discourse he will say, "The secret's keeping, eh? If anyone knew of it—I should be so ashamed. Makes a fellow look such a fool, you know. Crawling about on a ceiling and all that. . . ."

And now to elude Pyecraft, occupying, as he does, an admirable strategic position between me and the door.

The Words of Guru

BY C. M. KORNBLUTH

YESTERDAY, when I was going to meet Guru in the woods a man stopped me and said: "Child, what are you doing out at one in the morning? Does your mother know where you are? How old are you, walking around this late?"

I looked at him, and saw that he was white-haired, so I laughed. Old men never see; in fact men hardly see at all. Sometimes young women see part, but men rarely ever see at all. "I'm twelve on my next birthday," I said. And then, because I would not let him live to tell people, I said, "And I'm out this late to see Guru."

"Guru?" he asked. "Who is Guru? Some foreigner, I suppose? Bad business mixing with foreigners, young fellow. Who is Guru?"

So I told him who Guru was, and just as he began talking about cheap magazines and fairy tales I said one of the words that Guru taught me and he stopped talking. Because he was an old man and his joints were stiff he didn't crumple up but fell in one piece, hitting his head on the stone. Then I went on.

Even though I'm going to be only twelve on my next birthday I know many things that old people don't. And I remember things that other boys can't. I remember being born out of darkness, and I remember the noises that people made about me. Then when I was two months old I began to understand that the noises meant things like the things that were going on inside my head. I found out that I could make the noises too, and everybody was very much surprised. "Talking!" they said, again and again. "And so very young! Clara, what do you make of it?" Clara was my mother.

And Clara would say: "I'm sure I don't know. There never was any genius in my family, and I'm sure there was none in Joe's." Joe was my father.

Once Clara showed me a man I had never seen before, and told me that he was a reporter—that he wrote things in newspapers. The reporter tried to talk to me as if I were an ordinary baby. I didn't even answer him, but just kept looking at him until his eyes fell and he went away. Later Clara scolded me and read me a little piece in the reporter's newspaper that was supposed to be funny—about the reporter asking me very complicated questions and me answering with baby noises. It was not true, of course. I didn't say a word to the reporter, and he didn't ask me even one of the questions.

I heard her read the little piece, but while I listened I was watching the slug crawling on the wall. When Clara was finished I asked her: "What is that gray thing?"

She looked where I pointed, but couldn't see it. "What gray thing, Peter?" she asked. I had her call me by my whole name, Peter, instead of anything silly like Petey. "What gray thing?"

"It's as big as your hand, Clara, but soft. I don't think it has any bones at all. It's crawling up, but I don't see any face on the topward side. And there aren't any legs."

I think she was worried, but she tried to baby me by putting her hand on the wall and trying to find out where it was. I called out whether she was right or left of the thing. Finally she put her hand right through the slug. And then I realized that she really couldn't see it, and didn't believe it was there. I stopped talking about it then and only asked her a few days later: "Clara, what do you call a thing which one person can see and another person can't?"

"An illusion, Peter," she said. "If that's what you mean." I said nothing, but let her put me to bed as usual, but when she turned out the light and went away I waited a little while and then called out softly, "Illusion! Illusion!"

At once Guru came for the first time. He bowed, the way he always has since, and said: "I have been waiting."

"I didn't know that was the way to call you," I said.

"Whenever you want me I will be ready. I will teach you, Peter—if you want to learn. Do you know what I will teach you?"

"If you will teach me about the gray thing on the wall," I said, "I will listen. And if you will teach me about real things and unreal things I will listen."

"These things," he said thoughtfully, "very few wish to learn. And there are some things that nobody ever wished to learn. And there are some things that I will not teach."

Then I said: "The things nobody has ever wished to learn I will learn. And I will even learn the things you do not wish to teach."

He smiled mockingly. "A master has come," he said, half-laughing. "A master of Guru."

That was how I learned his name. And that night he taught me a word which would do little things, like spoiling food.

From that day, to the time I saw him last night he has not changed at all, though now I am as tall as he is. His skin is still as dry and shiny as ever it was, and his face is still bony, crowned by a head of very coarse, black hair.

When I was ten years old I went to bed one night only long enough to make Joe and Clara suppose I was fast asleep. I left in my place something which appears when you say one of the words of Guru and went down the drainpipe outside my window. It always was easy to climb down and up, ever since I was eight years old.

I met Guru in Inwood Hill Park. "You're late," he said.

"Not too late," I answered. "I know it's never too late for one of these things."

"How do you know?" he asked sharply. "This is your first."

"And maybe my last," I replied. "I don't like the idea of it. If I have nothing more to learn from my second than my first I shan't go to another."

"You don't know," he said. "You don't know what it's like—the voices, and the bodies slick with unguent, leaping flames, mind-filling ritual! You can have no idea at all until you've taken part."

"We'll see," I said. "Can we leave from here?"

"Yes," he said. Then he taught me the word I would need to know, and we both said it together.

The place we were in next was lit with red lights, and I think that the walls were of rock. Though of course there was no real seeing there, and so the lights only seemed to be red, and it was not real rock.

As we were going to the fire one of them stopped us. "Who's with you?" she asked, calling Guru by another name. I did not know that he was also the person bearing that name, for it was a very powerful one.

He cast a hasty, sidewise glance at me and then said: "This is Peter of whom I have often told you."

She looked at me then and smiled, stretching out her oily arms. "Ah," she said, softly, like the cats when they talk at night to me. "Ah, this is Peter. Will you come to me when I call you, Peter? And sometimes call for me—in the dark—when you are alone?"

"Don't do that!" said Guru, angrily pushing past her. "He's very young—you might spoil him for his work."

She screeched at our backs: "Guru and his pupil—fine pair! Boy, he's no more real than I am—you're the only real thing here!"

"Don't listen to her," said Guru. "She's wild and raving. They're always tight-strung when this time comes around."

We came near the fires then, and sat down on rocks. They were killing animals and birds and doing things with their bodies. The blood was being collected in a basin of stone, which passed through the crowd. The one to my left handed it to me. "Drink," she said, grinning to show me her fine, white teeth. I swallowed twice from it and passed it to Guru.

When the bowl had passed all around we took off our clothes. Some, like Guru, did not wear them, but many did. The one to my left sat closer to me, breathing heavily at my face. I moved away. "Tell her to stop, Guru," I said. "This isn't part of it, I know."

Guru spoke to her sharply in their own language, and she changed her seat, snarling.

Then we all began to chant, clapping our hands and beating our thighs. One of them rose slowly and circled about the fires in a slow pace, her eyes rolling wildly. She worked her jaws and flung her arms about so sharply that I could hear the elbows crack. Still shuffling her feet against the rock floor she bent her body backwards down to her feet. Her belly muscles were bands standing out from her skin, nearly, and the oil rolled down her body and legs. As the palms of her hands touched the ground she collapsed in a twitching heap and began to set up a thin wailing noise against the steady chant and hand-beat that the rest of us were keeping up.

Another of them did the same as the first, and we chanted louder for her and still louder for the third. Then, while we still beat our hands and thighs, one of them took up the third, laid her across the altar and made her ready with a stone knife. The fire's light gleamed off the chipped edge of obsidian. As her blood drained down the groove cut as a gutter into the rock of the altar, we stopped our chant and the fires were snuffed out.

But still we could see what was going on, for these things were, of course, not happening at all—only seeming to happen, really, just as all the people and things there only seemed to be what they were. Only I was real. That must be why they desired me so.

As the last of the fires died Guru excitedly whispered: "The Presence!" He was very deeply moved.

From the pool of blood from the third dancer's body there issued the Presence. It was the tallest one there, and when it spoke its voice was deeper, and when it commanded its commands were obeyed.

"Let blood!" it commanded, and we gashed ourselves with flints. It smiled and showed teeth bigger and sharper and whiter than any of the others.

"Make water!" it commanded, and we all spat on each other. It flapped its wings and rolled its eyes, that were bigger and redder than any of the others.

"Pass flame!" it commanded, and we breathed smoke and fire on our limbs. It stamped its feet, let blue flames roar from its mouth, and they were bigger and wilder than any of the others.

Then it returned to the pool of blood and we lit the fires again. Guru was staring straight before him; I tugged his arm. He bowed as though we were meeting for the first time that night.

"What are you thinking of?" I asked. "We shall go now."

"Yes," he said heavily. "Now we shall go." Then we said the word that had brought us there.

The first man I killed was Brother Paul, at the school where I went to learn the things that Guru did not teach me.

It was less than a year ago, but it seems like a very long time. I have killed so many times since then.

"You're a very bright boy, Peter," said the brother.

"Thank you, brother."

"But there are things about you that I don't understand. Normally I'd ask your parents but—I feel that they don't understand either. You were an infant prodigy, weren't you?"

"Yes, brother."

"There's nothing very unusual about that—glands, I'm told. You know what glands are?"

Then I was alarmed. I had heard of them, but I was not certain whether they were the short, thick green men who wear only metal or the things with many legs with whom I talked in the woods.

"How did you find out?" I asked him.

"But Peter! You look positively frightened, lad! I don't know a thing about them myself, but Father Frederick does. He has whole books about them, though I sometimes doubt whether he believes them himself."

"They aren't good books, brother," I said. "They ought to be burned."

"That's a savage thought, my son. But to return to your own problem—"

I could not let him go any further knowing what he did about me. I said one of the words Guru taught me and he looked at first very surprised and then seemed to be in great pain. He dropped across his desk and I felt his wrist to make sure, for I had not used that word before. But he was dead.

There was a heavy step outside and I made myself invisible. Stout Father Frederick entered, and I nearly killed him too with the word, but I knew that that would be very curious. I decided to wait, and went through the door as Father Frederick bent over the dead monk. He thought he was asleep.

I went down the corridor to the book-lined office of the stout priest and, working quickly, piled all his books in the center of the room and lit them with my breath. Then I went down to the schoolyard and made myself visible again when there was nobody looking. It was very easy. I killed a man I passed on the street the next day.

There was a girl named Mary who lived near us. She was fourteen then, and I desired her as those in the Cavern out of Time and Space had desired me.

So when I saw Guru and he had bowed, I told him of it, and he looked at me in great surprise. "You are growing older, Peter," he said.

"I am, Guru. And there will come a time when your words will not be strong enough for me."

He laughed. "Come, Peter," he said. "Follow me if you wish. There is something that is going to be done—" He licked his thin, purple lips and said: "I have told you what it will be like."

"I shall come," I said. "Teach me the word." So he taught me the word and we said it together.

The place we were in next was not like any of the other places I had been to before with Guru. It was No-place. Always before there had been the seeming passage of time and matter, but here there was not even that. Here Guru and the others cast off their forms and were what they were, and No-place was the only place where they could do this.

It was not like the Cavern, for the Cavern had been out of time and space, and this place was not enough of a place even for that. It was No-place.

What happened there does not bear telling, but I was made known to certain ones who never departed from there. All came to them as they existed. They had not color or the seeming of color, or any seeming of shape.

There I learned that eventually I would join with them; that I had been selected as the one of my planet who was to dwell without being forever in that No-place.

Guru and I left, having said the word.

"Well?" demanded Guru, staring me in the eye.

"I am willing," I said. "But teach me one word now—"

"Ah," he said grinning. "The girl?"

"Yes," I said. "The word that will mean much to her."

Still grinning, he taught me the word.

Mary, who had been fourteen, is now fifteen and what they call incurably mad.

Last night I saw Guru again and for the last time. He bowed as I approached him. "Peter," he said warmly.

"Teach me the word," said I.

"It is not too late."

"Teach me the word."

"You can withdraw—with what you master you can master also this world. Gold without reckoning; sardonyx and gems, Peter! Rich crushed velvet—stiff, scraping, embroidered tapestries!"

"Teach me the word."

"Think, Peter, of the house you could build. It could be of white marble, and every slab centered by a winking ruby. Its gate could be of beaten gold within and without and it could be built about one slender tower of carven ivory, rising mile after mile into the turquoise sky. You could see the clouds float underneath your eyes."

"Teach me the word."

"Your tongue could crush the grapes that taste like melted silver. You could hear always the song of the bulbul and the lark that sounds like the dawnstar made musical. Spikenard that will bloom a thousand thousand years could be ever in your nostrils. Your hands could feel the down of purple Himalayan swans that is softer than a sunset cloud."

"Teach me the word."

"You could have women whose skin would be from the black of ebony to the white of snow. You could have women who would be as hard as flints or as soft as a sunset cloud."

"Teach me the word."

Guru grinned and said the word.

Now, I do not know whether I will say that word, which was the last that Guru taught me, today or tomorrow or until a year has passed.

It is a word that will explode this planet like a stick of dynamite in a rotten apple.

Postpaid to Paradise

BY ROBERT ARTHUR

IT WAS Hobby Week at the Club, and Malcolm was displaying his stamp collection.

"Now take these triangulars," he said. "Their value is not definitely known, since they've never been sold as a unit. But they make up the rarest and most interesting complete set known to philatelists. They—"

"I once had a set of stamps that was even rarer and more interesting," Murchison Morks interrupted, his voice melancholy. Morks is a small, wispy man who usually sits by the fireplace and smokes his pipe, silently contemplating the coals. I do not believe he particularly cares for Malcolm, who is our only millionaire and likes what he owns to be better than what anybody else owns.

"You own a set of stamps *rarer* than my triangulars?" Malcolm asked incredulously, a dark tinge of annoyance creeping into his ruddy cheeks.

"Not own, no." Morks shook his head in gentle correction. "Owned."

"Oh!" Malcolm snorted. "I suppose they got burned? Or stolen?"

"No"—and Morks uttered a sigh—"I used them. For postage, I mean. Before I realized their utter uniqueness."

Malcolm gnawed at his lip.

"This set of stamps," he said with great positiveness, laying a possessive hand on the glass covering the triangular bits of paper, "cost the life of at least one man."

"Mine," Morks replied, "cost me my best friend."

"Cost you the *life* of your best friend?" Malcolm demanded.

Morks shook his head, his face expressing a reflective sadness, as if in his mind he were living again a bit of the past that it still hurt him to remember.

"I don't know," he answered the philatelist. "I really don't. I suspect not. I honestly think that Harry Norris—that was my friend—at this moment is a dozen times happier than any man here. And when I reflect that but for a bit of timidity on my part I might be with him—

"But I had better tell you the whole story," he said more briskly, "so you can fully understand."

I am not a stamp collector myself [he began, with a pleasant nod toward Malcolm] but my father was. He died some years ago, and among other things he left me his collection.

It was not a particularly good one—he had leaned more toward picturesqueness in his items than toward rarity or value—and when I sold it, I hardly got enough for it to repay me for the trouble I went to in having it appraised.

I even thought for a time of keeping it; for some of his collection, particularly those stamps from tropical countries that featured exotic birds and beasts, were highly decorative.

But in the end I sold them all—except one set of five which the dealer refused to take, because he said they were forgeries.

Forgeries! If he had only guessed.

But naturally I took his word for it. I assumed he knew. Especially since the five stamps differed considerably from any I had ever seen before, and had not even been pasted into my father's album. Instead, they had been loose in an envelope tucked in at the rear of the book.

But forgeries or not, they were both interesting and attractive. The five were in differing denominations: ten cents, fifty cents, one dollar, three dollars, and five dollars.

All were unused, in mint condition—that's the term, isn't it, Malcolm?—and in the gayest of colors: vermillion and ultramarine, emerald and yellow, orange and azure, chocolate and ivory, black and gold.

And since they were all large—their size was roughly four times that of the current airmail stamps, with which you are all familiar—the scenes they showed had great vividness and reality.

In particular the three-dollar one, portraying the native girl with the platter of fruit on her head—

However, that's getting ahead of my story. Let me say simply that, thinking they were forgeries, I put them away in my desk and forgot about them.

I found them again one night, quite by accident, when I was rummaging around in the back of a drawer, looking for an envelope in which to post a letter I had just written to my best friend, Harry Norris. Harry was at that time living in Boston.

It so happened that the only envelope I could find was the one in which I had been keeping those stamps of my father's. I emptied them out, addressed the envelope, and then, after I had sealed the letter inside, found my attention attracted to those five strange stamps.

I have mentioned that they were all large and rectangular: almost the size of baggage labels, rather than of conventional postage stamps. But then, of course, these were not conventional postage stamps.

Across the top of them was a line in bold print: FEDERATED STATES OF EL DORADO. Then, on either side, about the center, the denomination. And at the bottom, another line, *Rapid Post.*

Being unfamiliar with such things, I had assumed when first I found them that El Dorado was one of these small Indian states, or perhaps it was in Central America someplace. Rapid Post, I judged, would probably correspond to our own air mail.

Since the denominations were in cents and dollars, I rather leaned to the Latin America theory: there are a lot of little countries down there that I'm always getting confused, like San Salvador and Colombia. But until that moment I had never really given the matter much thought.

Now, staring at them, I began to wonder whether that dealer had known his business. They were done so well, the engraving executed with such superb verve, the colors so bold and attractive, that it hardly seemed likely any forger could have gotten them up.

It is true the subjects they depicted were far from usual. The ten-cent value, for instance, pictured a unicorn standing erect, head up, spiral horn pointing skyward, mane flowing, the very breathing image of life.

It was almost impossible to look at it without *knowing* that the artist had worked with a real unicorn for a model. Except, of course, that there aren't any unicorns any more.

The fifty-center showed Neptune, trident held aloft, riding a pair of harnessed dolphins through a foaming surf. It was just as real as the first.

The one-dollar value depicted Pan playing on his pipes, with a Greek temple in the background, and three fauns dancing on the grass. Looking at it, I could almost hear the music he was making.

I'm not exaggerating in the least. I must admit I was a little puzzled that a tropical country should be putting Pan on one of its stamps, for I thought he was purely a Greek monopoly. But when I moved on to the three-dollar stamp, I forgot all about him.

I probably can't put into words quite the impression that stamp made upon me—and upon Harry Norris, later.

The central figure was a girl; I believe I spoke of that.

A native girl, against a background of tropical flowers, a girl of about sixteen, I should say, just blossomed into womanhood, smiling a little secret smile that managed to combine the utter innocence of girlhood with all the inherited wisdom of a woman.

Or am I making myself clear? Not very? Well, no matter. Let it go at that. I'll only add that on her head, native fashion, she was carrying a great flat platter piled high with fruit of every kind you can imagine; and that platter, together with some flowers at her feet, was her only attire.

I looked at her for quite a long time, before I examined the last of the set—the five-dollar value.

This one was relatively uninteresting, by comparison—just a map. It showed several small islands set down in an expanse of water labeled, in neat letters, *Sea of El Dorado*. I assumed that the islands represented the Federated States of El Dorado itself, and that the little dot on the largest, marked by the word Nirvana, was the capital of the country.

Then an idea occurred to me. Harry had a nephew who collected stamps. Just for the fun of it, I might put one of those El Dorado forgeries—if they were forgeries—on my letter to Harry, along with the regular stamp, and see whether it wouldn't go through the post office. If it did, Harry's nephew might get a rarity, a foreign stamp with an American cancelation.

It was a silly idea, but it was late at night and finding the stamps had put me in a gay mood. I promptly licked the ten-cent El Dorado, pasted it onto the corner of Harry's letter, and then got up to hunt a regulation stamp to put with it.

The search took me into my bedroom, where I found the necessary postage in the wallet I had left in my coat. While I was gone, I left the letter itself lying in plain sight on my desk.

And when I got back into the library, the letter was gone.

I don't need to say I was puzzled. There wasn't any place it could have gone to. There wasn't anybody who could have taken it. The window was open, but it was a penthouse window overlooking twenty floors of empty space, and nobody had come in through it.

Nor was there any breeze that might have blown the envelope to the floor. I looked. In fact, I looked everywhere, growing steadily more puzzled.

And then, as I was about to give up, my phone began ringing.

It was Harry Norris, calling me from Boston. His voice, as he said hello, was a little strained. I quickly found out why.

Three minutes before, as he was getting ready for bed, the letter I had just finished giving up for lost had come swooping in his window, hung for a moment in midair as he stared at it, and then fluttered to the floor.

The next afternoon, Harry Norris arrived in New York. I had promised him over the phone, after explaining about the El Dorado stamp on the letter, not to touch the others except to put them safely away.

It was obvious that the stamp was responsible for what had happened. In some manner it had carried that letter from my library straight to Harry Norris' feet in an estimated time of three minutes, or at an average rate of approximately five thousand miles an hour.

It was a thought to stagger the imagination. Certainly it staggered mine.

Harry arrived just at lunch time, and over lunch I told him all I knew; just what I've told you now. He was disappointed at the meagerness of my information. But I couldn't add a thing to the facts we already knew, and those facts spoke for themselves.

Basically, they reduced to this: I had put the El Dorado stamp on Harry's letter, and promptly that letter had delivered itself to him with no intermediary processes whatever.

"No, that's not quite right!" Harry burst out. "Look. I brought the letter with me. And–"

He held it out to me, and I saw I had been wrong. There *had* been an intermediary process of some kind, for the stamp was canceled. Yes, and the envelope was postmarked, too, in a clearly legible, pale purple ink.

Federated States of El Dorado, the postmark said. It was circular, like our own; and in the center of the circle, where the time of cancellation usually is, was just the word *Thursday*.

"Today is Thursday," Harry remarked. "It was after midnight when you put the stamp on the letter?"

"Just after," I told him. "Seems queer these El Dorado people pay no attention to the hour and the minute, doesn't it?"

"Only proves they're a tropical country," Harry suggested. "Time means little or nothing in the tropics, you know. But what I was getting at, the Thursday postmark goes to show El Dorado is probably down in Central America, as you suggested. If it were in India, or the Orient, it would have been marked Wednesday, wouldn't it? On account of the time difference?"

"Or would it have been Friday?" I asked, rather doubtfully, not knowing much about those things. "In any case we can find out easily enough. We've just to look in the atlas. I don't know why I didn't think of it before."

Harry brightened.

"Of course," he said. "Where do you keep yours?"

But it turned out I hadn't any atlas in the house—not even a small one. So we phoned downtown to one of the big bookstores to send up their latest and largest atlas. And while we waited for it we examined the letter again and speculated upon the method by which it had been transmitted.

"Rapid post!" Harry explained. "I should say so! It beats airmail all hollow. Why, if that letter not only traveled from here to Boston between the time you missed it and it fell at my feet, but actually went all the way to Central America, was canceled and postmarked, and *then* went on to Boston, its average speed must have been—"

We did a little rough calculation and hit upon two thousand miles a minute as a probable speed. When we'd done that, we looked at each other.

"Good Lord!" Harry gasped. "The Federated States of El Dorado may be a tropical country, but they've really hit upon something new in this thing! I wonder why we haven't heard about it before?"

"May be keeping it a secret," I suggested. "No, that won't do, because I've had the stamps for several years, and of course, my father had them before that."

"I tell you, there's something queer here," Harry suggested, darkly. "Where are those others you told me about? I think we ought to make a few tests with them while we're waiting for that atlas."

With that I brought out the four remaining unused stamps, and handed them to him. Now Harry, among other things, was a rather good artist; and his whistle at the workmanship was appreciative. He examined each with care, but it was—I'd thought it would be—the three-dollar value that really caught his eye. The one with the native girl on it, you remember.

"Lord!" Harry said aloud. "What a beauty!"

Presently, however, Harry put that one aside and finished examining the others. Then he turned to me.

"The thing I can't get over," he commented, "is the *lifelikeness* of the figures. You know what I'd suspect if I didn't know better? I'd suspect these stamps were never engraved at all. I'd believe that the plates they came from were prepared from photographs."

"From photographs!" I exclaimed; and Harry nodded.

"Of course, you know and I know they can't have been," he added. "Unicorns and Neptunes and Pans aren't running around to be photographed, these days. But that's the feeling they give me."

I confessed that I had had the same feeling. But since we both agreed on the impossibility of its being so, we dismissed that phase of the matter and went back again to the problem of the method used in transporting the letter.

"You say you were out of the room when it vanished," Harry remarked. "That means you didn't see it go. You don't actually know what happened when you put that stamp on and turned your back, do you?"

I agreed that was so, and Harry sat in thoughtful silence.

At last he looked up.

"*I* think," he said, "we ought to find out by using one of these other stamps to mail something with."

Why that hadn't occurred to me before I can't imagine. As soon as Harry said it, I recognized the rightness of the idea. The only thing was to decide what to send, and to whom.

That held us up for several minutes. There wasn't anybody else either of us cared to know about this just now; and we couldn't send anything to each other very well, being both there together.

"I'll tell you!" Harry exclaimed at last. "We'll send something to El Dorado itself!"

I agreed to that readily enough, but how it came about that we decided to send, not a letter, but Thomas à Becket, my aged and ailing Siamese cat, I can't remember.

I do know that I told myself it would be a kind way to dispose of the creature. Transmission through space at the terrific velocity of one hundred and twenty thousand miles an hour would surely put him out of his sufferings, quickly and painlessly.

Thomas à Becket was asleep under the couch, breathing asthmatically and with difficulty. I found a cardboard box the right size and we punched some air holes in it. Then I gathered up Thomas and placed him in the container. He opened rheumy old eyes, gazed at me vaguely, and relapsed into slumber again. With a pang I put the lid on and we tied the box.

"Now," Harry said thoughtfully, "there's the question of how to address him, of course. However, any address will do for our purpose."

He took up a pen and wrote with rapidity. *Mr. Henry Smith, 711 Elysian Fields Avenue, Nirvana, Federated States of El Dorado.* And beneath that he added, *Perishable! Handle With Care!*

"But—" I began. Harry cut me off.

"No," he said, "of course I don't know of any such address. I just made it up. But the post-office people won't know that, will they?"

"But what will happen when—" I began again, and again he had had the answer before I'd finished the question.

"It'll go to the dead letter office, I expect," he told me. "And if he *is* dead, they'll dispose of him. If he's alive, I've no doubt they'll take good care of him. From the stamps I've gotten a notion living is easy there."

That silenced my questions, and Harry picked up a stamp—the fifty-cent value—licked it, and placed it firmly on the box. Then he withdrew his hand and stepped back beside me.

Intently, we watched the parcel.

For a moment, nothing whatever happened.

And then, just as disappointment was gathering on Harry Norris' countenance, the box holding Thomas à Becket rose slowly into the air, turned like a compass needle, and began to drift with increasing speed toward the open window.

By the time it reached the window, it was moving with race-horse velocity. It shot through and into the open. We rushed to the window and saw it moving upward in a westerly direction, above the Manhattan skyline.

And then, as we stared, it began to be vague in outline, misty; and an instant later had vanished entirely. Because of its speed, I suggested, the same way a rifle bullet is invisible.

But Harry had another idea. He shook his head as we stepped back toward the center of the room.

"No," he began, "I don't think that's the answer. I have a notion—"

What his notion was I never did find out. Because just then he stopped speaking, with his mouth still open, and I saw him stiffen. He was looking past me, and I turned to see what had affected him so.

Outside the window was the package we had just seen vanish. It hung there for a moment, then moved slowly into the room, gave a little swoop, and settled lightly onto the table from which, not two minutes before, it had left.

Harry and I rushed over to it, and our eyes must have bugged out a bit.

Because the package was all properly canceled and postmarked, just as the letter had been. With the addition that across the corner, in large purple letters, somebody had stamped, RETURN TO SENDER. NO SUCH PERSON AT THIS ADDRESS.

"Well!" Harry said at last. It wasn't exactly adequate, but it was all either of us could think of. Then, inside the box, Thomas à Becket let out a squawl.

I cut the cords and lifted the lid. Thomas à Becket leaped out with an animation he had not shown in years.

There was no denying it. Instead of killing him, his trip to El Dorado, brief as it was, had done him good. He looked five years younger.

Harry Norris was turning the box over in his hands, perplexed.

"What I can't get over," he remarked, "is that there really *is* such an address as 711 Elysian Fields Avenue. I swear I just made it up."

"There's more to it than that," I reminded him. "The very fact that the package came back. We didn't put any return address on it."

"So we didn't," Harry agreed. "Yet they knew just where to return it, didn't they?"

He pondered for a moment longer. Then he put the box down.

"I'm beginning to think," he said, an odd expression on his face, "that there is more to this than we realize. A great deal more. I suspect the whole truth is a lot more exciting than we have any notion. As for this Federated States of El Dorado, I have a theory—"

But he didn't tell me what his theory was. Instead, that three-dollar chocolate-and-ivory stamp caught his eye again.

"Jove!" he whispered, more to himself than to me—he was given occasionally to these archaic ejaculations—"she's beautiful. Heavenly! With a model like that an artist might paint—"

"He might forget to paint, too," I put in. Harry nodded.

"He might indeed," he agreed. "Though I think he'd be inspired in the end to work he'd never on earth have dreamed of doing, otherwise." His gaze at the stamp was almost hungry. "This girl," he declared, "is the one I've been waiting all my life to find. To meet her I'd give—I'd give— Well, almost anything."

"I'm afraid you'd have to go to El Dorado to do that," I suggested flippantly, and Harry started.

"So I would! And I'm perfectly willing to do it, too. Listen! These stamps suggest this El Dorado place must be rather fascinating. What do you say we both pay it a visit? We neither of us have any ties to keep us, and—"

"Go there just so you can meet the girl who was the model for that stamp?" I demanded.

"Why not? Can you think of a better reason?" he asked me. "I can give you more. For one thing, the climate. Look how much better the cat is. His little excursion took years off his age. Must be a highly healthful place. Maybe it'll make a young man of you again. And besides—"

But he didn't have to go on. I was already convinced.

"All right," I agreed. "We'll take the first boat. But when we get there, how will we—"

"By logic," Harry shot back. "Purely by logic. The girl must have posed for an artist, mustn't she? And the postmaster general of El Dorado must know who the artist is, mustn't he? We'll go straight to the postmaster general. He'll direct us to the artist. The artist will give us her name and address. Could anything be simpler?"

I hadn't realized how easy it would be. Now some of his impatience was getting into my own blood.

"Maybe we won't have to take a boat," I suggested. "Maybe there's a plane service. That would save—"

"Boat!" Harry Norris snorted, stalking back and forth across the room and waving his hands. "Plane! You can take boats and planes if you want to. I've got a better idea. I'm going to El Dorado by mail!"

Until I saw how beautifully simple his idea was, I was a bit stunned. But he quickly pointed out that Thomas à Becket had made the trip, and come back, without injury. If a cat could do it, a man could.

There wasn't a thing in the way except the choice of a destination. It would be rather wasted effort to go, only to be sent back ignominiously for want of proper addressing.

"I have that figured out too," Harry told me promptly when I voiced the matter. "The first person I'd go to see anyway when I got there would be the postmaster general. *He* must exist, certainly. And mail addressed to him would be the easiest of all to deliver. So why not kill two birds with one stone by posting myself to his office?"

That answered all my objections. It was as sound and sensible a plan as I'd ever heard.

"Why," Harry Norris added with rising excitement, "I may be having dinner with the girl tonight! Wine and pomegranates beneath a gold-washed moon, with Pan piping in the shadows and nymphs dancing on the velvet green!"

"But"—I felt I had to prepare him for possible disappointment—"suppose she's married by now?"

He shook his head.

"She won't be. I have a feeling. Just a feeling. Now to settle the details. We've got three stamps left—nine dollars' worth altogether. That should be enough. I'm a bit lighter; you've been taking on weight lately, I see. Four dollars should carry me—the one and the three. That leaves the five-dollar for you.

"As for the address, we'll write that on tags and tie them to our wrists. You have tags, haven't you? Yes, here's a couple in this drawer. Now give me that pen and ink. Something like this ought to do very well . . ."

He wrote, then held the tags out to me. They were just alike. *Office of the Postmaster General,* they said. *Nirvana, Federated States of El Dorado. Perishable. Handle With Care.*

"Now," he said, "we'll each tie one to our wrist—"

But I drew back. Somehow I couldn't quite nerve myself to it. Delightful as the prospects he had painted of the place, the idea of posting myself into the unknown, the way I had sent off Thomas à Becket, did something queer to me.

I told him I would join him. I would take the first boat, or plane, and meet him there, say at the principal hotel.

Harry was disappointed, but he was too impatient by now to argue.

"Well," he agreed, "all right. But if for any reason you can't get a boat or plane, you'll use that last stamp to join me?"

I promised faithfully that I would. With that he held out his right wrist and I tied a tag about it. Then he took up the one-dollar stamp, moistened it, and applied it to the tag. He had the three-dollar one in his hand when the doorbell rang.

"In a minute," he was saying, "or maybe in less, I shall probably be in the fairest land man's combined imagination has ever been able to picture."

"Wait!" I called, and hurried out to answer the bell. I don't know whether he heard me or not. He was just lifting that second stamp to his tongue to moisten it when I turned away, and that was the last I ever saw of him.

When I came back, with the package in my hands—the ring had been the messenger from the bookshop, with the atlas we had ordered—Harry Norris was gone.

Thomas à Becket was sitting up and staring toward the window. The curtains were still fluttering. I hurried over. But Norris was not in sight.

Well, I thought, he must have put on that stamp he had in his hand, not knowing I'd left the room. I could see him, in my mind's eye, that very moment being deposited on his feet in the office of an astonished postmaster general.

Then it occurred to me I might as well find out just where the Federated States of El Dorado were, after all. So I ripped the paper off the large volume the bookstore had sent and began to leaf through it.

When I had finished, I sat in silence for a while. From time to time I glanced at that unused tag, and that uncanceled stamp still lying on my desk. Then I made my decision.

I got up and fetched Harry's bag. It was summer, luckily, and he had brought mostly light clothing. To it I added anything of mine I thought he might be able to use, including a carton of cigarettes, and pen and ink on the chance he might want to write me.

As an afterthought I added a small Bible—just in case.

Then I strapped the bag shut and affixed the tag to it. I wrote *Harry Norris* above the address, pasted that last El Dorado stamp to it, and waited.

In a moment the bag rose in the air, floated to the window, out, and began to speed away.

It would reach there, I figured, before Harry had had time to leave the postmaster general's office, and I hoped he might send me a postcard or something by way of acknowledgment. But he didn't. Perhaps he couldn't.

. . . At this point Morks stopped, as if he had finished his story. But unnoticed Malcolm had left our little group for a moment. Now he came pushing back into it with a large atlas-gazeteer in his hands.

"So that's what became of your set of rarities!" he said, with a scarcely veiled sneer. "Very interesting and entertaining. But there's one point I want to clear up. The stamps were issued by the Federated States of El Dorado, you say. Well, I've just been looking through this atlas, and there's no such place on earth."

Morks looked at him, his melancholy countenance calm.

"I know it," he said. "That's why, after glancing through my own atlas that day, I didn't keep my promise to Harry Norris and use that last stamp to join him. I'm sorry now. When I think of how Harry must be enjoying himself there—

"But it's no good regretting what I did or didn't do. I couldn't help it. The truth is that my nerve failed me, just for a moment then, when I discovered there *was* no such place as the Federated States of El Dorado—on earth, I mean."

And sadly he shook his head.

"I've often wished I knew where my father got those stamps," he murmured, almost to himself; then fell into a meditative silence.

The White People

BY ARTHUR MACHEN

Prologue

"SORCERY and sanctity," said Ambrose, "these are the only realities. Each is an ecstasy, a withdrawal from the common life."

Cotgrave listened, interested. He had been brought by a friend to this moldering house in a northern suburb, through an old garden to the room where Ambrose the recluse dozed and dreamed over his books.

"Yes," he went on, "magic is justified of her children. There are many, I think, who eat dry crusts and drink water, with a joy infinitely sharper than anything within the experience of the 'practical' epicure."

"You are speaking of the saints?"

"Yes, and of the sinners, too. I think you are falling into the very general error of confining the spiritual world to the supremely good; but the supremely wicked, necessarily, have their portion in it. The merely carnal, sensual man can no more be a great sinner than he can be a great saint. Most of us are just indifferent, mixed-up creatures; we muddle through the world without realizing the meaning and the inner sense of things, and consequently, our wickedness and our goodness are alike second-rate, unimportant."

"And you think the great sinner, then, will be an ascetic, as well as the great saint?"

"Great people of all kinds forsake the imperfect copies and go to the perfect originals. I have no doubt but that many of the very highest among the saints have never done a 'good action' (using the words in their ordinary sense). And, on the other hand, there have been those who have sounded the very depths of sin, who all their lives have never done an 'ill deed.' "

He went out of the room for a moment, and Cotgrave, in high delight, turned to his friend and thanked him for the introduction.

"He's grand," he said. "I never saw that kind of lunatic before."

Ambrose returned with more whiskey and helped the two men in a liberal manner. He abused the teetotal sect with ferocity, as he handed out the seltzer, and pouring out a glass of water for himself, was about to resume his monologue, when Cotgrave broke in–

"I can't stand it, you know," he said, "your paradoxes are too monstrous. A man may be a great sinner and yet never do anything sinful! Come!"

"You're quite wrong," said Ambrose. "I never make paradoxes; I wish I could. I merely said that a man may have an exquisite taste in Romanée Conti, and yet never have even smelt sour ale. That's all, and it's more like a truism than a paradox, isn't it? Your surprise at my remark is due to the fact that you haven't realized what sin is. Oh, yes, there is a sort of connection between Sin with the capital letter, and actions which are commonly called sinful: with murder, theft, adultery, and so forth. Much the same connection that there is between the A, B, C and fine literature. But I believe that the misconception–it is all but universal–arises in great measure from our looking at the matter through social spectacles. We think that a man who does evil to *us* and to his neighbors must be very evil. So he is, from a social standpoint; but can't you realize that Evil in its essence is a lonely thing, a passion of the solitary, individual soul? Really, the average murderer, *qua* murderer, is not by any means a sinner in the true sense of the word. He is simply a wild beast that we have to get rid of to save our own necks from his knife. I should class him rather with tigers than with sinners."

"It seems a little strange."

"I think not. The murderer murders not from positive qualities, but from negative ones; he lacks something which non-murderers possess. Evil, of course, is wholly positive—only it is on the wrong side. You may believe me that sin in its proper sense is very rare; it is probable that there have been far fewer sinners than saints. Yes, your standpoint is all very well for practical, social purposes; we are naturally inclined to think that a person who is very disagreeable to us must be a very great sinner! It is very disagreeable to have one's pocket picked, and we pronounce the thief to be a very great sinner. In truth, he is merely an undeveloped man. He cannot be a saint, of course; but he may be, and often is, an infinitely better creature than thousands who have never broken a single commandment. He is a great nuisance to *us*, I admit, and we very properly lock him up if we catch him; but between his troublesome and unsocial action and evil—Oh, the connection is of the weakest."

It was getting very late. The man who had brought Cotgrave had probably heard all this before, since he assisted with a bland and judicious smile, but Cotgrave began to think that his "lunatic" was turning into a sage.

"Do you know," he said, "you interest me immensely? You think, then, that we do not understand the real nature of evil?"

"No, I don't think we do. We overestimate it and we underestimate it. We take the very numerous infractions of our social 'bylaws'—the very necessary and very proper regulations which keep the human company together—and we get frightened at the prevalence of 'sin' and 'evil.' But this is really nonsense. Take theft, for example. Have you any *horror* at the thought of Robin Hood, of the Highland caterans of the seventeenth century, of the mosstroopers, of the company promoters of our day?

"Then, on the other hand, we underrate evil. We attach such an enormous importance to the 'sin' of meddling with our pockets (and our wives) that we have quite forgotten the awfulness of real sin."

"And what is sin?" said Cotgrave.

"I think I must reply to your question by another. What would your feelings be, seriously, if your cat or your dog began to talk to you, and to dispute with you in human accents?

You would be overwhelmed with horror. I am sure of it. And if the roses in your garden sang a weird song, you would go mad. And suppose the stones in the road began to swell and grow before your eyes, and if the pebble that you noticed at night had shot out stony blossoms in the morning?

"Well, these examples may give you some notion of what sin really is."

"Look here," said the third man, hitherto placid, "you two seem pretty well wound up. But I'm going home. I've missed my tram, and I shall have to walk."

Ambrose and Cotgrave seemed to settle down more profoundly when the other had gone out into the early misty morning and the pale light of the lamps.

"You astonish me," said Cotgrave. "I have never thought of that. If that is really so, one must turn everything upside down. Then the essence of sin really is—"

"In the taking of heaven by storm, it seems to me," said Ambrose. "It appears to me that it is simply an attempt to penetrate into another and higher sphere in a forbidden manner. You can understand why it is so rare. There are few, indeed, who wish to penetrate into other spheres, higher or lower, in ways allowed or forbidden. Men, in the mass, are amply content with life as they find it. Therefore there are few saints, and sinners (in the proper sense) are fewer still, and men of genius, who partake sometimes of each character, are rare also. Yes, on the whole, it is, perhaps, harder to be a great sinner than a great saint."

"There is something profoundly unnatural about sin? Is that what you mean?"

"Exactly. Holiness requires as great, or almost as great, an effort; but holiness works on lines that *were* natural once; it is an effort to recover the ecstasy that was before the Fall. But sin is an effort to gain the ecstasy and the knowledge that pertain alone to angels, and in making this effort man becomes a demon. I told you that the mere murderer is not *therefore* a sinner; that is true, but the sinner is sometimes a murderer. Gilles de Raiz is an instance. So you see that while the good and the evil are unnatural to man as he now is—to man the social, civilized being—evil is unnatural in a much deeper sense than good. The saint endeavors to recover a gift which he has lost; the sinner tries to obtain something which was never his. In brief, he repeats the Fall."

"But are you a Catholic?" said Cotgrave.

"Yes, I am a member of the persecuted Anglican Church."

"Then, how about those texts which seem to reckon as sin that which you would set down as a mere trivial dereliction?"

"Yes, but in one place the word 'sorcerers' comes in the same sentence, doesn't it? That seems to me to give the keynote. Consider: can you imagine for a moment that a false statement which saves an innocent man's life is a sin? No. Very good, then, it is not the mere liar who is excluded by those words; it is, above all, the 'sorcerers' who use the material life, who use the failings incidental to material life as instruments to obtain their infinitely wicked ends. And let me tell you this: our higher senses are so blunted, we are so drenched with materialism, that we should probably fail to recognize real wickedness if we encountered it."

"But shouldn't we experience a certain horror—a terror such as you hinted we would experience if a rose tree sang—in the mere presence of an evil man?"

"We should if we were natural: children and women feel this horror you speak of, even animals experience it. But with most of us convention and civilization and education have blinded and deafened and obscured the natural reason. No, sometimes we may recognize evil by its hatred of the good—one doesn't need much penetration to guess at the influence which dictated, quite unconsciously, the 'Blackwood' review of Keats—but this is purely incidental; and, as a rule, I suspect that Hierarchs of Tophet pass quite unnoticed, or, perhaps, in certain cases, as good but mistaken men."

"But you used the word 'unconscious' just now, of Keats' reviewers. Is wickedness ever unconscious?"

"Always. It must be so. It is like holiness and genius in this as in other points; it is a certain rapture or ecstasy of the soul; a transcendent effort to surpass the ordinary bounds. So, surpassing these, it surpasses also the understanding, the faculty that takes note of that which comes before it. No, a man may be infinitely and horribly wicked and never suspect it. But I tell you, evil in this, its certain and true sense, is rare, and I think it is growing rarer."

"I am trying to get hold of it all," said Cotgrave. "From what you say, I gather that the true evil differs generically from that which we call evil?"

"Quite so. There is, no doubt, an analogy between the two; a resemblance such as enables us to use, quite legitimately, such terms as the 'foot of the mountain' and the 'leg of the table.' And, sometimes, of course, the two speak, as it were, in the same language. The rough miner, or 'puddler,' the untrained, undeveloped 'tiger-man,' heated by a quart or two above his usual measure, comes home and kicks his irritating and injudicious wife to death. He is a murderer. And Gilles de Raiz was a murderer. But you see the gulf that separates the two? The 'word,' if I may so speak, is accidentally the same in each case, but the 'meaning' is utterly different. It is flagrant 'Hobson Jobson' to confuse the two, or rather, it is as if one supposed that Juggernaut and the Argonauts had something to do etymologically with one another. And no doubt the same weak likeness, or analogy, runs between all the 'social' sins and the real spiritual sins, and in some cases, perhaps, the lesser may be 'schoolmasters' to lead one on to the greater—from the shadow to the reality. If you are anything of a theologian, you will see the importance of all this."

"I am sorry to say," remarked Cotgrave, "that I have devoted very little of my time to theology. Indeed, I have often wondered on what grounds theologians have claimed the title of Science of Sciences for their favorite study; since the 'theological' books I have looked into have always seemed to me to be concerned with feeble and obvious pieties, or with the kings of Israel and Judah. I do not care to hear about those kings."

Ambrose grinned.

"We must try to avoid theological discussion," he said. "I perceive that you would be a bitter disputant. But perhaps the 'dates of the kings' have as much to do with theology as the hobnails of the murderous puddler with evil."

"Then, to return to our main subject, you think that sin is an esoteric, occult thing?"

"Yes. It is the infernal miracle as holiness is the supernal. Now and then it is raised to such a pitch that we entirely fail to suspect its existence; it is like the note of the great pedal pipes of the organ, which is so deep that we cannot hear it. In other cases it may lead to the lunatic asylum, or to still stranger issues. But you must never confuse it with mere social misdoing. Remember how the apostle, speaking of the 'other side,' distinguishes between 'charitable' actions and charity. And as one may give all one's goods to the poor, and yet lack charity; so, remember, one may avoid every crime and yet be a sinner."

"Your psychology is very strange to me," said Cotgrave, "but I confess I like it, and I suppose that one might fairly deduce from your premises the conclusion that the real sinner might very possibly strike the observer as a harmless enough personage?"

"Certainly, because the true evil has nothing to do with social life or social laws, or if it has, only incidentally and accidentally. It is a lonely passion of the soul—or a passion of the lonely soul—whichever you like. If, by chance, we understand it, and grasp its full significance, then, indeed, it will fill us with horror and with awe. But this emotion is widely distinguished from the fear and the disgust with which we regard the ordinary criminal, since this latter is largely or entirely founded on the regard which we have for our own skins or purses. We hate a murderer, because we know that we should hate to be murdered, or to have anyone that we like murdered. So, on the 'other side,' we venerate the saints, but we don't 'like' them as we like our friends. Can you persuade yourself that you would have 'enjoyed' St. Paul's company? Do you think that you and I would have 'got on' with Sir Galahad?

"So with the sinners, as with the saints. If you met a very evil man, and recognized his evil, he would, no doubt, fill you with horror and awe; but there is no reason why you should 'dislike' him. On the contrary, it is quite possible that if you could succeed in putting the sin out of your mind you might find the sinner capital company, and in a little while you might have to reason yourself back into horror. Still, how awful it is. If the roses and the lilies suddenly sang on this coming morning; if the furniture began to move in procession, as in de Maupassant's tale!"

"I am glad you have come back to that comparison," said

Cotgrave, "because I wanted to ask you what it is that corresponds in humanity to these imaginary feats of inanimate things. In a word—what is sin? You have given me, I know, an abstract definition, but I should like a concrete example."

"I told you it was very rare," said Ambrose, who appeared willing to avoid the giving of a direct answer. "The materialism of the age, which has done a good deal to suppress sanctity, has done perhaps more to suppress evil. We find the earth so very comfortable that we have no inclination either for ascents or descents. It would seem as if the scholar who decided to 'specialize' in Tophet, would be reduced to purely antiquarian researches. No paleontologist could show you a *live* pterodactyl."

"And yet you, I think, have 'specialized,' and I believe that your researches have descended to our modern times."

"You are really interested, I see. Well, I confess, that I have dabbled a little, and if you like I can show you something that bears on the very curious subject we have been discussing."

Ambrose took a candle and went away to a far, dim corner of the room. Cotgrave saw him open a venerable bureau that stood there, and from some secret recess he drew out a parcel, and came back to the window where they had been sitting.

Ambrose undid a wrapping of paper, and produced a green pocketbook.

"You will take care of it?" he said. "Don't leave it lying about. It is one of the choicer pieces in my collection, and I should be very sorry if it were lost."

He fondled the faded binding.

"I knew the girl who wrote this," he said. "When you read it, you will see how it illustrates the talk we have had tonight. There is a sequel, too, but I won't talk of that.

"There was an odd article in one of the reviews some months ago," he began again, with the air of a man who changes the subject. "It was written by a doctor—Dr. Coryn, I think, was the name. He says that a lady, watching her little girl playing at the drawing-room window, suddenly saw the heavy sash give way and fall on the child's fingers. The lady fainted, I think, but at any rate the doctor was summoned, and when he had dressed the child's wounded and maimed fingers he was summoned to the mother. She was groaning with pain, and it was found that three fingers of her hand, corresponding with those that had been injured on the child's hand, were swollen and inflamed, and later, in the doctor's language, purulent sloughing set in."

Ambrose still handled delicately the green volume.

"Well, here it is," he said at last, parting with difficulty, it seemed, from his treasure.

"You will bring it back as soon as you have read it," he said, as they went out into the hall, into the old garden, faint with the odor of white lilies.

There was a broad red band in the east as Cotgrave turned to go, and from the high ground where he stood he saw that awful spectacle of London in a dream.

The Green Book

THE morocco binding of the book was faded, and the color had grown faint, but there were no stains nor bruises nor marks of usage. The book looked as if it had been bought "on a visit to London" some seventy or eighty years ago, and had somehow been forgotten and suffered to lie away out of sight. There was an old, delicate, lingering odor about it, such an odor as sometimes haunts an ancient piece of furniture for a century or more. The end papers, inside the binding, were oddly decorated with colored patterns and faded gold. It looked small, but the paper was fine, and there were many leaves, closely covered with minute, painfully formed characters.

I found this book (the manuscript began) in a drawer in the old bureau that stands on the landing. It was a very rainy day and I could not go out, so in the afternoon I got a candle and rummaged in the bureau. Nearly all the drawers were full of old dresses, but one of the small ones looked empty, and I found this book hidden right at the back. I wanted a book like this, so I took it to write in. It is full of secrets. I have a great many other books of secrets I have written, hidden in a safe place, and I am going to write here many of the old secrets and some new ones; but there are some I shall not put down at all. I must not write down the real names of the days and months which I found out a year ago, nor the way to make the Aklo letters, or the Chian language, or the great beautiful Circles, nor the Mao Games, nor the chief songs. I may write something about all these things but not the way to do them, for peculiar reasons. And I must not say who the Nymphs are, or the Dôls, or Jeelo, or what voolas mean. All these are most secret secrets, and I am glad when I remember what they are, and how many wonderful languages I know, but there are some things that I call the secrets of the secrets of the secrets that I dare not think of unless I am quite alone, and then I shut my eyes, and put my hands over them and whisper the word, and the Alala comes. I only do this at night in my room or in certain woods that I know, but I must not describe them, as they are secret woods. Then there are the Ceremonies, which are all of them important, but some are more delightful than others—there are the White Ceremonies, and the Green Ceremonies, and the Scarlet Ceremonies. The Scarlet Ceremonies are the best, but there is only one place where they can be performed properly, though there is a very nice imitation which I have done in other places. Besides these, I have the dances, and the Comedy, and I have done the Comedy sometimes when the others were looking, and they didn't understand anything about it. I was very little when I first knew about these things.

When I was very small, and mother was alive, I can remember remembering things before that, only it has all got confused. But I remember when I was five or six I heard them talking about me when they thought I was not noticing. They were saying how queer I was a year or two before, and how nurse had called my mother to come and listen to me talking all to myself, and I was saying words that nobody could understand. I was speaking the Xu language, but I only remember a very few of the words, as it was about the little white faces that used to look at me when I was lying in my cradle. They used to talk to me, and I learned their language and talked to them in it about some great white place where they lived, where the trees and the grass were all white, and there were white hills as high up as the moon, and a cold wind. I have often dreamed of it afterwards, but the faces went away when I was very little. But a wonderful thing happened when I was about five. My nurse was carrying me on her shoulder; there was a field of yellow corn, and we went through it; it was very hot. Then we came to a path through a wood, and a tall man came after us, and went with us till we came to a place where there was a deep pool, and it was very dark and shady. Nurse put me down on the soft moss under a tree, and she said: "She can't get to the pond now." So they left me there, and I sat quite still and watched, and out of the water and out of the wood came two wonderful white people, and they began to play and dance and sing. They were a kind of creamy white like the old ivory figure in the drawing room; one was a beautiful lady with kind dark eyes, and a grave face, and long black hair, and she smiled such a strange sad smile at the other, who laughed and came to her. They played together, and danced round and round the pool, and they sang a song till I fell asleep.

Nurse woke me up when she came back, and she was looking something like the lady had looked, so I told her all about it, and asked her why she looked like that. At first she cried, and then she looked very frightened, and turned quite pale. She put me down on the grass and stared at me, and I could see she was shaking all over. Then she said I had been dreaming, but I knew I hadn't. Then she made me promise not to say a word about it to anybody, and if I did I should be thrown into the black pit. I was not frightened at all, though nurse was, and I never forgot about it, because when I shut my eyes and it was quite quiet, and I was all alone, I could see them again, very faint and far away, but very splendid; and little bits of the song they sang came into my head, but I couldn't sing it.

I was thirteen, nearly fourteen, when I had a very singular adventure, so strange that the day on which it happened is always called the White Day. My mother had been dead for more than a year, and in the morning I had lessons, but they let me go out for walks in the afternoon. And this afternoon I walked a new way, and a little brook led me into a new country, but I tore my frock getting through some of the difficult places, as the way was through many bushes, and beneath the low branches of trees, and up thorny thickets on the hills, and by dark woods full of creeping thorns. And it was a long, long way. It seemed as if I was going on forever and ever, and I had to creep by a place like a tunnel where a brook must have been, but all the water had dried up, and the floor was rocky, and the bushes had grown overhead till they met, so that it was quite dark. And I went on and on through that dark place; it was a long, long way. And I came to a hill that I never saw before. I was in a dismal thicket full of black twisted boughs that tore me as I went through them, and I cried out because I was smarting all over, and then I found that I was climbing, and I went up and up a long way, till at last the thicket stopped and I came out crying just under the top of a big bare place, where there were ugly grey stones lying all about on the grass, and here and there a little twisted, stunted tree came out from under a stone, like a snake. And I went up, right to the top, a long way. I never saw such big ugly stones before; they came out of the earth some of them, and some looked as if they had been rolled to where they were, and they went on and on as far as I could see, a long, long way. I looked out from them and saw the country, but it was strange. It was winter time, and there were black terrible woods hanging from the hills all round; it was like seeing a large room hung with black curtains, and the shape of the trees seemed quite different from any I had ever seen before. I was afraid. Then beyond the woods there were other hills round in a great ring, but I had never seen any of them; it all looked black, and everything had a voor over it. It was all so still and silent, and the sky was heavy and gray and sad, like a wicked voorish dome in Deep Dendo. I went on into the dreadful rocks. There were hundreds and hundreds of them. Some were like horrid-grinning men; I could see their faces as if they would jump at me out of the stone, and catch hold of me, and drag me with them back into the rock, so that I should always be there. And there were other rocks that were like animals, creeping, horrible animals, putting out their tongues, and others were like words that I could not say, and others like dead people lying on the grass. I went on among them, though they frightened me, and my heart was full of wicked songs that they put into it; and I wanted to make faces and twist myself about in the way they did, and I went on and on a long way till at last I liked the rocks, and they didn't frighten me any more. I sang the songs I thought of; songs full of words that must not be spoken or written down. Then I made faces like the faces on the rocks, and I twisted myself about like the twisted ones, and I lay down flat on the ground like the dead ones, and I went up to one that was grinning, and put my arms round him and hugged him. And so I went on and on through the rocks till I came to a round mound in the middle of them. It was higher than a mound; it was nearly as high as our house, and it was like a great basin turned upside down, all smooth and round and green, with one stone, like a post, sticking up at the top. I climbed up the sides, but they were so steep I had to stop or I should have rolled all the way down again, and I should have knocked against the stones at the bottom, and perhaps been killed. But I wanted to get up to the very top of the big round mound, so I lay down flat on my face, and took hold of the grass with my hands and drew myself up, bit by bit, till I was at the top. Then I sat down on the stone in the middle, and looked all about. I felt I had come such a long, long way, just as if I were a hundred miles from home, or in some other country, or in one of the strange places I had read about in the *Tale of the Genie* and the *Arabian Nights,* or as if I had gone across the sea, far away, for years and I had found another world that nobody had ever seen or heard of before, or as if I had somehow flown through the sky and fallen on one of the stars I had read about where everything is dead and cold and gray, and there is no air, and the wind doesn't blow. I sat on the stone and looked all round and down and round about me. It was just as if I was sitting on a tower in the middle of a great empty town, because I could see nothing all around but the gray rocks on the ground. I couldn't make out their shapes any more, but I could see them on and on for a long way, and I looked at them, and they seemed as if they had been arranged into patterns, and shapes, and figures. I knew they couldn't be, because I had seen a lot of them coming right out of the earth, joined to the deep rocks below, so I looked again, but still I saw nothing but circles, and small circles inside big ones, and pyramids, and domes, and spires, and they seemed all to go round and round the place where I was sitting, and the more I looked, the more I saw great big rings of rocks, getting bigger and bigger, and I stared so long that it felt as if they were all moving and turning, like a great wheel, and I was turning, too, in the middle. I got quite dizzy and queer in the head, and everything began to be hazy and not clear, and I saw little sparks of blue light, and the stones looked as if they were springing and dancing and twisting as they went round and round and round. I was frightened again, and I cried aloud, and jumped up from the stone I was sitting on, and fell down. When I got up I was so glad they all looked still, and I sat down on the top and slid down the mound, and went on again. I danced as I went in the peculiar way the rocks had danced when I got giddy, and I was so glad I could do it quite well, and I danced and danced along, and sang extraordinary songs that came into my head. At last I came to the edge of that great flat hill, and there were no more rocks, and the way went again through a dark thicket in a hollow. It was just as bad as the other one I went through climbing up, but I didn't mind this one, because I was so glad I had seen those singular dances and could imitate them. I went down, creeping through the bushes, and a tall nettle stung me on my leg, and made me burn, but I didn't mind it, and I tingled with the boughs and the thorns, but I only laughed and sang. Then I got out of the thicket into a close valley, a little secret place like a dark passage that nobody ever knows of, because it was so narrow and deep and the woods were so thick round it. There is a steep bank with trees hanging over it, and there the ferns keep green all through the winter, when they are dead and brown upon the hill, and the ferns there have a sweet, rich smell like what oozes out of fir trees. There was a little stream of water running down this valley, so small that I could easily step across it. I drank the water with my hand, and it tasted like bright, yellow wine, and it sparkled and bubbled as it ran down over beautiful red and yellow and green stones, so that it seemed alive and all colors at once. I drank it, and I drank more with my hand, but I couldn't drink enough, so I lay down and bent my head and sucked the water up with my lips. It tasted much better, drinking it that way, and a ripple would come up to my mouth and give me a kiss, and I laughed, and drank again, and pretended there was a nymph, like the one in the old picture at home, who lived in the water and was kissing me. So I bent low down to the water, and put my lips softly to it, and whispered to the nymph that I would come again. I felt sure it could not be common water. I was so glad when I got up and went on; and I danced again and went up and up the valley, under hanging hills. And when I came to the top, the ground rose up in front of me, tall and steep as a wall, and there was nothing but the green wall and the sky. I thought of "forever and forever, world without end, Amen"; and I thought I must have really found the end of the world, because it was like the end of everything, as if there could be nothing at all beyond, except the kingdom of Voor, where the light goes when it is put out, and the water goes when the sun takes it away. I began to think of all the long, long way I had journeyed, how I had found a brook and followed it, and followed it on, and gone through bushes and thorny thickets, and dark woods full of creeping thorns. Then I had crept up a tunnel under trees, and climbed a thicket, and seen all the gray rocks, and sat in the middle of them when they turned round, and then I had gone on through the gray rocks and come down the hill through the stinging thicket and up the dark valley, all a long, long way. I wondered how I should get home again, if I could ever find the way, and if my home was there any more, or if it were turned and everybody in it into gray rocks, as in the *Arabian Nights.* So I sat down on the grass and thought what I should do next. I was tired, and my feet were hot with walking, and as I looked about I saw there was a wonderful well just under the high, steep wall of grass. All the ground round it was covered with bright, green, dripping moss; there was every kind of moss there, moss like beautiful little ferns, and like palms and fir trees, and it was all green as jewelry, and drops of water hung on it like diamonds. And in the middle was the great well, deep and shining and beautiful, so clear that it looked as if I could touch the red sand at the bottom, but it was far below. I stood by it and looked in, as if I were looking in a glass. At the bottom of the well, in the middle of it, the red grains of sand were moving and stirring all the time, and I saw how the water bubbled up, but at the top it was quite smooth, and full and brimming.

It was a great well, large like a bath, and with the shining, glittering green moss about it, it looked like a great white jewel, with green jewels all round. My feet were so hot and tired that I took off my boots and stockings, and let my feet down into the water, and the water was soft and cold, and when I got up I wasn't tired any more, and I felt I must go on, farther and farther, and see what was on the other side of the wall. I climbed up it very slowly, going sideways all the time, and when I got to the top and looked over, I was in the queerest country I had seen, stranger even than the hill of the gray rocks. It looked as if earth-children had been playing there with their spades, as it was all hills and hollows, and castles and walls made of earth and covered with grass. There were two mounds like big beehives, round and great and solemn, and then hollow basins, and then a steep mounting wall like the ones I saw once by the seaside where the big guns and the soldiers were. I nearly fell into one of the round hollows, it went away from under my feet so suddenly, and I ran fast down the side and stood at the bottom and looked up. It was strange and solemn to look up. There was nothing but the gray, heavy sky and the sides of the hollow; everything else had gone away, and the hollow was the whole world, and I thought that at night it must be full of ghosts and moving shadows and pale things when the moon shone down to the bottom at the dead of the night, and the wind wailed up above. It was so strange and solemn and lonely, like a hollow temple of dead heathen gods. It reminded me of a tale my nurse had told me when I was quite little; it was the same nurse that took me into the wood where I saw the beautiful white people. And I remembered how nurse had told me the story one winter night, when the wind was beating the trees against the wall, and crying and moaning in the nursery chimney. She said there was, somewhere or other, a hollow pit, just like the one I was standing in, everybody was afraid to go into it or near it, it was such a bad place. But once upon a time there was a poor girl who said she would go into the hollow pit, and everybody tried to stop her, but she would go. And she went down into the pit and came back laughing, and said there was nothing there at all, except green grass and red stones, and white stones and yellow flowers. And soon after, people saw she had most beautiful emerald earrings, and they asked how she got them, as she and her mother were quite poor. But she laughed, and said her earrings were not made of emeralds at all, but only of green grass. Then, one day, she wore on her breast the reddest ruby that anyone had ever seen, and it was as big as a hen's egg, and glowed and sparkled like a hot burning coal of fire. And they asked how she got it, as she and her mother were quite poor. But she laughed, and said it was not a ruby at all, but only a red stone. Then one day she wore round her neck the loveliest necklace that anyone had ever seen, much finer than the queen's finest, and it was made of great bright diamonds, hundreds of them, and they shone like all the stars on a night in June. So they asked her how she got it, as she and her mother were quite poor. But she laughed, and said they were not diamonds at all, but only white stones. And one day she went to the Court, and she wore on her head a crown of pure angel-gold, so nurse said, and it shone like the sun, and it was much more splendid than the crown the king was wearing himself, and in her ears she wore the emeralds, and the big ruby was the brooch on her breast, and the great diamond necklace was sparkling on her neck. And the king and queen thought she was some great princess from a long way off, and got down from their thrones and went to meet her, but somebody told the king and queen who she was, and that she was quite poor. So the king asked why she wore a gold crown, and how she got it, as she and her mother were so poor. And she laughed, and said it wasn't a gold crown at all, but only some yellow flowers she had put in her hair. And the king thought it was very strange, and said she should stay at the Court, and they would see what would happen next. And she was so lovely that everybody said that her eyes were greener than the emeralds, that her lips were redder than the ruby, and her skin was whiter than the diamonds, and that her hair was brighter than the golden crown. So the king's son said he would marry her, and the king said he might. And the bishop married them, and there was a great supper, and afterwards the king's son went to his wife's room. But just when he had his hand on the door, he saw a tall, black man, with a dreadful face, standing in front of the door, and a voice said—

Venture not upon your life,
This is mine own wedded wife.

Then the king's son fell down on the ground in a fit. And they came and tried to get into the room, but they couldn't, and they hacked at the door with hatchets, but the wood had turned hard as iron, and at last everybody ran away, they were so frightened at the screaming and laughing and shrieking and crying that came out of the room. But next day they went in, and found there was nothing in the room but thick black smoke, because the black man had come and taken her away. And on the bed there were two knots of faded grass and a red stone, and some white stones, and some faded yellow flowers. I remembered this tale of nurse's while I was standing at the bottom of the deep hollow; it was so strange and solitary there, and I felt afraid. I could not see any stones or flowers, but I was afraid of bringing them away without knowing, and I thought I would do a charm that came into my head to keep the black man away. So I stood right in the very middle of the hollow, and I made sure that I had none of those things on me, and then I walked round the place, and touched my eyes, and my lips, and my hair in a peculiar manner, and whispered some queer words that nurse taught me to keep bad things away. Then I felt safe and climbed up out of the hollow, and went on through all those mounds and hollows and walls, till I came to the end, which was high above all the rest, and I could see that all the different shapes of the earth were arranged in patterns, something like the gray rocks, only the pattern was different. It was getting late, and the air was indistinct, but it looked from where I was standing something like two great figures of people lying on the grass. And I went on, and at last I found a certain wood, which is too secret to be described, and nobody knows of the passage into it, which I found out in a very curious manner, by seeing some little animal run into the wood through it. So I went after the animal by a very narrow dark way, under thorns and bushes, and it was almost dark when I came to a kind of open place in the middle. And there I saw the most wonderful sight I have ever seen, but it was only for a minute, as I ran away directly, and crept out of the wood by the passage I had come by, and ran as fast as ever I could, because I was afraid, what I had seen was so wonderful and so strange and beautiful. But I wanted to get home and think of it, and I did not know what might not happen if I stayed by the wood. I was hot all over and trembling, and my heart was beating, and strange cries that I could not help came from me as I ran from the wood. I was glad that a great white moon came up from over a round hill and showed me the way, so I went back through the mounds and hollows and down the close valley, and up through the thicket over the place of the gray rocks, and so at last I got home again. My father was busy in his study, and the servants had not told about my not coming home, though they were frightened, and wondered what they ought to do, so I told them I had lost my way, but I did not let them find out the real way I had been. I went to bed and lay awake all through the night, thinking of what I had seen. When I came out of the narrow way, and it looked all shining, though the air was dark, it seemed so certain, and all the way home I was quite sure that I had seen it, and I wanted to be alone in my room, and be glad over it all to myself, and shut my eyes and pretend it was there, and do all the things I would have done if I had not been so afraid. But when I shut my eyes the sight would not come, and I began to think about my adventures all over again, and I remembered how dusky and queer it was at the end, and I was afraid it must be all a mistake, because it seemed impossible it could happen. It seemed like one of nurse's tales, which I didn't really believe in, though I was frightened at the bottom of the hollow; and the stories she told me when I was little came back into my head, and I wondered whether it was really there what I thought I had seen, or whether any of her tales could have happened a long time ago. It was so queer; I lay awake there in my room at the back of the house, and the moon was shining on the other side toward the river, so the bright light did not fall upon the wall. And the house was quite still. I had heard my father come upstairs, and just after the clock struck twelve, and after the house was still and empty, as if there was nobody alive in it. And though it was all dark and indistinct in my room, a pale glimmering kind of light shone in through the white blind, and once I got up and looked out, and there was a great black shadow of the house covering the garden, looking like a prison where men are hanged; and then beyond it was all white; and the wood shone white with black gulfs between the trees. It was still and clear, and there were no clouds on the sky. I wanted to think of what I had seen but I couldn't, and I began to think of all the tales that nurse had told me so long ago that I thought I had forgotten, but they all came back, and mixed up with the thickets and the gray rocks and the hollows in the earth and the secret wood, till I hardly knew what was new and what was old, or whether it was not all dreaming. And then I remembered that hot summer afternoon, so long ago, when nurse left me by myself in the shade, and the white people came out of the water and out of the wood, and played, and danced, and sang, and I began to fancy that nurse told me about something like it before I saw them, only I couldn't recollect exactly what she told me. Then I wondered whether she had been the white lady, as I remembered she was just as white and beautiful, and had the same dark eyes and black hair; and sometimes she smiled and looked like the lady had looked, when she was telling me some of her stories, beginning with "Once on a time," or "In the time of the fairies." But I thought she couldn't be the lady, as she seemed to have gone a different way into the wood, and I didn't think the man who came after us could be the other, or I couldn't have seen that wonderful secret in the secret wood. I thought of the moon: but it was afterwards when I was in the middle of the wild land, where the earth was made into the shape of great figures, and it was all walls, and mysterious hollows, and smooth round mounds, that I saw the great white moon come up over a round hill. I was wondering about all these things, till at last I got quite frightened, because I was afraid something had happened to me, and I remembered nurse's tale of the poor girl who went into the hollow pit, and was carried away at last by the black man. I knew I had gone into a hollow pit too, and perhaps it was the same, and I had done something dreadful. So I did the charm over again, and touched my eyes and my lips and my hair in a peculiar manner, and said the old words from the fairy language, so that I might be sure I had not been carried away. I tried again to see the secret wood, and to creep up the passage and see what

I had seen there, but somehow I couldn't, and I kept on thinking of nurse's stories. There was one I remembered about a young man who once upon a time went hunting, and all the day he and his hounds hunted everywhere, and they crossed the rivers and went into all the woods, and went round the marshes, but they couldn't find anything at all, and they hunted all day till the sun sank down and began to set behind the mountain. And the young man was angry because he couldn't find anything, and he was going to turn back, when just as the sun touched the mountain, he saw come out of a brake in front of him a beautiful white stag. And he cheered to his hounds, but they whined and would not follow, and he cheered to his horse, but it shivered and stood stock still, and the young man jumped off the horse and left the hounds and began to follow the white stag all alone. And soon it was quite dark, and the sky was black, without a single star shining in it, and the stag went away into the darkness. And though the man had brought his gun with him he never shot at the stag, because he wanted to catch it, and he was afraid he would lose it in the night. But he never lost it once, though the sky was so black and the air was so dark, and the stag went on and on till the young man didn't know a bit where he was. And they went through enormous woods where the air was full of whispers and a pale, dead light came out from the rotten trunks that were lying on the ground, and just as the man thought he had lost the stag, he would see it all white and shining in front of him, and he would run fast to catch it, but the stag always ran faster, so he did not catch it. And they went through the enormous woods, and they swam across rivers, and they waded through black marshes where the ground bubbled, and the air was full of will-o'-the-wisps, and the stag fled away down into rocky narrow valleys, where the air was like the smell of a vault, and the man went after it. And they went over the great mountain and the man heard the wind come down from the sky, and the stag went on and the man went after. At last the sun rose and the young man found he was in a country that he had never seen before; it was a beautiful valley with a bright stream running through it, and a great, big round hill in the middle. And the stag went down the valley, towards the hill, and it seemed to be getting tired and went slower and slower, and though the man was tired, too, he began to run faster, and he was sure he would catch the stag at last. But just as they got to the bottom of the hill, and the man stretched out his hand to catch the stag, it vanished into the earth, and the man began to cry; he was so sorry that he had lost it after all his long hunting. But as he was crying he saw there was a door in the hill, just in front of him, and he went in, and it was quite dark, but he went on, as he thought he would find the white stag. And all of a sudden it got light, and there was the sky, and the sun shining, and birds singing in the trees, and there was a beautiful fountain. And by the fountain a lovely lady was sitting, who was the queen of the fairies, and she told the man that she had changed herself into a stag to bring him there because she loved him so much. Then she brought out a great gold cup, covered with jewels, from her fairy palace, and she offered him wine in the cup to drink. And he drank, and the more he drank the more he longed to drink, because the wine was enchanted. So he kissed the lovely lady, and she became his wife and he stayed all that day and all that night in the hill where she lived, and when he woke he found he was lying on the ground, close to where he had seen the stag first, and his horse was there and his hounds were there waiting, and he looked up, and the sun sank behind the mountain. And he went home and lived a long time, but he would never kiss any other lady because he had kissed the queen of the fairies, and he would never drink common wine any more, because he had drunk enchanted wine. And sometimes nurse told me tales that she had heard from her great-grandmother, who was very old, and lived in a cottage on the mountain all alone, and most of these tales were about a hill where people used to meet at night long ago, and they used to play all sorts of strange games and do queer things that nurse told me of, but I couldn't understand, and now, she said, everybody but her great-grandmother had forgotten all about it, and nobody knew where the hill was, not even her great-grandmother. But she told me one very strange story about the hill, and I trembled when I remembered it. She said that people always went there in summer, when it was very hot, and they had to dance a good deal. It would be all dark at first, and there were trees there, which made it much darker, and people would come, one by one, from all directions, by a secret path which nobody else knew, and two persons would keep the gate, and every one as they came up had to give a very curious sign, which nurse showed me as well as she could, but she said she couldn't show me properly. And all kinds of people would come; there would be gentle folks and village folks, and some old people and the boys and girls, and quite small children, who sat and watched. And it would all be dark as they came in, except in one corner where someone was burning something that smelt strong and sweet, and made them laugh, and there one would see a glaring of coals, and the smoke mounting up red. So they would all come in, and when the last had come there was no door any more, so that no one else could get in, even if they knew there was anything beyond. And once a gentleman who was a stranger and had ridden a long way, lost his path at night, and his horse took him into the very middle of the wild country, where everything was upside down, and there were dreadful marshes and great stones everywhere, and holes underfoot, and the trees looked like gibbet-posts, because they had great black arms that stretched out across the way. And this strange gentleman was very frightened, and his horse began to shiver all over, and at last it stopped and wouldn't go any farther, and the gentleman got down and tried to lead the horse, but it wouldn't move, and it was all covered with a sweat, like death. So the gentleman went on all alone, going farther and farther into the wild country, till at last he came to a dark place, where he heard shouting and singing and crying, like nothing he had ever heard before. It all sounded quite close to him, but he couldn't get in, and so he began to call, and while he was calling, something came behind him, and in a minute his mouth and arms and legs were all bound up, and he fell into a swoon. And when he came to himself, he was lying by the roadside, just where he had first lost his way, under a blasted oak with a black trunk, and his horse was tied beside him. So he rode on to the town and told the people there what had happened, and some of them were amazed; but others knew. So when once everybody had come, there was no door at all for anybody else to pass in by. And when they were all inside, round in a ring, touching each other, someone began to sing in the darkness, and someone else would make a noise like thunder with a thing they had on purpose, and on still nights people would hear the thundering noise far, far away beyond the wild land, and some of them, who thought they knew what it was, used to make a sign on their breasts when they woke up in their beds at dead of night and heard that terrible deep noise, like thunder on the mountains. And the noise and the singing would go on and on for a long time, and the people who were in a ring swayed a little to and fro; and the song was in an old, old language that nobody knows now, and the tune was queer. Nurse said her great-grandmother had known someone who remembered a little of it, when she was quite a little girl, and nurse tried to sing some of it to me, and it was so strange a tune that I turned all cold and my flesh crept as if I had put my hand on something dead. Sometimes it was a man that sang and sometimes it was a woman, and sometimes the one who sang it did it so well that two or three of the people who were there fell to the ground shrieking and tearing with their hands. The singing went on, and the people in the ring kept swaying to and fro for a long time, and at last the moon would rise over a place they called the Tole Deol, and came up and showed them swinging and swaying from side to side, with the sweet thick smoke curling up from the burning coals, and floating in circles all around them. Then they had their supper. A boy and a girl brought it to them; the boy carried a great cup of wine, and the girl carried a cake of bread, and they passed the bread and the wine round and round, but they tasted quite different from common bread and common wine, and changed everybody that tasted them. Then they all rose up and danced, and secret things were brought out of some hiding place, and they played extraordinary games, and danced round and round and round in the moonlight, and sometimes people would suddenly disappear and never be heard of afterwards, and nobody knew what had happened to them. And they drank more of that curious wine, and they made images and worshipped them, and nurse showed me how the images were made one day when we were out for a walk, and we passed by a place where there was a lot of wet clay. So nurse asked me if I would like to know what those things were like that they made on the hill, and I said yes. Then she asked me if I would promise never to tell a living soul a word about it, and if I did I was to be thrown into the black pit with the dead people, and I said I wouldn't tell anybody, and she said the same thing again and again, and I promised. So she took my wooden spade and dug a big lump of clay and put it in my tin bucket, and told me to say if anyone met us that I was going to make pies when I went home. Then we went on a little way till we came to a little brake growing right down into the road, and nurse stopped, and looked up the road and down it, and then peeped through the hedge into the field on the other side, and then she said, "Quick!" and we ran into the brake, and crept in and out among the bushes till we had gone a good way from the road. Then we sat down under a bush, and I wanted so much to know what nurse was going to make with the clay, but before she would begin she made me promise again not to say a word about it, and she went again and peeped through the bushes on every side, though the lane was so small and deep that hardly anybody ever went there. So we sat down, and nurse took the clay out of the bucket, and began to knead it with her hands, and do queer things with it, and turn it about. And she hid it under a big dock leaf for a minute or two and then she brought it out again, and then she stood up and sat down, and walked round the clay in a peculiar manner, and all the time she was softly singing a sort of rhyme, and her face got very red. Then she sat down again, and took the clay in her hands and began to shape it into a doll, but not like the dolls I have at home, and she made the queerest doll I had ever seen, all out of the wet clay, and hid it under a bush to get dry and hard, and all the time she was making it she was singing these rhymes to herself, and her face got redder and redder. So we left the doll there, hidden away in the bushes where nobody would ever find it. And a few days later we went the same walk, and when we came to that narrow, dark part of the lane where the brake runs down to the bank, nurse made me promise all over again, and she looked about, just as she had done before, and we crept into the bushes till we got to the green place where the little clay man was hidden. I remember it all so well, though I was only eight, and it is eight years ago now as I am writing it down, but the sky was a deep violet blue, and in the middle of the brake where we were sitting there was a great elder tree covered with blossoms, and on the other side there was a clump of meadowsweet, and when I think of that day the smell of the meadowsweet and elder blossom seems to fill the room, and if I shut my eyes I can see the glaring blue sky, with little clouds very white floating across it, and nurse who went away long ago sitting opposite me and looking like the beautiful white lady in the wood. So we sat down and nurse took out the clay doll from the secret place where she had hidden it, and she said we must "pay our respects," and she would show me what to do, and I must watch her all the time. So she did all sorts of queer things with the little clay man, and I noticed she was all streaming with perspiration, though we had walked so slowly, and then she told me to "pay my respects," and I did everything she did because I liked her, and it was such an odd game. And she said that if one loved very much, the clay man was very good, if one did certain things with it, and if one hated very much, it was just as good, only one had to do different things, and we played with it a long time, and pretended all sorts of things. Nurse said her great-grandmother had told her all about these images, but what we did was no harm at all, only a game. But she told me a story about these images that frightened me very much, and that was what I remembered that night when I was lying awake in my room in the pale, empty darkness, thinking of what I had seen and the secret wood. Nurse said there was once a young lady of the high gentry, who lived in a great castle. And she was so beautiful that all the gentlemen wanted to marry her, because she was the loveliest lady that anybody had ever seen, and she was kind to everybody, and everybody thought she was very good. But though she was polite to all the gentlemen who wished to marry her, she put them off, and said she couldn't make up her mind, and she wasn't sure she wanted to marry anybody at all. And her father, who was a very great lord, was angry, though he was so fond of her, and he asked her why she wouldn't choose a bachelor out of all the handsome young men who came to the castle. But she only said she didn't love any of them very much, and she must wait, and if they pestered her, she said she would go and be a nun in a nunnery. So all the gentlemen said they would go away and wait for a year and a day, and when a year and a day were gone, they would come back again and ask her to say which one she would marry. So the day was appointed and they all went away; and the lady had promised that in a year and a day it would be her wedding day with one of them. But the truth was, that she was the queen of the people who danced on the hill on summer nights, and on the proper nights she would lock the door of her room, and she and her maid would steal out of the castle by a secret passage that only they knew of, and go away up to the hill in the wild land. And she knew more of the secret things than anyone else, and more than anyone knew before or after, because she would not tell anybody the most secret secrets. She knew how to do all the awful things, how to destroy young men, and how to put a curse on people, and other things that I could not understand. And her real name was the Lady Avelin, but the dancing people called her Cassap, which meant somebody very wise, in the old language. And she was whiter than any of them and taller, and her eyes shone in the dark like burning rubies; and she could sing songs that none of the others could sing, and when she sang they all fell down on their faces and worshipped her. And she could do what they called the shib-show, which was a very wonderful enchantment. She would tell the great lord, her father, that she wanted to go into the woods to gather flowers, so he let her go, and she and her maid went into the woods where nobody came, and the maid would keep watch. Then the lady would lie down under the trees and begin to sing a particular song, and she stretched out her arms, and from every part of the wood great serpents would come, hissing and gliding in and out among the trees, and shooting out their forked tongues as they crawled up to the lady. And they all came to her, and twisted round her, round her body, and her arms, and her neck, till she was covered with writhing serpents, and there was only her head to be seen. And she whispered to them, and she sang to them, and they writhed round and round, faster and faster, till she told them to go. And they all went away directly, back to their holes, and on the lady's breast there would be a most curious, beautiful stone, shaped something like an egg, and colored dark blue and yellow, and red and green, marked like a serpent's scales. It was called a glame stone, and with it one could do all sorts of wonderful things, and nurse said her great-grandmother had seen a glame stone with her own eyes, and it was for all the world shiny and scaly like a snake. And the lady could do a lot of other things as well, but she was quite fixed that she would not be married. And there were a great many gentlemen who wanted to marry her, but there were five of them who were chief, and their names were Sir Simon, Sir John, Sir Oliver, Sir Richard, and Sir Rowland. All the others believed she spoke the truth, and that she would choose one of them to be her man when a year and a day was done; it was only Sir Simon, who was very crafty, who thought she was deceiving them all, and he vowed he would watch and try if he could find out anything. And though he was very wise he was very young, and he had a smooth, soft face like a girl's, and he pretended, as the rest did, that he would not come to the castle for a year and a day, and he said he was going away beyond the sea to foreign parts. But he really only went a very little way, and came back dressed like a servant girl, and so he got a place in the castle to wash the dishes. And he waited and watched, and he listened and said nothing, and he hid in dark places, and woke up at night and looked out, and he heard things and he saw things that he thought were very strange. And he was so sly that he told the girl that waited on the lady that he was really a young man, and that he had dressed up as a girl because he loved her so very much and wanted to be in the same house with her, and the girl was so pleased that she told him many things, and he was more than ever certain that the Lady Avelin was deceiving him and the others. And he was so clever, and told the servant so many lies, that one night he managed to hide in the Lady Avelin's room behind the curtains. And he stayed quite still and never moved, and at last the lady came. And she bent down under the bed, and raised up a stone, and there was a hollow place underneath, and out of it she took a waxen image, just like the clay one that I and nurse had made in the brake. And all the time her eyes were burning like rubies.

And she took the little wax doll up in her arms and held it to her breast, and she whispered and she murmured, and she took it up and she laid it down again, and she held it high, and she held it low, and she laid it down again. And she said, "Happy is he that begat the bishop, that ordered the clerk, that married the man, that had the wife, that fashioned the hive, that harbored the bee, that gathered the wax that my own true love was made of." And she brought out of a pantry a great golden bowl, and she brought out of a closet a great jar of wine, and she poured some of the wine into the bowl, and she laid her manikin very gently in the wine, and washed it in the wine all over. Then she went to a cupboard and took a small round cake and laid it on the image's mouth, and then she bore it softly and covered it up. And Sir Simon, who was watching all the time, though he was terribly frightened, saw the lady bend down and stretch out her arms and whisper and sing, and then Sir Simon saw beside her a handsome young man, who kissed her on the lips. And they drank wine out of the golden bowl together, and they ate the cake together. But when the sun rose there was only the little wax doll, and the lady hid it again under the bed in the hollow place. So Sir Simon knew quite well what the lady was, and he waited and he watched, till the time she had said was nearly over, and in a week the year and a day would be done. And one night, when he was watching behind the curtains in her room, he saw her making more wax dolls. And she made five, and hid them away. And the next night she took one out, and held it up, and filled the golden bowl with water, and took the doll by the neck and held it under the water. Then she said—

Sir Dickon, Sir Dickon, your day is done,
You shall be drowned in the water wan.

And the next day news came to the castle that Sir Richard had been drowned at the ford. And at night she took another doll and tied a violet cord round its neck and hung it up on a nail. Then she said—

Sir Rowland, your life has ended its span,
High on a tree I see you hang.

And the next day news came to the castle that Sir Rowland had been hanged by robbers in the wood. And at night she took another doll, and drove her bodkin right into its heart. Then she said—

> Sir Noll, Sir Noll, so cease your life,
> Your heart piercèd with the knife.

And the next day news came to the castle that Sir Oliver had fought in a tavern, and a stranger had stabbed him to the heart. And at night she took another doll, and held it to a fire of charcoal till it was melted. Then she said—

> Sir John, return, and turn to clay,
> In fire of fever you waste away.

And the next day news came to the castle that Sir John had died in a burning fever. So then Sir Simon went out of the castle and mounted his horse and rode away to the bishop and told him everything. And the bishop sent his men, and they took the Lady Avelin, and everything she had done was found out. So on the day after the year and a day, when she was to have been married, they carried her through the town in her smock, and they tied her to a great stake in the marketplace, and burned her alive before the bishop with her wax image hung round her neck. And people said the wax man screamed in the burning of the flames. And I thought of this story again and again as I was lying awake in my bed, and I seemed to see the Lady Avelin in the marketplace, with the yellow flames eating up her beautiful white body. And I thought of it so much that I seemed to get into the story myself, and I fancied I was the lady, and that they were coming to take me to be burnt with fire, with all the people in the town looking at me. And I wondered whether she cared, after all the strange things she had done, and whether it hurt very much to be burned at the stake. I tried again and again to forget nurse's stories, and to remember the secret I had seen that afternoon, and what was in the secret wood, but I could only see the dark and a glimmering in the dark, and then it went away, and I only saw myself running, and then a great moon came up white over a dark round hill. Then all the old stories came back again, and the queer rhymes that nurse used to sing to me; and there was one beginning "Halsy cumsy Helen musty," that she used to sing very softly when she wanted me to go to sleep. And I began to sing it to myself inside of my head, and I went to sleep.

The next morning I was very tired and sleepy, and could hardly do my lessons, and I was very glad when they were over and I had had my dinner, as I wanted to go out and be alone. It was a warm day, and I went to a nice turfy hill by the river, and sat down on my mother's old shawl that I had brought with me on purpose. The sky was gray, like the day before, but there was a kind of white gleam behind it, and from where I was sitting I could look down on the town, and it was all still and quiet and white, like a picture. I remembered that it was on that hill that nurse taught me to play an old game called "Troy Town," in which one had to dance, and wind in and out on a pattern in the grass, and then when one had danced and turned long enough the other person asks you questions, and you can't help answering whether you want to or not, and whatever you are told to do you feel you have to do it. Nurse said there used to be a lot of games like that that some people knew of, and there was one by which people could be turned into anything you liked, and an old man her great-grandmother had seen had known a girl who had been turned into a large snake. And there was another very ancient game of dancing and winding and turning, by which you could take a person out of himself and hide him away as long as you liked, and his body went walking about quite empty, without any sense in it. But I came to that hill because I wanted to think of what had happened the day before, and of the secret of the wood. From the place where I was sitting I could see beyond the town, into the opening I had found, where a little brook had led me into an unknown country. And I pretended I was following the brook over again, and I went all the way in my mind, and at last I found the wood, and crept into it under the bushes, and then in the dusk I saw something that made me feel as if I were filled with fire, as if I wanted to dance and sing and fly up into the air, because I was changed and wonderful. But what I saw was not changed at all, and had not grown old, and I wondered again and again how such things could happen, and whether nurse's stories were really true, because in the daytime in the open air everything seemed quite different from what it was at night, when I was frightened, and thought I was to be burned alive. I once told my father one of her little tales, which was about a ghost, and asked him if it was true, and he told me it was not true at all, and that only common, ignorant people believed in such rubbish. He was very angry with nurse for telling me the story, and scolded her, and after that I promised her I would never whisper a word of what she told me, and if I did I should be bitten by the great black snake that lived in the pool in the wood. And all alone on the hill I wondered what was true. I had seen something very amazing and very lovely, and I knew a story, and if I had really seen it, and not made it up out of the dark, and the black bough, and the bright shining that was mounting up to the sky from over the great round hill, but had really seen it in truth, then there were all kinds of wonderful and lovely and terrible things to think of, so I longed and trembled, and I burned and got cold. And I looked down on the town, so quiet and still, like a little white picture, and I thought over and over if it could be true. I was a long time before I could make up my mind to anything; there was such a strange fluttering at my heart that seemed to whisper to me all the time that I had not made it up out of my head, and yet it seemed quite impossible, and I knew my father and everybody would say it was dreadful rubbish. I never dreamed of telling him or anybody else a word about it, because I knew it would be of no use, and I should only get laughed at or scolded, so for a long time I was very quiet, and went about thinking and wondering; and at night I used to dream of amazing things, and sometimes I woke up in the early morning and held out my arms with a cry. And I was frightened, too, because there were dangers, and some awful thing would happen to me, unless I took great care, if the story were true. These old tales were always in my head, night and morning, and I went over them and told them to myself over and over again, and went for walks in the places where nurse had told them to me; and when I sat in the nursery by the fire in the evenings I used to fancy nurse was sitting in the other chair, and telling me some wonderful story in a low voice, for fear anybody should be listening. But she used to like best to tell me about things when we were right out in the country, far from the house, because she said she was telling me such secrets, and walls have ears. And if it was something more-than-ever secret, we had to hide in brakes or woods; and I used to think it was such fun creeping along a hedge, and going very softly, and then we would get behind the bushes or run into the wood all of a sudden, when we were sure that none was watching us; so we knew that we had our secrets quite all to ourselves, and nobody else at all knew anything about them. Now and then, when we had hidden ourselves as I have described, she used to show me all sorts of odd things. One day, I remember, we were in a hazel brake, overlooking the brook, and we were so snug and warm, as though it was April; the sun was quite hot, and the leaves were just coming out. Nurse said she would show me something funny that would make me laugh, and then she showed me, as she said, how one could turn a whole house upside down, without anybody being able to find out, and the pots and pans would jump about, and the china would be broken, and the chairs would tumble over of themselves. I tried it one day in the kitchen, and I found I could do it quite well, and a whole row of plates on the dresser fell off it, and cook's little worktable tilted up and turned right over "before her eyes," as she said, but she was so frightened and turned so white that I didn't do it again, as I liked her. And afterward, in the hazel copse, when she had shown me how to make things tumble about, she showed me how to make rapping noises, and I learned how to do that, too. Then she taught me rhymes to say on certain occasions, and peculiar marks to make on other occasions, and other things that her great-grandmother had taught her when she was a little girl herself. And these were all the things I was thinking about in those days after the strange walk when I thought I had seen a great secret, and I wished nurse were there for me to ask her about it, but she had gone away more than two years before, and nobody seemed to know what had become of her, or where she had gone. But I shall always remember those days if I live to be quite old, because all the time I felt so strange, wondering and doubting, and feeling quite sure at one time, and making up my mind, and then I would feel quite sure that such things couldn't happen really, and it began all over again. But I took great care not to do certain things that might be very dangerous. So I waited and wondered for a long time, and though I was not sure at all, I never dared to try to find out. But one day I became sure that all that nurse said was quite true, and I was all alone when I found it out. I trembled all over with joy and terror, and as fast as I could I ran into one of the old brakes where we used to go—it was the one by the lane, where nurse made the little clay man—and I ran into it, and I crept into it; and when I came to the place where the elder was, I covered up my face with my hands and lay down flat on the grass, and I stayed there for two hours without moving, whispering to myself delicious, terrible things, and saying some words over and over again. It was all true and wonderful and splendid, and when I remembered the story I knew and thought of what I had really seen, I got hot and cold, and the air seemed full of scent, and flowers, and singing. And first I wanted to make a little clay man, like the one nurse had made so long ago, and I had to invent plans and stratagems, and to look about, and to think of things beforehand, because nobody must dream of anything that I was doing or going to do, and I was too old to carry clay about in a tin bucket. At last I thought of a plan, and I brought the wet clay to the brake, and did everything that nurse had done, only I made a much finer image than the one she had made; and when it was finished I did everything that I could imagine and much more than she did, because it was the likeness of something far better. And a few days later, when I had done my lessons early, I went for the second time by the way of the little brook that had led me into a strange country. And I followed the brook, and went through the bushes, and beneath the low branches of trees, and up thorny thickets on the hill, and by dark woods full of creeping thorns, a long, long way. Then I crept through the dark tunnel where the brook had been and the ground was stony, till at last I came to the thicket that climbed up the hill, and though the leaves were coming out upon the trees, everything looked almost as black as it was on the first day that I went there. And the thicket was just the same, and I went up slowly till I came out on the big bare hill, and began to walk among the wonderful rocks. I saw the terrible voor again on everything, for though the sky was brighter, the ring of wild hills all around was still dark, and the hanging woods looked dark and dreadful, and the strange rocks were as gray as ever; and when I looked down on them from the great mound, sitting on the stone, I saw all their amazing circles and rounds within rounds, and I had to sit quite still and watch them as they began to turn about me, and each stone danced in its place, and they seemed to go round and round in a great whirl, as if one were in the middle of all the stars and heard them rushing through the air. So I went down among the rocks to dance with them and to sing extraordinary songs; and I went down through the other thicket, and drank from the bright stream in the close and secret valley, putting my lips down to the bubbling water; and then I went on till I came to the deep, brimming well among the glittering moss, and I sat down. I looked before me into the secret darkness of the valley, and behind me was the great high wall of grass, and all around me there were the hanging woods that made the valley such a secret place. I knew there was nobody here at all besides myself, and that no one could see me. So I took off my boots and stockings, and let my feet down into the water, saying the words I knew. And it was not cold at all, as I expected, but warm and very pleasant, and when my feet were in it I felt as if they were in silk, or as if the nymph were kissing them. So when I had done, I said the other words and made the signs, and then I dried my feet with a towel I had brought on purpose, and put on my stockings and boots. Then I climbed up the steep wall, and went into the place where there are the hollows, and the two beautiful mounds, and the round ridges of land, and all the strange shapes. I did not go down into the hollow this time, but I turned at the end, and made out the figures quite plainly, as it was lighter, and I had remembered the story I had quite forgotten before, and in the story the two figures are called Adam and Eve, and only those who know the story understand what they mean. So I went on and on till I came to the secret wood which must not be described, and I crept into it by the way I had found. And when I had gone about halfway I stopped, and turned round, and got ready, and I bound the handkerchief tightly round my eyes, and made quite sure that I could not see at all, not a twig, nor the end of a leaf, nor the light of the sky, as it was an old red silk handkerchief with large yellow spots, that went round twice and covered my eyes, so that I could see nothing. Then I began to go on, step by step, very slowly. My heart beat faster and faster, and something rose in my throat that choked me and made me want to cry out, but I shut my lips, and went on. Boughs caught in my hair as I went, and great thorns tore me; but I went on to the end of the path. Then I stopped, and held out my arms and bowed, and I went round the first time, feeling with my hands, and there was nothing. I went round the second time, feeling with my hands, and there was nothing. Then I went round the third time, feeling with my hands, and the story was all true, and I wished that the years were gone by, and that I had not so long a time to wait before I was happy forever and ever.

Nurse must have been a prophet like those we read of in the Bible. Everything that she said began to come true, and since then other things that she told me of have happened. That was how I came to know that her stories were true and that I had not made up the secret myself out of my own head. But there was another thing that happened that day. I went a second time to the secret place. It was at the deep brimming well, and when I was standing on the moss I bent over and looked in, and then I knew who the white lady was that I had seen come out of the water in the wood long ago when I was quite little. And I trembled all over, because that told me other things. Then I remembered how sometime after I had seen the white people in the wood, nurse asked me more about them, and I told her all over again, and she listened, and said nothing for a long, long time, and at last she said, "You will see her again." So I understood what had happened and what was to happen. And I understood about the nymphs; how I might meet them in all kinds of places, and they would always help me, and I must always look for them, and find them in all sorts of strange shapes and appearances. And without the nymphs I could never have found the secret, and without them none of the other things could happen. Nurse had told me all about them long ago, but she called them by another name, and I did not know what she meant, or what her tales of them were about, only that they were very queer. And there were two kinds, the bright and the dark, and both were very lovely and very wonderful, and some people saw only one kind, and some only the other, but some saw them both. But usually the dark appeared first, and the bright ones came afterwards, and there were extraordinary tales about them. It was a day or two after I had come home from the secret place that I first really knew the nymphs. Nurse had shown me how to call them, and I had tried, but I did not know what she meant, and so I thought it was all nonsense. But I made up my mind I would try again, so I went to the wood where the pool was, where I saw the white people, and I tried again. The dark nymph, Alanna, came, and she turned the pool of water into a pool of fire. . . .

Epilogue

"That's a very queer story," said Cotgrave, handing back the green book to the recluse, Ambrose. "I see the drift of a good deal, but there are many things that I do not grasp at all. On the last page, for example, what does she mean by 'nymphs'?"

"Well, I think there are references throughout the manuscript to certain 'processes' which have been handed down by tradition from age to age. Some of these processes are just beginning to come within the purview of science, which has arrived at them—or rather at the steps which lead to them—by quite different paths. I have interpreted the reference to 'nymphs' as a reference to one of these processes."

"And you believe that there are such things?"

"Oh, I think so. Yes, I believe I could give you convincing evidence on that point. I am afraid you have neglected the study of alchemy? It is a pity, for the symbolism, at all events, is very beautiful, and moreover if you were acquainted with certain books on the subject, I could recall to your mind phrases which might explain a good deal in the manuscript that you have been reading."

"Yes, but I want to know whether you seriously think that

there is any foundation of fact beneath these fancies. Is it not all a department of poetry; a curious dream with which man has indulged himself?"

"I can only say that it is no doubt better for the great mass of people to dismiss it all as a dream. But if you ask my veritable belief—that goes quite the other way. No, I should not say belief, but rather knowledge. I may tell you that I have known cases in which men have stumbled quite by accident on certain of these 'processes,' and have been astonished by wholly unexpected results. In the cases I am thinking of there could have been no possibility of 'suggestion' or sub-conscious action of any kind. One might as well suppose a schoolboy 'suggesting' the existence of Æschylus to himself, while he plods mechanically through the declensions.

"But you have noticed the obscurity," Ambrose went on, "and in this particular case it must have been dictated by instinct, since the writer never thought that her manuscripts would fall into other hands. But the practice is universal, and for most excellent reasons. Powerful and sovereign medicines, which are, of necessity, virulent poisons also, are kept in a locked cabinet. The child may find the key by chance, and drink herself dead; but in most cases the search is educational, and the phials contain precious elixirs for him who has patiently fashioned the key for himself."

"You do not care to go into details?"

"No, frankly, I do not. No, you must remain unconvinced. But you saw how the manuscript illustrates the talk we had last week?"

"Is this girl still alive?"

"No. I was one of those who found her. I knew the father well; he was a lawyer, and had always left her very much to herself. He thought of nothing but deeds and leases, and the news came to him as an awful surprise. She was missing one morning; I suppose it was about a year after she had written what you have read. The servants were called, and they told things, and put the only natural interpretation on them—a perfectly erroneous one.

"They discovered that green book somewhere in her room, and I found her in the place that she described with so much dread, lying on the ground before the image."

"It was an image?"

"Yes, it was hidden by the thorns and the thick undergrowth that had surrounded it. It was a wild, lonely country; but you know what it was like by her description, though of course you will understand that the colors have been heightened. A child's imagination always makes the heights higher and the depths deeper than they really are; and she had, unfortunately for herself, something more than imagination. One might say, perhaps, that the picture in her mind which she succeeded in a measure in putting into words, was the scene as it would have appeared to an imaginative artist. But it is a strange, desolate land."

"And she was dead?"

"Yes. She had poisoned herself—in time. No, there was not a word to be said against her in the ordinary sense. You may recollect a story I told you the other night about a lady who saw her child's fingers crushed by a window?"

"And what was this statue?"

"Well, it was of Roman workmanship, of a stone that with the centuries had not blackened, but had become white and luminous. The thicket had grown up about it and concealed it, and in the Middle Ages the followers of a very old tradition had known how to use it for their own purposes. In fact it had been incorporated into the monstrous mythology of the Sabbath. You will have noted that those to whom a sight of that shining whiteness had been vouchsafed by chance, or rather, perhaps, by apparent chance, were required to blindfold themselves on their second approach. That is very significant."

"And is it there still?"

"I sent for tools, and we hammered it into dust and fragments.

"The persistence of tradition never surprises me," Ambrose went on after a pause. "I could name many an English parish where such traditions as that girl had listened to in her childhood are still existent in occult but unabated vigor. No, for me, it is the 'story' not the 'sequel,' which is strange and awful, for I have always believed that wonder is of the soul."

Extract from Captain Stormfield's Visit to Heaven

BY MARK TWAIN

1

WELL, when I had been dead about thirty years, I begun to get a little anxious. Mind you, I had been whizzing through space all that time, like a comet. *Like* a comet! Why, Peters, I laid over the lot of them! Of course there warn't any of them going my way, as a steady thing, you know, because they travel in a long circle like the loop of a lasso, whereas I was pointed as straight as a dart for the Hereafter; but I happened on one every now and then that was going my way for an hour or so, and then we had a bit of a brush together. But it was generally pretty one-sided, because I sailed by them the same as if they were standing still. An ordinary comet don't make more than about two hundred thousand miles a minute. Of course when I came across one of that sort—like Encke's and Halley's comets, for instance—it warn't anything but just a flash and a vanish, you see. You couldn't rightly call it a race. It was as if the comet was a gravel-train and I was a telegraph dispatch. But after I got outside of our astronomical system, I used to flush a comet occasionally that was something *like*. *We* haven't got any such comets—ours don't begin. One night I was swinging along at a good round gait, everything taut and trim, and the wind in my favor—I judged I was going about a million miles a minute; it might have been more, it couldn't have been less—when I flushed a most uncommonly big one about three points off my starboard bow. By his stern lights I judged he was bearing about northeast-by-north-half-east. Well, it was so near my course that I wouldn't throw away the chance; so I fell off a point, steadied my helm, and went for him. You should have heard me whiz, and seen the electric fur fly! In about a minute and a half I was fringed out with an electrical nimbus that flamed around for miles and miles and lit up all space like broad day. The comet was burning blue in the distance, like a sickly torch, when I first sighted him, but he begun to grow bigger and bigger as I crept up on him. I slipped up on him so fast that when I had gone about a hundred and fifty million miles I was close enough to be swallowed up in the phosphorescent glory of his wake, and I couldn't see anything for the glare. Thinks I, It won't do to run into him, so I shunted to one side and tore along. By and by I closed up abreast of his tail. Do you know what it was like? It was like a gnat closing up on the continent of America. I forged along. By and by I had sailed along his coast for a little upwards of a hundred and fifty million miles, and then I could see by the shape of him that I hadn't even got up to his waistband yet. Why, Peters, *we* don't know anything about comets, down here. If you want to see comets that *are* comets, you've got to go outside of our solar system—where there's room for them, you understand. My friend, I've seen comets out there that couldn't even lay down inside the *orbits* of our noblest comets without their tails hanging over.

Well, I boomed along another hundred and fifty million miles, and got up abreast his shoulder, as you may say. I was feeling pretty fine, I tell you; but just then I noticed the officer of the deck come to the side and hoist his glass in my direction. Straight off I heard him sing out:

"Below there, ahoy! Shake her up, shake her up! Heave on a hundred million billion tons of brimstone!"

"Aye, aye, sir!"

"Pipe the starboard watch! All hands on deck!"

"Aye, aye, sir!"

"Send two hundred thousand million men aloft to shake out royals and skyscrapers!"

"Aye, aye, sir!"

"Hand the stuns'ls! Hang out every rag you've got! Clothe her from stem to rudderpost!"

"Aye, aye, sir!"

In about a second I begun to see I'd woke up a pretty ugly customer, Peters. In less than ten seconds that comet was just a blazing cloud of red-hot canvas. It was piled up into the heavens clean out of sight—the old thing seemed to swell out and occupy all space; the sulfur smoke from the furnaces—oh, well, nobody can describe the way it rolled and tumbled up into the skies, and nobody can half describe the way it smelt. Neither can anybody begin to describe the way that monstrous craft begun to crash along. And such another powwow—thousands of bo's'n's whistles screaming at once, and a crew like the populations of a hundred thousand worlds like ours all swearing at once. Well, I never heard the like of it before.

We roared and thundered along side by side, both doing our level best, because I'd never struck a comet before that could lay over me, and so I was bound to beat this one or break something. I judged I had some reputation in space, and I calculated to keep it. I noticed I wasn't gaining as fast, now, as I was before, but still I was gaining. There was a power of excitement on board the comet. Upwards of a hundred billion passengers swarmed up from below and rushed to the side and begun to bet on the race. Of course this careened her and damaged her speed. My, but wasn't the mate mad! He jumped at that crowd, with his trumpet in his hand, and sung out:

"Amidships! amidships, you———!* or I'll brain the last idiot of you!"

Well, sir, I gained and gained, little by little, till at last I went skimming sweetly by the magnificent old conflagration's nose. By this time the captain of the comet had been rousted out, and he stood there in the red glare for'ard, by the mate, in his shirt sleeves and slippers, his hair all rats' nests and one suspender hanging, and how sick those two men did look! I just simply couldn't help putting my thumb to my nose as I glided away and singing out:

"Ta-ta! ta-ta! Any word to send to your family?"

* The Captain could not remember what this word was. He said it was in a foreign tongue.

Peters, it was a mistake. Yes, sir, I've often regretted that—it was a mistake. You see, the captain had given up the race, but that remark was too tedious for him—he couldn't stand it. He turned to the mate, and says he:

"Have we got brimstone enough of our own to make the trip?"

"Yes, sir."

"Sure?"

"Yes, sir—more than enough."

"How much have we got in cargo for Satan?"

"Eighteen hundred thousand billion quintillion kazarks."

"Very well, then, let his boarders freeze till the next comet comes. Lighten ship! Lively, now, lively, men! Heave the whole cargo overboard!"

Peters, look me in the eye, and be calm. I found out, over there, that a kazark is exactly the bulk of a *hundred and sixty-nine worlds like ours!* They hove all that load overboard. When it fell, it wiped out a considerable raft of stars just as clean as if they'd been candles and somebody blowed them out. As for the race, that was at an end. The minute she was lightened the comet swung along by me the same as if I was anchored. The captain stood on the stern, by the after davits, and put his thumb to his nose and sung out:

"Ta-ta! ta-ta! Maybe *you've* got some message to send your friends in the Everlasting Tropics!"

Then he hove up his other suspender and started for'ard, and inside of three-quarters of an hour his craft was only a pale torch again in the distance. Yes, it was a mistake, Peters—that remark of mine. I don't reckon I'll ever get over being sorry about it. I'd 'a' beat the bully of the firmament if I'd kept my mouth shut.

But I've wandered a little off the track of my tale; I'll get back on my course again. Now you see what kind of speed I was making. So, as I said, when I had been tearing along this way about thirty years I begun to get uneasy. Oh, it was pleasant enough, with a good deal to find out, but then it was kind of lonesome, you know. Besides, I wanted to get somewhere. I hadn't shipped with the idea of cruising forever. First off, I liked the delay, because I judged I was going to fetch up in pretty warm quarters when I got through; but towards the last I begun to feel that I'd rather go to—well, most any place, so as to finish up the uncertainty.

Well, one night—it was always night, except when I was rushing by some star that was occupying the whole universe with its fire and its glare; light enough then, of course, but I necessarily left it behind in a minute or two and plunged into a solid week of darkness again. The stars ain't so close together as they look to be— Where was I? Oh yes; one night I was sailing along, when I discovered a tremendous long row of blinking lights away on the horizon ahead. As I approached, they begun to tower and swell and look like mighty furnaces. Says I to myself:

"By George, I've arrived at last—and at the wrong place, just as I expected!"

Then I fainted. I don't know how long I was insensible, but it must have been a good while, for when I came to, the darkness was all gone and there was the loveliest sunshine and the balmiest, fragrantest air in its place. And there was such a marvelous world spread out before me—such a glowing, beautiful, bewitching country. The things I took for furnaces were gates, miles high, made all of flashing jewels, and they pierced a wall of solid gold that you couldn't see the top of, nor yet the end of, in either direction. I was pointed straight for one of these gates, and a-coming like a house afire. Now I noticed that the skies were black with millions of people, pointed for those gates. What a roar they made, rushing through the air! The ground was as thick as ants with people, too—billions of them, I judge.

I lit. I drifted up to a gate with a swarm of people, and when it was my turn the head clerk says, in a businesslike way:

"Well, quick! Where are you from?"

"San Francisco," says I.

"San Fran—*what?*" says he.

"San Francisco."

He scratched his head and looked puzzled. Then he says: "Is it a planet?"

By George, Peters, think of it! *"Planet?"* says I; "it's a city. And moreover, it's one of the biggest and finest and—"

"There, there!" says he. "No time here for conversation. We

don't deal in cities here. Where are you from in a *general* way?"

"Oh," I says, "I beg your pardon. Put me down for California."

I had him *again,* Peters! He puzzled a second, then he says, sharp and irritable:

"I don't know any such planet—is it a constellation?"

"Oh, my goodness!" says I. "Constellation, says you? No—it's a state."

"Man, we don't deal in states here. *Will* you tell me where you are from *in general—at large,* don't you understand?"

"Oh, now I get your idea," I says. "I'm from America—the United States of America."

Peters, do you know I had him *again?* If I hadn't I'm a clam! His face was as blank as a target after a militia shooting match. He turned to an under clerk and says:

"Where is America? *What* is America?"

The under clerk answered up prompt and says:

"There ain't any such orb."

"*Orb?*" says I. "Why, what are you talking about, young man? It ain't an orb; it's a country; it's a continent. Columbus discovered it; I reckon likely you've heard of *him,* anyway. America—why, sir, America—"

"Silence!" says the head clerk. "Once for all, where—are—you—*from?*"

"Well," says I, "I don't know anything more to say—unless I lump things, and just say I'm from the world."

"Ah," says he, brightening up, "now, that's something like! *What* world?"

Peters, he had *me,* that time. I looked at him, puzzled; he looked at me, worried. Then he burst out:

"Come, come, what world?"

Says I, "Why, *the* world, of course."

"*The* world!" he says. "H'm! there's billions of them! . . . Next!"

That meant for me to stand aside. I done so, and a sky-blue man with seven heads and only one leg hopped into my place. I took a walk. It just occurred to me then that all the myriads I had seen swarming to that gate, up to this time, were just like that creature. I tried to run across somebody I was acquainted with, but they were out of acquaintances of mine just then. So I thought the thing all over and finally sidled back there pretty meek and feeling rather stumped, as you may say.

"Well?" said the head clerk.

"Well, sir," I says, pretty humble, "I don't seem to make out which world it is I'm from. But you may know it from this—it's the one the Saviour saved."

He bent his head at the Name. Then he says, gently:

"The worlds He has saved are like to the gates of heaven in number—none can count them. What astronomical system is your world in?—perhaps that may assist."

"It's the one that has the sun in it—and the moon—and Mars"—he shook his head at each name; hadn't ever heard of them, you see—"and Neptune—and Uranus—and Jupiter—"

"Hold on!" says he. "Hold on a minute! Jupiter . . . Jupiter . . . Seems to me we had a man from there eight or nine hundred years ago—but people from that system very seldom enter by this gate." All of a sudden he begun to look me so straight in the eye that I thought he was going to bore through me. Then he says, very deliberate, "Did you come *straight here* from your system?"

"Yes, sir," I says—but I blushed the least little bit in the world when I said it.

He looked at me very stern, and says:

"That is not true; and this is not the place for prevarication. You wandered from your course. How did that happen?"

Says I, blushing again:

"I'm sorry, and I take back what I said, and confess. I raced a little with a comet one day—only just the least little bit—only the tiniest lit—"

"So—so," says he—and without any sugar in his voice to speak of.

I went on, and says:

"But I only fell off just a bare point, and I went right back on my course again the minute the race was over."

"No matter—that divergence has made all this trouble. It has brought you to a gate that is billions of leagues from the right one. If you had gone to your own gate they would have known all about your world at once and there would have been no delay. But we will try to accommodate you." He turned to an under clerk and says:

"What system is Jupiter in?"

"I don't remember, sir, but I think there is such a planet in one of the little new systems away out in one of the thinly worlded corners of the universe. I will see."

He got a balloon and sailed up and up and up, in front of a map that was as big as Rhode Island. He went on up till he was out of sight, and by and by he came down and got something to eat and went up again. To cut a long story short, he kept on doing this for a day or two, and finally he came down and said he thought he had found that solar system, but it might be flyspecks. So he got a microscope and went back. It turned out better than he feared. He had rousted out our system, sure enough. He got me to describe our planet and its distance from the sun, and then he says to his chief:

"Oh, I know the one he means now, sir. It is on the map. It is called the Wart."

Says I to myself, Young man, it wouldn't be wholesome for you to go down *there* and call it the Wart.

Well, they let me in then, and told me I was safe forever and wouldn't have any more trouble.

Then they turned from me and went on with their work, the same as if they considered my case all complete and shipshape. I was a good deal surprised at this, but I was diffident about speaking up and reminding them. I did so hate to do it, you know; it seemed a pity to bother them, they had so much on their hands. Twice I thought I would give up and let the thing go; so twice I started to leave, but immediately I thought what a figure I should cut stepping out amongst the redeemed in such a rig, and that made me hang back and come to anchor again. People got to eyeing me—clerks, you know—wondering why I didn't get under way. I couldn't stand this long—it was too uncomfortable. So at last I plucked up courage and tipped the head clerk a signal. He says:

"What, you here yet? What's wanting?"

Says I, in a low voice and very confidential, making a trumpet with my hands at his ear:

"I beg pardon, and you mustn't mind my reminding you and seeming to meddle, but hain't you forgot something?"

He studied a second, and says:

"Forgot something? . . . No, not that I know of."

"Think," says I.

He thought. Then he says:

"No, I can't seem to have forgot anything. What is it?"

"Look at me," says I; "look me all over."

He done it.

"Well?" says he.

"Well," says I, "you don't notice anything? If I branched out amongst the elect looking like this, wouldn't I attract considerable attention? Wouldn't I be a little conspicuous?"

"Well," he says, "I don't see anything the matter. What do you lack?"

"Lack! Why, I lack my harp, and my wreath, and my halo, and my hymnbook, and my palm branch—I lack everything that a body naturally requires up here, my friend."

Puzzled? Peters, he was the worst puzzled man you ever saw. Finally he says:

"Well, you seem to be a curiosity every way a body takes you. I never heard of these things before."

I looked at the man awhile in solid astonishment; then I says:

"Now, I hope you don't take it as an offense, for I don't mean any, but really, for a man that has been in the Kingdom as long as I reckon you have, you do seem to know powerful little about its customs."

"Its customs!" says he. "Heaven is a large place, good friend. Large empires have many and diverse customs. Even small dominions have, as you doubtless know by what you have seen of the matter on a small scale in the Wart. How can you imagine I could ever learn the varied customs of the countless kingdoms of heaven? It makes my head ache to think of it. I know the customs that prevail in those portions inhabited by peoples that are appointed to enter my own gate—and hark ye, that is quite enough knowledge for one individual to try to pack into his head in the thirty-seven millions of years I have devoted night and day to that study. But the idea of learning the customs of the whole appalling expanse of heaven—O man, how insanely you talk! Now, I don't doubt that this odd costume you talk about is the fashion in that district of heaven you belong to, but you won't be conspicuous in this section without it."

I felt all right if that was the case, so I bade him good day and left. All day I walked towards the far end of a prodigious hall of the office, hoping to come out into heaven any moment, but it was a mistake. That hall was built on the general heavenly plan—it naturally couldn't be small. At last I got so tired I couldn't go any farther; so I sat down to rest, and begun to tackle the queerest sort of strangers and ask for information, but I didn't get any; they couldn't understand my language, and I could not understand theirs. I got dreadfully lonesome. I was so downhearted and homesick I wished a hundred times I never had died. I turned back, of course. About noon next day, I got back at last and was on hand at the booking office once more. Says I to the head clerk:

"I begin to see that a man's got to be in his own heaven to be happy."

"Perfectly correct," says he: "Did you imagine the same heaven would suit all sorts of men?"

"Well, I had that idea—but I see the foolishness of it. Which way am I to go to get to my district?"

He called the under clerk that had examined the map, and he gave me general directions. I thanked him and started; but he says:

"Wait a minute; it is millions of leagues from here. Go outside and stand on that red wishing carpet; shut your eyes, hold your breath, and wish yourself there."

"I'm much obliged," says I; "why didn't you dart me through when I first arrived?"

"We have a good deal to think of here; it was your place to think of it and ask for it. Goodbye; we probably sha'n't see you in this region for a thousand centuries or so."

"In that case, *o revoor,*" says I.

I hopped onto the carpet and held my breath and shut my eyes and wished I was in the booking office of my own section. The very next instant a voice I knew sung out in a business kind of a way:

"A harp and a hymnbook, pair of wings and a halo, size thirteen, for Cap'n Eli Stormfield, of San Francisco! Make him out a clean bill of health, and let him in."

I opened my eyes. Sure enough, it was a Pi Ute Injun I used to know in Tulare County; mighty good fellow—I remembered being at his funeral, which consisted of him being burnt and the other Injuns gauming their faces with his ashes and howling like wildcats. He was powerful glad to see me, and you may make up your mind I was just as glad to see him, and felt that I was in the right kind of a heaven at last.

Just as far as your eye could reach, there was swarms of clerks, running and bustling around, tricking out thousands of Yanks and Mexicans and English and Arabs, and all sorts of people in their new outfits; and when they gave me my kit and I put on my halo and I took a look in the glass, I could have jumped over a house for joy, I was so happy. "Now, *this* is something like!" says I. "Now," says I, "I'm all right—show me a cloud."

Inside of fifteen minutes I was a mile on my way towards the cloud banks and about a million people along with me. Most of us tried to fly, but some got crippled and nobody made a success of it. So we concluded to walk, for the present, till we had had some wing practice.

We begun to meet swarms of folks who were coming back. Some had harps and nothing else; some had hymnbooks and nothing else; some had nothing at all; all of them looked meek and uncomfortable; one young fellow hadn't anything left but his halo, and he was carrying that in his hand; all of a sudden he offered it to me and says:

"Will you hold it for me a minute?"

Then he disappeared in the crowd. I went on. A woman asked me to hold her palm branch, and then *she* disappeared. A girl got me to hold her harp for her, and by George, *she* disappeared; and so on and so on, till I was about loaded down to the guards. Then comes a smiling old gentleman and asked me to hold *his* things. I swabbed off the perspiration and says, pretty tart:

"I'll have to get you to excuse me, my friend—*I* ain't no hat rack."

About this time I begun to run across piles of those traps,

lying in the road. I just quietly dumped my extra cargo along with them. I looked around, and, Peters, that whole nation that was following me were loaded down the same as I'd been. The return crowd had got them to hold their things a minute, you see. They all dumped their loads too, and we went on.

When I found myself perched on a cloud, with a million other people, I never felt so good in my life. Says I, "Now, this is according to the promises; I've been having my doubts, but now I *am* in heaven, sure enough." I gave my palm branch a wave or two, for luck, and then I tautened up my harp strings and struck in. Well, Peters, you can't imagine anything like the row we made. It was grand to listen to, and made a body thrill all over, but there was considerable many tunes going on at once, and that was a drawback to the harmony, you understand; and then there was a lot of Injun tribes, and they kept up such another war whooping that they kind of took the tuck out of the music. By and by I quit performing and judged I'd take a rest. There was quite a nice mild old gentleman sitting next to me, and I noticed he didn't take a hand; I encouraged him, but he said he was naturally bashful and was afraid to try before so many people. By and by the old gentleman said he never could seem to enjoy music somehow. The fact was, I was beginning to feel the same way, but I didn't say anything. Him and I had a considerable long silence then, of course it warn't noticeable in that place. After about sixteen or seventeen hours, during which I played and sung a little, now and then—always the same tune, because I didn't know any other—I laid down my harp and begun to fan myself with my palm branch. Then we both got to sighing pretty regular. Finally, says he:

"Don't you know any tune but the one you've been pegging at all day?"

"Not another blessed one," says I.

"Don't you reckon you could learn another one?" says he.

"Never," says I; "I've tried to, but I couldn't manage it."

"It's a long time to hang to the one—eternity, you know."

"Don't break my heart," says I; "I'm getting low-spirited enough already."

After another long silence, says he:

"Are you glad to be here?"

Says I, "Old man, I'll be frank with you. This *ain't* just as near my idea of bliss as I thought it was going to be when I used to go to church."

Says he, "What do you say to knocking off and calling it half a day?"

"That's me," says I. "I never wanted to get off watch so bad in my life."

So we started. Millions were coming to the cloud bank all the time, happy and hosannahing; millions were leaving it all the time, looking mighty quiet, I tell you. We laid for the newcomers, and pretty soon I'd got them to hold all my things a minute, and then I was a free man again and most outrageously happy. Just then I ran across old Sam Bartlett, who had been dead a long time, and stopped to have a talk with him. Says I:

"Now, tell me—is this to go on forever? Ain't there anything else for a change?"

Says he:

"I'll set you right on that point very quick. People take the figurative language of the Bible and the allegories for literal, and the first thing they ask for when they get here is a halo and a harp, and so on. Nothing that's harmless and reasonable is refused a body here, if he asks it in the right spirit. So they are outfitted with these things without a word. They go and sing and play just about one day, and that's the last you'll ever see them in the choir. They don't need anybody to tell them that that sort of thing wouldn't make a heaven—at least not a heaven that a sane man could stand a week and remain sane. That cloud bank is placed where the noise can't disturb the old inhabitants, and so there ain't any harm in letting everybody get up there and cure himself as soon as he comes.

"Now, you just remember this—heaven is as blissful and lovely as it can be, but it's just the busiest place you ever heard of. There ain't any idle people here after the first day. Singing hymns and waving palm branches through all eternity is pretty when you hear about it in the pulpit, but it's as poor a way to put in valuable time as a body could contrive. It would just make a heaven of warbling ignoramuses, don't you see? Eternal Rest sounds comforting in the pulpit too. Well, you try it once and see how heavy time will hang on your hands. Why, Stormfield, a man like you, that had been active and stirring all his life, would go mad in six months in a heaven where he hadn't anything to do. Heaven is the very last place to come to *rest* in—and don't you be afraid to bet on that!"

Says I:

"Sam, I'm as glad to hear it as I thought I'd be sorry. I'm glad I come, now."

Says he:

"Cap'n, ain't you pretty physically tired?"

Says I:

"Sam, it ain't any name for it! I'm dog-tired."

"Just so—just so. You've earned a good sleep, and you'll get it. You've earned a good appetite, and you'll enjoy your dinner. It's the same here as it is on earth—you've got to earn a thing, square and honest, before you enjoy it. You can't enjoy first and earn afterwards. But there's this difference here: you can choose your own occupation, and all the powers of heaven will be put forth to help you make a success of it, if you do your level best. The shoemaker on earth that had the soul of a poet in him won't have to make shoes here."

"Now, that's all reasonable and right," says I. "Plenty of work, and the kind you hanker after; no more pain, no more suffering—"

"Oh, hold on; there's plenty of pain here—but it don't kill. There's plenty of suffering here, but it don't last. You see, happiness ain't a *thing in itself*—it's only a *contrast* with something that ain't pleasant. That's all it is. There ain't a thing you can mention that is happiness in its own self—it's only so by contrast with the other thing. And so as soon as the novelty is over and the force of the contrast dulled, it ain't happiness any longer, and you have to get something fresh. Well, there's plenty of pain and suffering in heaven—consequently there's plenty of contrasts, and just no end of happiness."

Says I, "It's the sensiblest heaven I've heard of yet, Sam, though it's about as different from the one I was brought up on as a live princess is different from her own wax figger."

Along in the first months I knocked around about the Kingdom, making friends and looking at the country, and finally settled down in a pretty likely region, to have a rest before taking another start. I went on making acquaintances and gathering up information. I had a good deal of talk with an old bald-headed angel by the name of Sandy McWilliams. He was from somewhere in New Jersey. I went about with him considerable. We used to lay around, warm afternoons, in the shade of a rock, on some meadow ground that was pretty high and out of the marshy slush of his cranberry farm, and there we used to talk about all kinds of things, and smoke pipes. One day, says I:

"About how old might you be, Sandy?"

"Seventy-two."

"I judged so. How long you been in heaven?"

"Twenty-seven years come Christmas."

"How old was you when you come up?"

"Why, seventy-two, of course."

"You can't mean it!"

"Why can't I mean it?"

"Because, if you was seventy-two then, you are naturally ninety-nine now."

"No, but I ain't. I stay the same age I was when I come."

"Well," says I, "come to think, there's something just here that I want to ask about. Down below, I always had an idea that in heaven we would all be young, and bright, and spry."

"Well, you *can* be young if you want to. You've only got to wish."

"Well, then, why didn't you wish?"

"I did. They all do. You'll try it some day, like enough; but you'll get tired of the change pretty soon."

"Why?"

"Well, I'll tell you. Now, you've always been a sailor; did you ever try some other business?"

"Yes, I tried keeping grocery once, up in the mines, but I couldn't stand it. It was too dull—no stir, no storm, no life about it; it was like being part dead and part alive, both at the same time. I wanted to be one thing or t'other. I shut up shop pretty quick and went to sea."

"That's it. Grocery people like it, but you couldn't. You see, you wasn't used to it. Well, I wasn't used to being young, and I couldn't seem to take any interest in it. I was strong, and handsome, and had curly hair—yes, and wings, too!—gay wings like a butterfly. I went to picnics and dances and parties with the fellows, and tried to carry on and talk nonsense with the girls, but it wasn't any use; I couldn't take to it—fact is, it was an awful bore. What I wanted was early to bed and early to rise, and something to *do;* and when my work was done, I wanted to sit quiet, and smoke and think—not tear around with a parcel of giddy young kids. You can't think what I suffered whilst I was young."

"How long was you young?"

"Only two weeks. That was plenty for me. Laws, I was so lonesome! You see, I was full of the knowledge and experience of seventy-two years; the deepest subject those young folks could strike was only A-B-C to me. And to hear them argue—oh, my! it would have been funny if it hadn't been so pitiful. Well, I was so hungry for the ways and the sober talk I was used to that I tried to ring in with the old people, but they wouldn't have it. They considered me a conceited young upstart and gave me the cold shoulder. Two weeks was a-plenty for me. I was glad to get back my bald head again, and my pipe, and my old drowsy reflections in the shade of a rock or a tree."

"Well," says I, "do you mean to say you're going to stand still at seventy-two forever?"

"I don't know, and I ain't particular. But I ain't going to drop back to twenty-five any more—I know that mighty well. I know a sight more than I did twenty-seven years ago, and I enjoy learning all the time, but I don't seem to get any older. That is, bodily—my mind gets older, and stronger, and better seasoned, and more satisfactory."

Says I, "If a man comes here at ninety, don't he ever set himself back?"

"Of course he does. He sets himself back to fourteen; tries it a couple of hours, and feels like a fool; sets himself forward to twenty; it ain't much improvement; tries thirty, fifty, eighty, and finally ninety—finds he is more at home and comfortable at the same old figure he is used to than any other way. Or if his mind begun to fail him on earth at eighty, that's where he finally sticks up here. He sticks at the place where his mind was last at its best, for there's where his enjoyment is best, and his ways most set and established."

"Does a chap of twenty-five stay always twenty-five, and look it?"

"If he is a fool, yes, But if he is bright and ambitious and industrious, the knowledge he gains and the experience he has change his ways and thoughts and likings, and make him find his best pleasure in the company of people above that age; so he allows his body to take on that look of as many added years as he needs to make him comfortable and proper in that sort of society; he lets his body go on taking the look of age, according as he progresses, and by and by he will be bald and wrinkled outside, and wise and deep within."

"Babies the same?"

"Babies the same. Laws, what asses we used to be, on earth, about these things! We said we'd be always young in heaven. We didn't say *how* young—we didn't think of that, perhaps; that is, we didn't all think alike, anyway. When I was a boy of seven, I suppose I thought we'd all be twelve in heaven; when I was twelve, I suppose I thought we'd all be eighteen or twenty in heaven; when I was forty, I begun to go back; I remember I hoped we'd all be about *thirty* years old in heaven. Neither a man nor a boy ever thinks the age he *has* is exactly the best one—he puts the *right* age a few years older or a few years younger than he is. Then he makes the ideal age the general age of the heavenly people. And he expects everybody to *stick* at that age—stand stock-still—and expects them to enjoy it! Now, just think of the idea of standing still in heaven! Think of a heaven made up entirely of hoop-rolling, marble-playing cubs of seven years! Or of awkward, diffident, sentimental immaturities of nineteen! Or of vigorous people of thirty, healthy-minded, brimming with ambition, but chained hand and foot to that one age and its limitations like so many helpless galley slaves! Think of the dull sameness of a society made up of people all of one age and one set of looks, habits, tastes, and feelings. Think how superior to it earth would be, with its variety of types and faces and ages, and the enlivening attrition of the myriad interests that come into pleasant collision in such a variegated society."

"Look here," says I, "do you know what you're doing?"

"Well, what am I doing?"

"You are making heaven pretty comfortable in one way, but you are playing the mischief with it in another."

"How d'you mean?"

"Well," I says, "take a young mother that's lost her child, and—"

"Sh!" he says. "Look!"

It was a woman. Middle-aged, and had grizzled hair. She was walking slow, and her head was bent down, and her wings hanging limp and droopy; and she looked ever so tired, and was crying, poor thing! She passed along by, with her head down that way and the tears running down her face, and didn't see us. Then Sandy said, low and gentle, and full of pity:

"*She's* hunting for her child! No, *found* it, I reckon. Lord, how she's changed! But I recognized her in a minute, though it's twenty-seven years since I saw her. A young mother she was, about twenty-two or -four, or along there; and blooming and lovely and sweet—oh, just a flower! And all her heart and all her soul was wrapped up in her child, the little girl, two years old. And it died, and she went wild with grief, just wild! Well, the only comfort she had was that she'd see her child again in heaven—'never more to part,' she said, and kept on saying it over and over, 'never more to part.' And the words made her happy; yes, they did; they made her joyful; and when I was dying, twenty-seven years ago, she told me to find her child the first thing, and say she was coming—'soon, soon, *very* soon, she hoped and believed!' "

"Why, it's pitiful, Sandy."

He didn't say anything for a while, but sat looking at the ground, thinking. Then he says, kind of mournful:

"And now she's come!"

"Well? Go on."

"Stormfield, maybe she hasn't found the child, but *I* think she has. Looks so to me. I've seen cases before. You see, she's kept that child in her head just the same as it was when she jounced it in her arms a little chubby thing. But here it didn't elect to *stay* a child. No, it elected to grow up, which it did. And in these twenty-seven years it has learned all the deep scientific learning there is to learn, and is studying and studying and learning and learning more and more all the time, and don't give a damn for anything *but* learning; just learning, and discussing gigantic problems with people like herself."

"Well?"

"Stormfield, don't you see? Her mother knows *cranberries,* and how to tend them, and pick them, and put them up, and market them; and not another blamed thing! Her and her daughter can't be any more company for each other *now* than mud turtle and bird o' paradise. Poor thing, she was looking for a baby to jounce; *I* think she's struck a disapp'intment."

"Sandy, what will they do—stay unhappy forever in heaven?"

"No, they'll come together and get adjusted by and by. But not this year, and not next. By and by."

2

I had been having considerable trouble with my wings. The day after I helped the choir I made a dash or two with them, but was not lucky. First off, I flew thirty yards and then fouled an Irishman and brought him down—brought us both down, in fact. Next, I had a collision with a bishop—and bowled him down, of course. We had some sharp words, and I felt pretty cheap, to come banging into a grave old person like that, with a million strangers looking on and smiling to themselves.

I saw I hadn't got the hang of the steering, and so couldn't rightly tell where I was going to bring up when I started. I went afoot the rest of the day, and let my wings hang. Early next morning I went to a private place to have some practice. I got up on a pretty high rock and got a good start and went swooping down, aiming for a bush a little over three hundred yards off; but I couldn't seem to calculate for the wind, which was about two points abaft my beam. I could see I was going considerable to looard of the bush, so I worked my starboard wing slow and went ahead strong on the port one, but it wouldn't answer; I could see I was going to broach to, so I slowed down on both, and lit. I went back to the rock and took another chance at it. I aimed two or three points to starboard of the bush—yes, more than that—enough so as to make it nearly a head wind. I done well enough, but made pretty poor time. I could see plain enough that on a head wind, wings was a mistake. I could see that a body could sail pretty close to the wind, but he couldn't go in the wind's eye. I could see that if I wanted to go a-visiting any distance from home and the wind was ahead, I might have to wait days, maybe, for a change; and I could see, too, that these things could not be any use at all in a gale; if you tried to run before the wind, you would make a mess of it, for there isn't any way to shorten sail—like reefing, you know you have to take it *all* in—shut your feathers down flat to your sides. That would *land* you, of course. You could lay to, with your head to the wind—that is the best you could do, and right hard work you'd find it, too. If you tried any other game, you would founder sure.

I judge it was about a couple of weeks or so after this that I dropped old Sandy McWilliams a note one day—it was a Tuesday—and asked him to come over and take his manna and quails with me next day; and the first thing he did when he stepped in was to twinkle his eye in a sly way, and say:

"Well, Cap, what you done with your wings?"

I saw in a minute that there was some sarcasm done up in that rag somewheres, but I never let on. I only says:

"Gone to the wash."

"Yes," he says, in a dry sort of way, "they mostly go to the wash—about this time; I've often noticed it. Fresh angels are powerful neat. When do you look for 'em back?"

"Day after tomorrow," says I.

He winked at me and smiled.

Says I:

"Sandy, out with it. Come—no secrets among friends. I notice you don't ever wear wings—and plenty others don't. I've been making an ass of myself—is that it?"

"That is about the size of it. But it is no harm. We all do it at first. It's perfectly natural. You see, on earth we jumped to such foolish conclusions as to things up here. In the pictures we always saw the angels with wings on—and that was all right; but we jumped to the conclusion that that was their way of getting around—and that was all wrong. The wings ain't anything but a uniform, that's all. When they are in the field—so to speak—they always wear them; you never see an angel going with a message anywhere without his wings, any more than you would see a military officer presiding at a court-martial without his uniform, or a postman delivering letters, or a policeman walking his beat, in plain clothes. But they ain't to *fly* with! The wings are for show, not for use. Old experienced angels are like officers of the regular army—they dress plain when they are off duty. New angels are like the militia—never shed the uniform: always fluttering and floundering around in their wings, butting people down, flapping here and there and everywhere, always imagining they are attracting the admiring eye—well, they just think they are the very most important people in heaven. And when you see one of them come sailing around with one wing tipped up and t'other down, you make up your mind he is saying to himself: 'I wish Mary Ann in Arkansaw could see me now. I reckon she'd wish she hadn't shook me.' No, they're just for show, that's all—only just for show."

"I judge you've got it about right, Sandy," says I.

"Why, look at it yourself," says he. "*You* ain't built for wings—no man is. You know what a grist of years it took you to come here from the earth—and yet you were booming along faster than any cannon ball could go. Suppose you had to fly that distance with your wings—wouldn't eternity have been over before you got here? Certainly. Well, angels have to go to the earth every day—millions of them—to appear in visions to dying children and good people, you know—it's the heft of their business. They appear with their wings, of course, because they are on official service, and because the dying persons wouldn't know they were angels if they hadn't wings—but do you reckon they fly with them? It stands to reason they don't. The wings would wear out before they got halfway; even the pinfeathers would be gone; the wing frames would be as bare as kite sticks before the paper is pasted on. The distances in heaven are billions of times greater; angels have to go all over heaven every day. Could they do it with their wings alone? No, indeed; they wear the wings for style, but they travel any distance in an instant by *wishing*. The wishing carpet of the *Arabian Nights* was a sensible idea—but our earthly idea of angels flying these awful distances with their clumsy wings was foolish.

"Our young saints, of both sexes, wear wings all the time—blazing red ones, and blue and green, and gold, and variegated, and rainbowed, and ring-streaked-and-striped ones—and nobody finds fault. It is suitable to their time of life. The things are beautiful, and they set the young people off. They are the most striking and lovely part of their outfit—a halo don't *begin.*"

"Well," says I, "I've tucked mine away in the cupboard, and I allow to let them lay there till there's mud."

"Yes—or a reception."

"What's that?"

"Well, you can see one tonight if you want to. There's a barkeeper from Jersey City going to be received."

"Go on—tell me about it."

"This barkeeper got converted at a Moody and Sankey meeting in New York and started home on the ferryboat, and there was a collision and he got drowned. He is of a class that thinks all heaven goes wild with joy when a particularly hard lot like him is saved; they think all heaven turns out hosannahing to welcome them; they think there isn't anything talked about in the realms of the blest but their case, for that day. This barkeeper thinks there hasn't been such another stir here in years as his coming is going to raise. And I've always noticed this peculiarity about a dead barkeeper: he not only expects all hands to turn out when he arrives, but he expects to be received with a torchlight procession."

"I reckon he is disappointed, then."

"No, he isn't. No man is allowed to be disappointed here. Whatever he wants when he comes—that is, any reasonable and unsacrilegious thing—he can have. There's always a few millions or billions of young folks around who don't want any better entertainment than to fill up their lungs and swarm out with their torches and have a high time over a barkeeper. It tickles the barkeeper till he can't rest, it makes a charming lark for the young folks, it don't do anybody any harm, it don't cost a rap, and it keeps up the place's reputation for making all comers happy and content."

"Very good. I'll be on hand and see them land the barkeeper."

"It is manners to go in full dress. You want to wear your wings, you know, and your other things."

"Which ones?"

"Halo, and harp, and palm branch, and all that."

"Well," says I, "I reckon I ought to be ashamed of myself,

but the fact is I left them laying around that day I resigned from the choir. I haven't got a rag to wear but this robe and the wings."

"That's all right. You'll find they've been raked up and saved for you. Send for them."

"I'll do it, Sandy. But what was it you was saying about unsacrilegious things, which people expect to get and will be disappointed about?"

"Oh, there are a lot of such things that people expect and don't get. For instance, there's a Brooklyn preacher by the name of Talmage who is laying up a considerable disappointment for himself. He says, every now and then in his sermons, that the first thing he does when he gets to heaven, will be to fling his arms around Abraham, Isaac, and Jacob and kiss them and weep on them. There's millions of people down there on earth that are promising themselves the same thing. As many as sixty thousand people arrive here every single day that want to run straight to Abraham, Isaac, and Jacob and hug them and weep on them. Now, mind you, sixty thousand a day is a pretty heavy contract for those old people. If they were a mind to allow it, they wouldn't ever have anything to do, year in and year out, but stand up and be hugged and wept on thirty-two hours in the twenty-four. They would be tired out and as wet as muskrats all the time. What would heaven be to *them?* It would be a mighty good place to get out of—you know that yourself. Those are kind and gentle old Jews, but they ain't any fonder of kissing the emotional highlights of Brooklyn than you be. You mark my words, Mr. T.'s endearments are going to be declined, with thanks. There are limits to the privileges of the elect, even in heaven. Why, if Adam was to show himself to every newcomer that wants to call and gaze at him and strike him for his autograph, he would never have time to do anything else but just that. Talmage has said he is going to give Adam some of his attentions, as well as A., I., and J. But he will have to change his mind about that."

"Do you think Talmage will really come here?"

"Why, certainly he will. But don't you be alarmed; he will run with his own kind, and there's plenty of them. That is the main charm of heaven: there's all kinds here—which wouldn't be the case if you let the preachers tell it. Anybody can find the sort he prefers here, and he just lets the others alone, and they let him alone. When the Deity builds a heaven, it is built right, and on a liberal plan."

Sandy sent home for his things, and I sent for mine, and about nine in the evening we begun to dress. Sandy says:

"This is going to be a grand time for you, Stormy. Like as not some of the patriarchs will turn out."

"No, but will they?"

"Like as not. Of course, they are pretty exclusive. They hardly ever show themselves to the common public. I believe they never turn out except for an eleventh-hour convert. They wouldn't do it then, only earthly tradition makes a grand show pretty necessary on that kind of an occasion."

"Do they all turn out, Sandy?"

"Who—all the patriarchs? Oh, no—hardly ever more than a couple. You will be here fifty thousand years—maybe more—before you get a glimpse of all the patriarchs and prophets. Since I have been here, Job has been to the front once, and once Ham and Jeremiah both at the same time. But the finest thing that has happened in my day was a year or so ago; that was Charles Peace's reception—him they called 'the Bannercross Murderer'—an Englishman. There were four patriarchs and two prophets on the Grand Stand that time—there hasn't been anything like it since Captain Kidd came. Abel was there —the first time in twelve hundred years. A report got around that Adam was coming; well, of course, Abel was enough to bring a crowd all by himself, but there is nobody that can draw like Adam. It was a false report, but it got around anyway, as I say, and it will be a long day before I see the like of it again. The reception was in the English department, of course, which is eight hundred and eleven million miles from the New Jersey line. I went, along with a good many of my neighbors, and it was a sight to see, I can tell you. Flocks came from all the departments. I saw Eskimos there, and Tartars, Negroes, Chinamen—people from everywhere. You see a mixture like that in the Grand Choir the first day you land here, but you hardly ever see it again. There were billions of people; when they were singing or hosannahing, the noise was wonderful; and even when their tongues were still the drumming of the wings was nearly enough to burst your head, for all the sky was as thick as if it was snowing angels. Although Adam was not there, it was a great time anyway, because we had three archangels on the Grand Stand—it is a seldom thing that even one comes out."

"What did they look like, Sandy?"

"Well, they had shining faces, and shining robes, and wonderful rainbow wings, and they stood eighteen feet high, and wore swords, and held their heads up in a noble way, and looked like soldiers."

"Did they have halos?"

"No—anyway, not the hoop kind. The archangels and the upper-class patriarchs wear a finer thing than that. It is a round, solid, splendid glory of gold that is blinding to look at. You have often seen a patriarch in a picture, on earth, with that thing on—you remember it?—he looks as if he had his head in a brass platter. That don't give you the right idea of it at all—it is much more shining and beautiful."

"Did you talk with those archangels and patriarchs, Sandy?"

"Who—*I*? Why, what can you be thinking about, Stormy? I ain't worthy to speak to such as they."

"Is Talmage?"

"Of course not. You have got the same mixed-up idea about these things that everybody has down there. I had it once, but I got over it. Down there they talk of the heavenly King—and that is right—but then they go right on speaking as if this was a republic and everybody was on a dead level with everybody else, and privileged to fling his arms around anybody he comes across, and be hail-fellow-well-met with all the elect, from the highest down. How tangled up and absurd that is! How are you going to have a republic under a king? How are you going to have a republic at all, where the head of the government is absolute, holds his place forever, and has no parliament, no council to meddle or make in his affairs, nobody voted for, nobody elected, nobody in the whole universe with a voice in the government, nobody asked to take a hand in its matters, and nobody *allowed* to do it? Fine republic, ain't it?"

"Well, yes—it *is* a little different from the idea I had—but I thought I might go around and get acquainted with the grandees, anyway—not exactly splice the main brace with them, you know, but shake hands and pass the time of day."

"Could Tom, Dick, and Harry call on the Cabinet of Russia and do that? On Prince Gortschakoff, for instance?"

"I reckon not, Sandy."

"Well, this is Russia—only more so. There's not the shadow of a republic about it anywhere. There are ranks here. There are viceroys, princes, governors, subgovernors, sub-subgovernors, and a hundred orders of nobility, grading along down from grand-ducal archangels, stage by stage, till the general level is struck, where there ain't any titles. Do you know what a prince of the blood is, on earth?"

"No."

"Well, a prince of the blood don't belong to the royal family exactly, and he don't belong to the mere nobility of the kingdom; he is lower than the one and higher than t'other. That's about the position of the patriarchs and prophets here. There's some mighty high nobility here—people that you and I ain't worthy to polish sandals for—and *they* ain't worthy to polish sandals for the patriarchs and prophets. That gives you a kind of an idea of their rank, don't it? You begin to see how high up they are, don't you? Just to get a two-minute glimpse of one of them is a thing for a body to remember and tell about for a thousand years. Why, Captain, just think of this: if Abraham was to set his foot down here by this door, there would be a railing set up around that foot track right away, and a shelter put over it, and people would flock here from all over heaven for hundreds and hundreds of years to look at it. Abraham is one of the parties that Mr. Talmage, of Brooklyn, is going to embrace and kiss and weep on, when he comes. He wants to lay in a good stock of tears, you know, or five to one he will go dry before he gets a chance to do it."

"Sandy," says I, "I had an idea that *I* was going to be equal with everybody here too, but I will let that drop. It don't matter, and I am plenty happy enough anyway."

"Captain, you are happier than you would be the other way. These old patriarchs and prophets have got ages the start of you; they know more in two minutes than you know in a year.

Did you ever try to have a sociable, improving time discussing winds and currents and variations of compass with an undertaker?"

"I get your idea, Sandy. He couldn't interest me. He would be an ignoramus in such things—he would bore me, and I would bore him."

"You have got it. You would bore the patriarchs when you talked, and when they talked they would shoot over your head. By and by you would say, 'Good morning, your Eminence, I will call again'—but you wouldn't. Did you ever ask the slush boy to come up in the cabin and take dinner with you?"

"I get your drift again, Sandy. I wouldn't be used to such grand people as the patriarchs and prophets, and I would be sheepish and tongue-tied in their company, and mighty glad to get out of it. Sandy, which is the highest rank, patriarch or prophet?"

"Oh, the prophets hold over the patriarchs. The newest prophet, even, is of a sight more consequence than the oldest patriarch. Yes, sir, Adam himself has to walk behind Shakespeare."

"Was Shakespeare a prophet?"

"Of course he was; and so was Homer, and heaps more. But Shakespeare and the rest have to walk behind a common tailor from Tennessee by the name of Billings, and behind a horse doctor named Sakka from Afghanistan. Jeremiah and Billings and Buddha walk together, side by side, right behind a crowd from planets not in our astronomy; next come a dozen or two from Jupiter and other worlds; next come Daniel and Sakka and Confucius; next a lot from systems outside of ours; next come Ezekiel, Mahomet, Zoroaster, and a knife grinder from ancient Egypt; then there is a long string, and after them, away down toward the bottom, come Shakespeare and Homer and a shoemaker named Marais from the back settlements of France."

"Have they really rung in Mahomet and all those other heathens?"

"Yes—they all had their message, and they all get their reward. The man who don't get his reward on earth needn't bother—he will get it here sure."

"But why did they throw off on Shakespeare that way and put him away down there below those shoemakers and horse doctors and knife grinders—a lot of people nobody ever heard of?"

"That is the heavenly justice of it—they warn't rewarded according to their deserts on earth, but here they get their rightful rank. That tailor Billings, from Tennessee, wrote poetry that Homer and Shakespeare couldn't begin to come up to, but nobody would print it; nobody read it but his neighbors, an ignorant lot, and they laughed at it. Whenever the village had a drunken frolic and a dance, they would drag him in and crown him with cabbage leaves and pretend to bow down to him; and one night when he was sick and nearly starved to death, they had him out and crowned him, and then they rode him on a rail about the village, and everybody followed along, beating tin pans and yelling. Well, he died before morning. He wasn't ever expecting to go to heaven, much less that there was going to be any fuss made over him, so I reckon he was a good deal surprised when the reception broke on him."

"Was you there, Sandy?"

"Bless you, no!"

"Why? Didn't you know it was going to come off?"

"Well, I judge I did. It was the talk of these realms—not for a day, like this barkeeper business, but for twenty years before the man died."

"Why the mischief didn't you go, then?"

"Now, how you talk! The like of me go meddling around at the reception of a prophet? A mudsill like me trying to push in and help receive an awful grandee like Edward J. Billings? Why, I should have been laughed at for a billion miles around. I shouldn't ever have heard the last of it."

"Well, who did go, then?"

"Mighty few people that you and I will ever get a chance to see, Captain. Not a solitary commoner ever has the luck to see a reception of a prophet, I can tell you. All the nobility, and all the patriarchs and prophets—every last one of them—and all the archangels, and all the princes and governors and viceroys, were there, and *no* small fry—not a single one. And mind you, I'm not talking about only the grandees from *our* world, but the princes and patriarchs and so on from *all* the worlds that shine in our sky, and from billions more that belong in systems upon systems away outside of the one our sun is in. There were some prophets and patriarchs there that ours ain't a circumstance to, for rank and illustriousness and all that. Some were from Jupiter and other worlds in our own system, but the most celebrated were three poets, Saa, Bo, and Soof, from great planets in three different and very remote systems. These three names are common and familiar in every nook and corner of heaven, clear from one end of it to the other—fully as well known as the eighty Supreme Archangels, in fact—whereas our Moses, and Adam, and the rest have not been heard of outside of our world's little corner of heaven, except by a few very learned men scattered here and there—and they always spell their names wrong, and get the performances of one mixed up with the doings of another, and they almost always locate them simply *in our solar system,* and think that is enough without going into little details such as naming the particular world they are from. It is like a learned Hindoo showing off how much he knows by saying Longfellow lived in the United States—as if he lived all over the United States, and as if the country was so small you couldn't throw a brick there without hitting him. Between you and me, it does gravel me the cool way people from those monster worlds outside our system snub our little world, and even our system. Of course we think a good deal of Jupiter, because our world is only a potato to it, for size; but then there are worlds in other systems that Jupiter isn't even a mustard seed to—like the planet Goobra, for instance, which you couldn't squeeze inside the orbit of Halley's comet without straining the rivets. Tourists from Goobra (I mean parties that lived and died there—natives) come here, now and then, and inquire about our world, and when they find out it is so little that a streak of lightning can flash clear around it in the eighth of a second, they have to lean up against something to laugh. Then they screw a glass into their eye and go to examining *us,* as if we were a curious kind of foreign bug or something of that sort. One of them asked me how long our day was, and when I told him it was twelve hours long, as a general thing, he asked me if people where I was from considered it worthwhile to get up and wash for such a day as that. That is the way with those Goobra people—they can't seem to let a chance go by to throw it in your face that their day is three hundred and twenty-two of our years long. This young snob was just of age—he was six or seven thousand of his days old—say two million of our years—and he had all the puppy airs that belong to that time of life—that turning point when a person has got over being a boy and yet ain't quite a man exactly. If it had been anywhere else but in heaven, I would have given him a piece of my mind. Well, anyway, Billings had the grandest reception that has been seen in thousands of centuries, and I think it will have a good effect. His name will be carried pretty far, and it will make our system talked about, and maybe our world too, and raise us in the respect of the general public of heaven. Why, look here—Shakespeare walked backwards before that tailor from Tennessee and scattered flowers for him to walk on, and Homer stood behind his chair and waited on him at the banquet. Of course, that didn't go for much *there,* amongst all those big foreigners from other systems, as they hadn't heard of Shakespeare or Homer either, but it would amount to considerable down there on our little earth if they could know about it. I wish there was something *in* that miserable spiritualism, so we could send them word. That Tennessee village would set up a monument to Billings then, and his autograph would outsell Satan's. Well, they had grand times at that reception; a small-fry noble from Hoboken told me all about it—Sir Richard Duffer, Baronet."

"What, Sandy, a nobleman from Hoboken? How is that?"

"Easy enough. Duffer kept a sausage shop and never saved a cent in his life because he used to give all his spare meat to the poor, in a quiet way. Not tramps—no, the other sort—the sort that will starve before they will beg—honest square people out of work. Dick used to watch hungry-looking men and women and children, and track them home and find out all about them from the neighbors, and then feed them and find them work. As nobody ever *saw* him give anything to anybody, he had the reputation of being mean; he died with it, too, and everybody said it was a good riddance; but the minute he landed here they made him a baronet, and the very first words Dick the sausage maker of Hoboken heard when he stepped upon the heavenly shore were 'Welcome, Sir Richard Duffer!' It surprised him some, because he thought he had reasons to believe he was pointed for a warmer climate than this one."

All of a sudden the whole region fairly rocked under the crash of eleven hundred and one thunder blasts, all let off at once, and Sandy says:

"There, that's for the barkeep."

I jumped up and says:

"Then let's be moving along, Sandy; we don't want to miss any of this thing, you know."

"Keep your seat," he says; "he is only just telegraphed, that is all."

"How?"

"That blast only means that he has been sighted from the signal station. He is off Sandy Hook. The committees will go down to meet him now and escort him in. There will be ceremonies and delays; they won't be coming up the Bay for a considerable time yet. It is several billion miles away, anyway."

"*I* could have been a barkeeper and a hard lot just as well as not," says I, remembering the lonesome way I arrived, and how there wasn't any committee nor anything.

"I notice some regret in your voice," says Sandy, "and it is natural enough; but let bygones be bygones; you went according to your lights, and it is too late now to mend the thing."

"No, let it slide, Sandy, I don't mind. But you've got a Sandy Hook *here*, too, have you?"

"We've got everything here, just as it is below. All the states and territories of the Union, and all the kingdoms of the earth and the islands of the sea are laid out here just as they are on the globe—all the same shape they are down there, and all graded to the relative size, only each state and realm and island is a good many billion times bigger here than it is below. There goes another blast."

"What is that one for?"

"That is only another fort answering the first one. They each fire eleven hundred and one thunder blasts at a single dash—it is the usual salute for an eleventh-hour guest: a hundred for each hour and an extra one for the guest's sex; if it was a woman we would know it by their leaving off the extra gun."

"How do we know there's eleven hundred and one, Sandy, when they all go off at once?—and yet we certainly do know."

"Our intellects are a good deal sharpened up, here, in some ways, and that is one of them. Numbers and sizes and distances are so great here that we have to be made so we can *feel* them—our old ways of counting and measuring and ciphering wouldn't ever give us an idea of them, but would only confuse us and oppress us and make our heads ache."

After some more talk about this, I says, "Sandy, I notice that I hardly ever see a white angel; where I run across one white angel, I strike as many as a hundred million copper-colored ones—people that can't speak English. How is that?"

"Well, you will find it the same in any state or territory of the American corner of heaven you choose to go to. I have shot along a whole week on a stretch and gone millions and millions of miles, through perfect swarms of angels, without ever seeing a single white one, or hearing a word I could understand. You see, America was occupied a billion years and more by Injuns and Aztecs and that sort of folks before a white man ever set his foot in it. During the first three hundred years after Columbus's discovery, there wasn't ever more than one good lecture audience of white people all put together in America—I mean the whole thing, British possessions and all; in the beginning of our century there were only six or seven million—say seven; twelve or fourteen million in 1825; say twenty-three million in 1850; forty million in 1875. Our death rate has always been twenty in a thousand per annum. Well, a hundred and forty thousand died the first year of the century; two hundred and eighty thousand the twenty-fifth year; five hundred thousand the fiftieth year; about a million the seventy-fifth year. Now, I am going to be liberal about this thing and consider that fifty million whites have died in America from the beginning up to today—make it sixty, if you want to; make it a hundred million—it's no difference about a few millions one way or t'other. Well, now, you can see yourself that when you come to spread a little dab of people like that over these hundreds of billions of miles of American territory here in heaven, it is like scattering a ten-cent box of homeopathic pills over the Great Sahara and expecting to find them again. You can't expect us to amount to anything in heaven, and we *don't*—now, that is the simple fact, and we have got to do the best we can with it. The learned men from other planets and other systems come here and hang around awhile, when they are touring around the Kingdom, and then go back to their own section of heaven and write a book of travels, and they give America about five lines in it. And what do they say about us? They say this wilderness is populated with a scattering few hundred thousand billions of red angels, with now and then a curiously complected *diseased* one. You see, they think we whites and the occasional Negro are Injuns that have been bleached out or blackened by some leprous disease or other—for some peculiarly rascally *sin,* mind you. It is a mighty sour pill for us all, my friend—even the modestest of us, let alone the other kind, that think they are going to be received like a long-lost government bond, and hug Abraham into the bargain. I haven't asked you any of the particulars, Captain, but I judge it goes without saying—if my experience is worth anything—that there wasn't much of a hooraw made over you when you arrived—now, was there?"

"Don't mention it, Sandy," says I, coloring up a little; "I wouldn't have had the family see it for any amount you are a mind to name. Change the subject, Sandy, change the subject."

"Well, do you think of settling in the California department of bliss?"

"I don't know. I wasn't calculating on doing anything really definite in that direction till the family come. I thought I would just look around, meantime, in a quiet way and make up my mind. Besides, I know a good many dead people, and I was calculating to hunt them up and swap a little gossip with them about friends, and old times, and one thing or another, and ask them how they like it here, as far as they have got. I reckon my wife will want to camp in the California range, though, because most all her departed will be there, and she likes to be with folks she knows."

"Don't you let her. You see what the Jersey district of heaven is, for whites; well, the California district is a thousand times worse. It swarms with a mean kind of leather-headed mud-colored angels—and your nearest white neighbors is likely to be a million miles away. *What a man mostly misses, in heaven, is company*—company of his own sort and color and language. I have come near settling in the European part of heaven once or twice on that account."

"Well, why didn't you, Sandy?"

"Oh, various reasons. For one thing, although you *see* plenty of whites there, you can't understand any of them hardly, and so you go about as hungry for talk as you do here. I like to look at a Russian or a German or an Italian—I even like to look at a Frenchman if I ever have the luck to catch him engaged in anything that ain't indelicate—but *looking* don't cure the hunger; what you want is talk."

"Well, there's England, Sandy—the English district of heaven."

"Yes, but it is not so very much better than this end of the heavenly domain. As long as you run across Englishmen born this side of three hundred years ago, you are all right; but the minute you get back of Elizabeth's time the language begins to fog up, and the further back you go the foggier it gets. I had some talk with one Langland and a man by the name of Chaucer—old-time poets—but it was no use; I couldn't quite understand them and they couldn't quite understand me. I have had letters from them since, but it is such broken English I can't make it out. Back of those men's time the English are just simply foreigners, nothing more, nothing less; they talk Danish, German, Norman French, and sometimes a mixture of all three; back of *them,* they talk Latin, and ancient British, Irish, and Gaelic; and then back of these come billions and billions of pure savages that talk a gibberish that Satan himself couldn't understand. The fact is, where you strike one man in the English settlements that you can understand, you wade through awful swarms that talk something you can't make head nor tail of. You see, every country on earth has been overlaid so often, in the course of a billion years, with different kinds of people and different sorts of languages that this sort of mongrel business was bound to be the result in heaven."

"Sandy," says I, "did you see a good many of the great people history tells about?"

"Yes—plenty. I saw kings and all sorts of distinguished people."

"Do the kings rank just as they did below?"

"No; a body can't bring his rank up here with him. Divine right is a good-enough earthly romance, but it don't go here. Kings drop down to the general level as soon as they reach the realms of grace. I knew Charles the Second very well—one of the most popular comedians in the English section; draws first rate. There are better, of course—people that were never heard of on earth—but Charles is making a very good reputation indeed and is considered a rising man. Richard the Lionhearted is in the prize ring and coming into considerable favor. Henry the Eighth is a tragedian, and the scenes where he kills people are done to the very life. Henry the Sixth keeps a religious-book stand."

"Did you ever see Napoleon, Sandy?"

"Often—sometimes in the Corsican range, sometimes in the French. He always hunts up a conspicuous place and goes frowning around with his arms folded and his field glass under his arm, looking as grand, gloomy, and peculiar as his reputation calls for, and very much bothered because he don't stand as high here, for a soldier, as he expected to."

"Why, who stands higher?"

"Oh, a *lot* of people *we* never heard of before—the shoemaker and horse-doctor and knife-grinder kind, you know—clodhoppers from goodness knows where, that never handled a sword or fired a shot in their lives; but the soldiership was in them, though they never had a chance to show it. But here they take their right place, and Caesar and Napoleon and Alexander have to take a back seat. The greatest military genius our world ever produced was a bricklayer from somewhere back of Boston—died during the Revolution—by the name of Absalom Jones. Wherever he goes, crowds flock to see him. You see, everybody knows that if he had had a chance he would have shown the world some generalship that would have made all generalship before look like child's play and 'prentice work. But he never got a chance; he tried heaps of times to enlist as a private, but he had lost both thumbs and a couple of front teeth, and the recruiting sergeant wouldn't pass him. However, as I say, everybody knows, now, what he *would* have been, and so they flock by the million to get a glimpse of him whenever they hear he is going to be anywhere. Caesar and Hannibal and Alexander and

Napoleon are all on his staff, and ever so many more great generals; but the public hardly care to look at *them* when *he* is around. Boom! There goes another salute. The barkeeper's off quarantine now."

Sandy and I put on our things. Then we made a wish, and in a second we were at the reception place. We stood on the edge of the ocean of space and looked out over the dimness, but couldn't make out anything. Close by us was the Grand Stand—tier on tier of dim thrones rising up toward the zenith. From each side of it spread away the tiers of seats for the general public. They spread away for leagues and leagues—you couldn't see the ends. They were empty and still, and hadn't a cheerful look, but looked dreary, like a theater before anybody comes—gas turned down.

Sandy says:

"We'll sit down here and wait. We'll see the head of the procession come in sight away off yonder pretty soon now."

Says I:

"It's pretty lonesome, Sandy; I reckon there's a hitch somewheres. Nobody but just you and me—it ain't much of a display for the barkeeper."

"Don't you fret; it's all right. There'll be one more gunfire—then you'll see."

In a little while we noticed a sort of a lightish flush away off on the horizon.

"Head of the torchlight procession," says Sandy.

It spread, and got lighter and brighter; soon it had a strong glare like a locomotive headlight; it kept on getting brighter and brighter till it was like the sun peeping above the horizon line at sea—the big red rays shot high up into the sky.

"Keep your eyes on the Grand Stand and the miles of seats—sharp!" says Sandy. "And listen for the gunfire."

Just then it burst out, "Boom-boom-boom!" like a million thunderstorms in one, and made the whole heavens rock. Then there was a sudden and awful glare of light all about us, and in that very instant every one of the millions of seats was occupied, and as far as you could see, in both directions, was just a solid pack of people, and the place was all splendidly lit up! It was enough to take a body's breath away. Sandy says:

"That is the way we do it here. No time fooled away; nobody straggling in after the curtain's up. Wishing is quicker work than traveling. A quarter of a second ago these folks were millions of miles from here. When they heard the last signal, all they had to do was to wish, and here they are."

The prodigious choir struck up:

We long to hear thy voice,
To see thee face to face.

It was noble music, but the uneducated chipped in and spoilt it, just as the congregations used to do on earth.

The head of the procession begun to pass, now, and it was a wonderful sight. It swept along, thick and solid, five hundred thousand angels abreast, and every angel carrying a torch and singing—the whirring thunder of the wings made a body's head ache. You could follow the line of the procession back, and slanting upward into the sky, far away in a glittering snaky rope, till it was only a faint streak in the distance. The rush went on and on, for a long time, and at last, sure enough, along comes the barkeeper, and then everybody rose, and a cheer went up that made the heavens shake, I tell you! He was all smiles, and had his halo tilted over one ear in a cocky way, and was the most satisfied-looking saint I ever saw. While he marched up the steps of the Grand Stand, the choir struck up:

The whole wide heaven groans,
And waits to hear that voice.

There were four gorgeous tents standing side by side in the place of honor, on a broad railed platform in the center of the Grand Stand, with a shining guard of honor round about them. The tents had been shut up all this time. As the barkeeper climbed along up, bowing and smiling to everybody, and at last got to the platform, these tents were jerked up aloft all of a sudden and we saw four noble thrones of gold, all caked with jewels, and in the two middle ones sat old white-whiskered men, and in the two others a couple of the most glorious and gaudy giants, with platter halos and beautiful armor. All the millions went down on their knees, and stared, and looked glad, and burst out into a joyful kind of murmurs. They said:

"Two archangels!—that is splendid. Who can the others be?"

The archangels gave the barkeeper a stiff little military bow; the two old men rose; one of them said, "Moses and Esau welcome thee!" and then all the four vanished, and the thrones were empty.

The barkeeper looked a little disappointed, for he was calculating to hug those old people, I judge; but it was the gladdest and proudest multitude you ever saw—because they had seen Moses and Esau. Everybody was saying, "Did you see them?—I did—Esau's side face was to me, but I saw Moses full in the face, just as plain as I see you this minute!"

The procession took up the barkeeper and moved on with him again, and the crowd broke up and scattered. As we went along home, Sandy said it was a great success and the barkeeper would have a right to be proud of it forever. And he said *we* were in luck, too; said we might attend receptions for forty thousand years to come and not have a chance to see a brace of such grand moguls as Moses and Esau. We found afterwards that we had come near seeing another patriarch, and likewise a genuine prophet besides, but at the last moment they sent regrets. Sandy said there would be a monument put up there, where Moses and Esau had stood, with the date and circumstances and all about the whole business, and travelers would come for thousands of years and gawk at it, and climb over it, and scribble their names on it.

Will You Wait?

BY ALFRED BESTER

THEY keep writing those antiquated stories about bargains with the Devil. You know—sulphur, spells and pentagrams; tricks, snares and delusions. They don't know what they're talking about. Twentieth century diabolism is slick and streamlined, like jukeboxes and automatic elevators and television and all the other modern efficiencies that leave you helpless and infuriated.

A year ago I got fired from an agency job for the third time in ten months. I had to face the fact that I was a failure. I was also dead broke. I decided to sell my soul to the Devil, but the problem was how to find him. I went down to the main reference room of the library and read everything on demonology and devil-lore. Like I said, it was all just talk. Anyway, if I could have afforded the expensive ingredients which they claimed could raise the Devil, I wouldn't have had to deal with him in the first place.

I was stumped, so I did the obvious thing; I called Celebrity Service. A delicate young man answered.

I asked, "Can you tell me where the Devil is?"

"Are you a subscriber to Celebrity Service?"

"No."

"Then I can give you no information."

"I can afford to pay a small fee for one item."

"You wish limited service?"

"Yes."

"Who is the celebrity, please?"

"The Devil."

"Who?"

"The Devil . . . Satan, Lucifer, Scratch, Old Nick . . . The Devil."

"One moment, please." In five minutes he was back, extremely annoyed. "Veddy soddy. The Devil is no longer a celebrity."

He hung up. I did the sensible thing and looked through the telephone directory. On a page decorated with ads for Sardi's Restaurant I found Satan, Shaitan, Carnage & Bael, 477 Madison Avenue, Judson 3-1900. I called them. A bright young woman answered.

"SSC&B. Good morning."

"May I speak to Mr. Satan, please?"

"The lines are busy. Will you wait?"

I waited and lost my dime. I wrangled with the operator and lost another dime but got the promise of a refund in postage stamps. I called Satan, Shaitan, Carnage & Bael again.

"SSC&B. Good morning."

"May I speak to Mr. Satan? And please don't leave me hanging on the phone. I'm calling from a—"

The switchboard cut me off and buzzed. I waited. The coin box gave a warning click. At last a line opened.

"Miss Hogan's office."

"May I speak to Mr. Satan?"

"Who's calling?"

"He doesn't know me. It's a personal matter."

"I'm sorry. Mr. Satan is no longer with our organization."

"Can you tell me where I can find him?"

There was muffled discussion in broad Brooklyn and then Miss Hogan spoke in crisp Secretary: "Mr. Satan is now with Beelzebub, Belial, Devil & Orgy."

I looked them up in the phone directory. 383 Madison Avenue, Plaza 6-1900. I dialed. The phone rang once and then choked. A metallic voice spoke in sing-song: "The number you are dialing is not a working number. Kindly consult your directory for the correct number. This is a recorded message." I consulted my directory. It said Plaza 6-1900. I dialed again and got the same recorded message.

I finally broke through to a live operator who was persuaded to give me the new number of Beelzebub, Belial, Devil & Orgy. I called them. A bright young woman answered.

"B.B.D.O. Good morning."

"May I speak to Mr. Satan, please?"

"Who?"

"Mr. Satan."

"I'm sorry. There is no such person with our organization."

"Then give me Beelzebub or the Devil."

"One moment, please."

I waited. Every half minute she opened my wire long enough to gasp: "Still ringing the Dev—" and then cut off before I had a chance to answer. At last a bright young woman spoke. "Mr. Devil's office."

"May I speak to him?"

"Who's calling?"

I gave her my name.

"He's on another line. Will you wait?"

I waited. I was fortified with a dwindling reserve of nickels and dimes. After twenty minutes, the bright young woman spoke again: "He's just gone into an emergency meeting. Can he call you back?"

"No. I'll try again."

Nine days later I finally got him.

"Yes, sir? What can I do for you?"

I took a breath. "I want to sell you my soul."

"Have you got anything on paper?"

"What do you mean, anything on paper?"

"The Property, my boy. The Sell. You can't expect B.B.D.O. to buy a pig in a poke. We may drink out of dixie cups up here, but the sauce has got to be a hundred proof. Bring in your Presentation. My girl'll set up an appointment."

I prepared a Presentation of my soul with plenty of Sell. Then I called his girl.

"I'm sorry, he's on the Coast. Call back in two weeks."

Five weeks later she gave me an appointment. I went up and sat in the photo-montage reception room of B.B.D.O.

for two hours, balancing my Sell on my knees. Finally I was ushered into a corner office decorated with Texas brands in glowing neon. The Devil was lounging on his contour chair, dictating to an Iron Maiden. He was a tall man with the phony voice of a sales manager; the kind that talks loud in elevators. He gave me a Sincere handshake and immediately looked through my Presentation.

"Not bad," he said. "Not bad at all. I think we can do business. Now what did you have in mind? The usual?"

"Money, success, happiness."

He nodded. "The usual. Now we're square shooters in this shop. B.B.D.O. doesn't dry-gulch. We'll guarantee money, success and happiness."

"For how long?"

"Normal life span. No tricks, my boy. We take our estimates from the Actuary Tables. Offhand I'd say you're good for another forty, forty-five years. We can pinpoint that in the contract later."

"No tricks?"

He gestured impatiently. "That's all bad public relations, what you're thinking. I promise you, no tricks."

"Guaranteed?"

"Not only do we guarantee service; we *insist* on giving service. B.B.D.O. doesn't want any beefs going up to the Fair Practice Committee. You'll have to call on us for service at least twice a year or the contract will be terminated."

"What kind of service?"

He shrugged. "Any kind. Shine your shoes; empty ashtrays; bring you dancing girls. That can be pinpointed later. We just insist that you use us at least twice a year. We've got to give you a quid for your quo. *Quid pro quo*. Check?"

"But no tricks?"

"No tricks. I'll have our legal department draw up the contract. Who's representing you?"

"You mean an agent? I haven't got one."

He was startled. "Haven't got an agent? My boy, you're living dangerously. Why, we could skin you alive. Get yourself an agent and tell him to call me."

"Yes, sir. M-may I . . . Could I ask a question?"

"Shoot. Everything is open and aboveboard at B.B.D.O."

"What will it be like for me . . . wh-when the contract terminates?"

"You really want to know?"

"Yes."

"I don't advise it."

"I want to know."

He showed me. It was like a hideous session with a psychoanalyst, in perpetuity . . . an eternal, agonizing self-indictment. It was hell. I was shaken.

"I'd rather have inhuman fiends torturing me," I said.

He laughed. "They can't compare to man's inhumanity to himself. Well . . . changed your mind, or is it a deal?"

"It's a deal."

We shook hands and he ushered me out. "Don't forget," he warned. "Protect yourself. Get an agent. Get the best."

I signed with Sibyl & Sphinx. That was on March 3. I called S & S on March 15. Mrs. Sphinx said: "Oh yes, there's been a hitch. Miss Sibyl was negotiating with B.B.D.O. for you, but she had to fly to Sheol. I've taken over for her."

I called April 1. Miss Sibyl said: "Oh yes, there's been a slight delay. Mrs. Sphinx had to go to Salem for a tryout. A witch-burning. She'll be back next week."

I called April 15. Miss Sibyl's bright young secretary told me that there was some delay getting the contracts typed. It seemed that B.B.D.O. was reorganizing its legal department. On May 1, Sibyl & Sphinx told me that the contracts had arrived and that *their* legal department was looking them over.

I had to take a menial job in June to keep body and soul together. I worked in the stencil department of a network. At least once a week a script would come in about a bargain with the Devil which was signed, sealed and delivered before the opening commercial. I used to laugh at them. After four months of negotiation I was still threadbare.

I saw the Devil once, bustling down Park Avenue. He was running for Congress and was very busy being jolly and hearty with the electorate. He addressed every cop and doorman by first name. When I spoke to him he got a little frightened, thinking I was a Communist or worse. He didn't remember me at all.

In July, all negotiations stopped; everybody was away on

vacation. In August everybody was overseas for some Black Mass Festival. In September Sibyl & Sphinx called me to their office to sign the contract. It was thirty-seven pages long, and fluttered with pasted-in corrections and additions. There were half a dozen tiny boxes stamped on the margin of every page.

"If you only knew the work that went into this contract," Sibyl & Sphinx told me with satisfaction.

"It's kind of long, isn't it?"

"It's the short contracts that make all the trouble. Initial every box, and sign on the last page. All six copies."

I initialed and signed. When I was finished I didn't feel any different. I'd expected to start tingling with money, success and happiness.

"Is it a deal now?" I asked.

"Not until *he's* signed it."

"I can't hold out much longer."

"We'll send it over by messenger."

I waited a week and then called.

"You forgot to initial one of the boxes," they told me.

I went to the office and initialed. After another week I called.

"*He* forgot to initial one of the boxes," they told me that time.

On October 1st I received a special delivery parcel. I also received a registered letter. The parcel contained the signed, sealed and delivered contract between me and the Devil. I could at last be rich, successful and happy. The registered letter was from B.B.D.O. and informed me that in view of my failure to comply with Clause 27-A of the contract, it was considered terminated, and I was due for collection at their convenience. I rushed down to Sibyl & Sphinx.

"What's Clause 27-A?" they asked.

We looked it up. It was the clause that required me to use the services of the Devil at least once every six months.

"What's the date of the contract?" Sibyl & Sphinx asked.

We looked it up. The contract was dated March 1st, the day I'd had my first talk with the Devil in his office.

"March, April, May . . ." Miss Sibyl counted on her fingers. "That's right. Seven months have elapsed. Are you sure you didn't ask for *any* service?"

"How could I? I didn't have a contract."

"We'll see about this," Mrs. Sphinx said grimly. She called B.B.D.O. and had a spirited argument with the Devil and his legal department. Then she hung up. "He says you shook hands on the deal March 1st," she reported. "He was prepared in good faith to go ahead with his side of the bargain."

"How could I know? I didn't have a contract."

"Didn't you ask for anything?"

"No. I was waiting for the contract."

Sibyl & Sphinx called in their legal department and presented the case.

"You'll have to arbitrate," the legal department said, and explained that agents are forbidden to act as their client's attorney.

I hired the legal firm of Wizard, Warlock, Voodoo, Dowser & Hag (99 Watt Street, Exchange 3-1900) to represent me before the Arbitration Board (479 Madison Avenue, Lexington 5-1900). They asked for a $200 retainer plus twenty percent of the contract's benefits. I'd managed to save $34 during the four months I was working in the stencil department. They waived the retainer and went ahead with the Arbitration preliminaries.

On November 15 the network demoted me to the mail room, and I seriously contemplated suicide. Only the fact that my soul was in jeopardy in an arbitration stopped me.

The case came up December 12th. It was tried before a panel of three impartial Arbitrators and took all day. I was told they'd mail me their decision. I waited a week and called Wizard, Warlock, Voodoo, Dowser & Hag.

"They've recessed for the Christmas holidays," they told me.

I called January 2.

"One of them's out of town."

I called January 10.

"He's back, but the other two are out of town."

"When will I get a decision?"

"It could take months."

"How do you think my chances look?"

"Well, we've never lost an arbitration."

"That sounds pretty good."

"But there can always be a first time."

That sounded pretty bad. I got scared and figured I'd better copper my bets. I did the sensible thing and hunted through the telephone directory until I found Seraphim, Cherubim and Angel, 666 Fifth Avenue, Templeton 6-1900. I called them. A bright young woman answered.

"Seraphim, Cherubim and Angel. Good morning."

"May I speak to Mr. Angel, please?"

"He's on another line. Will you wait?"

I'm still waiting.

The King of the Cats

BY STEPHEN VINCENT BENÉT

"BUT, my *dear,*" said Mrs. Culverin, with a tiny gasp, "you can't actually mean—a *tail!*"

Mrs. Dingle nodded impressively. "Exactly. I've seen him. Twice. Paris, of course, and then, a command appearance at Rome—we were in the Royal box. He conducted—my dear, you've never heard such effects from an orchestra—and, my dear," she hesitated slightly, "he conducted *with it.*"

"How perfectly, fascinatingly too horrid for words!" said Mrs. Culverin in a dazed but greedy voice. "We *must* have him to dinner as soon as he comes over—he is coming over, isn't he?"

"The twelfth," said Mrs. Dingle with a gleam in her eyes. "The New Symphony people have asked him to be guest-conductor for three special concerts—I do hope you can dine with *us* some night while he's here—he'll be very busy, of course—but he's promised to give us what time he can spare—"

"Oh, thank you, dear," said Mrs. Culverin, abstractedly, her last raid upon Mrs. Dingle's pet British novelist still fresh in her mind. "You're always so delightfully hospitable—but you mustn't wear yourself out—the rest of us must do *our* part—I know Henry and myself would be only too glad to—"

"That's very sweet of you, darling." Mrs. Dingle also remembered the larceny of the British novelist. "But we're just going to give Monsieur Tibault—sweet name, isn't it! They say he's descended from the Tybalt in *Romeo and Juliet* and that's why he doesn't like Shakespeare—we're just going to give Monsieur Tibault the simplest sort of time—a little reception after his first concert, perhaps. He hates," she looked around the table, "large, mixed parties. And then, of course, his—er—little idiosyncrasy—" she coughed delicately. "It makes him feel a trifle shy with strangers."

"But I don't understand yet, Aunt Emily," said Tommy Brooks, Mrs. Dingle's nephew. "Do you really mean this Tibault bozo has a tail? Like a monkey and everything?"

"Tommy dear," said Mrs. Culverin, crushingly, "in the first place Monsieur Tibault is not a bozo—he is a very distinguished musician—the finest conductor in Europe. And in the second place—"

"He has," Mrs. Dingle was firm. "He has a tail. He conducts with it."

"Oh, but honestly!" said Tommy, his ears pinkening. "I mean—of course, if you say so, Aunt Emily, I'm sure he has—but still, it sounds pretty steep, if you know what I mean! How about it, Professor Tatto?"

Professor Tatto cleared his throat. "Tck," he said, putting his fingertips together cautiously, "I shall be very anxious to see this Monsieur Tibault. For myself, I have never observed a genuine specimen of *homo caudatus*, so I should be inclined to doubt, and yet. . . . In the Middle Ages, for instance, the belief in men—er—tailed or with caudal appendages of some sort, was both widespread and, as far as we can gather, well-founded. As late as the Eighteenth Century, a Dutch sea captain with some character for veracity recounts the discovery of a pair of such creatures in the island of Formosa. They were in a low state of civilization, I believe, but the appendages in question were quite distinct. And in 1860, Dr. Grimbrook, the English surgeon, claims to have treated no less than three African natives with short but evident tails—though his testimony rests upon his unsupported word. After all, the thing is not impossible, though doubtless unusual. Web feet—rudimentary gills—these occur with some frequency. The appendix we have with us always. The chain of our descent from the ape-like form is by no means complete. For that matter," he beamed around the table, "what can we call the last few vertebrae of the normal spine but the beginnings of a concealed and rudimentary tail? Oh, yes—yes—it's possible

—quite—that in an extraordinary case—a reversion to type—a survival—though, of course—"

"I told you so," said Mrs. Dingle triumphantly. "*Isn't* it fascinating? Isn't it, Princess?"

The Princess Vivrakanarda's eyes, blue as a field of larkspur, fathomless as the center of heaven, rested lightly for a moment on Mrs. Dingle's excited countenance.

"Ve-ry fascinating," she said, in a voice like stroked, golden velvet. "I should like—I should like ve-ry much to meet this Monsieur Tibault."

"Well, *I* hope he breaks his neck!" said Tommy Brooks, under his breath—but nobody ever paid much attention to Tommy.

Nevertheless as the time for Mr. Tibault's arrival in these States drew nearer and nearer, people in general began to wonder whether the Princess had spoken quite truthfully—for there was no doubt of the fact that, up till then, she had been the unique sensation of the season—and you know what social lions and lionesses are. . . .

It was, if you remember, a Siamese season, and genuine Siamese were at quite as much of a premium as Russian accents had been in the quaint old days when the Chauve-Souris was a novelty. The Siamese Art Theatre, imported at terrific expense, was playing to packed houses. *Gushuptzgu,* an epic novel of Siamese farm life, in nineteen closely-printed volumes, had just been awarded the Nobel prize. Prominent pet-and-newt dealers reported no cessation in the appalling demand for Siamese cats. And upon the crest of this wave of interest in things Siamese, the Princess Vivrakanarda poised with the elegant nonchalance of a Hawaiian waterbaby upon its surfboard. She was indispensable. She was incomparable. She was everywhere.

Youthful, enormously wealthy, allied on one hand to the Royal Family of Siam and on the other to the Cabots (and yet with the first eighteen of her twenty-one years shrouded from speculation in a golden zone of mystery), the mingling of races in her had produced an exotic beauty as distinguished as it was strange. She moved with a feline, effortless grace, and her skin was as if it had been gently powdered with tiny grains of the purest gold—yet the blueness of her eyes, set just a trifle slantingly, was as pure and startling as the sea on the rocks of

Maine. Her brown hair fell to her knees—she had been offered extraordinary sums by the Master Barbers' Protective Association to have it shingled. Straight as a waterfall tumbling over brown rocks, it had a vague perfume of sandalwood and suave spices and held tints of rust and the sun. She did not talk very much—but then she did not have to—her voice had an odd, small, melodious huskiness that haunted the mind. She lived alone and was reputed to be very lazy—at least it was known that she slept during most of the day—but at night she bloomed like a moon-flower and a depth came into her eyes.

It was no wonder that Tommy Brooks fell in love with her. The wonder was that she let him. There was nothing exotic or distinguished about Tommy—he was just one of those pleasant, normal young men who seem created to carry on the bond business by reading the newspapers in the University Club during most of the day, and can always be relied upon at night to fill an unexpected hole in a dinner party. It is true that the Princess could hardly be said to do more than tolerate any of her suitors—no one had ever seen those aloofly arrogant eyes enliven at the entrance of any male. But she seemed to be able to tolerate Tommy a little more than the rest—and that young man's infatuated daydreams were beginning to be beset by smart solitaires and imaginary apartments on Park Avenue, when the famous M. Tibault conducted his first concert at Carnegie Hall.

Tommy Brooks sat beside the Princess. The eyes he turned upon her were eyes of longing and love, but her face was as impassive as a mask, and the only remark she made during the preliminary bustlings was that there seemed to be a number of people in the audience. But Tommy was relieved, if anything, to find her even a little more aloof than usual, for, ever since Mrs. Culverin's dinner party, a vague disquiet as to the possible impression which this Tibault creature might make upon her had been growing in his mind. It shows his devotion that he was present at all. To a man whose simple Princetonian nature found in "Just a Little Love, a Little Kiss," the quintessence of musical art, the average symphony was a positive torture, and he looked forward to the evening's program itself with a grim, brave smile.

"Ssh!" said Mrs. Dingle, breathlessly. "He's coming!" It seemed to the startled Tommy as if he were suddenly back in the trenches under a heavy barrage, as M. Tibault made his entrance to a perfect bombardment of applause.

Then the enthusiastic noise was sliced off in the middle and a gasp took its place—a vast, windy sigh, as if every person in that multitude had suddenly said, "Ah." For the papers had not lied about him. The tail was there.

They called him theatric—but how well he understood the uses of theatricalism! Dressed in unrelieved black from head to foot (the black dress shirt had been a special token of Mussolini's esteem), he did not walk on, he strolled, leisurely, easily, aloofly, the famous tail curled nonchalantly about one wrist—a suave, black panther lounging through a summer garden with that little mysterious weave of the head that panthers have when they pad behind bars—the glittering darkness of his eyes unmoved by any surprise or elation. He nodded, twice, in regal acknowledgment, as the clapping reached an apogee of frenzy. To Tommy there was something dreadfully reminiscent of the Princess in the way he nodded. Then he turned to his orchestra.

A second and louder gasp went up from the audience at this point, for, as he turned, the tip of that incredible tail twined with dainty carelessness into some hidden pocket and produced a black baton. But Tommy did not even notice. He was looking at the Princess instead.

She had not even bothered to clap, at first, but now. . . . He had never seen her moved like this, never. She was not applauding, her hands were clenched in her lap, but her whole body was rigid—rigid as a steel bar, and the blue flowers of her eyes were bent upon the figure of M. Tibault in a terrible concentration. The pose of her entire figure was so still and intense that for an instant Tommy had the lunatic idea that any moment she might leap from her seat beside him as lightly as a moth, and land, with no sound, at M. Tibault's side to—yes—to rub her proud head against his coat in worship. Even Mrs. Dingle would notice in a moment.

"Princess—" he said, in a horrified whisper, "Princess—"

Slowly the tenseness of her body relaxed, her eyes veiled again, she grew calm.

"Yes, Tommy?" she said, in her usual voice, but there was still something about her . . .

"Nothing, only—oh, hang—he's starting!" said Tommy, as M. Tibault, his hands loosely clasped before him, turned and *faced* the audience. His eyes dropped, his tail switched once impressively, then gave three little preliminary taps with his baton on the floor.

Seldom has Gluck's overture to "Iphigenie in Aulis" received such an ovation. But it was not until the Eighth Symphony that the hysteria of the audience reached its climax. Never before had the New Symphony played so superbly—and certainly never before had it been led with such genius. Three prominent conductors in the audience were sobbing with the despairing admiration of envious children toward the close, and one at least was heard to offer wildly ten thousand dollars to a well-known facial surgeon there present for a shred of evidence that tails of some variety could by any stretch of science be grafted upon a normally decaudate form. There was no doubt about it—no mortal hand and arm, be they ever so dexterous, could combine the delicate élan and powerful grace displayed in every gesture of M. Tibault's tail.

A sable staff, it dominated the brasses like a flicker of black lightning; an ebon, elusive whip, it drew the last exquisite breath of melody from the woodwinds and ruled the stormy strings like a magician's rod. M. Tibault bowed and bowed again—roar after roar of frenzied admiration shook the hall to its foundations—and when he finally staggered, exhausted, from the platform, the president of the Wednesday Sonata Club was only restrained by force from flinging her ninety-thousand-dollar string of pearls after him in an excess of aesthetic appreciation. New York had come and seen—and New York was conquered. Mrs. Dingle was immediately besieged by reporters, and Tommy Brooks looked forward to the "little party" at which he was to meet the new hero of the hour with feelings only a little less lugubrious than those that would have come to him just before taking his seat in the electric chair.

The meeting between his Princess and M. Tibault was worse and better than he expected. Better because, after all, they did not say much to each other—and worse because it seemed to him, somehow, that some curious kinship of mind between them made words unnecessary. They were certainly the most distinguished looking couple in the room, as he bent over her hand. "So darlingly foreign, both of them, and yet so different," babbled Mrs. Dingle—but Tommy couldn't agree.

They were different, yes—the dark, lithe stranger with the bizarre appendage tucked carelessly in his pocket, and the blue-eyed, brown-haired girl. But that difference only accentuated what they had in common—something in the way they moved, in the suavity of their gestures, in the set of their eyes. Something deeper, even, than race. He tried to puzzle it out—then, looking around at the others, he had a flash of revelation. It was as if that couple were foreign, indeed—not only to New York but to all common humanity. As if they were polite guests from a different star.

Tommy did not have a very happy evening, on the whole. But his mind worked slowly, and it was not until much later that the mad suspicion came upon him in full force.

Perhaps he is not to be blamed for his lack of immediate comprehension. The next few weeks were weeks of bewildered misery for him. It was not that the Princess's attitude toward him had changed—she was just as tolerant of him as before, but M. Tibault was always there. He had a faculty of appearing as out of thin air—he walked, for all his height, as lightly as a butterfly—and Tommy grew to hate that faintest shuffle on the carpet that announced his presence.

And then, hang it all, the man was so smooth, so infernally, unrufflably smooth! He was never out of temper, never embarrassed. He treated Tommy with the extreme of urbanity, and yet his eyes mocked, deep-down, and Tommy could do nothing. And, gradually, the Princess became more and more drawn to this stranger, in a soundless communion that found little need for speech—and that, too, Tommy saw and hated, and that, too, he could not mend.

He began to be haunted not only by M. Tibault in the flesh, but by M. Tibault in the spirit. He slept badly, and when he slept, he dreamed—of M. Tibault, a man no longer, but a shadow, a specter, the limber ghost of an animal whose words came purringly between sharp little pointed teeth. There was certainly something odd about the whole shape of the fellow—his fluid ease, the mold of his head, even the cut of his fingernails—but just what it was escaped Tommy's intensest cogitation. And when he did put his finger on it at length, at first he refused to believe.

A pair of petty incidents decided him, finally, against all reason. He had gone to Mrs. Dingle's, one winter afternoon, hoping to find the Princess. She was out with his aunt, but was expected back for tea, and he wandered idly into the library to wait. He was just about to switch on the lights, for the library was always dark even in summer, when he heard a sound of light breathing that seemed to come from the leather couch in the corner. He approached it cautiously and dimly made out the form of M. Tibault, curled up on the couch, peacefully asleep.

The sight annoyed Tommy so that he swore under his breath and was back near the door on his way out, when the feeling we all know and hate, the feeling that eyes we cannot see are watching us, arrested him. He turned back—M. Tibault had not moved a muscle of his body to all appearance—but his eyes were open now. And those eyes were black and human no longer. They were green—Tommy could have sworn it—and he could have sworn that they had no bottom and gleamed like little emeralds in the dark. It only lasted a moment, for Tommy pressed the light-button automatically—and there was M. Tibault, his normal self, yawning a little but urbanely apologetic, but it gave Tommy time to think. Nor did what happened a trifle later increase his peace of mind.

They had lit a fire and were talking in front of it—by now Tommy hated M. Tibault so thoroughly that he felt that odd yearning for his company that often occurs in such cases. M. Tibault was telling some anecdote and Tommy was hating him worse than ever for basking with such obvious enjoyment in the heat of the flames and the ripple of his own voice.

Then they heard the street door open, and M. Tibault jumped up—and jumping, caught one sock on a sharp corner of the brass firerail and tore it open in a jagged flap. Tommy looked down mechanically at the tear—a second's glance, but enough—for M. Tibault, for the first time in Tommy's experience, lost his temper completely. He swore violently in some spitting, foreign tongue—his face distorted suddenly—he clapped his hand over his sock. Then, glaring furiously at Tommy, he fairly sprang from the room, and Tommy could hear him scaling the stairs in long, agile bounds.

Tommy sank into a chair, careless for once of the fact that he heard the Princess's light laugh in the hall. He didn't want to see the Princess. He didn't want to see anybody. There had been something revealed when M. Tibault had torn that hole in his sock—and it was not the skin of a man. Tommy had caught a glimpse of—black plush. Black velvet. And then had come M. Tibault's sudden explosion of fury. Good *Lord*—did the man wear black velvet stockings under his ordinary socks? Or could he—could he—but here Tommy held his fevered head in his hands.

He went to Professor Tatto that evening with a series of hypothetical questions, but as he did not dare confide his real suspicions to the professor, the hypothetical answers he received served only to confuse him the more. Then he thought of Billy Strange. Billy was a good sort, and his mind had a turn for the bizarre. Billy might be able to help.

He couldn't get hold of Billy for three days and lived through the interval in a fever of impatience. But finally they had dinner together at Billy's apartment where his queer books were, and Tommy was able to blurt out the whole disordered jumble of his suspicions.

Billy listened without interrupting until Tommy was quite through. Then he pulled at his pipe. "But, my dear *man*—" he said, protestingly.

"Oh, I know—I know—" said Tommy, and waved his hands, "I know I'm crazy—you needn't tell me that—but I tell you, the man's a cat all the same—no, I don't see how he could be, but he is—why, hang it, in the first place, everybody knows he's got a tail!"

"Even so," said Billy, puffing. "Oh, my dear Tommy, I don't doubt you saw, or think you saw, everything you say. But, even so—" He shook his head.

"But what about those other birds, werewolves and things?" said Tommy.

Billy looked dubious. "We-ll," he admitted, "you've got me there, of course. At least—a tailed man *is* possible. And the yarns about werewolves go back far enough, so that—well, I wouldn't say there aren't or haven't been werewolves—but then I'm willing to believe more things than most people. But a were-cat—or a man that's a cat and a cat that's a man—honestly, Tommy—"

"If I don't get some real advice I'll go clean off my hinge. For Heaven's sake, tell me something to *do!*"

"Lemme think," said Billy. "First, you're pizen-sure this man is—"

"A cat. Yeah," and Tommy nodded violently.

"Check. And second—if it doesn't hurt your feelings, Tommy—you're afraid this girl you're in love with has—er—at least a streak of—felinity—in her—and so she's drawn to him?"

"Oh, Lord, Billy, if I only knew!"

"Well—er—suppose she really is, too, you know—would you still be keen on her?"

"I'd marry her if she turned into a dragon every Wednesday!" said Tommy, fervently.

Billy smiled. "H'm," he said, "then the obvious thing to do is to get rid of this M. Tibault. Lemme think."

He thought about two pipes full, while Tommy sat on pins and needles. Then, finally, he burst out laughing.

"What's so darn funny?" said Tommy, aggrievedly.

"Nothing, Tommy, only I've just thought of a stunt—something so blooming crazy—but if he is—h'm—what you think he is—it *might* work—" And, going to the bookcase, he took down a book.

"If you think you're going to quiet my nerves by reading me a bedtime story—"

"Shut up, Tommy, and listen to this—if you really want to get rid of your feline friend."

"What is it?"

"Book of Agnes Repplier's. About cats. Listen.

" 'There is also a Scandinavian version of the ever famous story which Sir Walter Scott told to Washington Irving, which Monk Lewis told to Shelley and which, in one form or another, we find embodied in the folklore of every land'—now, Tommy, pay attention—'the story of the traveler who saw within a ruined abbey, a procession of cats, lowering into a grave a little coffin with a crown upon it. Filled with horror, he hastened from the spot; but when he had reached his destination, he could not forbear relating to a friend the wonder he had seen. Scarcely had the tale been told when his friend's cat, who lay curled up tranquilly by the fire, sprang to its feet, cried out, "Then I am the King of the Cats!" and disappeared in a flash up the chimney.'

"Well?" said Billy, shutting the book.

"By gum!" said Tommy, staring. "By gum! Do you think there's a chance?"

"*I* think we're both in the booby-hatch. But if you want to try it–"

"Try it! I'll spring it on him the next time I see him. But–listen–I can't make it a ruined abbey–"

"Oh, use your imagination! Make it Central Park–anywhere. Tell it as if it happened to you–seeing the funeral procession and all that. You can lead into it somehow–let's see–some general line–oh, yes–'Strange, isn't it, how fact so often copies fiction. Why, only yesterday–' See?"

"Strange, isn't it, how fact so often copies fiction," repeated Tommy dutifully. "Why, only yesterday–"

"I happened to be strolling through Central Park when I saw something very odd."

"I happened to be strolling through–here, gimme that book!" said Tommy; "I want to learn the rest of it by heart!"

Mrs. Dingle's farewell dinner to the famous Monsieur Tibault, on the occasion of his departure for his Western tour, was looked forward to with the greatest expectations. Not only would everybody be there, including the Princess Vivrakanarda, but Mrs. Dingle, a hinter if there ever was one, had let it be known that at this dinner an announcement of very unusual interest to Society might be made. So everyone, for once, was almost on time, except for Tommy. He was at least fifteen minutes early, for he wanted to have speech with his aunt alone. Unfortunately, however, he had hardly taken off his overcoat when she was whispering some news in his ear so rapidly that he found it difficult to understand a word of it.

"And you mustn't breathe it to a soul!" she ended, beaming.

"That is, not before the announcement—I think we'll have *that* with the salad—people never pay very much attention to salad—"

"Breathe what, Aunt Emily?" said Tommy, confused.

"The Princess, darling—the dear Princess and Monsieur Tibault—they just got engaged this afternoon, dear things! Isn't it *fascinating?*"

"Yeah," said Tommy, and started to walk blindly through the nearest door. His aunt restrained him.

"Not there, dear—not in the library. You can congratulate them later. They're just having a sweet little moment alone there now—" And she turned away to harry the butler, leaving Tommy stunned.

But his chin came up after a moment. He wasn't beaten yet.

"Strange, isn't it, how often fact copies fiction?" he repeated to himself in dull mnemonics, and, as he did so, he shook his fist at the library door.

Mrs. Dingle was wrong, as usual. The Princess and M. Tibault were not in the library—they were in the conservatory, as Tommy discovered when he wandered aimlessly past the glass doors.

He didn't mean to look, and after a second he turned away. But that second was enough.

Tibault was seated in a chair and she was crouched on a stool at his side, while his hand, softly, smoothly, stroked her brown hair. Black cat and Siamese kitten. Her face was hidden from Tommy, but he could see Tibault's face. And he could hear.

They were not talking, but there was a sound between them. A warm and contented sound like the murmur of giant bees in a hollow tree—a golden, musical rumble, deep-throated, that came from Tibault's lips and was answered by hers—a golden purr.

Tommy found himself back in the drawing room, shaking hands with Mrs. Culverin, who said, frankly, that she had seldom seen him look so pale.

The first two courses of the dinner passed Tommy like dreams, but Mrs. Dingle's cellar was notable, and by the middle of the meat course, he began to come to himself. He had only one resolve now.

For the next few moments he tried desperately to break into the conversation, but Mrs. Dingle was talking, and even Gabriel will have a time interrupting Mrs. Dingle. At last, though, she paused for breath and Tommy saw his chance.

"Speaking of that," said Tommy, piercingly, without knowing in the least what he was referring to, "Speaking of that—"

"As I was saying," said Professor Tatto. But Tommy would not yield. The plates were being taken away. It was time for salad.

"Speaking of that," he said again, so loudly and strangely that Mrs. Culverin jumped and an awkward hush fell over the table. "Strange, isn't it, how often fact copies fiction?" There, he was started. His voice rose even higher. "Why, only today I was strolling through—" and, word for word, he repeated his lesson. He could see Tibault's eyes glowing at him, as he described the funeral. He could see the Princess, tense.

He could not have said what he had expected might happen when he came to the end; but it was not bored silence, everywhere, to be followed by Mrs. Dingle's acrid, "Well, Tommy, is that *quite* all?"

He slumped back in his chair, sick at heart. He was a fool and his last resource had failed. Dimly he heard his aunt's voice, saying, "Well, then—" and realized that she was about to make the fatal announcement.

But just then Monsieur Tibault spoke.

"One moment, Mrs. Dingle," he said, with extreme politeness, and she was silent. He turned to Tommy.

"You are—positive, I suppose, of what you saw this afternoon, Brooks?" he said, in tones of light mockery.

"Absolutely," said Tommy sullenly. "Do you think I'd—"

"Oh, no, no, no," Monsieur Tibault waved the implication aside, "but—such an interesting story—one likes to be sure of the details—and, of course, you *are* sure—*quite* sure—that the kind of crown you describe was on the coffin?"

"Of course," said Tommy, wondering, "but—"

"Then I'm the King of the Cats!" cried Monsieur Tibault in a voice of thunder, and, even as he cried it, the house lights blinked—there was the soft thud of an explosion that seemed muffled in cotton wool from the minstrel gallery—and the scene was lit for a second by an obliterating and painful burst of light that vanished in an instant and was succeeded by heavy blinding clouds of white, pungent smoke.

"Oh, those *horrid* photographers," came Mrs. Dingle's voice in a melodious wail. "I *told* them not to take the flashlight picture till dinner was over, and now they've taken it *just* as I was nibbling lettuce!"

Someone tittered a little nervously. Someone coughed. Then, gradually the veils of smoke dislimned and the green-and-black spots in front of Tommy's eyes died away.

They were blinking at each other like people who have just come out of a cave into brilliant sun. Even yet their eyes stung with the fierceness of that abrupt illumination and Tommy found it hard to make out the faces across the table from him.

Mrs. Dingle took command of the half-blinded company with her accustomed poise. She rose, glass in hand. "And now, dear friends," she said in a clear voice, "I'm sure all of us are very happy to—" Then she stopped, open-mouthed, an expression of incredulous horror on her features. The lifted glass began to spill its contents on the tablecloth in a little stream of amber. As she spoke, she had turned directly to Monsieur Tibault's place at the table—and Monsieur Tibault was no longer there.

Some say there was a bursting flash of fire that disappeared up the chimney—some say it was a giant cat that leaped through the window at a bound, without breaking the glass. Professor Tatto puts it down to a mysterious chemical disturbance operating only over M. Tibault's chair. The butler, who is pious, believes the devil in person flew away with him, and Mrs. Dingle hesitates between witchcraft and a malicious ectoplasm dematerializing on the wrong cosmic plane. But be that as it may, one thing is certain—in the instant of fictive darkness which followed the glare of the flashlight, Monsieur Tibault, the great conductor, disappeared forever from mortal sight, tail and all.

Mrs. Culverin swears he was an international burglar and that she was just about to unmask him, when he slipped away under cover of the flashlight smoke, but no one else who sat at that historic dinner table believes her. No, there are no sound explanations, but Tommy thinks he knows, and he will never be able to pass a cat again without wondering.

Mrs. Tommy is quite of her husband's mind regarding cats —she was Gretchen Woolwine, of Chicago—for Tommy told her his whole story, and while she doesn't believe a great deal of it, there is no doubt in her heart that one person concerned in the affair was a *perfect* cat. Doubtless it would have been more romantic to relate how Tommy's daring finally won him his Princess—but, unfortunately, it would not be veracious. For the Princess Vivrakanarda, also, is with us no longer. Her nerves, shattered by the spectacular denouement of Mrs. Dingle's dinner, required a sea voyage, and from that voyage she has never returned to America.

Of course, there are the usual stories—one hears of her, a nun in a Siamese convent, or a masked dancer at Le Jardin de ma Soeur—one hears that she has been murdered in Patagonia or married in Trebizond—but as far as can be ascertained, not one of these gaudy fables has the slightest basis of fact. I believe that Tommy, in his heart of hearts, is quite convinced that the sea voyage was only a pretext, and that by some unheard-of means, she has managed to rejoin the formidable Monsieur Tibault, wherever in the world of the visible or the invisible he may be—in fact, that in some ruined city or subterranean palace they reign together now, King and Queen of all the mysterious Kingdom of Cats. But that, of course, is quite impossible.

The Word of Unbinding

BY URSULA K. LE GUIN

WHERE was he? The floor was hard and slimy, the air black and stinking, and that was all there was. Except a headache. Lying flat on the clammy floor, Festin moaned, and then said, "Staff!" When his alderwood wizard's staff did not come to his hand, he knew he was in peril. He sat up, and not having his staff with which to make a proper light, he struck a spark between finger and thumb, muttering a certain Word. A blue will o' the wisp sprang from the spark and rolled feebly through the air, sputtering. "Up," said Festin, and the fireball wobbled upward till it lit a vaulted trapdoor very high above, so high that Festin projecting into the fireball momentarily saw his own face forty feet below as a pale dot in the darkness. The light struck no reflections on the damp walls; they had been woven out of night, by magic. He rejoined himself and said, "Out." The ball expired. Festin sat in the dark, cracking his knuckles.

He must have been overspelled from behind, by surprise; for the last memory he had was of walking through his own woods at evening talking with the trees. Lately, in these lone years in the middle of his life, he had been burdened with a sense of waste, of unspent strength; so, needing to learn patience, he had left the villages and gone to converse with trees, especially oaks, chestnuts, and the gray alders whose roots are in profound communication with running water. It had been six months since he had spoken to a human being, or even a gnome. He had been busy with essentials, casting no spells and bothering no one. So who had spellbound him and shut him in this reeking well? "Who?" he demanded of the walls, and slowly a name gathered on them and ran down to him like a thick black drop sweated out from pores of stone and spores of fungus: "Voll."

For a moment Festin was in a cold sweat himself.

He had heard first long ago of Voll the Fell, who was said to be more than wizard yet less than man; who passed from island to island of the Outer Reach, undoing the works of the Ancients, enslaving men, cutting forests and spoiling fields, and sealing in underground tombs any wizard or mage who tried to combat him. Refugees from ruined islands told always the same tale, that he came at evening on a dark wind over the sea. His slaves followed in ships, a band of huge rock-trolls; these they had seen. But none of them had ever seen Voll. . . . There were many men and creatures of evil will among the Islands, and Festin, a young warlock intent on his training, had not paid much heed to these tales of Voll the Fell. "I can protect this island," he had thought, knowing his untried power, and had returned to his oaks and alders, the sound of wind in their leaves, the rhythm of growth in their round trunks and limbs and twigs, the taste of sunlight on leaves or dark groundwater around roots. Where were they now, the trees his old companions? Had Voll destroyed the forest?

Awake at last and up on his feet, Festin made two broad motions with rigid hands, shouting aloud a Name that would burst all locks and break open any man-made door. But these walls impregnated with night and the name of their builder did not heed, did not hear. The name re-echoed back clapping in Festin's ears so that he fell on his knees, hiding his head in his arms till the echoes died away in the vaults above him. Then, still shaken by the backfire, he sat brooding.

They were right; Voll was strong. Here on his own ground, within this spell-built dungeon, his magic would withstand any direct attack; and Festin's strength was halved by the loss of his staff. But not even his captor could take from him his powers, relative only to himself, of Projecting and Transforming. So, after rubbing his own doubly aching head, he transformed. Quietly his body melted away into a cloud of fine mist.

Lazy, trailing, the mist rose off the floor, drifting up along the slimy walls until it found, where vault met wall, a hairline crack. Through this, droplet by droplet, it seeped. It was almost all through the crack when a hot wind, hot as a furnace-blast, struck at it scattering the mist-drops, drying them. Hurriedly the mist sucked itself back into the vault, spiralled to the floor, took on Festin's own form and lay there panting. Transformation is an emotional strain to introverted warlocks of Festin's sort; when to that strain is added the shock of facing unhuman death in one's assumed shape, the experience becomes horrible. Festin lay for a while merely breathing. He was also angry with himself. It had been a pretty simple-minded notion to escape as a mist, after all. Every fool vampire knew that trick. Voll had probably just left a hot wind waiting. Festin gathered himself into a small black bat, flew up to the ceiling, retransformed into a thin stream of plain air, and seeped through the crack.

This time he got clear out and was blowing softly down the hall in which he found himself toward a window, when a sharp sense of peril made him pull together, snapping himself into the first small, coherent shape that came to mind—a gold ring. It was just as well. The hurricane of arctic air that would have dispersed his air-form in unrecallable chaos merely chilled his ring-form slightly. As the storm passed he lay on the marble pavement, wondering which form might get out the window quickest.

Too late, he began to roll away. An enormous blank-faced troll strode cataclysmically across the floor, stooped, caught the quick-rolling ring and picked it up in a huge limestone-like hand. The troll strode to the trapdoor, lifted it by an iron handle and a muttered charm, and dropped Festin down into the darkness. He fell straight for forty feet and landed on the stone floor—clink.

Resuming his true form he sat up, ruefully rubbing a bruised elbow. Enough of this transformation on an empty stomach. He longed bitterly for his staff, with which he could have summoned up any amount of dinner. Without it, though he could change his own form and exert certain spells and powers, he could not transform or summon to him any material thing—neither lightning nor a lamb chop.

"Patience," Festin told himself, and when he had got his breath he dissolved his body into the infinite delicacy of volatile oils, becoming the aroma of a frying lamb chop. He drifted once more through the crack. The waiting troll sniffed suspiciously, but already Festin had regrouped himself into a falcon, winging straight for the window. The troll lunged after him, missed by yards, and bellowed in a vast stony voice, "The hawk, get the hawk!" Swooping over the enchanted castle toward his forest that lay dark to westward, sunlight and sea-glare dazzling his eyes, Festin rode the wind like an arrow. But a quicker arrow found him. Crying out, he fell. Sun and sea and towers spun around him and went out.

He woke again on the dank floor of the dungeon, hands and hair and lips wet with his own blood. The arrow had struck his pinion as a falcon, his shoulder as a man. Lying still, he mumbled a spell to close the wound. Presently he was able to sit up, and recollect a longer, deeper spell of healing. But he had lost a good deal of blood, and with it, power. A chill had settled in the marrow of his bones which even the healing-spell could not warm. There was darkness in his eyes, even when he struck a will o' the wisp and lit the reeking air: the same dark mist he had seen, as he flew, overhanging his forest and the little towns of his land.

It was up to him to protect that land.

He could not attempt direct escape again. He was too weak and tired. Trusting his power too much, he had lost his strength. Now whatever shape he took would share his weakness, and be trapped.

Shivering with cold, he crouched there, letting the fire-ball sputter out with a last whiff of methane—marsh gas. The smell brought to his mind's eye the marshes stretching from the forest wall down to the sea, his beloved marshes where no men came, where in fall the swans flew long and level, where between still pools and reed-islands the quick, silent, seaward streamlets ran. Oh, to be a fish in one of those streams; or better yet to be farther upstream, near the springs, in the forest in the shadow of the trees, in the clear brown backwater under an alder's roots, resting hidden . . .

This was a great magic. Festin had no more performed it than has any man who in exile or danger longs for the earth and waters of his home, seeing and yearning over the doorsill of his house, the table where he has eaten, the branches outside the window of the room where he has slept. Only in dreams do any but the great Mages realize this magic of going home. But Festin, with the cold creeping out from his marrow into nerves and veins, stood up between the black walls, gathered his will together till it shone like a candle in the darkness of his flesh, and began to work the great and silent magic.

The walls were gone. He was in the earth, rocks and veins of granite for bones, groundwater for blood, the roots of things for nerves. Like a blind worm he moved through the earth westward, slowly, darkness before and behind. Then all at once coolness flowed along his back and belly, a buoyant, unresisting, inexhaustible caress. With his sides he tasted the water, felt current-flow; and with lidless eyes he saw before him the deep brown pool between the great buttress-roots of an alder. He darted forward, silvery, into shadow. He had got free. He was home.

The water ran timelessly from its clear spring. He lay on the sand of the pool's bottom letting running water, stronger than any spell of healing, soothe his wound and with its coolness wash away the bleaker cold that had entered him. But as he rested he felt and heard a shaking and trampling in the earth. Who walked now in his forest? Too weary to try to change form, he hid his gleaming trout-body under the arch of the alder root, and waited.

Huge gray fingers groped in the water, roiling the sand. In the dimness above water, vague faces, blank eyes loomed and vanished, reappeared. Nets and hands groped, missed, missed again, then caught and lifted him writhing up into the air. He struggled to take back his own shape and could not; his own spell of homecoming bound him. He writhed in the net, gasping in the dry, bright, terrible air, drowning. The agony went on, and he knew nothing beyond it.

After a long time and little by little he became aware that

he was in his human form again; some sharp, sour liquid was being forced down his throat. Time lapsed again, and he found himself sprawled face down on the dank floor of the vault. He was back in the power of his enemy. And, though he could breathe again, he was not very far from death.

The chill was all through him now; and the trolls, Voll's servants, must have crushed the fragile trout-body, for when he moved, his ribcage and one forearm stabbed with pain. Broken and without strength, he lay at the bottom of the well of night. There was no power in him to change shape; there was no way out, but one.

Lying there motionless, almost but not quite beyond the reach of pain, Festin thought: Why has he not killed me? Why does he keep me here alive?

Why has he never been seen? With what eyes can he be seen, on what ground does he walk?

He fears me, though I have no strength left.

They say that all the wizards and men of power whom he has defeated, live on sealed in tombs like this, live on year after year trying to get free. . . .

But if one chose not to live?

So Festin made his choice. His last thought was, If I am wrong, men will think I was a coward. But he did not linger on this thought. Turning his head a little to the side he closed his eyes, took a last deep breath, and whispered the word of unbinding, which is only spoken once.

This was not transformation. He was not changed. His body, the long legs and arms, the clever hands, the eyes that had liked to look on trees and streams, lay unchanged, only still, perfectly still and full of cold. But the walls were gone. The vaults built by magic were gone, and the rooms and towers; and the forest, and the sea, and the sky of evening. They were all gone, and Festin went slowly down the far slope of the hill of being, under new stars.

In life he had had great power; so here he did not forget. Like a candle flame he moved in the darkness of the wider land. And remembering he called out his enemy's name: "Voll!"

Called, unable to withstand, Voll came toward him, a thick

pale shape in the starlight. Festin approached, and the other cowered and screamed as if burnt. Festin followed when he fled, followed him close. A long way they went, over dry lava-flows from the great extinct volcanoes rearing their cones against the unnamed stars, across the spurs of silent hills, through valleys of short black grass, past towns or down their unlit streets between houses through whose windows no face looked. The stars hung in the sky; none set, none rose. There was no change here. No day would come. But they went on, Festin always driving the other before him, till they reached a place where once a river had run, very long ago: a river from the living lands. In the dry stream-bed, among boulders, a dead body lay: that of an old man, naked, flat eyes staring at the stars that are innocent of death.

"Enter it," Festin said. The Voll-shadow whimpered, but Festin came closer. Voll cowered away, stooped, and entered in the open mouth of his own dead body.

At once the corpse vanished. Unmarked, stainless, the dry boulders gleamed in starlight. Festin stood still a while, then slowly sat down among the great rocks to rest. To rest, not sleep; for he must keep guard here until Voll's body, sent back to its grave, had turned to dust, all evil power gone, scattered by the wind and washed seaward by the rain. He must keep watch over this place where once death had found a way back into the other land. Patient now, infinitely patient, Festin waited among the rocks where no river would ever run again, in the heart of the country which has no seacoast. The stars stood still above him; and as he watched them slowly, very slowly he began to forget the voice of streams and the sound of rain on the leaves of the forests of life.

Magic, Inc.

BY ROBERT A. HEINLEIN

"WHOSE spells are you using, buddy?"

That was the first thing this bird said after coming into my place of business. He had hung around maybe twenty minutes, until I was alone, looking at samples of waterproof pigment, fiddling with plumbing catalogues, and monkeying with the hardware display.

I didn't like his manner. I don't mind a legitimate business inquiry from a customer, but I resent gratuitous snooping.

"Various of the local licensed practitioners of thaumaturgy," I told him in a tone that was chilly but polite. "Why do you ask?"

"You didn't answer my question," he pointed out. "Come on—speak up. I ain't got all day."

I restrained myself. I require my clerks to be polite, and, while I was pretty sure this chap would never be a customer, I didn't want to break my own rules. "If you are thinking of buying anything," I said, "I will be happy to tell you what magic, if any, is used in producing it, and who the magician is."

"Now you're not being cooperative," he complained. "We like for people to be cooperative. You never can tell what bad luck you may run into not cooperating."

"Who d'you mean by 'we,'" I snapped, dropping all pretense of politeness, "and what do you mean by 'bad luck'?"

"Now we're getting somewhere," he said with a nasty grin, and settled himself on the edge of the counter so that he breathed into my face. He was short and swarthy—Sicilian, I judged—and dressed in a suit that was overtailored. His clothes and haberdashery matched perfectly in a color scheme that I didn't like. "I'll tell you what I mean by 'we'; I'm a field representative for an organization that protects people from bad luck—if they're smart, and cooperative. That's why I asked you whose charms you're usin'. Some of the magicians around here aren't cooperative; it spoils their luck, and that bad luck follows their products."

"Go on," I said. I wanted him to commit himself as far as he would.

"I knew you were smart," he answered. "F'r instance—how would you like for a salamander to get loose in your shop, setting fire to your goods and maybe scaring your customers? Or you sell the materials to build a house, and it turns out there's a poltergeist living in it, breaking the dishes and souring the milk and kicking the furniture around. That's what can come of dealing with the wrong magicians. A little of that and your business is ruined. We wouldn't want that to happen, *would we?*" He favored me with another leer.

I said nothing; he went on, "Now, we maintain a staff of the finest demonologists in the business, expert magicians themselves, who can report on how a magician conducts himself in the Half World, and whether or not he's likely to bring his clients bad luck. Then we advise our clients whom to deal with, and keep them from having bad luck. See?"

I saw all right. I wasn't born yesterday. The magicians I dealt with were local men that I had known for years, men with established reputations both here and in the Half World. They didn't do anything to stir up the elementals against them, and they did not have bad luck.

What this slimy item meant was that I should deal only with the magicians they selected at whatever fees they chose to set, and they would take a cut on the fees and also on the profits of my business. If I didn't choose to "cooperate," I'd be persecuted by elementals they had an arrangement with—renegades, probably, with human vices—my stock in trade spoiled and my customers frightened away. If I still held out, I could expect some really dangerous black magic that would injure or kill me. All this under the pretense of selling me protection from men I knew and liked.

A neat racket!

I had heard of something of the sort back East, but had not expected it in a city as small as ours.

He sat there, smirking at me, waiting for my reply, and twisting his neck in his collar, which was too tight. That caused me to notice something. In spite of his foppish clothes a thread showed on his neck just above the collar in back. It seemed likely that it was there to support something next to his skin—an amulet. If so, he was superstitious, even in this day and age.

"There's something you've omitted," I told him. "I'm a seventh son, born under a caul, and I've got second sight. My luck's all right, but I can see bad luck hovering over you like cypress over a grave!" I reached out and snatched at the thread. It snapped and came loose in my hand. There was an amulet on it, right enough, an unsavory little wad of nothing in particular and about as appetizing as the bottom of a bird cage. I dropped it on the floor and ground it into the dirt.

He had jumped off the counter and stood facing me, breathing hard. A knife showed up in his right hand; with his left hand he was warding off the evil eye, the first and little fingers pointed at me, making the horns of Asmodeus. I knew I had him—for the time being.

"Here's some magic you may not have heard of," I rapped out, and reached into a drawer behind the counter. I hauled out a pistol and pointed it at his face. "Cold iron! Now go back to your owner and tell him there's cold iron waiting for him, too—both ways!"

He backed away, never taking his eyes off my face. If looks could kill, and so forth. At the door he paused and spat on the doorsill, then got out of sight very quickly.

I put the gun away and went about my work, waiting on two customers who came in just as Mr. Nasty Business left. But I will admit that I was worried. A man's reputation is his most valuable asset. I've built up a name, while still a young man, for dependable products. It was certain that this bird and his pals would do all they could to destroy that name—which might be plenty if they were hooked in with black magicians!

Of course the building-materials game does not involve as much magic as other lines dealing in less durable goods. People like to know, when they are building a home, that the bed won't fall into the basement some night, or the roof disappear and leave them out in the rain.

Besides, building involves quite a lot of iron, and there are very few commercial sorcerers who can cope with cold iron. The few that can are so expensive it isn't economical to use them in building. Of course if one of the café-society crowd, or somebody like that, wants to boast that they have a summer-house or a swimming pool built entirely by magic, I'll accept the contract, charging accordingly, and sublet it to one of the expensive, first-line magicians. But by and large my business uses magic only in the side issues—perishable items and doodads which people like to buy cheap and change from time to time.

So I was not worried about magic *in* my business, but about what magic could *do* to my business—if someone set out deliberately to do me mischief. I had the subject of magic on my mind, anyhow, because of an earlier call from a chap named Ditworth—not a matter of vicious threats, just a business proposition that I was undecided about. But it worried me, just the same. . . .

I closed up a few minutes early and went over to see Jedson—a friend of mine in the cloak-and-suit business. He is considerably older than I am, and quite a student, without holding a degree, in all forms of witchcraft, white and black magic, necrology, demonology, spells, charms, and the more practical forms of divination. Besides that, Jedson is a shrewd, capable man in every way, with a long head on him. I set a lot of store by his advice.

I expected to find him in his office, and more or less free, at that hour, but he wasn't. His office boy directed me up to a room he used for sales conferences. I knocked and then pushed the door.

"Hello, Archie," he called out as soon as he saw who it was. "Come on in. I've got something." And he turned away.

I came in and looked around. Besides Joe Jedson there was a handsome, husky woman about thirty years old in a nurse's uniform, and a fellow named August Welker, Jedson's foreman. He was a handy all-around man with a magician's license, third class. Then I noticed a fat little guy, Zadkiel Feldstein, who was agent for a good many of the second-rate magicians along the street, and some few of the first-raters. Naturally, his religion prevented him from practicing magic himself, but, as I understand it, there was no theological objection to his turning an honest commission. I had had dealings with him; he was all right.

This ten-percenter was clutching a cigar that had gone out, and watching intently Jedson and another party, who was slumped in a chair.

This other party was a girl, not over twenty-five, maybe not that old. She was blond, and thin to the point that you felt that light would shine through her. She had big, sensitive hands with long fingers, and a big, tragic mouth. Her hair was silver-white, but she was not an albino. She lay back in the chair, awake but apparently done in. The nurse was chafing her wrists.

"What's up?" I asked. "The kid faint?"

"Oh no," Jedson assured me, turning around. "She's a white witch—works in a trance. She's a little tired now, that's all."

"What's her specialty?" I inquired.

"Whole garments."

"Huh?" I had a right to be surprised. It's one thing to create yard goods; another thing entirely to turn out a dress, or a suit, all finished and ready to wear. Jedson produced and merchandised a full line of garments in which magic was used throughout. They were mostly sportswear, novelty goods, ladies' fashions, and the like, in which style, rather than wearing qualities, was the determining factor. Usually they were marked "One Season Only," but they were perfectly satisfactory for that one season, being backed up by the consumers' groups.

But they were not turned out in one process. The yard goods involved were made first, usually by Welker. Dyes and designs were added separately. Jedson had some very good connections among the Little People, and could obtain shades and patterns from the Half World that were exclusive with him. He used both the old methods and magic in assembling garments, and employed some of the most talented artists in the business. Several of his dress designers free-lanced their magic in Hollywood under an arrangement with him. All he asked for was screen credit.

But to get back to the blond girl—

"That's what I said," Jedson answered, "whole garments, with good wearing qualities too. There's no doubt that she is the real McCoy; she was under contract to a textile factory in Jersey City. But I'd give a thousand dollars to see her do that whole-garment stunt of hers just once. We haven't had any luck, though I've tried everything but red-hot pincers."

The kid looked alarmed at this, and the nurse looked indignant. Feldstein started to expostulate, but Jedson cut him short. "That was just a figure of speech; you know I don't hold with black magic. Look, darling," he went on, turning back to the girl, "do you feel like trying again?" She nodded, and he added, "All right—sleepy time now!"

And she tried again, going into her act with a minimum of groaning and spitting. The ectoplasm came out freely and, sure enough, it formed into a complete dress instead of yard goods. It was a neat little dinner frock, about a size sixteen, sky blue in a watered silk. It had class in a refined way, and I knew that any jobber who saw it would be good for a sizable order.

Jedson grabbed it, cut off a swatch of cloth and applied his usual tests, finishing by taking the swatch out of the microscope and touching a match to it.

He swore. "Damn it," he said, "there's no doubt about it. It's not a new integration at all; she's just reanimated an old rag!"

"Come again," I said. "What of it?"

"Huh? Archie, you really ought to study up a bit. What she just did isn't really creative magic at all. This dress"—he picked it up and shook it—"had a real existence someplace at some time. She's gotten hold of a piece of it, a scrap or maybe just a button, and applied the laws of homeopathy and contiguity to produce a simulacrum of it."

I understood him, for I had used it in my own business. I had once had a section of bleachers, suitable for parades and athletic events, built on my own grounds by old methods, using skilled master mechanics and the best materials—no iron, of course. Then I cut it to pieces. Under the law of contiguity, each piece remained part of the structure it had once been in. Under the law of homeopathy, each piece was potentially the entire structure. I would contract to handle a Fourth of July crowd, or the spectators for a circus parade, and send out a couple of magicians armed with as many fragments of the original stands as we needed sections of bleachers. They would bind a spell to last twenty-four hours around each piece. That way the stands cleared themselves away automatically.

I had had only one mishap with it; an apprentice magician, who had the chore of being on hand as each section vanished and salvaging the animated fragment for further use, happened one day to pick up the wrong piece of wood from where one section had stood. The next time we used it, for the Shrine convention, we found we had thrown up a brand-new four-room bungalow at the corner of Fourteenth and Vine instead of a section of bleachers. It could have been embarrassing, but I stuck a sign on it

MODEL HOME NOW ON DISPLAY

and ran up another section on the end.

An out-of-town concern tried to chisel me out of the business one season, but one of their units fell, either through faulty workmanship on the pattern or because of unskilled magic, and injured several people. Since then I've had the field pretty much to myself.

I could not understand Joe Jedson's objection to reanimation. "What difference does it make?" I persisted. "It's a dress, isn't it?"

"Sure, it's a dress, but it's not a new one. That style is registered somewhere and doesn't belong to me. And even if it were one of my numbers she had used, reanimation isn't what I'm after. I can make better merchandise cheaper without it; otherwise I'd be using it now."

The blond girl came to, saw the dress, and said, "Oh, Mr. Jedson, did I do it?"

He explained what had happened. Her face fell, and the dress melted away at once. "Don't you feel bad about it, kid," he added, patting her on the shoulder, "you were tired. We'll try again tomorrow. I know you can do it when you're not nervous and overwrought."

She thanked him and left with the nurse. Feldstein was full of explanations, but Jedson told him to forget it, and to have them all back there at the same time tomorrow. When we were alone I told him what had happened to me.

He listened in silence, his face serious, except when I told him how I had kidded my visitor into thinking I had second sight. That seemed to amuse him.

"You may wish that you really had it—second sight, I mean," he said at last, becoming solemn again. "This is an unpleasant prospect. Have you notified the Better Business Bureau?"

I told him I hadn't.

"Very well then. I'll give them a ring and the Chamber of Commerce too. They probably can't help much, but they are entitled to notification, so they can be on the lookout for it."

I asked him if he thought I ought to notify the police. He shook his head. "Not just yet. Nothing illegal has been done, and, anyhow, all the chief could think of to cope with the situation would be to haul in all the licensed magicians in town and sweat them. That wouldn't do any good, and would just cause hard feeling to be directed against you by the legitimate members of the profession. There isn't a chance in ten that the sorcerers connected with this outfit are licensed to perform magic; they are almost sure to be clandestine. If the police know about them, it's because they are protected. If they don't know about them, then they probably can't help you."

"What do you think I ought to do?"

"Nothing just yet. Go home and sleep on it. This Charlie may be playing a lone hand, making small-time shakedowns purely on bluff. I don't really think so; his type sounds like a mobster. But we need more data; we can't do anything until they expose their hand a little more."

We did not have long to wait. When I got down to my place of business the next morning I found a surprise waiting for me—several of them, all unpleasant.

It was as if it had been ransacked by burglars, set fire to, then gutted by a flood. I called up Jedson at once. He came right over. He didn't have anything to say at first, but went poking through the ruins, examining a number of things. He stopped at the point where the hardware storeroom had stood, reached down and gathered up a handful of the wet ashes and muck. "Notice anything?" he asked, working his fingers so that the debris sloughed off and left in his hand some small metal objects—nails, screws, and the like.

"Nothing in particular. This is where the hardware bins were located; that's some of the stuff that didn't burn."

"Yes, I know," he said impatiently, "but don't you see anything else? Didn't you stock a lot of brass fittings?"

"Yes."

"Well, find one!"

I poked around with my toe in a spot where there should have been a lot of brass hinges and drawer pulls mixed in with the ashes. I did not find anything but the nails that had held the bins together. I oriented myself by such landmarks as I could find, and tried again. There were plenty of nuts and bolts, casement hooks, and similar junk, but no brass.

Jedson watched me with a sardonic grin on his face.

"Well?" I said, somewhat annoyed at his manner.

"Don't you see?" he answered. "It's magic, all right. In this entire yard there is not one scrap of metal left, *except cold iron!*"

It was plain enough. I should have seen it myself.

He messed around awhile longer. Presently we came across an odd thing. It was a slimy, wet track that meandered through my property, and disappeared down one of the drains. It looked as if a giant slug, about the size of a Crosley car, had wandered through the place.

"Undine," Jedson announced, and wrinkled his nose at the smell. I once saw a movie, a Megapix superproduction called the *Water King's Daughter*. According to it undines were luscious enough to have interested Earl Carroll, but if they left trails like that I wanted none of them.

He took out his handkerchief and spread it for a clean place to sit down on what had been sacks of cement—a fancy, quick-setting variety, with a trade name of Hydrolith. I had been getting eighty cents a sack for the stuff; now it was just so many big boulders.

He ticked the situation off on his fingers. "Archie, you've been kicked in the teeth by at least three of the four different types of elementals—earth, fire, and water. Maybe there was a sylph of the air in on it, too, but I can't prove it. First the gnomes came and cleaned out everything you had that came out of the ground, except cold iron. A salamander followed them and set fire to the place, burning everything that was burnable, and scorching and smoke-damaging the rest. Then the undine turned the place into a damned swamp, ruining anything that wouldn't burn, like cement and lime. You're insured?"

"Naturally." But then I started to think. I carried the usual fire, theft, and flood insurance, but business-risk insurance comes pretty high; I was not covered against the business I would lose in the meantime, nor did I have any way to complete current contracts. It was going to cost me quite a lot to cover those contracts; if I let them slide it would ruin the good will of my business, and lay me open to suits for damage.

The situation was worse than I had thought, and looked worse still the more I thought about it. Naturally I could not accept any new business until the mess was cleaned up, the place rebuilt, and new stock put in. Luckily most of my papers were in a fireproof steel safe; but not all, by any means. There would be accounts receivable that I would never collect because I had nothing to show for them. I work on a slim margin of profit, with all of my capital at work. It began to look as if the firm of Archibald Fraser, Merchant and Contractor, would go into involuntary bankruptcy.

I explained the situation to Jedson.

"Don't get your wind up too fast," he reassured me. "What magic can do, magic can undo. What we need is the best wizard in town."

"Who's going to pay the fee?" I objected. "Those boys don't work for nickels, and I'm cleaned out."

"Take it easy, son," he advised, "the insurance outfit that carries your risks is due to take a bigger loss than you are. If we can show them a way to save money on this, we can do business. Who represents them here?"

I told him—a firm of lawyers downtown in the Professional Building.

I got hold of my office girl and told her to telephone such of our customers as were due for deliveries that day. She was to stall where possible and pass on the business that could not wait to a firm that I had exchanged favors with in the past. I sent the rest of my help home—they had been standing around since eight o'clock, making useless remarks and getting in the way—and told them not to come back until I sent for them. Luckily it was Saturday; we had the best part of forty-eight hours to figure out some answer.

We flagged a magic carpet that was cruising past and headed for the Professional Building. I settled back and determined to enjoy the ride and forget my troubles. I like taxicabs—they give me a feeling of luxury—and I've liked them even better since they took the wheels off them. This happened to be one of the new Cadillacs with the teardrop shape and air cushions. We went scooting down the boulevard, silent as thought, not six inches off the ground.

Perhaps I should explain that we have a local city ordinance against apportation unless it conforms to traffic regulations—ground traffic, I mean, not air. That may surprise you, but it came about as a result of a mishap to a man in my own line of business. He had an order for eleven-odd tons of glass brick to be delivered to a restaurant being remodeled on the other side of town from his yard. He employed a magician with a common carrier's license to deliver for him. I don't know whether he was careless or just plain stupid, but he dropped those eleven tons of brick through the roof of the Prospect Boulevard Baptist Church. Anybody knows that magic won't work over consecrated ground; if he had consulted a map he would have seen that the straight-line route took his load over the church. Anyhow, the janitor was killed, and it might just as well have been the whole congregation. It caused such a commotion that apportation was limited to the streets, near the ground.

It's people like that who make it inconvenient for everybody else.

Our man was in—Mr. Wiggin, of the firm of Wiggin, Snead, McClatchey & Wiggin. He had already heard about my "fire," but when Jedson explained his conviction that magic was at the bottom of it he balked. It was, he said, most irregular. Jedson was remarkably patient.

"Are you an expert in magic, Mr. Wiggin?" he asked.

"I have not specialized in thaumaturgic jurisprudence, if that is what you mean, sir."

"Well, I don't hold a license myself, but it has been my hobby for a good many years. I'm sure of what I say in this case; you can call in all the independent experts you wish—they'll confirm my opinion. Now suppose we stipulate, for the sake of argument, that this damage was caused by magic. If that is true, there is a possibility that we may be able to save much of the loss. You have authority to settle claims, do you not?"

"Well, I think I may say yes to that—bearing in mind the legal restrictions and the terms of the contract." I don't believe he would have conceded that he had five fingers on his right hand without an auditor to back him up.

"Then it is your business to hold your company's losses down to a minimum. If I find a wizard who can undo a part, or all, of the damage, will you guarantee the fee, on behalf of your company, up to a reasonable amount, say twenty-five per cent of the indemnity?"

He hemmed and hawed some more, and said he did not see how he could possibly do it, and that if the fire had been magic, then to restore by magic might be compounding a felony, as we could not be sure what the connections of the magicians involved might be in the Half World. Besides that, my claim had not been allowed as yet; I had failed to notify the company of my visitor of the day before, which possibly might prejudice my claim. In any case, it was a very serious precedent to set; he must consult the home office.

Jedson stood up. "I can see that we are simply wasting each other's time, Mr. Wiggin. Your contention about Mr. Fraser's possible responsibility is ridiculous, and you know it. There is no reason under the contract to notify you, and even if there were, he is within the twenty-four hours allowed for any notification. I think it best that we consult the home office ourselves." He reached for his hat.

Wiggin put up his hand. "Gentlemen, gentlemen, please! Let's not be hasty. Will Mr. Fraser agree to pay half of the fee?"

"No. Why should he? It's your loss, not his. *You* insured *him*."

Wiggin tapped his teeth with his spectacles, then said, "We must make the fee contingent on results."

"Did you ever hear of anyone in his right mind dealing with a wizard on any other basis?"

Twenty minutes later we walked out with a document which enabled us to hire any witch or wizard to salvage my place of business on a contingent fee not to exceed 25 per cent of the value reclaimed. "I thought you were going to throw up the whole matter," I told Jedson with a sigh of relief.

He grinned. "Not in the wide world, old son. He was simply trying to horse you into paying the cost of saving them some money. I just let him know that I knew."

It took some time to decide whom to consult. Jedson admitted frankly that he did not know of a man nearer than New York who could, with certainty, be trusted to do the job, and that was out of the question for the fee involved. We stopped in a bar, and he did some telephoning while I had a beer. Presently he came back and said, "I think I've got the man. I've never done business with him before, but he has the reputation and the training, and everybody I talked to seemed to think that he was the one to see."

"Who is it?" I wanted to know.

"Dr. Fortescue Biddle. He's just down the street—the Railway Exchange Building. Come on, we'll walk it."

I gulped down the rest of my beer and followed him.

Dr. Biddle's place was impressive. He had a corner suite on the fourteenth floor, and he had not spared expense in furnishing and decorating it. The style was modern; it had the austere elegance of a society physician's layout. There was a frieze around the wall of the signs of the zodiac done in intaglio glass, backed up by aluminum. That was the only decoration of any sort, the rest of the furnishing being very plain, but rich, with lots of plate glass and chromium.

We had to wait about thirty minutes in the outer office; I

spent the time trying to estimate what I could have done the suite for, subletting what I had to and allowing 10 per cent. Then a really beautiful girl with a hushed voice ushered us in. We found ourselves in another smaller room, alone, and had to wait about ten minutes more. It was much like the waiting room, but had some glass bookcases and an old print of Aristotle. I looked at the bookcases with Jedson to kill time. They were filled with a lot of rare old classics on magic. Jedson had just pointed out the *Red Grimoire* when we heard a voice behind us.

"Amusing, aren't they? The ancients knew a surprising amount. Not scientific, of course, but remarkably clever—" The voice trailed off. We turned around; he introduced himself as Dr. Biddle.

He was a nice enough looking chap, really handsome in a spare, dignified fashion. He was about ten years older than I am—fortyish, maybe—with iron-gray hair at the temples and a small, stiff, British major's mustache. His clothes could have been out of the style pages of *Esquire*. There was no reason for me not to like him; his manners were pleasant enough. Maybe it was the supercilious twist to his expression.

He led us into his private office, sat us down, and offered us cigarettes before business was mentioned. He opened up with, "You're Jedson, of course. I suppose Mr. Ditworth sent you?"

I cocked an ear at him; the name was familiar. But Jedson simply answered, "Why, no. Why would you think that he had?"

Biddle hesitated for a moment, then said, half to himself, "That's strange. I was certain that I had heard him mention your name. Do either one of you," he added, "know Mr. Ditworth?"

We both nodded at once and surprised each other. Biddle seemed relieved and said, "No doubt that accounts for it. Still—I need some more information. Will you gentlemen excuse me while I call him?"

With that he vanished. I had never seen it done before. Jedson says there are two ways to do it, one is hallucination, the other is an actual exit through the Half World. Whichever way it's done, I think it's bad manners.

"About this chap Ditworth," I started to say to Jedson. "I had intended to ask you—"

"Let it wait," he cut me off, "there's not time now."

At this Biddle reappeared. "It's all right," he announced, speaking directly to me. "I can take your case. I suppose you've come about the trouble you had last night with your establishment?"

"Yes," I agreed. "How did you know?"

"Methods," he replied, with a deprecatory little smile. "My profession has its means. Now, about your problem. What is it you desire?"

I looked at Jedson; he explained what he thought had taken place and why he thought so. "Now I don't know whether you specialize in demonology or not," he concluded, "but it seems to me that it should be possible to evoke the powers responsible and force them to repair the damage. If you can do it, we are prepared to pay any reasonable fee."

Biddle smiled at this and glanced rather self-consciously at the assortment of diplomas hanging on the walls of his office. "I feel that there should be reason to reassure you," he purred. "Permit me to look over the ground—" And he was gone again.

I was beginning to be annoyed. It's all very well for a man to be good at his job, but there is no reason to make a side show out of it. But I didn't have time to grouse about it before he was back.

"Examination seems to confirm Mr. Jedson's opinion; there should be no unusual difficulties," he said. "Now as to the—ah—business arrangements—" He coughed politely and gave a little smile, as if he regretted having to deal with such vulgar matters.

Why do some people act as if making money offended their delicate minds? I am out for a legitimate profit, and not ashamed of it; the fact that people will pay money for my goods and services shows that my work is useful.

However, we made a deal without much trouble, then Biddle told us to meet him at my place in about fifteen minutes. Jedson and I left the building and flagged another cab. Once inside I asked him about Ditworth.

"Where'd you run across him?" I said.

"Came to me with a proposition."

"Hm-m-m—" This interested me; Ditworth had made me a proposition, too, and it had worried me. "What kind of a proposition?"

Jedson screwed up his forehead. "Well, that's hard to say—there was so much impressive sales talk along with it. Briefly, he said he was the local executive secretary of a nonprofit association which had as its purpose the improvement of standards of practicing magicians."

I nodded. It was the same story I had heard. "Go ahead."

"He dwelt on the inadequacy of the present licensing laws and pointed out that anyone could pass the examinations and hang out his shingle after a couple of weeks' study of a *grimoire* or black book without any fundamental knowledge of the arcane laws at all. His organization would be a sort of bureau of standards to improve that, like the American Medical Association, or the National Conference of Universities and Colleges, or the Bar Association. If I signed an agreement to patronize only those wizards who complied with their requirements, I could display their certificate of quality and put their seal of approval on my goods."

"Joe, I've heard the same story," I cut in, "and I didn't know quite what to make of it. It sounds all right, but I wouldn't want to stop doing business with men who have given me good value in the past, and I've no way of knowing that the association would approve them."

"What answer did you give him?"

"I stalled him a bit—told him that I couldn't sign anything as binding as that without discussing it with my attorney."

"Good boy! What did he say to that?"

"Well, he was really quite decent about it, and honestly seemed to want to be helpful. Said he thought I was wise and left me some stuff to look over. Do you know anything about him? Is he a wizard himself?"

"No, he's not. But I did find out some things about him. I knew vaguely that he was something in the Chamber of Commerce; what I didn't know is that he is on the board of a dozen or more blue-ribbon corporations. He's a lawyer, but not in practice. Seems to spend all his time on his business interests."

"He sounds like a responsible man."

"I would say so. He seems to have had considerably less publicity than you would expect of a man of his business importance—probably a retiring sort. I ran across something that seemed to confirm that."

"What was it?" I asked.

"I looked up the incorporation papers for his association on file with the Secretary of State. There were just three names, his own and two others. I found that both of the others were employed in his office—his secretary and his receptionist."

"Dummy setup?"

"Undoubtedly. But there is nothing unusual about that. What interested me was this: I recognized one of the names."

"Huh?"

"You know, I'm on the auditing committee for the state committee of my party. I looked up the name of his secretary where I thought I had seen it. It was there all right. His secretary, a chap by the name of Mathias, was down for a whopping big contribution to the governor's personal campaign fund."

We did not have any more time to talk just then, as the cab had pulled up at my place. Dr. Biddle was there before us and had already started his preparations. He had set up a little crystal pavilion, about ten feet square, to work in. The entire lot was blocked off from spectators on the front by an impalpable screen. Jedson warned me not to touch it.

I must say he worked without any of the usual hocus-pocus. He simply greeted us and entered the pavilion, where he sat down on a chair and took a loose-leaf notebook from a pocket and commenced to read. Jedson says he used several pieces of paraphernalia too. If so, I didn't see them. He worked with his clothes on.

Nothing happened for a few minutes. Gradually the walls of the shed became cloudy, so that everything inside was indistinct. It was about then that I became aware that there was something else in the pavilion besides Biddle. I could not see clearly what it was, and, to tell the truth, I didn't want to.

We could not hear anything that was said on the inside, but there was an argument going on—that was evident. Biddle stood up and began sawing the air with his hands. The thing threw back its head and laughed. At that Biddle threw a worried look in our direction and made a quick gesture with his right hand. The walls of the pavilion became opaque at once and we didn't see any more.

About five minutes later Biddle walked out of his workroom, which promptly disappeared behind him. He was a sight—his hair all mussed, sweat dripping from his face, and his collar wrinkled and limp. Worse than that, his aplomb was shaken.

"Well?" said Jedson.

"There is nothing to be done about it, Mr. Jedson—nothing at all."

"Nothing you can do about it, eh?"

He stiffened a bit at this. "Nothing *anyone* can do about it, gentlemen. Give it up. Forget about it. That is my advice."

Jedson said nothing, just looked at him speculatively. I kept quiet. Biddle was beginning to regain his self-possession. He straightened his hat, adjusted his necktie, and added, "I must return to my office. The survey fee will be five hundred dollars."

I was stonkered speechless at the barefaced gall of the man, but Jedson acted as if he hadn't understood him. "No doubt it would be," he observed. "Too bad you didn't earn it. I'm sorry."

Biddle turned red, but preserved his urbanity. "Apparently you misunderstand me, sir. Under the agreement I have signed with Mr. Ditworth, thaumaturgists approved by the association are not permitted to offer free consultation. It lowers the standards of the profession. The fee I mentioned is the minimum fee for a magician of my classification, irrespective of services rendered."

"I see," Jedson answered calmly; "that's what it costs to step inside your office. But you didn't tell us that, so it doesn't apply. As for Mr. Ditworth, an agreement you sign with him does not bind us in any way. I advise you to return to your office and reread our contract. We owe you nothing."

I thought this time that Biddle would lose his temper, but all he answered was, "I shan't bandy words with you. You will hear from me later." He vanished then without so much as a by-your-leave.

I heard a snicker behind me and whirled around, ready to

bite somebody's head off. I had had an upsetting day and didn't like to be laughed at behind my back. There was a young chap there, about my own age. "Who are you, and what are you laughing at?" I snapped. "This is private property."

"Sorry, bud," he apologized with a disarming grin. "I wasn't laughing at you; I was laughing at the stuffed shirt. Your friend ticked him off properly."

"What are you doing here?" asked Jedson.

"Me? I guess I owe you an explanation. You see, I'm in the business myself—"

"Building?"

"No—magic. Here's my card." He handed it to Jedson, who glanced at it and passed it on to me. It read:

JACK BODIE
LICENSED MAGICIAN, 1ST CLASS
TELEPHONE CREST 3840

"You see, I heard a rumor in the Half World that one of the big shots was going to do a hard one here today. I just stopped in to see the fun. But how did you happen to pick a false alarm like Biddle? He's not up to this sort of thing."

Jedson reached over and took the card back. "Where did you take your training, Mr. Bodie?"

"Huh? I took my bachelor's degree at Harvard and finished up postgraduate at Chicago. But that's not important; my old man taught me everything I know, but he insisted on my going to college because he said a magician can't get a decent job these days without a degree. He was right."

"Do you think you could handle this job?" I asked.

"Probably not, but I wouldn't have made the fool of myself that Biddle did. Look here—you want to find somebody who *can* do this job?"

"Naturally," I said. "What do you think we're here for?"

"Well, you've gone about it the wrong way. Biddle's got a reputation simply because he's studied at Heidelberg and Vienna. That doesn't mean a thing. I'll bet it never occurred to you to look up an old-style witch for the job."

Jedson answered this one. "That's not quite true. I inquired around among my friends in the business, but didn't find anyone who was willing to take it on. But I'm willing to learn; whom do you suggest?"

"Do you know Mrs. Amanda Todd Jennings? Lives over in the old part of town, beyond the Congregational cemetery."

"Jennings—Jennings. Hm-m-m—no, can't say that I do. Wait a minute! Is she the old girl they call Granny Jennings? Wears Queen Mary hats and does her own marketing?"

"That's the one."

"But she's not a witch; she's a fortuneteller."

"That's what you think. She's not in regular commercial practice, it's true, being ninety years older than Santy Claus, and feeble to boot. But she's got more magic in her little finger than you'll find in Solomon's Book."

Jedson looked at me. I nodded, and he said:

"Do you think you could get her to attempt this case?"

"Well, I think she might do it, if she liked you."

"What arrangement do you want?" I asked. "Is ten per cent satisfactory?"

He seemed rather put out at this. "Hell," he said, "I couldn't take a cut; she's been good to me all my life."

"If the tip is good, it's worth paying for," I insisted.

"Oh, forget it. Maybe you boys will have some work in my line someday. That's enough."

Pretty soon we were off again, without Bodie. He was tied up elsewhere, but promised to let Mrs. Jennings know that we were coming.

The place wasn't too hard to find. It was on an old street, arched over with elms, and the house was a one-story cottage, set well back. The veranda had a lot of that old scroll-saw gingerbread. The yard was not very well taken care of, but there was a lovely old climbing rose arched over the steps.

Jedson gave a twist to the hand bell set in the door, and we waited for several minutes. I studied the colored-glass triangles set in the door's side panels and wondered if there was anyone left who could do that sort of work.

Then she let us in. She really was something incredible. She was so tiny that I found myself staring down at the crown of her head, and noting that the clean pink scalp showed plainly through the scant, neat threads of hair. She couldn't have weighed seventy pounds dressed for the street, but stood proudly erect in lavender alpaca and white collar, and sized us up with lively black eyes that would have fitted Catherine the Great or Calamity Jane.

"Good morning to you," she said. "Come in."

She led us through a little hall, between beaded portieres, said, "Scat, Seraphin!" to a cat on a chair, and sat us down in her parlor. The cat jumped down, walked away with an unhurried dignity, then sat down, tucked his tail neatly around his carefully placed feet, and stared at us with the same calm appraisal as his mistress.

"My boy Jack told me that you were coming," she began. "You are Mr. Fraser and you are Mr. Jedson," getting us sorted out correctly. It was not a question; it was a statement. "You want your futures read, I suppose. What method do you prefer—your palms, the stars, the sticks?"

I was about to correct her misapprehension when Jedson cut in ahead of me. "I think we'd best leave the method up to you, Mrs. Jennings."

"All right, we'll make it tea leaves then. I'll put the kettle on; 'twon't take a minute." She bustled out. We could hear her in the kitchen, her light footsteps clicking on the linoleum, utensils scraping and clattering in a busy, pleasant disharmony.

When she returned I said, "I hope we aren't putting you out, Mrs. Jennings."

"Not a bit of it," she assured me. "I like a cup of tea in the morning; it does a body comfort. I just had to set a love philter off the fire—that's what took me so long."

"I'm sorry—"

" 'Twon't hurt it to wait."

"The Zekerboni formula?" Jedson inquired.

"My goodness gracious, no!" She was plainly upset by the suggestion. "I wouldn't kill all those harmless little creatures. Hares and swallows and doves—the very idea! I don't know what Pierre Mora was thinking about when he set that recipe down. I'd like to box his ears!

"No, I use Emula campana, orange, and ambergris. It's just as effective."

Jedson then asked if she had ever tried the juice of vervain. She looked closely into his face before replying, "You have the sight yourself, son. Am I not right?"

"A little, mother," he answered soberly, "a little, perhaps."

"It will grow. Mind how you use it. As for vervain, it is efficacious, as you know."

"Wouldn't it be simpler?"

"Of course it would. But if that easy a method became generally known, anyone and everyone would be making it and using it promiscuously—a bad thing. And witches would starve for want of clients—perhaps a good thing!" She flicked up one white eyebrow. "But if it is simplicity you want, there is no need to bother even with vervain. Here—" She reached out and touched me on the hand. "'*Bestarberto corrumpit viscera ejus virilis.*'" That is as near as I can reproduce her words. I may have misquoted it.

But I had no time to think about the formula she had pronounced. I was fully occupied with the startling thing that had come over me. I was in love, ecstatically, deliciously in love—with Granny Jennings! I don't mean that she suddenly looked like a beautiful young girl—she didn't. I still saw her as a little, old, shriveled-up woman with the face of a shrewd monkey, and ancient enough to be my great-grandmother. It didn't matter. She was she—the Helen that all men desire, the object of romantic adoration.

She smiled into my face with a smile that was warm and full of affectionate understanding. Everything was all right, and I was perfectly happy. Then she said, "I would not mock you, boy," in a gentle voice, and touched my hand a second time while whispering something else.

At once it was all gone. She was just any nice old woman, the sort that would bake a cake for a grandson or sit up with a sick neighbor. Nothing was changed, and the cat had not even blinked. The romantic fascination was an emotionless memory. But I was poorer for the difference.

The kettle was boiling. She trotted out to attend to it, and returned shortly with a tray of tea things, a plate of seed cake, and thin slices of homemade bread spread with sweet butter.

When we had drunk a cup apiece with proper ceremony, she took Jedson's cup from him and examined the dregs. "Not much money there," she announced, "but you shan't need much; it's a fine full life." She touched the little pool of tea with the tip of her spoon and sent tiny ripples across it. "Yes, you have the sight, and the need for understanding that should go with it, but I find you in business instead of pursuing the great art, or even the lesser arts. Why is that?"

Jedson shrugged his shoulders and answered half apologetically, "There is work at hand that needs to be done. I do it."

She nodded. "That is well. There is understanding to be gained in any job, and you will gain it. There is no hurry; time is long. When your own work comes you will know it and be ready for it. Let me see your cup," she finished, turning to me.

I handed it to her. She studied it for a moment and said, "Well, you have not the clear sight such as your friend has, but you have the insight you need for your proper work. Any more would make you dissatisfied, for I see money here. You will make much money, Archie Fraser."

"Do you see any immediate setback in my business?" I said quickly.

"No. See for yourself." She motioned toward the cup. I leaned forward and stared at it. For a matter of seconds it seemed as if I looked through the surface of the dregs into a living scene beyond. I recognized it readily enough. It was my own place of business, even to the scars on the driveway gateposts where clumsy truck drivers had clipped the corner too closely.

But there was a new annex wing on the east side of the lot, and there were two beautiful new five-ton dump trucks drawn up in the yard with my name painted on them!

While I watched I saw myself step out of the office door and go walking down the street. I was wearing a new hat, but the suit was the one I was wearing in Mrs. Jennings's parlor, and so was the necktie—a plaid one from the tartan of my clan. I reached up and touched the original.

Mrs. Jennings said, "That will do for now," and I found myself staring at the bottom of the teacup. "You have seen," she went on, "your business need not worry you. As for love and marriage and children, sickness and health and death—let us look." She touched the surface of the dregs with a finger tip; the tea leaves moved gently. She regarded them closely for a moment. Her brow puckered; she started to speak, apparently thought better of it, and looked again. Finally she said, "I do not fully understand this. It is not clear; my own shadow falls across it."

"Perhaps I can see," offered Jedson.

"Keep your peace!" She surprised me by speaking tartly, and placed her hand over the cup. She turned back to me with compassion in her eyes. "It is not clear. You have two possible futures. Let your head rule your heart, and do not fret your soul with that which cannot be. Then you will marry, have children, and be content." With that she dismissed the matter, for she said at once to both of us, "You did not come here for divination; you came here for help of another sort." Again it was a statement, not a question.

"What sort of help, mother?" Jedson inquired.

"For this." She shoved my cup under his nose.

He looked at it and answered, "Yes, that is true. Is there help?" I looked into the cup, too, but saw nothing but tea leaves.

She answered, "I think so. You should not have employed Biddle, but the mistake was natural. Let us be going." Without further parley she fetched her gloves and purse and coat, perched a ridiculous old hat on the top of her head, and bustled us out of the house. There was no discussion of terms; it didn't seem necessary.

When we got back to the lot her workroom was already up. It was not anything fancy like Biddle's, but simply an old, square tent, like a gypsy's pitch, with a peaked top and made in several gaudy colors. She pushed aside the shawl that closed the door and invited us inside.

It was gloomy, but she took a big candle, lighted it and stuck it in the middle of the floor. By its light she inscribed five circles on the ground—first a large one, then a somewhat smaller one in front of it. Then she drew two others, one on each side the first and biggest circle. These were each big enough for a man to stand in, and she told us to do so. Finally she made one more circle off to one side and not more than a foot across.

I've never paid much attention to the methods of magicians, feeling about them the way Thomas Edison said he felt about mathematicians—when he wanted one he could hire one. But Mrs. Jennings was different. I wish I could understand the things she did—and why.

I know she drew a lot of cabalistic signs in the dirt within the circles. There were pentacles of various sizes, and some writing in what I judged to be Hebraic script, though Jedson says not. In particular there was, I remember, a sign like a long flat Z, with a loop in it, woven in and out of a Maltese cross. Two more candles were lighted and placed on each side of this.

Then she jammed the dagger—arthame, Jedson called it—with which she had scribed the figures into the ground at the top of the big circle so hard that it quivered. It continued to vibrate the whole time.

She placed a little folding stool in the center of the biggest circle, sat down on it, drew out a small book, and commenced to read aloud in a voiceless whisper. I could not catch the words, and presume I was not meant to. This went on for some time. I glanced around and saw that the little circle off to one side was now occupied—by Seraphin, her cat. We had left him shut up in her house. He sat quietly, watching everything that took place with dignified interest.

Presently she shut the book and threw a pinch of powder into the flame of the largest candle. It flared up and threw out a great puff of smoke. I am not quite sure what happened next, as the smoke smarted my eyes and made me blink, besides which, Jedson says I don't understand the purpose of fumigations at all. But I prefer to believe my eyes. Either that cloud of smoke solidified into a body or it covered up an entrance, one or the other.

Standing in the middle of the circle in front of Mrs. Jennings was a short, powerful man about four feet high or less. His shoulders were inches broader than mine, and his upper arms were thick as my thighs, knotted and bowed with muscle. He was dressed in a breechcloth, buskins, and a little hooded cap. His skin was hairless, but rough and earthy in texture. It was dull, lusterless. Everything about him was the same dull monotone, except his eyes, which shone green with repressed fury.

"Well!" said Mrs. Jennings crisply, "you've been long enough getting here! What have you to say for yourself?"

He answered sullenly, like an incorrigible boy caught but not repentant, in a language filled with rasping gutturals and sibilants. She listened awhile, then cut him off.

"I don't care who told you to; you'll account to me! I require this harm repaired—in less time than it takes to tell it!"

He answered back angrily, and she dropped into his language, so that I could no longer follow the meaning. But it was clear that I was concerned in it; he threw me several dirty looks, and finally glared and spat in my direction.

Mrs. Jennings reached out and cracked him across the mouth with the back of her hand. He looked at her, killing in his eye, and said something.

"So?" she answered, put out a hand and grabbed him by the nape of the neck and swung him across her lap, face down. She snatched off a shoe and whacked him soundly with it. He let out one yelp, then kept silent, but jerked every time she struck him.

When she was through she stood up, spilling him to the ground. He picked himself up and hurriedly scrambled back into his own circle, where he stood, rubbing himself. Mrs. Jennings's eyes snapped and her voice crackled; there was nothing feeble about her now. "You gnomes are getting above yourselves," she scolded. "I never heard of such a thing! One more slip on your part and I'll fetch your people to see you spanked! Get along with you. Fetch your people for your task, and summon your brother and your brother's brother. By the great Tetragrammaton, get hence to the place appointed for you!"

He was gone.

Our next visitant came almost at once. It appeared first as a tiny spark hanging in the air. It grew into a living flame, a fireball, six inches or more across. It floated above the center of the second circle at the height of Mrs. Jennings's eyes. It danced and whirled and flamed, feeding on nothing. Although I had never seen one, I knew it to be a salamander. It couldn't be anything else.

Mrs. Jennings watched it for a little time before speaking.

I could see that she was enjoying its dance, as I was. It was a perfect and beautiful thing, with no fault in it. There was life in it, a singing joy, with no concern for—with no *relation* to—matters of right and wrong, or anything human. Its harmonies of color and curve were their own reason for being.

I suppose I'm pretty matter-of-fact. At least I've always lived by the principle of doing my job and letting other things take care of themselves. But here was something that was worth while in itself, no matter what harm it did by my standards. Even the cat was purring.

Mrs. Jennings spoke to it in a clear, singing soprano that had no words to it. It answered back in pure liquid notes while the colors of its nucleus varied to suit the pitch. She turned to me and said, "It admits readily enough that it burned your place, but it was invited to do so and is not capable of appreciating your point of view. I dislike to compel it against its own nature. Is there any boon you can offer it?"

I thought for a moment. "Tell it that it makes me happy to watch it dance." She sang again to it. It spun and leaped, its flame tendrils whirling and floating in intricate, delightful patterns.

"That was good, but not sufficient. Can you think of anything else?"

I thought hard. "Tell it that if it likes, I will build a fireplace in my house where it will be welcome to live whenever it wishes."

She nodded approvingly and spoke to it again. I could almost understand its answer, but Mrs. Jennings translated. "It likes you. Will you let it approach you?"

"Can it hurt me?"

"Not here."

"All right then."

She drew a T between our two circles. It followed closely behind the arthame, like a cat at an opening door. Then it swirled about me and touched me lightly on my hands and face. Its touch did not burn, but tingled, rather, as if I felt its vibrations directly instead of sensing them as heat. It flowed over my face. I was plunged into a world of light, like the heart of the aurora borealis. I was afraid to breathe at first, but finally had to. No harm came to me, though the tingling was increased.

It's an odd thing, but I have not had a single cold since the salamander touched me. I used to sniffle all winter.

"Enough, enough," I heard Mrs. Jennings saying. The cloud of flame withdrew from me and returned to its circle. The musical discussion resumed, and they reached an agreement almost at once, for Mrs. Jennings nodded with satisfaction and said:

"Away with you then, fire child, and return when you are needed. Get hence—" She repeated the formula she had used on the gnome king.

The undine did not show up at once. Mrs. Jennings took out her book again and read from it in a monotonous whisper. I was beginning to be a bit sleepy—the tent was stuffy—when the cat commenced to spit. It was glaring at the center circle, claws out, back arched, and tail made big.

There was a shapeless something in that circle, a thing that dripped and spread its slimy moisture to the limit of the magic ring. It stank of fish and kelp and iodine, and shone with a wet phosphorescence.

"You're late," said Mrs. Jennings. "You got my message; why did you wait until I compelled you?"

It heaved with a sticky, sucking sound, but made no answer.

"Very well," she said firmly, "I shan't argue with you. You know what I want. You will do it!" She stood up and grasped the big center candle. Its flame flared up into a torch a yard high, and hot. She thrust it past her circle at the undine.

There was a hiss, as when water strikes hot iron, and a burbling scream. She jabbed at it again and again. At last she stopped and stared down at it, where it lay, quivering and drawing into itself. "That will do," she said. "Next time you will heed your mistress. Get hence!" It seemed to sink into the ground, leaving the dust dry behind it.

When it was gone she motioned for us to enter her circle, breaking our own with the dagger to permit us. Seraphin jumped lightly from his little circle to the big one and rubbed against her ankles, buzzing loudly. She repeated a meaningless series of syllables and clapped her hands smartly together.

There was a rushing and roaring. The sides of the tent

billowed and cracked. I heard the chuckle of water and the crackle of flames, and, through that, the bustle of hurrying footsteps. She looked from side to side, and wherever her gaze fell the wall of the tent became transparent. I got hurried glimpses of unintelligible confusion.

Then it all ceased with a suddenness that was startling. The silence rang in our ears. The tent was gone; we stood in the loading yard outside my main warehouse.

It was there! It was back—back unharmed, without a trace of damage by fire or water. I broke away and ran out the main gate to where my business office had faced on the street. It was there, just as it used to be, the show windows shining in the sun, the Rotary Club emblem in one corner, and up on the roof my big two-way sign:

ARCHIBALD FRASER

BUILDING MATERIALS & GENERAL CONTRACTING

Jedson strolled out presently and touched me on the arm. "What are you bawling about, Archie?"

I stared at him. I wasn't aware that I had been.

We were doing business as usual on Monday morning. I thought everything was back to normal and that my troubles were over. I was too hasty in my optimism.

It was nothing you could put your finger on at first—just the ordinary vicissitudes of business, the little troubles that turn up in any line of work and slow up production. You expect them and charge them off to overhead. No one of them would be worth mentioning alone, except for one thing: they were happening too frequently.

You see, in any business run under a consistent management policy the losses due to unforeseen events should average out in the course of a year to about the same percentage of total cost. You allow for that in your estimates. But I started having so many small accidents and little difficulties that my margin of profit was eaten up.

One morning two of my trucks would not start. We could not find the trouble; I had to put them in the shop and rent a truck for the day to supplement my one remaining truck. We got our deliveries made, but I was out the truck rent, the repair bill, and four hours' overtime for drivers at time and a half. I had a net loss for the day.

The very next day I was just closing a deal with a man I had been trying to land for a couple of years. The deal was not important, but it would lead to a lot more business in the future, for he owned quite a bit of income property—some courts and an apartment house or two, several commercial corners, and held title or options on well-located lots all over town. He always had repair jobs to place and very frequently new building jobs. If I satisfied him, he would be a steady customer with prompt payment, the kind you can afford to deal with on a small margin of profit.

We were standing in the showroom just outside my office, and talking, having about reached an agreement. There was a display of Sunprufe paint about three feet from us, the cans stacked in a neat pyramid. I swear that neither one of us touched it, but it came crashing to the floor, making a din that would sour milk.

That was nuisance enough, but not the pay-off. The cover flew off one can, and my prospect was drenched with red paint. He let out a yelp; I thought he was going to faint. I managed to get him back into my office, where I dabbed futilely at his suit with my handkerchief, while trying to calm him down.

He was in a state, both mentally and physically. "Fraser," he raged, "you've got to fire the clerk that knocked over those cans! Look at me! Eighty-five dollars' worth of suit ruined!"

"Let's not be hasty," I said soothingly, while holding my own temper in. I won't discharge a man to suit a customer, and don't like to be told to do so. "There wasn't anyone near those cans but ourselves."

"I suppose you think I did it?"

"Not at all. I know you didn't." I straightened up, wiped my hands, and went over to my desk and got out my check-book.

"Then you must have done it!"

"I don't think so," I answered patiently. "How much did you say your suit was worth?"

"Why?"

"I want to write you a check for the amount." I was quite

willing to; I did not feel to blame, but it had happened through no fault of his in my shop.

"You can't get out of it as easily as that!" he answered unreasonably. "It isn't the cost of the suit I mind—" He jammed his hat on his head and stumped out. I knew his reputation; I'd seen the last of him.

That is the sort of thing I mean. Of course it could have been an accident caused by clumsy stacking of the cans. But it might have been a poltergeist. Accidents don't make themselves.

Ditworth came to see me a day or so later about Biddle's phony bill. I had been subjected night and morning to this continuous stream of petty annoyances, and my temper was wearing thin. Just that day a gang of colored bricklayers had quit one of my jobs because some moron had scrawled some chalk marks on some of the bricks. "Voodoo marks," they said they were, and would not touch a brick. I was in no mood to be held up by Mr. Ditworth; I guess I was pretty short with him.

"Good day to you, Mr. Fraser," he said quite pleasantly, "can you spare me a few minutes?"

"Ten minutes, perhaps," I conceded, glancing at my wrist watch.

He settled his brief case against the legs of his chair and took out some papers. "I'll come to the point at once then. It's about Dr. Biddle's claim against you. You and I are both fair men; I feel sure that we can come to some equitable agreement."

"Biddle has no claim against me."

He nodded. "I know just how you feel. Certainly there is nothing in the written contract obligating you to pay him. But there can be implied contracts just as binding as written contracts."

"I don't follow you. All my business is done in writing."

"Certainly," he agreed; "that's because you are a businessman. In the professions the situation is somewhat different. If you go to a dental surgeon and ask him to pull an aching tooth, and he does, you are obligated to pay his fee, even though a fee has never been mentioned—"

"That's true," I interrupted, "but there is no parallel. Biddle didn't 'pull the tooth.' "

"In a way he did," Ditworth persisted. "The claim against you is for the survey, which was a service rendered you before this contract was written."

"But no mention was made of a service fee."

"That is where the implied obligation comes in, Mr. Fraser; you told Dr. Biddle that you had talked with me. He assumed quite correctly that I had previously explained to you the standard system of fees under the association—"

"But I did not join the association!"

"I know, I know. And I explained that to the other directors, but they insist that some sort of an adjustment must be made. I don't feel myself that you are fully to blame, but you will understand our position, I am sure. We are unable to accept you for membership in the association until this matter is adjusted—in fairness to Dr. Biddle."

"What makes you think I intend to join the association?"

He looked hurt. "I had not expected you to take that attitude, Mr. Fraser. The association needs men of your caliber. But in your own interest, you will necessarily join, for presently it will be very difficult to get efficient thaumaturgy except from members of the association. We want to help you. Please don't make it difficult for us."

I stood up. "I am afraid you had better sue me and let a court decide the matter, Mr. Ditworth. That seems to be the only satisfactory solution."

"I am sorry," he said, shaking his head. "It will prejudice your position when you come up for membership."

"Then it will just have to do so," I said shortly, and showed him out.

After he had gone I crabbed at my office girl for doing something I told her to do the day before, and then had to apologize. I walked up and down a bit, stewing, although there was plenty of work I should have been doing. I was nervous; things had begun to get my goat—a dozen things that I haven't mentioned—and this last unreasonable demand from Ditworth seemed to be the last touch needed to upset me completely. Not that he could collect by suing me—that was preposterous—but it was an annoyance just the same.

They say the Chinese have a torture that consists in letting one drop of water fall on the victim every few minutes. That's the way I felt.

Finally I called up Jedson and asked him to go to lunch with me.

I felt better after lunch. Jedson soothed me down, as he always does, and I was able to forget and put in the past most of the things that had been annoying me simply by telling him about them. By the time I had had a second cup of coffee and smoked a cigarette I was almost fit for polite society.

We strolled back toward my shop, discussing his problems for a change. It seems the blond girl, the white witch from Jersey City, had finally managed to make her synthesis stunt work on foot-gear. But there was still a hitch; she had turned out over eight hundred left shoes—and no right ones.

We were just speculating as to the probable causes of such a contretemps when Jedson said, "Look, Archie. The candid-camera fans are beginning to take an interest in you."

I looked. There was a chap standing at the curb directly across from my place of business and focusing a camera on the shop.

Then I looked again. "Joe," I snapped, "that's the bird I told you about, the one that came into my shop and started the trouble!"

"Are you sure?" he asked, lowering his voice.

"Positive." There was no doubt about it; he was only a short distance away on the same side of the street that we were. It was the same racketeer who had tried to blackmail me into buying "protection," the same Mediterranean look to him, the same flashy clothes.

"We've got to grab him," whispered Jedson.

But I had already thought of that. I rushed at him and had grabbed him by his coat collar and the slack of his pants before he knew what was happening, and pushed him across the street ahead of me. We were nearly run down, but I was so mad I didn't care. Jedson came pounding after us.

The yard door of my office was open. I gave the mug a final heave that lifted him over the threshold and sent him sprawling on the floor. Jedson was right behind; I bolted the door as soon as we were both inside.

Jedson strode over to my desk, snatched open the middle drawer, and rummaged hurriedly through the stuff that accumulates in such places. He found what he wanted, a carpenter's blue pencil, and was back alongside our gangster before he had collected himself sufficiently to scramble to his feet. Jedson drew a circle around him on the floor, almost tripping over his own feet in his haste, and closed the circle with an intricate flourish.

Our unwilling guest screeched when he saw what Joe was doing, and tried to throw himself out of the circle before it could be finished. But Jedson had been too fast for him—the circle was closed and sealed; he bounced back from the boundary as if he had struck a glass wall, and stumbled again to his knees. He remained so for the time, and cursed steadily in a language that I judged to be Italian, although I think there were bad words in it from several other languages—certainly some English ones.

He was quite fluent.

Jedson pulled out a cigarette, lighted it, and handed me one. "Let's sit down, Archie," he said, "and rest ourselves until our boy friend composes himself enough to talk business."

I did so, and we smoked for several minutes while the flood of invective continued. Presently Jedson cocked one eyebrow at the chap and said, "Aren't you beginning to repeat yourself?"

That checked him. He just sat and glared. "Well," Jedson continued, "haven't you anything to say for yourself?"

He growled under his breath and said, "I want to call my lawyer."

Jedson looked amused. "You don't understand the situation," he told him. "You're not under arrest, and we don't give a damn about your legal rights. We might just conjure up a hole and drop you in it, then let it relax." The guy paled a little under his swarthy skin. "Oh yes," Jedson went on, "we are quite capable of doing that—or worse. You see, we don't like you.

"Of course," he added meditatively, "we might just turn you over to the police. I get a soft streak now and then." The chap looked sour. "You don't like that either? Your fingerprints, maybe?" Jedson jumped to his feet and in two quick strides was standing over him, just outside the circle. "All right then," he rapped, "answer up and make 'em good! Why were you taking photographs?"

The chap muttered something, his eyes lowered. Jedson brushed it aside. "Don't give me that stuff—we aren't children! Who told you to do it?"

He looked utterly panic-stricken at that and shut up completely.

"Very well," said Jedson, and turned to me. "Have you some wax, or modeling clay, or anything of the sort?"

"How would putty do?" I suggested.

"Just the thing." I slid out to the shed where we stow glaziers' supplies and came back with a five-pound can. Jedson pried it open and dug out a good big handful, then sat at my desk and worked the linseed oil into it until it was soft and workable. Our prisoner watched him with silent apprehension.

"There! That's about right," Jedson announced at length, and slapped the soft lump down on my blotter pad. He commenced to fashion it with his fingers, and it took shape slowly as a little doll about ten inches high. It did not look like much of anything or anybody—Jedson is no artist—but Jedson kept glancing from the figurine to the man in the circle and back again, like a sculptor making a clay sketch directly from a model. You could see the chap's nervous terror increase by the minute.

"Now!" said Jedson, looking once more from the putty figure to his model. "It's just as ugly as you are. Why did you take that picture?"

He did not answer, but slunk farther back in the circle, his face nastier than ever.

"Talk!" snorted Jedson, and twisted a foot of the doll between a thumb and forefinger. The corresponding foot of our prisoner jerked out from under him and twisted violently. He fell heavily to the floor with a yelp of pain.

"You were going to cast a spell on this place, weren't you?"

He made his first coherent answer. "No, no, mister! Not me!"

"Not you? I see. You were just the errand boy. Who was to do the magic?"

"I don't know—Ow! Oh, God!" He grabbed at his left calf and nursed it. Jedson had jabbed a pen point into the leg of the doll. "I really *don't* know. Please, please!"

"Maybe you don't," Jedson grudged, "but at least you know who gives you your orders, and who some of the other members of your gang are. Start talking."

He rocked back and forth and covered his face with his hands. "I don't dare, mister," he groaned. "Please don't try to make me—" Jedson jabbed the doll with the pen again; he jumped and flinched, but this time he bore it silently with a look of gray determination.

"O.K.," said Jedson, "if you insist—" He took another drag from his cigarette, then brought the lighted end slowly toward the face of the doll. The man in the circle tried to shrink away from it, his hands up to protect his face, but his efforts were futile. I could actually see the skin turn red and angry and the blisters blossom under his hide. It made me sick to watch it, and, while I didn't feel any real sympathy for the rat, I turned to Jedson and was about to ask him to stop when he took the cigarette away from the doll's face.

"Ready to talk?" he asked. The man nodded feebly, tears pouring down his scorched cheeks. He seemed about to collapse. "Here—don't faint," Jedson added, and slapped the face of the doll with a finger tip. I could hear the smack land, and the chap's head rocked to the blow, but he seemed to take a brace from it.

"All right, Archie, you take it down." He turned back. "And you, my friend, talk—and talk lots. Tell us everything you know. If you find your memory failing you, stop to think how you would like my cigarette poked into dolly's eyes!"

And he did talk—babbled, in fact. His spirit seemed to be completely broken, and he even seemed anxious to talk, stopping only occasionally to sniffle, or wipe at his eyes. Jedson questioned him to bring out points that were not clear.

There were five others in the gang that he knew about, and the setup was roughly as we had guessed. It was their object to levy tribute on everyone connected with magic in this end of town, magicians and their customers alike. No, they did not have any real protection to offer except from their own mischief. Who was his boss? He told us. Was his boss the top man in the racket? No, but he did not know who the top man was. He was quite sure that his boss worked for someone else, but he did not know who. Even if we burned him again he could not tell us. But it was a big organization—he was sure of that. He himself had been brought from a city in the East to help organize here.

Was he a magician? So help him, no! Was his section boss one? No—he was sure; all that sort of thing was handled from higher up. That was all he knew, and could he go now? Jedson pressed him to remember other things; he added a number of details, most of them insignificant, but I took them all down. The last thing he said was that he thought both of us had been marked down for special attention because we had been successful in overcoming our first "lesson."

Finally Jedson let up on him. "I'm going to let you go now," he told him. "You'd better get out of town. Don't let me see you hanging around again. But don't go too far; I may want you again. See this?" He held up the doll and squeezed it gently around the middle. The poor devil immediately commenced to gasp for breath as if he were being compressed in a strait jacket. "Don't forget that I've got you any time I want you." He let up on the pressure, and his victim panted his relief. "I'm going to put your alter ego—doll to you!—where it will be safe, behind cold iron. When I want you, you'll feel a pain like that"—he nipped the doll's left shoulder with his fingernails; the man yelped—"then you telephone me, no matter where you are."

Jedson pulled a penknife from his vest pocket and cut the circle three times, then joined the cuts. "Now get out!"

I thought he would bolt as soon as he was released, but he did not. He stepped hesitantly over the pencil mark, stood still for a moment, and shivered. Then he stumbled toward the door. He turned just before he went through it and looked back at us, his eyes wide with fear. There was a look of appeal in them, too, and he seemed about to speak. Evidently he thought better of it, for he turned and went on out.

When he was gone I looked back at Jedson. He had picked up my notes and was glancing through them. "I don't know," he mused, "whether it would be better to turn this stuff at once over to the Better Business Bureau and let them handle it, or whether to have a go at it ourselves. It's a temptation."

I was not interested just then. "Joe," I said, "I wish you hadn't burned him!"

"Eh? How's that?" He seemed surprised and stopped scratching his chin. "I didn't burn him."

"Don't quibble," I said, somewhat provoked. "You burned him through the doll, I mean with magic."

"But I didn't, Archie. Really I didn't. He did that to himself —and it wasn't magic. I didn't do a thing!"

"What the hell do you mean?"

"Sympathetic magic isn't really magic at all, Archie. It's just an application of neuropsychology and colloidal chemistry. He did all that to himself, because he believed in it. I simply correctly judged his mentality."

The discussion was cut short; we heard an agony-loaded scream from somewhere outside the building. It broke off sharply, right at the top. "What was that?" I said, and gulped.

"I don't know," Jedson answered, and stepped to the door. He looked up and down before continuing. "It must be some distance away. I didn't see anything." He came back into the room. "As I was saying, it would be a lot of fun to—"

This time it was a police siren. We heard it from far away, but it came rapidly nearer, turned a corner, and yowled down our street. We looked at each other. "Maybe we'd better go see," we both said, right together, then laughed nervously.

It was our gangster acquaintance. We found him half a block down the street, in the middle of a little group of curious passers-by who were being crowded back by cops from the squad car at the curb.

He was quite dead.

He lay on his back, but there was no repose in the position. He had been raked from forehead to waist, laid open to the bone in three roughly parallel scratches, as if slashed by the talons of a hawk or an eagle. But the bird that made those wounds must have been the size of a five-ton truck.

There was nothing to tell from his expression. His face and throat were covered by, and his mouth choked with, a yellowish substance shot with purple. It was about the consistency of thin cottage cheese, but it had the most sickening smell I have ever run up against.

I turned to Jedson, who was not looking any too happy himself, and said, "Let's get back to the office."

We did.

We decided at last to do a little investigating on our own before taking up what we had learned with the Better Business Bureau or with the police. It was just as well that we did; none of the gang whose names we had obtained was any longer to be found in the haunts which we had listed. There was plenty of evidence that such persons had existed and that they had lived at the addresses which Jedson had sweated out of their pal. But all of them, without exception, had done a bunk for parts unknown the same afternoon that their accomplice had been killed.

We did not go to the police, for we had no wish to be associated with an especially unsavory sudden death. Instead, Jedson made a cautious verbal report to a friend of his at the Better Business Bureau, who passed it on secondhand to the head of the racket squad and elsewhere, as his judgment indicated.

I did not have any more trouble with my business for some time thereafter, and I was working very hard, trying to show a profit for the quarter in spite of setbacks. I had put the whole matter fairly well out of my mind, except that I dropped over to call on Mrs. Jennings occasionally and that I had used her young friend Jack Bodie once or twice in my business, when I needed commercial magic. He was a good workman —no monkey business and value received.

I was beginning to think I had the world on a leash when I ran into another series of accidents. This time they did not threaten my business; they threatened *me*—and I'm just as fond of my neck as the next man.

In the house where I live the water heater is installed in the kitchen. It is a storage type, with a pilot light and a thermostatically controlled main flame. Right alongside it is a range with a pilot light.

I woke up in the middle of the night and decided that I wanted a drink of water. When I stepped into the kitchen—don't ask me why I did not look for a drink in the bathroom, because I don't know—I was almost gagged by the smell of gas. I ran over and threw the window wide open, then ducked back out the door and ran into the living room, where I opened a big window to create a cross draft.

At that point there was a dull *whoosh* and a *boom,* and I found myself sitting on the living-room rug.

I was not hurt, and there was no damage in the kitchen except for a few broken dishes. Opening the windows had released the explosion, cushioned the effect. Natural gas is not an explosive unless it is confined. What had happened was clear enough when I looked over the scene. The pilot light on the heater had gone out; when the water in the tank cooled, the thermostat turned on the main gas jet, which continued indefinitely to pour gas into the room. When an explosive mixture was reached, the pilot light of the stove was waiting, ready to set it off.

Apparently I wandered in at the zero hour.

I fussed at my landlord about it, and finally we made a dicker whereby he installed one of the electrical water heaters which I supplied at cost and for which I donated the labor.

No magic about the whole incident, eh? That is what I thought. Now I am not so sure.

The next thing that threw a scare into me occurred the same week, with no apparent connection. I keep dry mix—sand, rock, gravel—in the usual big bins set up high on concrete stanchions, so that the trucks can drive under the hoppers for loading. One evening after closing time I was walking past the bins when I noticed that someone had left a scoop shovel in the driveway pit under the hoppers.

I have had trouble with my men leaving tools out at night; I decided to put this one in my car and confront someone with it in the morning. I was about to jump down into the pit when I heard my name called.

"Archibald!" it said—and it sounded remarkably like Mrs. Jennings's voice. Naturally I looked around. There was no one there. I turned back to the pit in time to hear a cracking sound and to see that scoop covered with twenty tons of medium gravel.

A man can live through being buried alive, but not when he has to wait overnight for someone to miss him and dig him out. A crystallized steel forging was the prima-facie cause of the mishap. I suppose that will do.

There was never anything to point to but natural causes, yet for about two weeks I stepped on banana peels both figuratively and literally. I saved my skin with a spot of fast footwork at least a dozen times. I finally broke down and told Mrs. Jennings about it.

"Don't worry too much about it, Archie," she reassured me. "It is not too easy to kill a man with magic unless he himself is involved with magic and sensitive to it."

"Might as well kill a man as scare him to death!" I protested.

She smiled that incredible smile of hers and said, "I don't think you have been really frightened, lad. At least you have not shown it."

I caught an implication in that remark and taxed her with it. "You've been watching me and pulling me out of jams, haven't you?"

She smiled more broadly and replied, "That's my business, Archie. It is not well for the young to depend on the old for help. Now get along with you. I want to give this matter more thought."

A couple of days later a note came in the mail addressed to me in a spidery, Spencerian script. The penmanship had the dignified flavor of the last century, and was the least bit shaky, as if the writer were unwell or very elderly. I had never seen the hand before, but guessed who it was before I opened it. It read:

MY DEAR ARCHIBALD:

This is to introduce my esteemed friend, Dr. Royce Worthington. You will find him staying at the Belmont Hotel; he is expecting to hear from you. Dr. Worthington is exceptionally well qualified to deal with the matters that have been troubling you these few weeks past. You may repose every confidence in his judgment, especially where unusual measures are required.

Please to include your friend, Mr. Jedson, in this introduction, if you wish.

I am, sir,

Very sincerely yours,

AMANDA TODD JENNINGS

I rang up Joe Jedson and read the letter to him. He said that he would be over at once, and for me to telephone Worthington.

"Is Dr. Worthington there?" I asked as soon as the room clerk had put me through.

"Speaking," answered a cultured British voice with a hint of Oxford in it.

"This is Archibald Fraser, Doctor. Mrs. Jennings has written to me, suggesting that I look you up."

"Oh yes!" he replied, his voice warming considerably. "I shall be delighted. When will be a convenient time?"

"If you are free, I could come right over."

"Let me see—" He paused about long enough to consult a watch. "I have occasion to go to your side of the city. Might I stop by your office in thirty minutes, or a little later?"

"That will be fine, Doctor, if it does not discommode you—"

"Not at all. I will be there."

Jedson arrived a little later and asked me at once about Dr. Worthington. "I haven't seen him yet," I said, "but he sounds like something pretty swank in the way of an English-university don. He'll be here shortly."

My office girl brought in his card a half hour later. I got up to greet him and saw a tall, heavy-set man with a face of great dignity and evident intelligence. He was dressed in rather conservative, expensively tailored clothes and carried gloves, stick, and a large brief case. But he was black as draftsman's ink!

I tried not to show surprise. I hope I did not, for I have an utter horror of showing that kind of rudeness. There was no reason why the man should not be a Negro. I simply had not been expecting it.

Jedson helped me out. I don't believe he would show surprise if a fried egg winked at him. He took over the conversation for the first couple of minutes after I introduced him; we all found chairs, settled down, and spent a few minutes in the polite, meaningless exchanges that people make when they are sizing up strangers.

Worthington opened the matter. "Mrs. Jennings gave me to believe," he observed, "that there was some fashion in which I might possibly be of assistance to one, or both, of you—"

I told him that there certainly was, and sketched out the background for him from the time the racketeer contact man first showed up at my shop. He asked a few questions, and Jedson helped me out with some details. I got the impression that Mrs. Jennings had already told him most of it, and that he was simply checking.

"Very well," he said at last, his voice a deep, mellow rumble that seemed to echo in his big chest before it reached the air, "I am reasonably sure that we will find a way to cope with your problems, but first I must make a few examinations before we can complete the diagnosis." He leaned over and commenced to unstrap his brief case.

"Uh—Doctor," I suggested, "hadn't we better complete our arrangements before you start to work?"

"Arrangements?" He looked momentarily puzzled, then smiled broadly. "Oh, you mean payment. My dear sir, it is a privilege to do a favor for Mrs. Jennings."

"But—but—see here, Doctor, I'd feel better about it. I assure you I am quite in the habit of paying for magic—"

He held up a hand. "It is not possible, my young friend, for two reasons: In the first place, I am not licensed to practice in your state. In the second place, I am not a magician."

I suppose I looked as inane as I sounded. "Huh? What's that? Oh! Excuse me, Doctor, I guess I just naturally assumed that since Mrs. Jennings had sent you, and your title, and all—"

He continued to smile, but it was a smile of understanding rather than amusement at my discomfiture. "That is not surprising; even some of your fellow citizens of my blood make that mistake. No, my degree is an honorary doctor of laws of Cambridge University. My proper pursuit is anthropology, which I sometimes teach at the University of South Africa. But anthropology has some odd bypaths; I am here to exercise one of them."

"Well, then, may I ask—"

"Certainly, sir. My avocation, freely translated from its quite unpronounceable proper name, is 'witch smeller.' "

I was still puzzled. "But doesn't that involve magic?"

"Yes and no. In Africa the hierarchy and the categories in these matters are not the same as in this continent. I am not considered a wizard, or witch doctor, but rather an antidote for such."

Something had been worrying Jedson. "Doctor," he inquired, "you were not originally from South Africa?"

Worthington gestured toward his own face. I suppose that Jedson read something there that was beyond my knowledge. "As you have discerned. No, I was born in a bush tribe south of the Lower Congo."

"From there, eh? That's interesting. By any chance, are you nganga?"

"Of the Ndembo, but not by chance." He turned to me and explained courteously. "Your friend asked me if I was a member of an occult fraternity which extends throughout Africa, but which has the bulk of its members in my native territory. Initiates are called nganga."

Jedson persisted in his interest. "It seems likely to me, Doctor, that Worthington is a name of convenience—that you have another name."

"You are again right—naturally. My tribal name—do you wish to know it?"

"If you will."

"It is"—I cannot reproduce the odd clicking, lip-smacking noise he uttered—"or it is just as proper to state it in English, as the meaning is what counts—Man-Who-Asks-Inconvenient-Questions. Prosecuting attorney is another reasonably idiomatic, though not quite literal, translation, because of the tribal function implied. But it seems to me," he went on, with a smile of unmalicious humor, "that the name fits you even better than it does me. May I give it to you?"

Here occurred something that I did not understand, except that it must have its basis in some African custom completely foreign to our habits of thought. I was prepared to laugh at the doctor's witticism, and I am sure he meant it to be funny, but Jedson answered him quite seriously:

"I am deeply honored to accept."

"It is you who honor me, brother."

From then on, throughout our association with him, Dr. Worthington invariably addressed Jedson by the African name he had formerly claimed as his own, and Jedson called him "brother" or "Royce." Their whole attitude toward each other underwent a change, as if the offer and acceptance of a name had in fact made them brothers, with all of the privileges and obligations of the relationship.

"I have not left you without a name," Jedson added. "You had a third name, your real name?"

"Yes, of course," Worthington acknowledged, "a name which we need not mention."

"Naturally," Jedson agreed, "a name which must not be mentioned. Shall we get to work, then?"

"Yes, let us do so." He turned to me. "Have you someplace here where I may make my preparations? It need not be large—"

"Will this do?" I offered, getting up and opening the door of a cloak- and washroom which adjoins my office.

"Nicely, thank you," he said, and took himself and his brief case inside, closing the door after him. He was gone ten minutes at least.

Jedson did not seem disposed to talk, except to suggest that I caution my girl not to disturb us or let anyone enter from the outer office. We sat and waited.

Then he came out of the cloakroom, and I got my second big surprise of the day. The urbane Dr. Worthington was gone. In his place was an African personage who stood over six feet tall in his bare black feet, and whose enormous, arched chest was overlaid with thick, sleek muscles of polished obsidian. He was dressed in a loin skin of leopard, and carried certain accouterments, notably a pouch, which hung at his waist.

But it was not his equipment that held me, nor yet the John Henry–like proportions of that warrior frame, but the face. The eyebrows were painted white and the hairline had been outlined in the same color, but I hardly noticed these things. It was the expression—humorless, implacable, filled with a dignity and strength which must be felt to be appreciated.

The eyes gave a conviction of wisdom beyond my comprehension, and there was no pity in them—only a stern justice that I myself would not care to face.

We white men in this country are inclined to underestimate the black man—I know I do—because we see him out of his cultural matrix. Those we know have had their own culture wrenched from them some generations back and a servile pseudo culture imposed on them by force. We forget that the black man has a culture of his own, older than ours and more solidly grounded, based on character and the power of the mind rather than the cheap, ephemeral tricks of mechanical gadgets. But it is a stern, fierce culture with no sentimental concern for the weak and the unfit, and it never quite dies out.

I stood up in involuntary respect when Dr. Worthington entered the room.

"Let us begin," he said in a perfectly ordinary voice, and squatted down, his great toes spread and grasping the floor. He took several things out of the pouch—a dog's tail, a wrinkled black object the size of a man's fist, and other things hard to identify. He fastened the tail to his waist so that it hung down behind. Then he picked up one of the things that he had taken from the pouch—a small item, wrapped and tied in red silk—and said to me, "Will you open your safe?"

I did so, and stepped back out of his way. He thrust the little bundle inside, clanged the door shut, and spun the knob. I looked inquiringly at Jedson.

"He has his—well—soul in that package, and has sealed it away behind cold iron. He does not know what dangers he may encounter," Jedson whispered. "See?" I looked and saw him pass his thumb carefully all around the crack that joined the safe to its door.

He returned to the middle of the floor and picked up the wrinkled black object and rubbed it affectionately. "This is my mother's father," he announced. I looked at it more closely and saw that it was a mummified human head with a few wisps of hair still clinging to the edge of the scalp! "He is very wise," he continued in a matter-of-fact voice, "and I shall need his advice. Grandfather, this is your new son and his friend." Jedson bowed, and I found myself doing so. "They want our help."

He started to converse with the head in his own tongue, listening from time to time, and then answering. Once they seemed to get into an argument, but the matter must have been settled satisfactorily, for the palaver soon quieted down. After a few minutes he ceased talking and glanced around the room. His eye lit on a bracket shelf intended for an electric fan, which was quite high off the floor.

"There!" he said. "That will do nicely. Grandfather needs a high place from which to watch." He went over and placed the little head on the bracket so that it faced out into the room.

When he returned to his place in the middle of the room he dropped to all fours and commenced to cast around with his nose like a hunting dog trying to pick up a scent. He ran back and forth, snuffling and whining, exactly like a pack leader worried by mixed trails. The tail fastened to his waist stood up tensely and quivered, as if still part of a live animal. His gait and his mannerisms mimicked those of a hound so convincingly that I blinked my eyes when he sat down suddenly and announced:

"I've never seen a place more loaded with traces of magic. I can pick out Mrs. Jennings' very strongly and your own business magic. But after I eliminate them the air is still crowded. You must have had everything but a rain dance and a sabbat going on around you!"

He dropped back into his character of a dog without giving us a chance to reply, and started making his casts a little wider. Presently he appeared to come to some sort of an impasse, for he settled back, looked at the head, and whined vigorously. Then he waited.

The reply must have satisfied him; he gave a sharp bark and dragged open the bottom drawer of a file cabinet, working clumsily, as if with paws instead of hands. He dug into the back of the drawer eagerly and hauled out something which he popped into his pouch.

After that he trotted very cheerfully around the place for a short time, until he had poked his nose into every odd corner. When he had finished he returned to the middle of the floor, squatted down again, and said, "That takes care of everything here for the present. This place is the center of their attack, so grandfather has agreed to stay and watch here until I can bind a cord around your place to keep witches out."

I was a little perturbed at that. I was sure the head would scare my office girl half out of her wits if she saw it. I said so as diplomatically as possible.

"How about that?" he asked the head, then turned back to me after a moment of listening. "Grandfather says it's all right; he won't let anyone see him he has not been introduced to." It turned out that he was perfectly correct; nobody noticed it, not even the scrubwoman.

"Now then," he went on, "I want to check over my brother's place of business at the earliest opportunity, and I want to smell out both of your homes and insulate them against mischief. In the meantime, here is some advice for each of you to follow carefully: Don't let anything of yourself fall into the hands of strangers—nail parings, spittle, hair cuttings—guard it all. Destroy them by fire, or engulf them in running water. It will make our task much simpler. I am finished." He got up and strode back into the cloakroom.

Ten minutes later the dignified and scholarly Dr. Worthington was smoking a cigarette with us. I had to look up at his grandfather's head to convince myself that a jungle lord had actually been there.

Business was picking up at that time, and I had no more screwy accidents after Dr. Worthington cleaned out the place. I could see a net profit for the quarter and was beginning to feel cheerful again. I received a letter from Ditworth, dunning me about Biddle's phony claim, but I filed it in the wastebasket without giving it a thought.

One day shortly before noon Feldstein, the magicians' agent, dropped into my place. "Hi, Zack!" I said cheerfully when he walked in. "How's business?"

"Mr. Fraser, of all questions, that you should ask me that one," he said, shaking his head mournfully from side to side. "Business—it is terrible."

"Why do you say that?" I asked. "I see lots of signs of activity around—"

"Appearances are deceiving," he insisted, "especially in my business. Tell me—have you heard of a concern calling themselves 'Magic, Incorporated'?"

"That's funny," I told him. "I just did, for the first time. This just came in the mail"—and I held up an unopened letter. It had a return address on it of "Magic, Incorporated, Suite 700, Commonwealth Building."

Feldstein took it gingerly, as if he thought it might poison him, and inspected it. "That's the parties I mean," he confirmed. "The gonophs!"

"Why, what's the trouble, Zack?"

"They don't want that a man should make an honest living —Mr. Fraser," he interrupted himself anxiously, "you wouldn't quit doing business with an old friend who had always done right by you?"

"Of course not, Zack, but what's it all about?"

"Read it. Go ahead." He shoved the letter back at me.

I opened it. The paper was a fine quality, watermarked, rag bond, and the letter was chaste and dignified. I glanced over the stuffed-shirt committee and was quite agreeably impressed by the caliber of men they had as officers and directors—big men, all of them, except for a couple of names among the executives that I did not recognize.

The letter itself amounted to an advertising prospectus. It was a new idea; I suppose you could call it a holding company for magicians. They offered to provide any and all kinds of magical service. The customer could dispense with shopping around; he could call this one number, state his needs, and the company would supply the service and bill him. It seemed fair enough—no more than an incorporated agency.

I glanced on down. "—fully guaranteed service, backed by the entire assets of a responsible company—" "—surprisingly low standard fees, made possible by elimination of fee splitting with agents and by centralized administration—" "The gratifying response from the members of the great profession enables us to predict that Magic, Incorporated, will be the natural source to turn to for competent thaumaturgy in any line—probably the only source of truly first-rate magic—"

I put it down. "Why worry about it, Zack? It's just another agency. As for their claims—I've heard you say that you have all the best ones in your stable. You didn't expect to be believed, did you?"

"No," he conceded, "not quite, maybe—among us two. But this is really serious, Mr. Fraser. They've hired away most of my really first-class operators with salaries and bonuses I can't match. And now they offer magic to the public at a price that undersells those I've got left. It's ruin, I'm telling you."

It was hard lines. Feldstein was a nice little guy who grabbed the nickels the way he did for a wife and five beady-eyed kids, to whom he was devoted. But I felt he was exaggerating; he has a tendency to dramatize himself. "Don't worry," I said, "I'll stick by you, and so, I imagine, will most of your customers. This outfit can't get all the magicians together; they're too independent. Look at Ditworth. He tried with his association. What did it get him?"

"Ditworth—aagh!" He started to spit, then remembered he was in my office. "This *is* Ditworth—this company!"

"How do you figure that? He's not on the letterhead."

"I found out. You think he wasn't successful because you held out. They held a meeting of the directors of the association—that's Ditworth and his two secretaries—and voted the contracts over to the new corporation. Then Ditworth resigns and his stooge steps in as front for the nonprofit association, and Ditworth runs both companies. You will see! If we could open the books of Magic, Incorporated, you will find he has voting control. I know it!"

"It seems unlikely," I said slowly.

"You'll see! Ditworth with all his fancy talk about a no-profit service for the improvement of standards shouldn't be any place around Magic, Incorporated, should he, now? You call up and ask for him—"

I did not answer, but dialed the number on the letterhead. When a girl's voice said, "Good morning—Magic, Incorporated," I said:

"Mr. Ditworth, please."

She hesitated quite a long time, then said, "Who is calling, please?"

That made it my turn to hesitate. I did not want to talk to Ditworth; I wanted to establish a fact. I finally said, "Tell him it's Dr. Biddle's office."

Whereupon she answered readily enough, but with a trace of puzzlement in her voice, "But Mr. Ditworth is not in the suite just now; he was due in Dr. Biddle's office half an hour ago. Didn't he arrive?"

"Oh," I said, "perhaps he's with the chief and I didn't see him come in. Sorry." And I rang off.

"I guess you are right," I admitted, turning back to Feldstein.

He was too worried to be pleased about it. "Look," he said, "I want you should have lunch with me and talk about it some more."

"I was just on my way to the Chamber of Commerce luncheon. Come along and we'll talk on the way. You're a member."

"All right," he agreed dolefully. "Maybe I can't afford it much longer."

We were a little late and had to take separate seats. The treasurer stuck the kitty under my nose and "twisted her tail." He wanted a ten-cent fine from me for being late. The kitty is an ordinary frying pan with a mechanical bicycle bell mounted on the handle. We pay all fines on the spot, which is good for the treasury and a source of innocent amusement. The treasurer shoves the pan at you and rings the bell until you pay up.

I hastily produced a dime and dropped it in. Steve Harris, who has an automobile agency, yelled, "That's right! Make the Scotchman pay up!" and threw a roll at me.

"Ten cents for disorder," announced our chairman, Norman Somers, without looking up. The treasurer put the bee on Steve. I heard the coin clink into the pan, then the bell was rung again.

"What's the trouble?" asked Somers.

"More of Steve's tricks," the treasurer reported in a tired voice. "Fairy gold, this time." Steve had chucked in a synthetic coin that some friendly magician had made up for him. Naturally, when it struck cold iron it melted away.

"Two bits more for counterfeiting," decided Somers, "then handcuff him and ring up the United States attorney." Steve is quite a card, but he does not put much over on Norman.

"Can't I finish my lunch first?" asked Steve, in tones that simply dripped with fake self-pity. Norman ignored him and he paid up.

"Steve, better have fun while you can," commented Al Donahue, who runs a string of drive-in restaurants. "When you sign up with Magic, Incorporated, you will have to cut out playing tricks with magic." I sat up and listened.

"Who said I was going to sign up with them?"

"Huh? Of course you are. It's the logical thing to do. Don't be a dope."

"Why should I?"

"Why should you? Why, it's the direction of progress, man. Take my case: I put out the fanciest line of vanishing desserts of any eating place in town. You can eat three of them if you like, and not feel full and not gain an ounce. Now I've been losing money on them, but kept them for advertising because of the way they bring in the women's trade. Now Magic, Incorporated, comes along and offers me the same thing at a price I can make money with them too. Naturally, I sign up."

"You would. Suppose they raise the prices on you after they have hired, or driven out of business, every competent wizard in town?"

Donahue laughed in a superior, irritating way. "I've got a contract."

"So? How long does it run? And did you read the cancellation clause?"

I knew what he was talking about, even if Donahue didn't; I had been through it. About five years ago a Portland cement firm came into town and began buying up the little dealers and cutting prices against the rest. They ran sixty-cent cement down to thirty-five cents a sack and broke their competitors. Then they jacked it back up by easy stages until cement sold for a dollar twenty-five. The boys took a whipping before they knew what had happened to them.

We all had to shut up about then, for the guest speaker, old B. J. Timken, the big subdivider, started in. He spoke on "Co-operation and Service." Although he is not exactly a scintillating speaker, he had some very inspiring things to say about how businessmen could serve the community and help each other; I enjoyed it.

After the clapping died down, Norman Somers thanked B. J. and said, "That's all for today, gentlemen, unless there is some new business to bring before the house—"

Jedson got up. I was sitting with my back to him, and had not known he was present. "I think there is, Mr. Chairman—a very important matter. I ask the indulgence of the Chair for a few minutes of informal discussion."

Somers answered, "Certainly, Joe, if you've got something important."

"Thanks. I think it is. This is really an extension of the discussion between Al Donahue and Steve Harris earlier in the meeting. I think there has been a major change in business conditions going on in this city right under our noses and we haven't noticed it, except where it directly affected our own businesses. I refer to the trade in commercial magic. How many of you use magic in your business? Put your hands up." All the hands went up, except for a couple of lawyers'. Personally, I had always figured they were magicians themselves.

"O.K.," Jedson went on, "put them down. We knew that; we all use it. I use it for textiles. Hank Manning here uses nothing else for cleaning and pressing, and probably uses it for some of his dye jobs too. Wally Haight's Maple Shop uses it to assemble and finish fine furniture. Stan Robertson will tell you that Le Bon Marché's slick window displays are thrown together with spells, as well as two thirds of the merchandise in his store, especially in the kids' toy department. Now I want to ask you another question: In how many cases is the percentage of your cost charged to magic greater than your margin of profit? Think about it for a moment before answering." He paused, then said: "All right—put up your hands."

Nearly as many hands went up as before.

"That's the point of the whole matter. We've got to have magic to stay in business. If anyone gets a strangle hold on magic in this community, we are all at his mercy. We would have to pay any prices that are handed us, charge the prices we are told to, and take what profits we are allowed to—or go out of business!"

The chairman interrupted him. "Just a minute, Joe. Granting that what you say is true—it is, of course—do you have any reason to feel that we are confronted with any particular emergency in the matter?"

"Yes, I do have." Joe's voice was low and very serious. "Little reasons, most of them, but they add up to convince me that someone is engaged in a conspiracy in restraint of trade." Jedson ran rapidly over the history of Ditworth's attempt to organize magicians and their clients into an association, presumably to raise the standards of the profession, and how alongside the nonprofit association had suddenly appeared a capital corporation which was already in a fair way to becoming a monopoly.

"Wait a second, Joe," put in Ed Parmelee, who has a produce jobbing business. "I think that association is a fine idea. I was threatened by some rat who tried to intimidate me into letting him pick my magicians. I took it up with the association, and they took care of it; I didn't have any more trouble. I think an organization which can clamp down on racketeers is a pretty fine thing."

"You had to sign with the association to get their help, didn't you?"

"Why, yes, but that's entirely reasonable—"

"Isn't it possible that your gangster got what he wanted when you signed up?"

"Why, that seems pretty farfetched."

"I don't say," persisted Joe, "that is the explanation, but it is a distinct possibility. It would not be the first time that monopolists used goon squads with their left hands to get by coercion what their right hands could not touch. I wonder whether any of the rest of you have had similar experiences?"

It developed that several of them had. I could see them beginning to think.

One of the lawyers present formally asked a question through the chairman. "Mr. Chairman, passing for the moment from the association to Magic, Incorporated, is this corporation anything more than a union of magicians? If so, they have a legal right to organize."

Norman turned to Jedson. "Will you answer that, Joe?"

"Certainly. It is not a union at all. It is a parallel to a situation in which all the carpenters in town are employees of one contractor; you deal with that contractor or you don't build."

"Then it's a simple case of monopoly—if it is a monopoly. This state has a Little Sherman Act; you can prosecute."

"I think you will find that it is a monopoly. Have any of you noticed that there are no magicians present at today's meeting?"

We all looked around. It was perfectly true. "I think you can expect," he added, "to find magicians represented hereafter in this chamber by some executive of Magic, Incorporated. With respect to the possibility of prosecution"—he hauled a folded newspaper out of his hip pocket—"have any of you paid any attention to the governor's call for a special session of the legislature?"

Al Donahue remarked superciliously that he was too busy making a living to waste any time on the political game. It was a deliberate dig at Joe, for everybody knew that he was a committeeman, and spent quite a lot of time on civic affairs. The dig must have gotten under Joe's skin, for he said pityingly, "Al, it's a damn good thing for you that some of us are willing to spend a little time on government, or you would wake up some morning to find they had stolen the sidewalks in front of your house."

The chairman rapped for order; Joe apologized. Donahue muttered something under his breath about the whole political business being dirty, and that anyone associated with it was bound to turn crooked. I reached out for an ash tray and knocked over a glass of water, which spilled into Donahue's lap. It diverted his mind. Joe went on talking.

"Of course we knew a special session was likely for several reasons, but when they published the agenda of the call last night, I found tucked away toward the bottom an item 'Regulation of Thaumaturgy.' I couldn't believe that there was any reason to deal with such a matter in a special session unless something was up. I got on the phone last night and called a friend of mine at the capitol, a fellow committee member. She did not know anything about it, but she called me back later. Here's what she found out: The item was stuck into the agenda at the request of some of the governor's campaign backers; he has no special interest in it himself. Nobody seems to know what it is all about, but one bill on the subject has already been dropped in the hopper—" There was an interruption; somebody wanted to know what the bill said.

"I'm trying to tell you," Joe said patiently. "The bill was submitted by title alone; we won't be likely to know its contents until it is taken up in committee. But here is the title: 'A Bill to Establish Professional Standards for Thaumaturgists, Regulate the Practice of the Thaumaturgic Profession, Provide for the Appointment of a Commission to Examine, License, and Administer—' and so on. As you can see, it isn't even a proper title; it's just an omnibus onto which they can hang any sort of legislation regarding magic, including an abridgment of antimonopoly regulation if they choose."

There was a short silence after this. I think all of us were trying to make up our minds on a subject that we were not really conversant with—politics. Presently someone spoke up and said, "What do you think we ought to do about it?"

"Well," he answered, "we at least ought to have our own representative at the capitol to protect us in the clinches. Besides that, we at least ought to be prepared to submit our own bill, if this one has any tricks in it, and bargain for the best compromise we can get. We should at least get an implementing amendment out of it that would put some real teeth into the state antitrust act, at least insofar as magic is concerned." He grinned. "That's four 'at leasts,' I think."

"Why can't the state Chamber of Commerce handle it for us? They maintain a legislative bureau."

"Sure, they have a lobby, but you know perfectly well that the state chamber doesn't see eye to eye with us little businessmen. We can't depend on them; we may actually be fighting them."

There was quite a powwow after Joe sat down. Everybody had his own ideas about what to do and tried to express them all at once. It became evident that there was no general agreement, whereupon Somers adjourned the meeting with the announcement that those interested in sending a representative to the capitol should stay. A few of the diehards like Donahue left, and the rest of us reconvened with Somers again in the chair. It was suggested that Jedson should be the one to go, and he agreed to do it.

Feldstein got up and made a speech with tears in his eyes.

He wandered and did not seem to be getting anyplace, but finally he managed to get out that Jedson would need a good big war chest to do any good at the capitol, and also should be compensated for his expenses and loss of time. At that he astounded us by pulling out a roll of bills, counting out one thousand dollars, and shoving it over in front of Joe.

That display of sincerity caused him to be made finance chairman by general consent, and the subscriptions came in very nicely. I held down my natural impulses and matched Feldstein's donation, though I did wish he had not been quite so impetuous. I think Feldstein had a slight change of heart a little later, for he cautioned Joe to be economical and not to waste a lot of money buying liquor for "those schlemiels at the capitol."

Jedson shook his head at this, and said that while he intended to pay his own expenses, he would have to have a free hand in the spending of the fund, particularly with respect to entertainment. He said the time was too short to depend on sweet reasonableness and disinterested patriotism alone—that some of those lunkheads had no more opinions than a weather vane and would vote to favor the last man they had had a drink with.

Somebody made a shocked remark about bribery. "I don't intend to bribe anyone," Jedson answered with a brittle note in his voice. "If it comes to swapping bribes, we're licked to start with. I am just praying that there are still enough unpledged votes up there to make a little persuasive talking and judicious browbeating worth while."

He got his own way, but I could not help agreeing privately with Feldstein. And I made a resolution to pay a little more attention to politics thereafter; I did not even know the name of my own legislator. How did I know whether or not he was a high-caliber man or just a cheap opportunist?

And that is how Jedson, Bodie, and myself happened to find ourselves on the train, headed for the capitol.

Bodie went along because Jedson wanted a first-rate magician to play bird dog for him. He said he did not know what might turn up. I went along because I wanted to. I had never been to the capitol before, except to pass through, and was interested to see how this lawmaking business is done.

Jedson went straight to the Secretary of State's office to register as a lobbyist, while Jack and I took our baggage to the Hotel Constitution and booked some rooms. Mrs. Logan, Joe's friend the committeewoman, showed up before he got back.

Jedson had told us a great deal about Sally Logan during the train trip. He seemed to feel that she combined the shrewdness of Machiavelli with the greathearted integrity of Oliver Wendell Holmes. I was surprised at his enthusiasm, for I have often heard him grouse about women in politics.

"But you don't understand, Archie," he elaborated. "Sally isn't a woman politician, she is simply a politician, and asks no special consideration because of her sex. She can stand up and trade punches with the toughest manipulators on the Hill. What I said about women politicians is perfectly true, as a statistical generalization, but it proves nothing about any particular woman.

"It's like this: Most women in the United States have a short-sighted, peasant individualism resulting from the male-created romantic tradition of the last century. They were told that they were superior creatures, a little nearer to the angels than their men-folks. They were not encouraged to think, nor to assume social responsibility. It takes a strong mind to break out of that sort of conditioning, and most minds simply aren't up to it, male or female.

"Consequently, women as electors are usually suckers for romantic nonsense. They can be flattered into misusing their ballot even more easily than men. In politics their self-righteous feeling of virtue, combined with their essentially peasant training, resulted in their introducing a type of cut-rate, petty chiseling that should make Boss Tweed spin in his coffin.

"But Sally's not like that. She's got a tough mind which could reject the hokum."

"You're not in love with her, are you?"

"Who, me? Sally's happily married and has two of the best kids I know."

"What does her husband do?"

"Lawyer. One of the governor's supporters. Sally got started in politics through pinch-hitting for her husband one campaign."

"What is her official position up here?"

"None. Right hand for the governor. That's her strength. Sally has never held a patronage job, nor been paid for her services."

After this build-up I was anxious to meet the paragon. When she called I spoke to her over the house phone and was about to say that I would come down to the lobby when she announced that she was coming up, and hung up. I was a little startled at the informality, not yet realizing that politicians did not regard hotel rooms as bedrooms, but as business offices.

When I let her in she said, "You're Archie Fraser, aren't you? I'm Sally Logan. Where's Joe?"

"He'll be back soon. Won't you sit down and wait?"

"Thanks." She plopped herself into a chair, took off her hat and shook out her hair. I looked her over.

I had unconsciously expected something pretty formidable in the way of a mannish matron. What I saw was a young, plump, cheerful-looking blonde, with an untidy mass of yellow hair and frank blue eyes. She was entirely feminine, not over thirty at the outside, and there was something about her that was tremendously reassuring.

She made me think of county fairs and well water and sugar cookies.

"I'm afraid this is going to be a tough proposition," she began at once. "I didn't think there was much interest in the matter, and I still don't think so, but just the same someone has a solid bloc lined up for Assembly Bill Twenty-two—that's the bill I wired Joe about. What do you boys plan to do, make a straight fight to kill it or submit a substitute bill?"

"Jedson drew up a fair-practices act with the aid of some of our Half World friends and a couple of lawyers. Would you like to see it?"

"Please. I stopped by the State Printing Office and got a few copies of the bill you are against—AB Twenty-two. We'll swap."

I was trying to translate the foreign language lawyers use when they write statutes when Jedson came in. He patted Sally's cheek without speaking, and she reached up and squeezed his hand and went on with her reading. He commenced reading over my shoulder. I gave up and let him have it. It made a set of building specifications look simple.

Sally asked, "What do you think of it, Joe?"

"Worse than I expected," he replied. "Take Paragraph Seven—"

"I haven't read it yet."

"So? Well, in the first place it recognizes the association as a semipublic body like the Bar Association or the Community Chest, and permits it to initiate actions before the commission. That means that every magician had better by a damn sight belong to Ditworth's association and be careful not to offend it."

"But how can that be legal?" I asked. "It sounds unconstitutional to me—a private association like that—"

"Plenty of precedent, son. Corporations to promote world's fairs, for example. They're recognized, and even voted tax money. As for unconstitutionality, you'd have to prove that the law was not equal in application—which it isn't!—but awfully hard to prove."

"But, anyhow, a witch gets a hearing before the commission?"

"Sure, but there's the rub. The commission has very broad powers, almost unlimited powers over everything connected with magic. The bill is filled with phrases like 'reasonable and proper,' which means the sky's the limit, with nothing but the good sense and decency of the commissioners to restrain them. That's my objection to commissions in government—the law can never be equal in application under them. They have delegated legislative powers, and the law is what they say it is. You might as well face a drumhead court-martial.

"There are nine commissioners provided for in this case, six of whom must be licensed magicians, first-class. I don't suppose it is necessary to point out that a few ill-advised appointments to the original commission will turn it into a tight little self-perpetuating oligarchy—through its power to license."

Sally and Joe were going over to see a legislator who they thought might sponsor our bill, so they dropped me off at the capitol. I wanted to listen to some of the debate.

It gave me a warm feeling to climb up the big, wide steps

of the statehouse. The old, ugly mass of masonry seemed to represent something tough in the character of the American people, the determination of free men to manage their own affairs. Our own current problem seemed a little smaller, not quite so overpoweringly important—still worth working on, but simply one example in a long history of the general problem of self-government.

I noticed something else as I was approaching the great bronze doors; the contractor for the outer construction of the building must have made his pile; the mix for the mortar was not richer than one to six!

I decided on the Assembly rather than the Senate because Sally said they generally put on a livelier show. When I entered the hall they were discussing a resolution to investigate the tarring and feathering the previous month of three agricultural-worker organizers up near the town of Six Points. Sally had remarked that it was on the calendar for the day, but that it would not take long because the proponents of the resolution did not really want it. However, the Central Labor Council had passed a resolution demanding it, and the labor-supported members were stuck with it.

The reason why they could only go through the motions of asking for an investigation was that the organizers were not really human beings at all, but mandrakes, a fact that the state council had not been aware of when they asked for an investigation. Since the making of mandrakes is the blackest kind of black magic, and highly illegal, they needed some way to drop it quietly. The use of mandrakes has always been opposed by organized labor, because it displaces real men—men with families to support. For the same reasons they oppose synthetic facsimiles and homunculi. But it is well known that the unions are not above using mandrakes, or mandragoras, as well as facsimiles, when it suits their purpose, such as for pickets, pressure groups, and the like. I suppose they feel justified in fighting fire with fire. Homunculi they can't use on account of their size, since they are too small to be passed off as men.

If Sally had not primed me, I would not have understood what took place. Each of the labor members got up and demanded in forthright terms a resolution to investigate. When they were all through, someone proposed that the matter be tabled until the grand jury of the county concerned held its next meeting. This motion was voted on without debate and without a roll call; although practically no members were present except those who had spoken in favor of the original resolution, the motion passed easily.

There was the usual crop of oil-industry bills on the agenda, such as you read about in the newspapers every time the legislature is in session. One of them was the next item on the day's calendar—a bill which proposed that the governor negotiate a treaty with the gnomes, under which the gnomes would aid the petroleum engineers in prospecting and, in addition, would advise humans in drilling methods so as to maintain the natural gas pressure underground needed to raise the oil to the surface. I think that is the idea, but I am no petroleum engineer.

The proponent spoke first. "Mr. Speaker," he said, "I ask for a 'Yes' vote on this bill, AB Seventy-nine. Its purpose is quite simple and the advantages obvious. A very large part of the overhead cost of recovering crude oil from the ground lies in the uncertainties of prospecting and drilling. With the aid of the Little People this item can be reduced to an estimated seven per cent of its present dollar cost, and the price of gasoline and other petroleum products to the people can be greatly lessened.

"The matter of underground gas pressure is a little more technical, but suffice it to say that it takes, in round numbers, a thousand cubic feet of natural gas to raise one barrel of oil to the surface. If we can get intelligent supervision of drilling operations far underground, where no human being can go, we can make the most economical use of this precious gas pressure.

"The only rational objection to this bill lies in whether or not we can deal with the gnomes on favorable terms. I believe that we can, for the Administration has some excellent connections in the Half World. The gnomes are willing to negotiate in order to put a stop to the present condition of chaos in which human engineers drill blindly, sometimes wrecking their homes and not infrequently violating their sacred places. They not unreasonably claim everything under the surface as their kingdom, but are willing to make any reasonable concession to abate what is to them an intolerable nuisance.

"If this treaty works out well, as it will, we can expect to arrange other treaties which will enable us to exploit all of the metal and mineral resources of this state under conditions highly advantageous to us and not hurtful to the gnomes. Imagine, if you please, having a gnome with his X-ray eyes peer into a mountainside and locate a rich vein of gold for you!"

It seemed very reasonable, except that, having once seen the king of the gnomes, I would not trust him very far, unless Mrs. Jennings did the negotiating.

As soon as the proponent sat down, another member jumped up and just as vigorously denounced it. He was older than most of the members, and I judged him to be a country lawyer. His accent placed him in the northern part of the state, well away from the oil country. "Mr. Speaker," he bellowed, "I ask for a vote of 'No'! Who would dream that an American legislature would stoop to such degrading nonsense? Have any of you ever seen a gnome? Have you any reason to believe that gnomes exist? This is just a cheap piece of political chicanery to do the public out of its proper share of the natural resources of our great state—"

He was interrupted by a question. "Does the honorable member from Lincoln County mean to imply that he has no belief in magic? Perhaps he does not believe in the radio or the telephone either."

"Not at all. If the Chair will permit, I will state my position so clearly that even my respected colleague on the other side of the house will understand it. There are certain remarkable developments in human knowledge in general use which are commonly referred to by the laity as magic. These principles are well understood and are taught, I am happy to say, in our great publicly owned institutions for higher learning. I have every respect for the legitimate practitioners thereof. But, as I understand it, although I am not myself a practitioner of the great science, there is nothing in it that requires a belief in the Little People.

"But let us stipulate, for the sake of argument, that the Little People do exist. Is that any reason to pay them blackmail?

Should the citizens of this commonwealth pay cumshaw to the denizens of the underworld——" He waited for his pun to be appreciated. It wasn't. "—for that which is legally and rightfully ours? If this ridiculous principle is pushed to its logical conclusion, the farmers and dairymen I am proud to number among my constituents will be required to pay toll to the elves before they can milk their cows!"

Someone slid into the seat beside me. I glanced around, saw that it was Jedson, and questioned him with my eyes. "Nothing doing now," he whispered. "We've got some time to kill and might as well do it here"—and he turned to the debate.

Somebody had gotten up to reply to the old duck with the Daniel Webster complex. "Mr. Speaker, if the honored member is quite through with his speech—I did not quite catch what office he is running for!—I would like to invite the attention of this body to the precedented standing in jurisprudence of elements of every nature, not only in Mosaic law, Roman law, the English common law, but also in the appellate court of our neighboring state to the south. I am confident that anyone possessing even an elementary knowledge of the law will recognize the case I have in mind without citation, but for the benefit of—"

"Mr. Speaker! I move to amend by striking out the last word."

"A stratagem to gain the floor," Joe whispered.

"Is it the purpose of the honorable member who preceded me to imply—"

It went on and on. I turned to Jedson and asked, "I can't figure out this chap who is speaking; awhile ago he was hollering about cows. What's he afraid of, religious prejudices?"

"Partly that; he's from a very conservative district. But he's lined up with the independent oilmen. They don't want the state setting the terms; they think they can do better dealing with the gnomes directly."

"But what interest has he got in oil? There's no oil in his district."

"No, but there is outdoor advertising. The same holding company that controls the so-called independent oilmen holds a voting trust in the Countryside Advertising Corporation. And that can be awfully important to him around election time."

The Speaker looked our way, and an assistant sergeant at arms threaded his way toward us. We shut up. Someone moved the order of the day, and the oil bill was put aside for one of the magic bills that had already come out of committee. This was a bill to outlaw every sort of magic, witchcraft, thaumaturgy.

No one spoke for it but the proponent, who launched into a diatribe that was more scholarly than logical. He quoted extensively from Blackstone's *Commentaries* and the records of the Massachusetts trials, and finished up with his head thrown back, one finger waving wildly to heaven and shouting, " 'Thou shalt not suffer a witch to live!' "

No one bothered to speak against it; it was voted on immediately without roll call, and, to my complete bewilderment, passed without a single nay! I turned to Jedson and found him smiling at the expression on my face.

"It doesn't mean a thing, Archie," he said quietly.

"Huh?"

"He's a party wheel horse who had to introduce that bill to please a certain bloc of his constituents."

"You mean he doesn't believe in the bill himself?"

"Oh no, he believes in it all right, but he also knows it is hopeless. It has evidently been agreed to let him pass it over here in the Assembly this session so that he would have something to take home to his people. Now it will go to the senate committee and die there; nobody will ever hear of it again."

I guess my voice carries too well, for my reply got us a really dirty look from the Speaker. We got up hastily and left.

Once outside I asked Joe what had happened that he was back so soon. "He would not touch it," he told me. "Said that he couldn't afford to antagonize the association."

"Does that finish us?"

"Not at all. Sally and I are going to see another member right after lunch. He's tied up in a committee meeting at the moment."

We stopped in a restaurant where Jedson had arranged to meet Sally Logan. Jedson ordered lunch, and I had a couple of cans of devitalized beer, insisting on their bringing it to the booth in the unopened containers. I don't like to get even a little bit tipsy, although I like to drink. On another occasion I had paid for wizard-processed liquor and had received intoxicating liquor instead. Hence the unopened containers.

I sat there, staring into my glass and thinking about what I had heard that morning, especially about the bill to outlaw all magic. The more I thought about it the better the notion seemed. The country had gotten along all right in the old days before magic had become popular and commercially widespread. It was unquestionably a headache in many ways, even leaving out our present troubles with racketeers and monopolists. Finally I expressed my opinion to Jedson.

But he disagreed. According to him prohibition never does work in any field. He said that anything which can be supplied and which people want will be supplied—law or no law. To prohibit magic would simply be to turn over the field to the crooks and the black magicians.

"I see the drawbacks of magic as well as you do," he went on, "but it is like firearms. Certainly guns made it possible for almost anyone to commit murder and get away with it. But once they were invented the damage was done. All you can do is to try to cope with it. Things like the Sullivan Act—they don't keep the crooks from carrying guns and using them; they simply took guns out of the hands of honest people.

"It's the same with magic. If you prohibit it, you take from decent people the enormous boons to be derived from a knowledge of the great arcane laws, while the nasty, harmful secrets hidden away in black grimoires and red grimoires will still be bootlegged to anyone who will pay the price and has no respect for law.

"Personally, I don't believe there was any less black magic practiced between, say, 1750 and 1950 than there is now, or was before then. Take a look at Pennsylvania and the hex country. Take a look at the Deep South. But since that time we have begun to have the advantages of white magic too."

Sally came in, spotted us, and slid into one side of the booth. "My," she said with a sigh of relaxation, "I've just fought my way across the lobby of the Constitution. The 'third house' is certainly out in full force this trip. I've never seen 'em so thick, especially the women."

"Third house?" I said.

"She means lobbyists, Archie," Jedson explained. "Yes, I

noticed them. I'd like to make a small bet that two thirds of them are synthetic."

"I *thought* I didn't recognize many of them," Sally commented. "Are you sure, Joe?"

"Not entirely. But Bodie agrees with me. He says that the women are almost all mandrakes, or androids of some sort. Real women are never quite so perfectly beautiful—nor so tractable. I've got him checking on them now."

"In what way?"

"He says he can spot the work of most of the magicians capable of that high-powered stuff. If possible we want to prove that all these androids were made by Magic, Incorporated—though I'm not sure just what use we can make of the fact.

"Bodie has even located some zombies," he added.

"Not really!" exclaimed Sally. She wrinkled her nose and looked disgusted. "Some people have odd tastes."

They started discussing aspects of politics that I know nothing about, while Sally put away a very sizable lunch topped off by a fudge ice-cream cake slice. But I noticed that she ordered from the left-hand side of the menu—all vanishing items, like the alcohol in my beer.

I found out more about the situation as they talked. When a bill is submitted to the legislature, it is first referred to a committee for hearings. Ditworth's bill, AB Twenty-two, had been referred to the Committee on Professional Standards. Over in the Senate an identical bill had turned up and had been referred by the lieutenant governor, who presides in the Senate, to the Committee on Industrial Practices.

Our immediate object was to find a sponsor for our bill; if possible, one for each house, and preferably sponsors who were members, in their respective houses, of the committees concerned. All of this needed to be done before Ditworth's bills came up for hearing.

I went with them to see their second-choice sponsor for the Assembly. He was not on the Professional Standards Committee, but he was on the Ways and Means Committee, which meant that he carried a lot of weight in any committee.

He was a pleasant chap named Spence—Luther B. Spence—and I could see that he was quite anxious to please Sally—for past favors, I suppose. But they had no more luck with him than with their first-choice man. He said that he did not have time to fight for our bill, as the chairman of the Ways and Means Committee was sick and he was chairman pro tem.

Sally put it to him flatly. "Look here, Luther, when you have needed a hand in the past, you've gotten it from me. I hate to remind a man of obligations, but you will recall that matter of the vacancy last year on the Fish and Game Commission. Now I want action on this matter, and not excuses!"

Spence was plainly embarrassed. "Now, Sally, please don't feel like that. You're getting your feathers up over nothing. You know I'll always do anything I can for you, but you don't really need this, and it would necessitate my neglecting things that I can't afford to neglect."

"What do you mean, I don't need it?"

"I mean you should not worry about AB Twenty-two. It's a cinch bill."

Jedson explained that term to me later. A cinch bill, he said, was a bill introduced for tactical reasons. The sponsors never intended to try to get it enacted into law, but simply used it as a bargaining point. It's like an "asking price" in a business deal.

"Are you sure of that?"

"Why, yes, I think so. The word has been passed around that there is another bill coming up that won't have the bugs in it that this bill has."

After we left Spence's office, Jedson said, "Sally, I hope Spence is right, but I don't trust Ditworth's intentions. He's out to get a strangle hold on the industry. I know it!"

"Luther usually has the correct information, Joe."

"Yes, that is no doubt true, but this is a little out of his line. Anyhow, thanks, kid. You did your best."

"Call on me if there is anything else, Joe. And come out to dinner before you go; you haven't seen Bill or the kids yet."

"I won't forget."

Jedson finally gave up as impractical trying to submit our bill, and concentrated on the committees handling Ditworth's bills. I did not see much of him. He would go out at four in the afternoon to a cocktail party and get back to the hotel at three in the morning, bleary-eyed, with progress to report.

He woke me up the fourth night and announced jubilantly, "It's in the bag, Archie!"

"You killed those bills?"

"Not quite. I couldn't manage that. But they will be reported out of committee so amended that we won't care if they do pass. Furthermore, the amendments are different in each committee."

"Well, what of that?"

"That means that even if they do pass their respective houses they will have to go to conference committee to have their differences ironed out, then back for final passage in each house. The chances of that this late in a short session are negligible. Those bills are dead."

Jedson's predictions were justified. The bills came out of committee with a "do pass" recommendation late Saturday evening. That was the actual time; the statehouse clock had been stopped forty-eight hours before to permit first and second readings of an administration "must" bill. Therefore it was officially Thursday. I know that sounds cockeyed, and it is, but I am told that every legislature in the country does it toward the end of a crowded session.

The important point is that, Thursday or Saturday, the session would adjourn sometime that night. I watched Ditworth's bill come up in the Assembly. It was passed, without debate, in the amended form. I sighed with relief. About midnight Jedson joined me and reported that the same thing had happened in the Senate. Sally was on watch in the conference committee room, just to make sure that the bills stayed dead.

Joe and I remained on watch in our respective houses. There was probably no need for it, but it made us feel easier. Shortly before two in the morning Bodie came in and said we were to meet Jedson and Sally outside the conference committee room.

"What's that?" I said, immediately all nerves. "Has something slipped?"

"No, it's all right and it's all over. Come on."

Joe answered my question, as I hurried up with Bodie trailing, before I could ask it. "It's O.K., Archie. Sally was present when the committee adjourned *sine die,* without acting on those bills. It's all over; we've won!"

We went over to the bar across the street to have a drink in celebration.

In spite of the late hour the bar was moderately crowded.

Lobbyists, local politicians, legislative attachés, all the swarm of camp followers who throng the capitol whenever the legislature is sitting—all such were still up and around, and many of them had picked this bar as a convenient place to wait for news of adjournment.

We were lucky to find a stool at the bar for Sally. We three men made a tight little cluster around her and tried to get the attention of the overworked bartender. We had just managed to place our orders when a young man tapped on the shoulder the customer on the stool to the right of Sally. He immediately got down and left. I nudged Bodie to tell him to take the seat.

Sally turned to Joe. "Well, it won't be long now. There go the sergeants at arms." She nodded toward the young man, who was repeating the process farther down the line.

"What does that mean?" I asked Joe.

"It means they are getting along toward the final vote on the bill they were waiting on. They've gone to 'call of the house' now, and the Speaker has ordered the sergeant at arms to send his deputies out to arrest absent members."

"Arrest them?" I was a little bit shocked.

"Only technically. You see, the Assembly has had to stall until the Senate was through with this bill, and most of the members have wandered out for a bite to eat, or a drink. Now they are ready to vote, so they round them up."

A fat man took a stool near us which had just been vacated by a member. Sally said, "Hello, Don."

He took a cigar from his mouth and said, "How are yuh, Sally? What's new? Say, I thought you were interested in that bill on magic?"

We were all four alert at once. "I am," Sally admitted. "What about it?"

"Well, then, you had better get over there. They're voting on it right away. Didn't you notice the 'call of the house'?"

I think we set a new record getting across the street, with Sally leading the field in spite of her plumpness. I was asking Jedson how it could be possible, and he shut me up with, "I don't know, man! We'll have to see."

We managed to find seats on the main floor back of the rail. Sally beckoned to one of the pages she knew and sent him up to the clerk's desk for a copy of the bill that was pending. In front of the rail the Assemblymen gathered in groups. There was a crowd around the desk of the administration floor leader and a smaller cluster around the floor leader of the opposition. The whips had individual members buttonholed here and there, arguing with them in tense whispers.

The page came back with the copy of the bill. It was an appropriation bill for the Middle Counties Improvement Project —the last of the "must" bills for which the session had been called—but pasted to it, as a rider, *was Ditworth's bill in its original, most damnable form!*

It had been added as an amendment in the Senate, probably as a concession to Ditworth's stooges in order to obtain their votes to make up the two-thirds majority necessary to pass the appropriation bill to which it had been grafted.

The vote came almost at once. It was evident, early in the roll call, that the floor leader had his majority in hand and that the bill would pass. When the clerk announced its passage, a motion to adjourn *sine die* was offered by the opposition floor leader and it was carried unanimously. The Speaker called the two floor leaders to his desk and instructed them to wait on the governor and the presiding officer of the Senate with notice of adjournment.

The crack of his gavel released us from stunned immobility. We shambled out.

We got in to see the governor late the next morning. The appointment, squeezed into an overcrowded calendar, was simply a concession to Sally and another evidence of the high regard in which she was held around the capitol. For it was evident that he did not want to see us and did not have time to see us.

But he greeted Sally affectionately and listened patiently while Jedson explained in a few words why we thought the combined Ditworth-Middle Counties bill should be vetoed.

The circumstances were not favorable to reasoned exposition. The governor was interrupted by two calls that he had to take, one from his director of finance and one from Washington. His personal secretary came in once and shoved a memorandum under his eyes, at which the old man looked worried, then scrawled something on it and handed it back. I could tell that his attention was elsewhere for some minutes after that.

When Jedson stopped talking, the governor sat for a moment, looking down at his blotter pad, an expression of deep-rooted weariness on his face. Then he answered in slow words, "No, Mr. Jedson, I can't see it. I regret as much as you do that this business of the regulation of magic has been tied in with an entirely different matter. But I cannot veto part of a bill and sign the rest—even though the bill includes two widely separated subjects.

"I appreciate the work you did to help elect my administration"—I could see Sally's hand in that remark—"and wish that we could agree in this. But the Middle Counties Project is something that I have worked toward since my inauguration. I hope and believe that it will be the means whereby the most depressed area in our state can work out its economic problems without further grants of public money. If I thought that the amendment concerning magic would actually do a grave harm to the state—"

He paused for a moment. "But I don't. When Mrs. Logan called me this morning I had my legislative counsel analyze the bill. I agree that the bill is unnecessary, but it seems to do nothing more than add a little more bureaucratic red tape. That's not good, but we manage to do business under a lot of it; a little more can't wreck things."

I butted in—rudely, I suppose—but I was all worked up. "But, Your Excellency, if you would just take time to examine this matter yourself, in detail, you would see how much damage it will do!"

I would not have been surprised if he had flared back at me. Instead, he indicated a file basket that was stacked high and spilling over. "Mr. Fraser, there you see fifty-seven bills passed by this session of the legislature. Every one of them has some defect. Every one of them is of vital importance to some, or all, of the people of this state. Some of them are as long to read as an ordinary novel. In the next nine days I must decide what ones shall become law and what ones must wait for revision at the next regular session. During that nine days at least a thousand people will want me to see them about some one of those bills—"

His aide stuck his head in the door. "Twelve-twenty, chief! You're on the air in forty minutes."

The governor nodded absently and stood up. "You will excuse me? I'm expected at a luncheon." He turned to his aide, who was getting out his hat and gloves from a closet. "You have the speech, Jim?"

"Of course, sir."

"Just a minute!" Sally had cut in. "Have you taken your tonic?"

"Not yet."

"You're not going off to one of those luncheons without it!" She ducked into his private washroom and came out with a medicine bottle. Joe and I bowed out as quickly as possible.

Outside I started fuming to Jedson about the way we had been given the run-around, as I saw it. I made some remark about dunderheaded, compromising politicians when Joe cut me short.

"Shut up, Archie! Try running a state sometime instead of a small business and see how easy you find it!"

I shut up.

Bodie was waiting for us in the lobby of the capitol. I could see that he was excited about something, for he flipped away a cigarette and rushed toward us. "Look!" he commanded. "Down there!"

We followed the direction of his finger and saw two figures just going out the big doors. One was Ditworth, the other was a well-known lobbyist with whom he had worked. "What about it?" Joe demanded.

"I was standing here behind this phone booth, leaning against the wall and catching a cigarette. As you can see, from here that big mirror reflects the bottom of the rotunda stairs. I kept an eye on it for you fellows. I noticed this lobbyist, Sims, coming downstairs by himself, but he was gesturing as if he were talking to somebody. That made me curious, so I looked around the corner of the booth and saw him directly. He was not alone; he was with Ditworth. I looked back at the mirror and he appeared to be alone. *Ditworth cast no reflection in the mirror!*"

Jedson snapped his fingers. "A demon!" he said in an amazed voice. "And I never suspected it!"

I am surprised that more suicides don't occur on trains. When a man is down, I know of nothing more depressing than staring at the monotonous scenery and listening to the maddening *lickety-tock* of the rails. In a way I was glad to have this new development of Ditworth's inhuman status to think about; it kept my mind off poor old Feldstein and his thousand dollars.

Startling as it was to discover that Ditworth was a demon, it made no real change in the situation except to explain the efficiency and speed with which we had been outmaneuvered and to confirm as a certainty our belief that the racketeers and Magic, Incorporated, were two heads of the same beast. But we had no way of proving that Ditworth was a Half World monster. If we tried to haul him into court for a test, he was quite capable of lying low and sending out a facsimile, or a mandrake, built to look like him and immune to the mirror test.

We dreaded going back and reporting our failure to the committee—at least I did. But at least we were spared that. The Middle Counties Act carried an emergency clause which put it into effect the day it was signed. Ditworth's bill, as an amendment, went into action with the same speed. The newspapers on sale at the station when we got off the train carried the names of the new commissioners for thaumaturgy.

Nor did the commission waste any time in making its power felt. They announced their intention of raising the standards of magical practice in all fields, and stated that new and more thorough examinations would be prepared at once. The association formerly headed by Ditworth opened a coaching school in which practicing magicians could take a refresher course in thaumaturgic principles and arcane law. In accordance with the high principles set forth in their charter, the school was not restricted to members of the association.

That sounds bighearted of the association. It wasn't. They managed to convey a strong impression in their classes that membership in the association would be a big help in passing the new examinations. Nothing you could put your finger on to take into court—just a continuous impression. The association grew.

A couple of weeks later all licenses were canceled and magicians were put on a day-to-day basis in their practice, subject to call for re-examination at a day's notice. A few of the outstanding holdouts against signing up with Magic, Incorporated, were called up, examined, and licenses refused them. The squeeze was on. Mrs. Jennings quietly withdrew from any practice. Bodie came around to see me; I had an uncompleted contract with him involving some apartment houses.

"Here's your contract, Archie," he said bitterly. "I'll need some time to pay the penalties for noncompletion; my bond was revoked when they canceled the licenses."

I took the contract and tore it in two. "Forget that talk about penalties," I told him. "You take your examinations and we'll write a new contract."

He laughed unhappily. "Don't be a Pollyanna."

I changed my tack. "What are you going to do? Sign up with Magic, Incorporated?"

He straightened himself up. "I've never temporized with demons; I won't start now."

"Good boy," I said. "Well, if the eating gets uncertain, I reckon we can find a job of some sort here for you."

It was a good thing that Bodie had some money saved, for I was a little too optimistic in my offer. Magic, Incorporated, moved quickly into the second phase of their squeeze, and it began to be a matter of speculation as to whether I myself would eat regularly. There were still quite a number of licensed magicians in town who were not employed by Magic, Incorporated—it would have been an evident, actionable frame-up to freeze out everyone—but those available were all incompetent bunglers, not fit to mix a philter. There was no competent, legal magical assistance to be gotten at any price—except through Magic, Incorporated.

I was forced to fall back on old-fashioned methods in every respect. Since I don't use much magic in any case, it was possible for me to do that, but it was the difference between making money and losing money.

I had put Feldstein on as a salesman after his agency folded up under him. He turned out to be a crackajack and helped to reduce the losses. He could smell a profit even farther than I could—farther than Dr. Worthington could smell a witch.

But most of the other businessmen around me were simply forced to capitulate. Most of them used magic in at least one phase of their business; they had their choice of signing a contract with Magic, Incorporated, or closing their doors. They had wives and kids—they signed.

The fees for thaumaturgy were jacked up until they were all the traffic would bear, to the point where it was just cheaper to do business with magic than without it. The magicians got none of the new profits; it all stayed with the corporation. As a matter of fact, the magicians got less of the proceeds than when they had operated independently, but they took what they could get and were glad of the chance to feed their families.

Jedson was hard hit—disastrously hit. He held out, naturally, preferring honorable bankruptcy to dealing with demons, but he used magic throughout his business. He was through. They started by disqualifying August Welker, his foreman, then cut off the rest of his resources. It was intimated that Magic, Incorporated, did not care to deal with him, even had he wished it.

We were all over at Mrs. Jennings's late one afternoon for tea—myself, Jedson, Bodie, and Dr. Royce Worthington, the witch smeller. We tried to keep the conversation away from our troubles, but we just could not do it. Anything that was said led back somehow to Ditworth and his damnable monopoly.

After Jack Bodie had spent ten minutes explaining carefully and mendaciously that he really did not mind being out of witchcraft, that he did not have any real talent for it, and had only taken it up to please his old man, I tried to change the subject. Mrs. Jennings had been listening to Jack with such pity and compassion in her eyes that I wanted to bawl myself.

I turned to Jedson and said inanely, "How is Miss Megeath?"

She was the white witch from Jersey City, the one who did creative magic in textiles. I had no special interest in her welfare.

He looked up with a start. "Ellen? She's—she's all right. They took her license away a month ago," he finished lamely.

That was not the direction I wanted the talk to go. I turned it again. "Did she ever manage to do that whole-garment stunt?"

He brightened a little. "Why, yes, she did—once. Didn't I

tell you about it?" Mrs. Jennings showed polite curiosity, for which I silently thanked her. Jedson explained to the others what they had been trying to accomplish. "She really succeeded too well," he continued. "Once she had started, she kept right on, and we could not bring her out of her trance. She turned out over thirty thousand little striped sports dresses, all the same size and pattern. My lofts were loaded with them. Nine tenths of them will melt away before I dispose of them.

"But she won't try it again," he added. "Too hard on her health."

"How?" I inquired.

"Well, she lost ten pounds doing that one stunt. She's not hardy enough for magic. What she really needs is to go out to Arizona and lie around in the sun for a year. I wish to the Lord I had the money. I'd send her."

I cocked an eyebrow at him. "Getting interested, Joe?" Jedson is an inveterate bachelor, but it pleases me to pretend otherwise. He generally plays up, but this time he was downright surly. It showed the abnormal state of nerves he was in.

"Oh, for cripes' sake, Archie! Excuse me, Mrs. Jennings! But can't I take a normal humane interest in a person without you seeing an ulterior motive in it?"

"Sorry."

"That's all right." He grinned. "I shouldn't be so touchy. Anyhow, Ellen and I have cooked up an invention between us that might be a solution for all of us. I'd been intending to show it to all of you just as soon as we had a working model. Look, folks!" He drew what appeared to be a fountain pen out of a vest pocket and handed it to me.

"What is it? A pen?"

"No."

"A fever thermometer?"

"No. Open it up."

I unscrewed the cap and found that it contained a miniature parasol. It opened and closed like a real umbrella, and was about three inches across when opened. It reminded me of one of those clever little Japanese favors one sometimes gets at parties, except that it seemed to be made of oiled silk and metal instead of tissue paper and bamboo.

"Pretty," I said, "and very clever. What's it good for?"

"Dip it in water."

I looked around for some. Mrs. Jennings poured some into an empty cup, and I dipped it in.

It seemed to crawl in my hands.

In less than thirty seconds I was holding a full-sized umbrella in my hands and looking as silly as I felt. Bodie smacked a palm with a fist.

"It's a lulu, Joe! I wonder why somebody didn't think of it before."

Jedson accepted congratulations with a fatuous grin, then added, "That's not all—look." He pulled a small envelope out of a pocket and produced a tiny transparent raincoat, suitable for a six-inch doll. "This is the same gag. And this." He hauled out a pair of rubber overshoes less than an inch long. "A man could wear these as a watch fob, or a woman could carry them on a charm bracelet. Then, with either the umbrella or the raincoat, one need never be caught in the rain. The minute the rain hits them, presto!—full size. When they dry out they shrink up."

We passed them around from hand to hand and admired them. Joe went on. "Here's what I have in mind. This business needs a magician—that's you, Jack—and a merchandiser—that's you, Archie. It has two major stockholders: that's Ellen and me. She can go take the rest cure she needs, and I'll retire and resume my studies, same as I always wanted to."

My mind immediately started turning over the commercial possibilities, then I suddenly saw the hitch. "Wait a minute, Joe. We can't set up business in this state."

"No."

"It will take some capital to move out of the state. How are you fixed? Frankly, I don't believe I could raise a thousand dollars if I liquidated."

He made a wry face. "Compared with me you are rich."

I got up and began wandering nervously around the room. We would just have to raise the money somehow. It was too good a thing to be missed, and would rehabilitate all of us. It was clearly patentable, and I could see commercial possibilities that would never occur to Joe. Tents for camping, canoes, swimming suits, traveling gear of every sort. We had a gold mine.

Mrs. Jennings interrupted in her sweet and gentle voice. "I

am not sure it will be too easy to find a state in which to operate."

"Excuse me, what did you say?"

"Dr. Royce and I have been making some inquiries. I am afraid you will find the rest of the country about as well sewed up as this state."

"What? Fifty states?"

"Demons don't have the same limitations in time that we have."

That brought me up short. Ditworth again.

Gloom settled down on us like fog. We discussed it from every angle and came right back to where we had started. It was no help to have a clever, new business; Ditworth had us shut out of every business. There was an awkward silence.

I finally broke it with an outburst that surprised myself. "Look here!" I exclaimed. "This situation is intolerable. Let's quit kidding ourselves and admit it. As long as Ditworth is in control we're whipped. Why don't we do something?"

Jedson gave me a pained smile. "God knows I'd like to, Archie, if I could think of anything useful to do."

"But we know who our enemy is—Ditworth! Let's tackle him—legal or not, fair means or dirty!"

"But that is just the point. Do we know our enemy? To be sure, we know he is a demon, but what demon, and where? Nobody has seen him in weeks."

"Huh? But I thought just the other day—"

"Just a dummy, a hollow shell. The real Ditworth is somewhere out of sight."

"But, look, if he is a demon, can't he be invoked, and compelled—"

Mrs. Jennings answered this time. "Perhaps—though it's uncertain and dangerous. But we lack one essential—his name. To invoke a demon you must know his real name, otherwise he will not obey you, no matter how powerful the incantation. I have been searching the Half World for weeks, but I have not learned that necessary name."

Dr. Worthington cleared his throat with a rumble as deep as a cement mixer, and volunteered, "My abilities are at your disposal, if I can help to abate this nuisance—"

Mrs. Jennings thanked him. "I don't see how we can use you as yet, Doctor. I knew we could depend on you."

Jedson said suddenly, "White prevails over black."

She answered, "Certainly."

"Everywhere?"

"Everywhere, since darkness is the absence of light."

He went on, "It is not good for the white to wait on the black."

"It is not good."

"With my brother Royce to help, we might carry light into darkness."

She considered this. "It is possible, yes. But very dangerous."

"You have been there?"

"On occasion. But you are not I, nor are these others."

Everyone seemed to be following the thread of the conversation but me. I interrupted with, "Just a minute, please. Would it be too much to explain what you are talking about?"

"There was no rudeness intended, Archibald," said Mrs. Jennings in a voice that made it all right. "Joseph has suggested that, since we are stalemated here, we make a sortie into the Half World, smell out this demon, and attack him on his home ground."

It took me a moment to grasp the simple audacity of the scheme. Then I said, "Fine! Let's get on with it. When do we start?"

They lapsed back into a professional discussion that I was unable to follow. Mrs. Jennings dragged out several musty volumes and looked up references on points that were sheer Sanskrit to me. Jedson borrowed her almanac, and he and the doctor stepped out into the back yard to observe the moon.

Finally it settled down into an argument—or rather discussion; there could be no argument, as they all deferred to Mrs. Jennings's judgment concerning liaison. There seemed to be no satisfactory way to maintain contact with the real world, and Mrs. Jennings was unwilling to start until it was worked out. The difficulty was this: not being black magicians, not having signed a compact with Old Nick, they were not citizens of the Dark Kingdom and could not travel through it with certain impunity.

Bodie turned to Jedson. "How about Ellen Megeath?" he inquired doubtfully.

"Ellen? Why, yes, of course. She would do it. I'll telephone her. Mrs. Jennings, do any of your neighbors have a phone?"

"Never mind," Bodie told him, "just think about her for a few minutes so that I can get a line—" He stared at Jedson's face for a moment, then disappeared suddenly.

Perhaps three minutes later Ellen Megeath dropped lightly out of nothing. "Mr. Bodie will be along in a few minutes," she said. "He stopped to buy a pack of cigarettes." Jedson took her over and presented her to Mrs. Jennings. She did look sickly, and I could understand Jedson's concern. Every few minutes she would swallow and choke a little, as if bothered by an enlarged thyroid.

As soon as Jack was back they got right down to details. He had explained to Ellen what they planned to do, and she was entirely willing. She insisted that one more session of magic would do her no harm. There was no advantage in waiting; they prepared to depart at once. Mrs. Jennings related the marching orders. "Ellen, you will need to follow me in trance, keeping in close rapport. I think you will find that couch near the fireplace a good place to rest your body. Jack, you will remain here and guard the portal." The chimney of Mrs. Jennings's living room fireplace was to be used as most convenient. "You will keep in touch with us through Ellen."

"But, Granny, I'll be needed in the Half—"

"No, Jack." She was gently firm. "You are needed here much more. Someone has to guard the way and help us back, you know. Each to his task."

He muttered a bit, but gave in. She went on, "I think that is all. Ellen and Jack here; Joseph, Royce, and myself to make the trip. You will have nothing to do but wait, Archibald, but we won't be longer than ten minutes, world time, if we are to come back." She bustled away toward the kitchen, saying something about the unguent and calling back to Jack to have the candles ready. I hurried after her.

"What do you mean," I demanded, "about me having nothing to do but wait? I'm going along!"

She turned and looked at me before replying, troubled concern in her magnificent eyes. "I don't see how that can be, Archibald."

Jedson had followed us and now took me by the arm. "See here, Archie, do be sensible. It's utterly out of the question. You're not a magician."

I pulled away from him. "Neither are you."

"Not in a technical sense, perhaps, but I know enough to be useful. Don't be a stubborn fool, man; if you come, you'll simply handicap us."

That kind of an argument is hard to answer and manifestly unfair. "How?" I persisted.

"Hell's bells, Archie, you're young and strong and willing, and there is no one I would rather have at my back in a roughhouse, but this is not a job for courage, or even intelligence alone. It calls for special knowledge and experience."

"Well," I answered, "Mrs. Jennings has enough of that for a regiment. But—if you'll pardon me, Mrs. Jennings!—she is old and feeble. I'll be her muscles if her strength fails."

Joe looked faintly amused, and I could have kicked him. "But that is not what is required in—"

Dr. Worthington's double-bass rumble interrupted him from somewhere behind us. "It occurs to me, brother, that there may possibly be a use for our young friend's impetuous ignorance. There are times when wisdom is too cautious."

Mrs. Jennings put a stop to it. "Wait—all of you," she commanded, and trotted over to a kitchen cupboard. This she opened, moved aside a package of rolled oats, and took down a small leather sack. It was filled with slender sticks.

She cast them on the floor, and the three of them huddled around the litter, studying the patterns. "Cast them again," Joe insisted. She did so.

I saw Mrs. Jennings and the doctor nod solemn agreement to each other. Jedson shrugged and turned away. Mrs. Jennings addressed me, concern in her eyes. "You will go," she said softly. "It is not safe, but you will go."

We wasted no more time. The unguent was heated and we took turns rubbing it on each other's backbone. Bodie, as gatekeeper, sat in the midst of his pentacles, mekagrans, and runes, and intoned monotonously from the great book. Worthington elected to go in his proper person, ebony in a breechcloth, parasymbols scribed on him from head to toe, his grandfather's head cradled in an elbow.

There was some discussion before they could decide on a final form for Joe, and the metamorphosis was checked and changed several times. He finished up with paper-thin gray flesh stretched over an obscenely distorted skull, a sloping back, the thin flanks of an animal, and a long, bony tail, which he twitched incessantly. But the whole composition was near enough to human to create a revulsion much greater than would be the case for a more outlandish shape. I gagged at the sight of him, but he was pleased. "There!" he exclaimed in a voice like scratched tin. "You've done a beautiful job, Mrs. Jennings. Asmodeus would not know me from his own nephew."

"I trust not," she said. "Shall we go?"

"How about Archie?"

"It suits me to leave him as he is."

"Then how about your own transformation?"

"I'll take care of that," she answered, somewhat tartly. "Take your places."

Mrs. Jennings and I rode double on the same broom, with me in front, facing the candle stuck in the straws. I've noticed All Hallow's Eve decorations which show the broom with the handle forward and the brush trailing. That is a mistake. Custom is important in these matters. Royce and Joe were to follow close behind us. Seraphin leaped quickly to his mistress' shoulder and settled himself, his whiskers quivering with eagerness.

Bodie pronounced the word, our candle flared up high, and we were off. I was frightened nearly to panic, but tried not to show it as I clung to the broom. The fireplace gaped at us, and swelled to a monster arch. The fire within roared up like a burning forest and swept us along with it. As we swirled up I caught a glimpse of a salamander dancing among the flames, and felt sure that it was my own—the one that had honored me with its approval and sometimes graced my new fireplace. It seemed a good omen.

We had left the portal far behind—if the word "behind" can be used in a place where directions are symbolic—the shrieking din of the fire was no longer with us, and I was beginning to regain some part of my nerve. I felt a reassuring hand at my waist, and turned my head to speak to Mrs. Jennings.

I nearly fell off the broom.

When we left the house there had mounted behind me an old, old woman, a shrunken, wizened body kept alive by an indomitable spirit. She whom I now saw was a young woman, strong, perfect, and vibrantly beautiful. There is no way to describe her; she was without defect of any sort, and imagination could suggest no improvement.

Have you ever seen the bronze Diana of the Woods? She was something like that, except that metal cannot catch the live, dynamic beauty that I saw.

But it was the same woman!

Mrs. Jennings—Amanda Todd, that was—at perhaps her twenty-fifth year, when she had reached the full maturity of her gorgeous womanhood, and before time had softened the focus of perfection.

I forgot to be afraid. I forgot everything except that I was in the presence of the most compelling and dynamic female I had ever known. I forgot that she was at least sixty years older than myself, and that her present form was simply a triumph of sorcery. I suppose if anyone had asked me at that time if I were in love with Amanda Jennings, I would have answered, "Yes!" But at the time my thoughts were much too confused to be explicit. She was there, and that was sufficient.

She smiled, and her eyes were warm with understanding. She spoke, and her voice was the voice I knew, even though it was rich contralto in place of the accustomed clear, thin soprano. "Is everything all right, Archie?"

"Yes," I answered in a shaky voice. "Yes, Amanda, everything is all right!"

As for the Half World . . . How can I describe a place that has no single matching criterion with what I have known? How can I speak of things for which no words have been invented? One tells of things unknown in terms of things which are known. Here there is no relationship by which to link; all is irrelevant. All I can hope to do is tell how matters affected my human senses, how events influenced my human emotions, knowing that there are two falsehoods involved—the falsehood I saw and felt, and the falsehood that I tell.

I have discussed this matter with Jedson, and he agrees with me that the difficulty is insuperable, yet some things may be said with a partial element of truth—truth of a sort, with respect to how the Half World impinged on me.

There is one striking difference between the real world and the Half World. In the real world there are natural laws which persist through changes of custom and culture; in the Half World only custom has any degree of persistence, and of natural law there is none. Imagine, if you please, a condition in which the head of a state might repeal the law of gravitation and have his decree really effective—a place where King Canute could order back the sea and have the waves obey him. A place where "up" and "down" were matters of opinion, and directions might read as readily in days or colors as in miles.

And yet it was not a meaningless anarchy, for they were constrained to obey their customs as unavoidably as we comply with the rules of natural phenomena.

We made a sharp turn to the left in the formless grayness that surrounded us in order to survey the years for a sabbat meeting. It was Amanda's intention to face the Old One with the matter directly rather than to search aimlessly through ever changing mazes of the Half World for a being hard to identify at best.

Royce picked out the sabbat, though I could see nothing until we let the ground come up to meet us and proceeded on foot. Then there was light and form. Ahead of us, perhaps a quarter of a mile away, was an eminence surmounted by a great throne which glowed red through the murky air. I could not make out clearly the thing seated there, but I knew it was "himself"—our ancient enemy.

We were no longer alone. Life—sentient, evil undeadness—boiled around us and fogged the air and crept out of the ground. The ground itself twitched and pulsated as we walked over it. Faceless things sniffed and nibbled at our heels. We were aware of unseen presences about us in the fog-shot gloom: beings that squeaked, grunted, and sniggered; voices that were slobbering whimpers, that sucked and retched and bleated.

They seemed vaguely disturbed by our presence—Heaven knows that I was terrified by them!—for I could hear them flopping and shuffling out of our path, then closing cautiously in behind, as they bleated warnings to one another.

A shape floundered into our path and stopped, a shape with great bloated head and moist, limber arms. "Back!" it wheezed.

"Go back! Candidates for witchhood apply on the lower level." It did not speak English, but the words were clear.

Royce smashed it in the face and we stamped over it, its chalky bones crunching underfoot. It pulled itself together again, whining its submission, then scurried out in front of us and thereafter gave us escort right up to the great throne.

"That's the only way to treat these beings," Joe whispered in my ear. "Kick 'em in the teeth first, and they'll respect you."

There was a clearing before the throne which was crowded with black witches, black magicians, demons in every foul guise, and lesser unclean things. On the left side the caldron boiled. On the right some of the company were partaking of the witches' feast. I turned my head away from that. Directly before the throne, as custom calls for, the witches' dance was being performed for the amusement of the Goat. Some dozens of men and women, young and old, comely and hideous, cavorted and leaped in impossible acrobatic adagio.

The dance ceased and they gave way uncertainly before us as we pressed up to the throne. "What's this? What's this?" came a husky, phlegm-filled voice. "It's my little sweetheart! Come up and sit beside me, my sweet! Have you come at last to sign my compact?"

Jedson grasped my arm; I checked my tongue.

"I'll stay where I am," answered Amanda in a voice crisp with contempt. "As for your compact, you know better."

"Then why are you here? And why such *odd* companions." He looked down at us from the vantage of his throne, slapped his hairy thigh and laughed immoderately. Royce stirred and muttered; his grandfather's head chattered in wrath. Seraphin spat.

Jedson and Amanda put their heads together for a moment, then she answered, "By the treaty with Adam, I claim the right to examine."

He chuckled, and the little devils around him covered their ears. "You claim privileges here? With no compact?"

"Your customs," she answered sharply.

"Ah yes, the customs! Since you invoke them, so let it be. And whom would you examine?"

"I do not know his name. He is one of your demons who has taken improper liberties outside your sphere."

"One of my demons, and you know not his name? I have

seven million demons, my pretty. Will you examine them one by one, or all together?" His sarcasm was almost the match of her contempt.

"All together."

"Never let it be said that I would not oblige a guest. If you will go forward—let me see—exactly five months and three days, you will find my gentlemen drawn up for inspection."

I do not recollect how we got there. There was a great, brown plain, and no sky. Drawn up in military order for review by their evil lord were all the fiends of the Half World, legion on legion, wave after wave. The Old One was attended by his cabinet; Jedson pointed them out to me—Lucifugé, the prime minister; Sataniacha, field marshal; Beelzebub and Leviathan, wing commanders; Ashtoreth, Abaddon, Mammon, Theutus, Asmodeus, and Incubus, the Fallen Thrones. The seventy princes each commanded a division, and each remained with his command, leaving only the dukes and the thrones to attend their lord, Satan Mekratrig.

He himself still appeared as the Goat, but his staff took every detestable shape they fancied. Asmodeus sported three heads, each evil and each different, rising out of the hind quarters of a swollen dragon. Mammon resembled, very roughly, a particularly repulsive tarantula. Ashtoreth I cannot describe at all. Only the Incubus affected a semblance of human form, as the only vessel adequate to display his lecherousness.

The Goat glanced our way. "Be quick about it," he demanded. "We are not here for your amusement."

Amanda ignored him, but led us toward the leading squadron. "Come back!" he bellowed. And indeed we were back; our steps had led us no place. "You ignore the customs. Hostages first!"

Amanda bit her lip. "Admitted," she retorted, and consulted briefly with Royce and Jedson. I caught Royce's answer to some argument.

"Since I am to go," he said, "it is best that I choose my companion, for reasons that are sufficient to me. My grandfather advises me to take the youngest. That one, of course, is Fraser."

"What's this?" I said when my name was mentioned. I had

been rather pointedly left out of all the discussions, but this was surely my business.

"Royce wants you to go with him to smell out Ditworth," explained Jedson.

"And leave Amanda here with these fiends? I don't like it."

"I can look out for myself, Archie," she said quietly. "If Dr. Worthington wants you, you can help me most by going with him."

"What is this hostage stuff?"

"Having demanded the right of examination," she explained, "you must bring back Ditworth—or the hostages are forfeit."

Jedson spoke up before I could protest. "Don't be a hero, son. This is serious. You can serve us all best by going. If you two don't come back, you can bet that they'll have a fight on their hands before they claim their forfeit!"

I went. Worthington and I had hardly left them before I realized acutely that what little peace of mind I had came from the nearness of Amanda. Once out of her immediate influence the whole mind-twisting horror of the place and its grisly denizens hit me. I felt something rub against my ankles and nearly jumped out of my shoes. But when I looked down I saw that Seraphin, Amanda's cat, had chosen to follow me. After that things were better with me.

Royce assumed his dog pose when we came to the first rank of demons. He first handed me his grandfather's head. Once I would have found that mummified head repulsive to touch; it seemed a friendly, homey thing here. Then he was down on all fours, scalloping in and out of the ranks of infernal warriors. Seraphin scampered after him, paired up and hunted with him. The hound seemed quite content to let the cat do half the work, and I have no doubt he was justified. I walked as rapidly as possible down the aisles between adjacent squadrons while the animals cast out from side to side.

It seems to me that this went on for many hours, certainly so long that fatigue changed to a wooden automatism and horror died down to a dull unease. I learned not to look at the eyes of the demons, and was no longer surprised at any *outré* shape.

Squadron by squadron, division by division, we combed them, until at last, coming up the left wing, we reached the end. The animals had been growing increasingly nervous. When they had completed the front rank of the leading squadron, the hound trotted up to me and whined. I suppose he sought his grandfather, but I reached down and patted his head.

"Don't despair, old friend," I said, "we have still these." I motioned toward the generals, princes all, who were posted before their divisions. Coming up from the rear as we had, we had yet to examine the generals of the leading divisions on the left wing. But despair already claimed me; what were half a dozen possibilities against an eliminated seven million?

The dog trotted away to the post of the nearest general, the cat close beside him, while I followed as rapidly as possible. He commenced to yelp before he was fairly up to the demon, and I broke into a run. The demon stirred and commenced to metamorphose. But even in this strange shape there was something familiar about it. "Ditworth!" I yelled, and dived for him.

I felt myself buffeted by leather wings, raked by claws. Royce came to my aid, a dog no longer, but two hundred pounds of fighting Negro. The cat was a ball of fury, teeth and claws. Nevertheless, we would have been lost, done in completely, had not an amazing thing happened. A demon broke ranks and shot toward us. I sensed him rather than saw him, and thought that he had come to succor his master, though I had been assured that their customs did not permit it. But he helped us—us, his natural enemies—and attacked with such vindictive violence that the gage was turned to our favor.

Suddenly it was all over. I found myself on the ground, clutching at not a demon prince but Ditworth in his pseudo-human form—a little mild businessman, dressed with restrained elegance, complete to brief case, spectacles, and thinning hair.

"Take that thing off me," he said testily. "That thing" was grandfather, who was clinging doggedly with toothless gums to his neck.

Royce spared a hand from the task of holding Ditworth and resumed possession of his grandfather. Seraphin stayed where he was, claws dug into our prisoner's leg.

The demon who had rescued us was still with us. He had Ditworth by the shoulders, talons dug into their bases. I cleared my throat and said, "I believe we owe this to you—" I had not the slightest notion of the proper thing to say. I think the situation was utterly without precedent.

The demon made a grimace that may have been intended to be friendly, but which I found frightening. "Let me introduce myself," he said in English. "I'm Federal Agent William Kane, Bureau of Investigation."

I think that was what made me faint.

I came to, lying on my back. Someone had smeared a salve on my wounds and they were hardly stiff, and not painful in the least, but I was mortally tired. There was talking going on somewhere near me. I turned my head and saw all the members of my party gathered together. Worthington and the friendly demon who claimed to be a G-man held Ditworth between them, facing Satan. Of all the mighty infernal army I saw no trace.

"So it was my nephew Nebiros," mused the Goat, shaking his head and clucking. "Nebiros, you are a bad lad and I'm proud of you. But I'm afraid you will have to try your strength against their champion now that they have caught you." He addressed Amanda. "Who is your champion, my dear?"

The friendly demon spoke up. "That sounds like my job."

"I think not," countered Amanda. She drew him to one side and whispered intently. Finally he shrugged his wings and gave in.

Amanda rejoined the group. I struggled to my feet and came up to them. "A trial to the death, I think," she was saying. "Are you ready, Nebiros?" I was stretched between heart-stopping fear for Amanda and a calm belief that she could do anything she attempted. Jedson saw my face and shook his head. I was not to interrupt.

But Nebiros had no stomach for it. Still in his Ditworth form and looking ridiculously human, he turned to the Old One. "I dare not, Uncle. The outcome is certain. Intercede for me."

"Certainly, Nephew. I had rather hoped she would destroy you. You'll trouble me someday." Then to Amanda, "Shall we say—ah—ten thousand thousand years?"

Amanda gathered our votes with her eyes, including me, to my proud pleasure, and answered, "So be it." It was not a stiff sentence as such things go, I'm told—about equal to six months in jail in the real world—but he had not offended their customs; he had simply been defeated by white magic.

Old Nick brought down one arm in an emphatic gesture. There was a crashing roar and a burst of light and Ditworth-Nebiros was spread-eagled before us on a mighty boulder, his limbs bound with massive iron chains. He was again in demon form. Amanda and Worthington examined the bonds. She pressed a seal ring against each hasp and nodded to the Goat. At once the boulder receded with great speed into the distance until it was gone from sight.

"That seems to be about all, and I suppose you will be going now," announced the Goat. "All except this one—" He smiled at the demon G-man. "I have plans for him."

"No." Amanda's tone was flat.

"What's that, my little one? He has not the protection of your party, and he has offended our customs."

"No!"

"Really, I must insist."

"Satan Mekratrig," she said slowly, "do you wish to try your strength with me?"

"With you, madame?" He looked at her carefully, as if inspecting her for the first time. "Well, it's been a trying day, hasn't it? Suppose we say no more about it. Till another time, then—"

He was gone.

The demon faced her. "Thanks," he said simply. "I wish I had a hat to take off." He added anxiously, "Do you know your way out of here?"

"Don't you?"

"No, that's the trouble. Perhaps I should explain myself. I'm assigned to the antimonopoly division; we got a line on this chap Ditworth, or Nebiros. I followed him in here, thinking he was simply a black wizard and that I could use his portal to get back. By the time I knew better it was too late, and I was trapped. I had about resigned myself to an eternity as a fake demon."

I was very much interested in his story. I knew, of course,

that all G-men are either lawyers, magicians, or accountants, but all that I had ever met were accountants. This calm assumption of incredible dangers impressed me and increased my already high opinion of Federal agents.

"You may use our portal to return," Amanda said. "Stick close to us." Then to the rest of us, "Shall we go now?"

Jack Bodie was still intoning the lines from the book when we landed. "Eight and a half minutes," he announced, looking at his wrist watch. "Nice work. Did you turn the trick?"

"Yes, we did," acknowledged Jedson, his voice muffled by the throes of his remetamorphosis. "Everything that—"

But Bodie interrupted. "Bill Kane—you old scoundrel!" he shouted. "How did you get in on this party?" Our demon had shucked his transformation on the way and landed in his natural form—lean, young, and hard-bitten, in a quiet gray suit and snap-brim hat.

"Hi, Jack," he acknowledged. "I'll look you up tomorrow and tell you all about it. Got to report in now." With which he vanished.

Ellen was out of her trance, and Joe was bending solicitously over her to see how she had stood up under it. I looked around for Amanda.

Then I heard her out in the kitchen and hurried out there. She looked up and smiled at me, her lovely young face serene and coolly beautiful. "Amanda," I said, "Amanda—"

I suppose I had the subconscious intention of kissing her, making love to her. But it is very difficult to start anything of that sort unless the woman in the case in some fashion indicates her willingness. She did not. She was warmly friendly, but there was a barrier of reserve I could not cross. Instead, I followed her around the kitchen, talking inconsequentially, while she made hot cocoa and toast for all of us.

When we rejoined the others I sat and let my cocoa get cold, staring at her with vague frustration in my heart while Jedson told Ellen and Jack about our experiences. He took Ellen home shortly thereafter, and Jack followed them out.

When Amanda came back from telling them good night at the door, Dr. Royce was stretched out on his back on the hearthrug, with Seraphin curled up on his broad chest. They were both snoring softly. I realized suddenly that I was wretchedly tired. Amanda saw it, too, and said, "Lie down on the couch for a little and nap if you can."

I needed no urging. She came over and spread a shawl over me and kissed me tenderly. I heard her going upstairs as I fell asleep.

I was awakened by sunlight striking my face. Seraphin was sitting in the window, cleaning himself. Dr. Worthington was gone, but must have just left, for the nap on the hearthrug had not yet straightened up. The house seemed deserted. Then I heard her light footsteps in the kitchen. I was up at once and quickly out there.

She had her back toward me and was reaching up to the old-fashioned pendulum clock that hung on her kitchen wall. She turned as I came in—tiny, incredibly aged, her thin white hair brushed neatly into a bun.

It was suddenly clear to me why a motherly good-night kiss was all that I had received the night before; she had had enough sense for two of us, and had refused to permit me to make a fool of myself.

She looked up at me and said in a calm, matter-of-fact voice, "See, Archie, my old clock stopped yesterday"—she reached up and touched the pendulum—"but it is running again this morning."

There is not anything more to tell. With Ditworth gone, and Kane's report, Magic, Incorporated, folded up almost overnight. The new licensing laws were an unenforced dead letter even before they were repealed.

We all hang around Mrs. Jennings's place just as much as she will let us. I'm really grateful that she did not let me get involved with her younger self, for our present relationship is something solid, something to tie to. Just the same, if I had been born sixty years sooner, Mr. Jennings would have had some rivalry to contend with.

I helped Ellen and Joe organize their new business, then put Bodie in as manager, for I decided that I did not want to give up my old line. I've built the new wing and bought those two trucks, just as Mrs. Jennings predicted. Business is good. •

Anything Box

BY ZENNA HENDERSON

I SUPPOSE it was about the second week of school that I noticed Sue-lynn particularly. Of course, I'd noticed her name before and checked her out automatically for maturity and ability and probable performance the way most teachers do with their students during the first weeks of school. She had checked out mature and capable and no worry as to performance as I had pigeonholed her—setting aside for the moment the little nudge that said, "Too quiet"—with my other no-worrys until the fluster and flurry of the first days had died down a little.

I remember my noticing day. I had collapsed into my chair for a brief respite from guiding hot little hands through the intricacies of keeping a crayola within reasonable bounds and the room was full of the relaxed, happy hum of a pleased class as they worked away, not realizing that they were rubbing "blue" into their memories as well as onto their papers. I was meditating on how individual personalities were beginning to emerge among the thirty-five or so heterogeneous first graders I had, when I noticed Sue-lynn—really noticed her—for the first time.

She had finished her paper—far ahead of the others as usual—and was sitting at her table facing me. She had her thumbs touching in front of her on the table and her fingers curving as though they held something between them—something large enough to keep her fingertips apart and angular enough to bend her fingers as if for corners. It was something pleasant that she held—pleasant and precious. You could tell that by the softness of her hold. She was leaning forward a little, her lower ribs pressed against the table, and she was looking, completely absorbed, at the table between her hands. Her face was relaxed and happy. Her mouth curved in a tender half-smile, and as I watched, her lashes lifted and she looked at me with a warm share-the-pleasure look. Then her eyes blinked and the shutters came down inside them. Her hand flicked into the desk and out. She pressed her thumbs to her forefingers and rubbed them slowly together. Then she laid one hand over the other on the table and looked down at them with the air of complete denial and ignorance children can assume so devastatingly.

The incident caught my fancy and I began to notice Sue-lynn. As I consciously watched her, I saw that she spent most of her free time staring at the table between her hands, much too unobtrusively to catch my busy attention. She hurried through even the fun-est of fun papers and then lost herself in looking. When Davie pushed her down at recess, and blood streamed from her knee to her ankle, she took her bandages and her tear-smudged face to that comfort she had so readily—if you'll pardon the expression—at hand, and emerged minutes later, serene and dry-eyed. I think Davie pushed her down because of her Looking. I know the day before he had come up to me, red-faced and squirming.

"Teacher," he blurted. "She Looks!"

"Who looks?" I asked absently, checking the vocabulary list in my book, wondering how on earth I'd missed *where,* one of those annoying *wh* words that throw the children for a loss.

"Sue-lynn. She Looks and Looks!"

"At you?" I asked.

"Well—" He rubbed a forefinger below his nose, leaving a clean streak on his upper lip, accepted the proffered tissue and put it in his pocket. "She looks at her desk and tell lies. She says she can see—"

"Can see what?" My curiosity picked up its ears.

"Anything," said Davie. "It's her Anything Box. She can see anything she wants to."

"Does it hurt you for her to Look?"

"Well," he squirmed. Then he burst out: "She says she saw me with a dog biting me because I took her pencil—she said." He started a pell-mell verbal retreat. "She *thinks* I took her pencil. I only found—" His eyes dropped. "I'll give it back."

"I hope so," I smiled. "If you don't want her to look at you, then don't do things like that."

"Durn girls," he muttered and clomped back to his seat.

So I think he pushed her down the next day to get back at her for the dog-bite.

Several times after that I wandered to the back of the room, casually in her vicinity, but always she either saw or felt me coming and the quick sketch of her hand disposed of the evidence. Only once I thought I caught a glimmer of something —but her thumb and forefinger brushed in sunlight, and it must have been just that.

Children don't retreat for no reason at all, and, though Sue-lynn did not follow any overt pattern of withdrawal, I started to wonder about her. I watched her on the playground, to see how she tracked there. That only confused me more.

She had a very regular pattern. When the avalanche of children first descended at recess, she avalanched along with them and nothing in the shrieking, running, dodging mass resolved itself into a withdrawn Sue-lynn. But after ten minutes or so, she emerged from the crowd, tousle-haired, rosy-cheeked, smutched with dust, one shoelace dangling and, through some alchemy that I coveted for myself, she suddenly became untousled, undusty and unsmutched. And there she was, serene and composed on the narrow little step at the side of the flight of stairs just where they disappeared into the base of the pseudo-Corinthian column that graced Our Door and her cupped hands received whatever they received and her absorption in what she saw became so complete that the bell came as a shock every time.

And each time, before she joined the rush to Our Door, her hand would sketch a gesture to her pocket, if she had one, or to the tiny ledge that extended between the hedge and the building. Apparently she always had to put the Anything Box away, but never had to go back to get it.

I was so intrigued by her putting whatever it was on the ledge that once I actually went over and felt along the grimy little outset. I sheepishly followed my children into the hall, wiping the dust from my fingertips, and Sue-lynn's eyes brimmed amusement at me without her mouth's smiling. Her hands mischievously squared in front of her and her thumbs caressed a solidness as the line of children swept into the room.

I smiled too because she was so pleased with having outwitted me. This seemed to be such a gay withdrawal that I let my worry die down. Better this manifestation than any number of other ones that I could name.

Someday, perhaps, I'll learn to keep my mouth shut. I wish I had before that long afternoon when we primary teachers worked together in a heavy cloud of ditto fumes, the acrid smell of India ink, drifting cigarette smoke and the constant current of chatter, and I let Alpha get me started on what to do with our behavior problems. She was all steamed up about the usual rowdy loudness of her boys and the eternal clack of her girls, and I—bless my stupidity—gave her Sue-lynn as an example of what should be our deepest concern rather than the outbursts from our active ones.

"You mean she just sits and looks at nothing?" Alpha's voice grated into her questioning tone.

"Well, I can't see anything," I admitted. "But apparently she can."

"But that's having hallucinations!" Her voice went up a notch. "I read a book once—"

"Yes." Marlene leaned across the desk to flick ashes into the ashtray. "So we have heard and heard and heard."

"Well!" sniffed Alpha. "It's better than *never* reading a book."

"We're waiting," Marlene leaked smoke from her nostrils, "for the day when you read another book. This one must have been uncommonly long."

"Oh, I don't know." Alpha's forehead wrinkled with concentration. "It was only about—" Then she reddened and turned her face angrily away from Marlene.

"Apropos of *our* discussion—" she said pointedly. "It sounds to me like that child has a deep personality disturbance. Maybe even a psychotic—whatever—" Her eyes glistened faintly as she turned the thought over.

"Oh, I don't know," I said, surprised into echoing her words at my sudden need to defend Sue-lynn. "There's something about her. She doesn't have that apprehensive, hunched-shoulder, don't-hit-me-again air about her that so many withdrawn children have." And I thought achingly of one of mine from last year that Alpha had now and was verbally bludgeoning back into silence after all my work with him. "She seems to have a happy, adjusted personality, only with this odd little—*plus*."

"Well, I'd be worried if she were mine," said Alpha. "I'm glad all my kids are so normal." She sighed complacently. "I guess I really haven't anything to kick about. I seldom ever have problem children except wigglers and yakkers, and a holler and a smack can straighten them out."

Marlene caught my eye mockingly, tallying Alpha's class with me, and I turned away with a sigh. To be so happy—well, I suppose ignorance does help.

"You'd better do something about that girl," Alpha shrilled as she left the room. "She'll probably get worse and worse as time goes on. Deteriorating, I think the book said."

I had known Alpha a long time and I thought I knew how much of her talk to discount, but I began to worry about Sue-lynn. Maybe this *was* a disturbance that was more fundamental than the usual run-of-the-mill that I had met up with. Maybe a child *can* smile a soft, contented smile and still have little maggots of madness flourishing somewhere inside.

Or, by gorry! I said to myself defiantly, maybe she *does* have an Anything Box. Maybe she *is* looking at something precious. Who am I to say no to anything like that?

An Anything Box! What could you see in an Anything Box? Heart's desire? I felt my own heart lurch—just a little—the next time Sue-lynn's hands curved. I breathed deeply to hold me in my chair. If it was *her* Anything Box, I wouldn't be able to see my heart's desire in it. Or would I? I propped my cheek up on my hand and doodled aimlessly on my time-schedule sheet. How on earth, I wondered—not for the first time—do I manage to get myself off on these tangents?

Then I felt a small presence at my elbow and turned to meet Sue-lynn's wide eyes.

"Teacher?" The word was hardly more than a breath.

"Yes?" I could tell that for some reason Sue-lynn was loving me dearly at the moment. Maybe because her group had gone into new books that morning. Maybe because I had noticed her new dress, the ruffles of which made her feel very feminine and lovable, or maybe just because the late autumn sun lay so golden across her desk. Anyway, she was loving me to overflowing, and since, unlike most of the children, she had no casual hugs or easy moist kisses, she was bringing her love to me in her encompassing hands.

"See my box, Teacher? It's my Anything Box."

"Oh, my!" I said. "May I hold it?"

After all, I have held—tenderly or apprehensively or bravely—tiger magic, live rattlesnakes, dragon's teeth, poor little dead butterflies and two ears and a nose that dropped off Sojie one cold morning—none of which I could see any more than I could the Anything Box. But I took the squareness from her carefully, my tenderness showing in my fingers and my face.

And I received weight and substance and actuality!

I almost let it slip out of my surprised fingers, but Sue-lynn's apprehensive breath helped me catch it and I curved my fingers around the precious warmness and looked down, down, past a faint shimmering, down into Sue-lynn's Anything Box.

I was running barefoot through the whispering grass. The swirl of my skirts caught the daisies as I rounded the gnarled appletree at the corner. The warm wind lay along each of my cheeks and chuckled in my ears. My heart outstripped my flying feet and melted with a rush of delight into warmness as his arms—

I closed my eyes and swallowed hard, my palms tight against the Anything Box. "It's beautiful!" I whispered. "It's wonderful, Sue-lynn. Where did you get it?"

Her hands took it back hastily. "It's mine," she said defiantly. "It's mine."

"Of course," I said. "Be careful now. Don't drop it."

She smiled faintly as she sketched a motion to her pocket. "I won't." She patted the pocket on her way back to her seat.

Next day she was afraid to look at me at first for fear I might say something or look something or in some way remind her of what must seem like a betrayal to her now, but after I only smiled my usual smile, with no added secret knowledge, she relaxed.

A night or so later when I leaned over my moon-drenched

window sill and let the shadow of my hair hide my face from such ebullient glory, I remembered about the Anything Box. Could I make one for myself? Could I square off this aching waiting, this out-reaching, this silent cry inside me, and make it into an Anything Box? I freed my hands and brought them together thumb to thumb, framing a part of the horizon's darkness between my upright forefingers. I stared into the empty square until my eyes watered. I sighed, and laughed a little, and let my hands frame my face as I leaned out into the night. To have magic so near—to feel it tingle off my fingertips and then to be so bound that I couldn't receive it. I turned away from the window—turning my back on brightness.

It wasn't long after this that Alpha succeeded in putting sharp points of worry back in my thoughts of Sue-lynn. We had ground duty together, and one morning when we shivered while the kids ran themselves rosy in the crisp air, she sizzed in my ear.

"Which one is it? The abnormal one, I mean."

"I don't have any abnormal children," I said, my voice sharpening before the sentence ended because I suddenly realized whom she meant.

"Well, I call it abnormal to stare at nothing." You could almost taste the acid in her words. "Who is it?"

"Sue-lynn," I said reluctantly. "She's playing on the bars now."

Alpha surveyed the upside-down Sue-lynn, whose brief skirts were belled down from her bare pink legs and half covered her face as she swung from one of the bars by her knees. Alpha clutched her wizened blue hands together and breathed on them. "She looks normal enough," she said.

"She *is* normal!" I snapped.

"*Well,* bite my head off!" cried Alpha. "You're the one that said she wasn't, not me—or is it 'not I'? I never could remember. Not me? Not I?"

The bell saved Alpha from a horrible end. I never knew a person so serenely unaware of essentials and so sensitive to trivia. But she had succeeded in making me worry about Sue-lynn again, and the worry exploded into distress a few days later.

Sue-lynn came to school sleepy-eyed and quiet. She didn't

finish any of her work and she fell asleep during rest time. I cussed TV and drive-ins and assumed a night's sleep would put it right. But next day Sue-lynn burst into tears and slapped Davie clear off his chair.

"Why Sue-lynn!" I gathered Davie up in all his astonishment and took Sue-lynn's hand. She jerked it away from me and flung herself at Davie again. She got two handfuls of his hair and had him out of my grasp before I knew it. She threw him bodily against the wall with a flip of her hands, then doubled up her fists and pressed them to her streaming eyes. In the shocked silence of the room, she stumbled over to Isolation and, seating herself, back to the class, on the little chair, she leaned her head into the corner and sobbed quietly in big gulping sobs.

"What on earth goes on?" I asked the stupefied Davie who sat spraddle-legged on the floor fingering a detached tuft of hair. "What did you do?"

"I only said 'Robber Daughter,'" said Davie. "It said so in the paper. My mamma said her daddy's a robber. They put him in jail cause he robbered a gas station." His bewildered face was trying to decide whether or not to cry. Everything had happened so fast that he didn't know yet if he was hurt.

"It isn't nice to call names," I said weakly. "Get back into your seat. I'll take care of Sue-lynn later."

He got up and sat gingerly down in his chair, rubbing his ruffled hair, wanting to make more of a production of the situation but not knowing how. He twisted his face experimentally to see if he had tears available and had none.

"Durn girls," he muttered and tried to shake his fingers free of a wisp of hair.

I kept my eye on Sue-lynn for the next half hour as I busied myself with the class. Her sobs soon stopped and her rigid shoulders relaxed. Her hands were softly in her lap and I knew she was taking comfort from her Anything Box. We had our talk together later, but she was so completely sealed off from me by her misery that there was no communication between us. She sat quietly watching me as I talked, her hands trembling in her lap. It shakes the heart, somehow, to see the hands of a little child quiver like that.

That afternoon I looked up from my reading group, startled, as though by a cry, to catch Sue-lynn's frightened eyes. She looked around bewildered and then down at her hands again—her empty hands. Then she darted to the Isolation corner and reached under the chair. She went back to her seat slowly, her hands squared to an unseen weight. For the first time, apparently, she had had to go get the Anything Box. It troubled me with a vague unease for the rest of the afternoon.

Through the days that followed while the trial hung fire, I had Sue-lynn in attendance bodily, but that was all. She sank into her Anything Box at every opportunity. And always, if she had put it away somewhere, she had to go back for it. She roused more and more reluctantly from these waking dreams, and there finally came a day when I had to shake her to waken her.

I went to her mother, but she couldn't or wouldn't understand me, and made me feel like a frivolous gossip-monger taking her mind away from her husband, despite the fact that I didn't even mention him—or maybe because I didn't mention him.

"If she's being a bad girl, spank her," she finally said, wearily shifting the weight of a whining baby from one hip to another and pushing her tousled hair off her forehead. "Whatever you do is all right by me. My worrier is all used up. I haven't got any left for the kids right now."

Well, Sue-lynn's father was found guilty and sentenced to the State Penitentiary and school was less than an hour old the next day when Davie came up, clumsily a-tiptoe, braving my wrath for interrupting a reading group, and whispered hoarsely, "Sue-lynn's asleep with her eyes open again, Teacher."

We went back to the table and Davie slid into his chair next to a completely unaware Sue-lynn. He poked her with a warning finger. "I told you I'd tell on you."

And before our horrified eyes, she toppled, as rigidly as a doll, sideways off the chair. The thud of her landing relaxed her and she lay limp on the green asphalt tile—a thin paper-doll of a girl, one hand still clenched open around something. I pried her fingers loose and almost wept to feel enchantment dissolve under my heavy touch. I carried her down to the nurse's room and we worked over her with wet towels and prayer and she finally opened her eyes.

"Teacher," she whispered weakly.

"Yes, Sue-lynn." I took her cold hands in mine.

"Teacher, I almost got in my Anything Box."

"No," I answered. "You couldn't. You're too big."

"Daddy's there," she said. "And where we used to live."

I took a long, long look at her wan face. I hope it was genuine concern for her that prompted my next words. I hope it wasn't envy or the memory of the niggling nagging of Alpha's voice that put firmness in my voice as I went on. "That's play-like," I said. "Just for fun."

Her hands jerked protestingly in mine. "Your Anything Box is just for fun. It's like Davie's cowpony that he keeps in his desk or Sojie's jet plane, or when the big bear chases all of you at recess. It's fun-for-play, but it's not for real. You mustn't think it's for real. It's only play."

"No!" she denied. "*No!*" she cried frantically and, hunching herself up on the cot, peering through her tear-swollen eyes, she scrabbled under the pillow and down beneath the rough blanket that covered her.

"Where is it?" she cried. "Where is it? Give it back to me, Teacher!"

She flung herself toward me and pulled open both my clenched hands.

"Where did you put it? Where did you put it?"

"There is no Anything Box," I said flatly, trying to hold her to me and feeling my heart breaking along with hers.

"You took it!" she sobbed. "You took it away from me!" And she wrenched herself out of my arms.

"Can't you give it back to her?" whispered the nurse. "If it makes her feel so bad? Whatever it is—"

"It's just imagination," I said, almost sullenly. "I can't give her back something that doesn't exist."

Too young! I thought bitterly. Too young to learn that heart's desire is only play-like.

Of course the doctor found nothing wrong. Her mother dismissed the matter as a fainting spell and Sue-lynn came back to class next day, thin and listless, staring blankly out the window, her hands palm down on the desk. I swore by the pale hollow of her cheek that never, *never* again would I take any belief from anyone without replacing it with something better. What had I given Sue-lynn? What had she better than I had taken from her? How did I know but that her Anything Box was on purpose to tide her over rough spots in her life like this? And what now, now that I had taken it from her?

Well, after a time she began to work again, and later, to play. She came back to smiles, but not to laughter. She puttered along quite satisfactorily except that she was a candle blown out. The flame was gone wherever the brightness of belief goes. And she had no more sharing smiles for me, no overflowing love to bring to me. And her shoulder shrugged subtly away from my touch.

Then one day I suddenly realized that Sue-lynn was searching our classroom. Stealthily, casually, day by day she was searching, covering every inch of the room. She went through every puzzle box, every lump of clay, every shelf and cupboard, every box and bag. Methodically she checked behind every row of books and in every child's desk until finally, after almost a week, she had been through everything in the place except my desk. Then she began to materialize suddenly at my elbow every time I opened a drawer. And her eyes would probe quickly and sharply before I slid it shut again. But if I tried to intercept her looks, they slid away and she had some legitimate errand that had brought her up to the vicinity of the desk.

She believes it again, I thought hopefully. She won't accept the fact that her Anything Box is gone. She wants it again.

But it *is* gone, I thought drearily. It's really-for-true gone.

My head was heavy from troubled sleep, and sorrow was a weariness in all my movements. Waiting is sometimes a burden almost too heavy to carry. While my children hummed happily over their fun stuff, I brooded silently out the window until I managed a laugh at myself. It was a shaky laugh that threatened to dissolve into something else, so I brisked back to my desk.

As good a time as any to throw out useless things, I thought, and to see if I can find that colored chalk I put away so carefully. I plunged my hands into the wilderness of the bottom right-hand drawer of my desk. It was deep with a huge accumulation of anything—just anything—that might need a temporary hiding place. I knelt to pull out leftover Jack Frost pictures, and a broken bean shooter, a chewed red ribbon, a roll of cap-gun ammunition, one striped sock, six Numbers papers, a rubber dagger, a copy of *The Gospel According to St. Luke,* a miniature coal shovel, patterns for jack-o'-lanterns, and a pink plastic pelican. I retrieved my Irish linen hankie I thought lost forever and Sojie's report card that he had told me solemnly had blown out of his hand and landed on a jet and broke the sound barrier so loud that it busted all to flitters. Under the welter of miscellany, I felt a squareness. Oh, happy! I thought, this *is* where I put the colored chalk! I cascaded papers off both sides of my lifting hands and shook the box free.

We were together again. Outside, the world was an enchanting wilderness of white, the wind shouting softly through the windows, tapping wet, white fingers against the warm light. Inside all the worry and waiting, the apartness and loneliness were over and forgotten, their hugeness dwindled by the comfort of a shoulder, the warmth of clasping hands—and nowhere, nowhere was the fear of parting, nowhere the need to do without again. This was the happy ending. This was—

This was Sue-lynn's Anything Box!

My racing heart slowed as the dream faded—and rushed again at the realization. I had it here! In my junk drawer! It had been here all the time!

It stood up shakily, concealing the invisible box in the flare of my skirts. I sat down and put the box carefully in the center of my desk, covering the top of it with my palms lest I should drown again in delight. I looked at Sue-lynn. She was finishing her fun paper, competently but unjoyously. Now would come her patient sitting with quiet hands until told to do something else.

Alpha would approve. And very possibly, I thought, Alpha would, for once in her limited life, be right. We may need "hallucinations" to keep us going—all of us but the Alphas—but when we go so far as to try to force ourselves, physically, into the Never-never land of heart's desire. . . .

I remembered Sue-lynn's thin rigid body toppling doll-like off its chair. Out of her deep need she had found—or created? —who could tell?—something too dangerous for a child. I could so easily bring the brimming happiness back to her eyes—but at what a possible price!

No, I had a duty to protect Sue-lynn. Only maturity—the maturity born of the sorrow and loneliness that Sue-lynn was only beginning to know—could be trusted to use an Anything Box safely and wisely.

My heart thudded as I began to move my hands, letting the palms slip down from the top to shape the sides of—

I had moved them back again before I really saw, and I have now learned almost to forget that glimpse of what heart's desire is like when won at the cost of another's heart.

I sat there at the desk trembling and breathless, my palms moist, feeling as if I had been on a long journey away from the little schoolroom. Perhaps I had. Perhaps I had been shown all the kingdoms of the world in a moment of time.

"Sue-lynn," I called. "Will you come up here when you're through?"

She nodded unsmilingly and snipped off the last paper from the edge of Mistress Mary's dress. Without another look at her handiwork, she carried the scissors safely to the scissors box, crumpled the scraps of paper in her hand and came up to the waste basket by the desk.

"I have something for you, Sue-lynn," I said, uncovering the box.

Her eyes dropped to the desk top. She looked indifferently up at me. "I did my fun paper already."

"Did you like it?"

"Yes." It was a flat lie.

"Good," I lied right back. "But look here." I squared my hands around the Anything Box.

She took a deep breath and the whole of her little body stiffened.

"I found it," I said hastily, fearing anger. "I found it in the bottom drawer."

She leaned her chest against my desk, her hands caught tightly between, her eyes intent on the box, her face white with the aching want you see on children's faces pressed to Christmas windows.

"Can I have it?" she whispered.

"It's yours," I said, holding it out.

Still she leaned against her hands, her eyes searching my face. "Can I have it?" she asked again.

"Yes!" I was impatient with this anticlimax. "But—"

Her eyes flickered. She had sensed my reservation before I had. "But you must never try to get into it again."

"O.K.," she said, the word coming out on a long relieved sigh. "O.K., Teacher."

She took the box and tucked it lovingly into her small pocket. She turned from the desk and started back to her table. My mouth quirked with a small smile. It seemed to me that everything about her had suddenly turned upward—even the ends of her straight taffy-colored hair. The subtle flame about her that made her Sue-lynn was there again. She scarcely touched the floor as she walked.

I sighed heavily and traced on the desk top with my finger a probable size for an Anything Box. What would Sue-lynn choose to see first? How like a drink after a drought it would seem to her.

I was startled as a small figure materialized at my elbow. It was Sue-lynn, her fingers carefully squared before her.

"Teacher," she said softly, all the flat emptiness gone from her voice. "Any time you want to take my Anything Box, you just say so."

I groped through my astonishment and incredulity for words. She couldn't possibly have had time to look into the Box yet.

"Why, thank you, Sue-lynn," I managed. "Thanks a lot. I would like very much to borrow it sometime."

"Would you like it now?" she asked, proffering it.

"No, thank you," I said, around the lump in my throat. "I've had a turn already. You go ahead."

"O.K.," she murmured. Then—"Teacher?"

"Yes?"

Shyly she leaned against me, her cheek on my shoulder. She looked up at me with her warm, unshuttered eyes, then both arms were suddenly around my neck in a brief awkward embrace.

"Watch out!" I whispered laughing into the collar of her blue dress. "You'll lose it again!"

"No I won't," she laughed back, patting the flat pocket of her dress. "Not ever, ever again!"

Artist Unknown

BY HEYWOOD BROUN

THE ragged man eased himself over to the fat customer who sat alone in a far corner of the bar.

"Charlie, the barkeep, tells me you're a newspaperman," he began in a wheedling way.

"So what?"

"I was just wondering whether you'd buy a fellow a couple of drinks if he told you a story that maybe you would write up for a paper or something."

"Let's hear the story."

"Oh," said the ragged man who by this time had eased himself into a chair, "I couldn't do that unless you bought me one of the drinks right now to get started on."

"Bring him a whiskey," called the fat reporter without much enthusiasm.

The interloper reached eagerly for the drink when it was set before him. It was a thin hand with long tapering fingers. It was a fine hand, but that might have passed unnoticed because it trembled so violently. The drink being done, the man with a story began, "I used to be an etcher and a drypoint man."

"You mean you were an artist?"

"I guess that's what you'd call it. And I was a good one. I studied in Paris and in Rome before I came here and in those days I only got drunk once and so often. Nobody in particular knew anything about me, but take it from me I was good. If you're a lefthanded pitcher somebody'll discover you, but there's nobody scouting around for etchers. Maybe that's why I got drunk. And this time I was good and drunk. It started on Easter Sunday and finally it was Monday morning and somehow or other I was in a cell in the West Forty-seventh Street police station with a cut over my left eye. When I woke up, the sun was streaming into that first cell. It only gets the light early in the morning.

"I should have had the shakes and the jitters but, for some reason, I felt fine. There was an energy in me. Sometime during the night I'd dreamed of a picture. The whole thing was complete in my mind. All I had to do was to find a surface and set it down. In my pocket there was an etcher's needle. I looked at the wall of the cell. It was steel and just recently they'd put a coat of dark green paint on it. The surface was soft but not gummy. It was all right. Something like wax. The steel underneath was bright like silver. If you know anything about etching you understand that you don't try to cut into the metal with your needle. That's left for the acid.

"With the bright metal underneath and the dark paint my fine lines showed up sharp and clear. I never worked so fast or intently in my life. I did the Crucifixion.

"You wouldn't understand about composition, I suppose, but the idea was this. Although there was a lot of detail—Roman soldiers and servants of the High Priest and all that and not skimped at all—the emphasis went on two faces. You wouldn't be interested in the technical details, but it's as simple as this. Everything in the composition led the eye to the Man on the cross and his mother, Mary, who watched afar off. And I made the face of Jesus serene, exalted. There was no suggestion of agony in his expression. Already he felt the surge of resurrection. It was his mother's face which mirrored the agony. It was as if the nails pierced her hands and feet and as if she bore Him again. Do you get what I'm driving at?"

The fat man nodded slowly.

"I worked fast and full of fever but I hadn't quite finished when I heard a cop coming down the hall to take us off to court. I slipped the etching tool into my pocket and the cop didn't even come into the cell. He simply called, 'Get a move on, bum, the wagon's waiting.' In court the Magistrate said, 'Learn to hold your liquor like a gentleman,' and turned me loose a free man.

"By now I did have the jitters and it was almost a week before I thought of the picture again. Then I tried to do it in the regular way on a zinc plate. It was no good. Something was gone. I destroyed the plate. In the last six months I've tried a dozen times, copper as well as zinc. No go any time. I can't get what I put on the wall of that cell Easter Monday morning.

"And then one day about a month ago I picked up an evening paper and saw what I guess you call a feature story—a two-column head. It said, MIRACLE IN WEST 47TH ST. POLICE STATION. And the story went on to say that for a long time the cops have been wondering about a marvelous picture scratched in the paint of cell No. 1. According to this newspaper story, there's no record of anybody having been in the cell the night they think the picture must have been made. Of course, the truth is that it may have been there for weeks before any cop noticed it. Lots of people scratch things on the walls of cells. All sorts of things, but not like my picture. And the newspaper story goes on to say that several great artists have looked at the picture in cell No. 1 and that they all say it's a work of genius. And then, to nail down the miracle theory, the police say that the cell has a curious influence on prisoners. They put the worst drunks in there and in the morning they come out sane, sober and exalted."

The reporter interrupted. "Why don't you go down to the station and explain that you did the picture and get the credit? After all they've got your name on the blotter and in the police record."

"Who would believe me? And it isn't my name. I can't even remember what name I did give or what address. You see this was all of six months ago and at that time I thought I might be disgraced if anybody knew I'd been picked up as drunk and disorderly. It wouldn't matter now."

"Well," said the reporter, "even if you have got the shakes you could draw something like the picture. That would prove you did it. How would you know otherwise?"

"That's too late, too. That feature story has a reproduction of the picture. Anybody could copy that. Anybody can copy that, but drunk or sober I'm the only man who can finish it. My name wouldn't matter. I could sign myself with every one of those last missing lines. Drunk or sober. That was the scheme.

"Two weeks ago I tried it. I would be the first and the worst drunk of the night and they would put me in the cell which brings sanity and exaltation to even the lowest bum. I took no chances. I put what was left of my pride in my pocket and also my etcher's needle. I got myself roaring. And I chose a saloon just around the corner from the West Forty-seventh Street Station. At that I miscalculated the time. It slipped by on me and so, although I was probably the worst drunk in the precinct, I wasn't the first. The sun was already up when I staggered around and lay me down on the steps of the police station. I didn't have long to wait. In a few minutes a couple of cops came swinging down the street heading for the station. They seemed a little surprised to find me there on the steps and one of them clubbed me on the soles of the feet. 'Come along, bum,' he said. 'This is the shortest haul I've ever had in my fifteen years on the force.' They jerked me to my feet and started to rough me up a little and out from the station came a young cop with his face all aglow. 'Boys,' he called out to them, 'let that poor old bum alone.'

" 'What's biting you?' asked the one who clubbed me.

" 'It's like this, Mike,' answered the young cop. 'I'm just after putting a drunk in cell No. 1 and I saw that picture. I never saw it like this before. The sun is shining on those faces. It is a miracle.'

" 'Here,' he said, taking a dollar out of his pocket, 'give me fifty cents, Mike, and let me have what you've got, Tom.'

"It amounted to a dollar and ninety-five cents. The young cop called a taxi from in front of the bail bond office across the street and said to the man, 'Take this poor fellow and drive him around till he sobers up. See that he gets a good breakfast and then turn him loose in God's bright sunshine.'

"And so," said the ragged man, "I remain mute, sodden and inglorious and there's nothing can be done about it."

"Well," said the fat reporter, "you can have that other drink."

The Silence

BY VENARD MCLAUGHLIN

THREE DAYS before The Silence came the old man touched Luciffe's hand and fell over dead. That was on May 3, 1974.

Sorkt saw it and he heard what the old man said. It was the old man's one-hundred-and-tenth birthday anniversary, and the people of Lum were gathered to honor him. They filed by, shaking hands. Only Luciffe the blacksmith stood back.

Sorkt remembered that. All the others had passed by. Then Luciffe came forward. He reached out a hand.

"But you made the whistles!" cried the old man. Then he touched Luciffe's hand and fell over dead. That was all.

But Sorkt remembered it. And because he did, he blamed himself. He said he should have known.

But how could he? That was three days before The Silence! No man could know.

Yet Sorkt said he should have; that he almost did. I will leave that to you gentlemen. These are the facts.

Already it is hard for you to remember Earth as it was. Or even Lum Village. Yet you all remember Luciffe. You remember the smithy south of town. You remember him standing in the door, spread-legged, before his flaming forge. Always red-flaming. Remember?

Yes, that's right, he did. He made whistles of willow shoots for you when you were boys—whenever you had the courage to go ask him—Yes, you remember Luciffe, all of you.

On the old man's birthday, Sorkt said, Luciffe came to the celebration in his long black apron, black beard and hair well brushed. Sorkt couldn't remember ever before seeing him away from the smithy.

Do any of you? Ah—you see?

Sorkt watched Luciffe. He watched him stand back from the crowd. He saw him come forward, touch the old man, and when the old man fell dead, go quietly away. And seeing that, Sorkt said, he knew instinctively a dread had come.

He thought about it, worried over it. The rest of the day back at his Paln on the local level he couldn't work. He kept feeling a dread.

At sundown he took the ground-beam and went out toward his home, walking. He said it was still. Just at sundown, no one in the streets, no wind. He walked slower and slower and once he stopped, listening to the silence.

The trees didn't move. Black iron against the sky, no wind. He walked on and he didn't go home. He went to Luciffe's.

You remember the gravel road running through brambles? The smithy standing alone in a patch of thorns and weeds?

He walked out there. Just before he came opposite the smithy he stopped. He felt the silence grow deeper. He stopped and stood still, even holding his breath. Right then, he was near knowing.

He looked up and Luciffe was watching him from the smithy door. For a moment they looked at each other. Then Sorkt said, "Good evening."

Luciffe stood silently. "What are you doing?"

Sorkt gave a little laugh as a man does caught at something foolish. He didn't like to admit that he was listening to silence. "Trying to see what bird that was," he pretended, and craned his neck as though he was trying to see a bird.

It was the wrong thing. Sorkt said even then—three days before—the birds were gone. Did any of you notice? Three days before?

"You were hearing The Silence," Luciffe said.

"Well—"

"Come in," Luciffe said. "I've been expecting you."

"Expecting me?"

"I chose you," Luciffe said.

Sorkt said he crossed the brambles to the door scarcely knowing what he was doing. He couldn't see anything but Luciffe's eyes, and The Silence was starting to press.

Did any of you notice that three days before?

He did. In that moment the hot smell of the smithy, the fiery forge, The Silence, and Luciffe were all together in his mind. He was very near knowing, you see.

He went inside and sat on a long bench against the wall. The Silence wasn't so painful in there. There was a spit of sound from the forge. Luciffe followed him and stood before him with his back to the forge.

There was no bellows, Sorkt said.

He felt better sitting down and the spit of sound helped. He wasn't frightened exactly, but he felt funny. He felt as you all did the day before it came, or maybe not until that morning.

"You were listening to The Silence," Luciffe said. His eyes were glowing.

"It *was* mighty quiet," Sorkt said with a little laugh.

"Yes. Don't you remember?"

"Remember?"

"Yes. Don't you—a little? Think!"

Sorkt looked hard at those eyes. He said for that instant everything seemed like a repetition. Everything was familiar. It seemed all to have happened before. It was like that dream all men have of falling which is remembered before it comes. A race-memory.

"Remember?"

"Silence," Sorkt said. He took a deep breath and looked all around, but he could see only the eyes. "The Silence—" but he couldn't get any farther.

"You don't remember," Luciffe said, and his shoulders seemed to sag a little. They straightened right away and he rubbed his beard. "You will, one time. When you do, I can go back."

Sorkt looked up blankly. Luciffe was staring over his head, sighing. He seemed to be seeing a long way off.

It got dark outside. It was dark inside except for the forge. For a long while Sorkt just sat there and Luciffe stood in front of him staring over his head.

Finally Luciffe sighed again and looked down at Sorkt. "Well—so it is. Come with me. I'll show you the place."

"The—place?"

"Come on."

Sorkt followed him toward the end of the shop. It was a long way. He got tired. Dark all around. He could hear footsteps ahead of him, and his own. It took a long time.

At last Luciffe stopped. There was a sound of chains, a sudden burst of light from the floor. Sorkt blinked.

When he could see again, Luciffe was already halfway down a ladder calling him to follow. He had lifted a trapdoor and light rushed up from below.

Dazed, Sorkt followed. He couldn't see around him much. The ladder was slippery and kept twisting around in his hands. He had to watch it. He had an impression of sunlight and breezes and brooks flowing, but he wasn't sure. The trapdoor closed over his head. The Silence let up and he breathed easier.

He felt ground under his feet and started to look around but there were those eyes again.

"Come on," Luciffe said, and they walked.

They walked a long time. Sorkt began to have a feeling of simultaneousness, as though he'd been walking forever and would go on walking forever, but that he'd done and would do millions of other things at the same time, and forever, too. And that anyhow it didn't make any difference, that there wasn't any Forever—only an eternal Now. But that that was a Forever too.

It was like being a separate person for every act and thought. He lifted an arm and knew that the arm went on lifting eternally, and that it always had been lifting eternally. He felt as though his life in Lum had been looking through a microscope at an amoeba, and down here he was lifting his head and seeing the whole world for the first time.

He grew tired and he couldn't see much but he kept having impressions. There seemed to be a lot going on. Everything that had ever happened or ever was going to happen seemed to be taking place right then and there. When Luciffe stopped again everything was quiet and fresh-smelling.

They were in a park of some kind, blossoming trees, flowers, birds, soft sunlight. They sat down and someone brought Sorkt a frosted mug of something thick and sweet like a honey malted milk.

He drank it with Luciffe watching him with a sad or discouraged expression.

"Here we are again," Luciffe said, sighing. He smoothed his hands on the black leather apron, looking about. "See if you can't do better this time."

Sorkt wiped his mouth wishing for more of the honey malted. He frowned. "Just what am I supposed to do?"

Luciffe stared at him. He stood up suddenly. He sat again. "Don't you even know that?"

"Well–" Sorkt began. He glanced suddenly at his hand and saw it was holding a fresh mug of honey malted. It was good stuff. He drank.

"The Struggle–" Luciffe suggested. "Remember?–the Struggle–?"

Sorkt became suddenly full and sleepy. He shook his head. "I'm afraid not."

"The Struggle," Luciffe said, more loudly. Then he bowed his head and rubbed his hand all over his face and beard. He drew in a big breath. "Well, then–listen again–"

Sorkt yawned. He felt fine. He liked it in that park.

"The Struggle," Luciffe said. "There is but one supreme struggle and that is between The Silence and The Truce–" He looked at Sorkt. "Remember? The Silence–The Truce? What are the earth, the sun–the planets, the stars–?"

"The Truce," Sorkt said sleepily.

"And what surrounds The Truce, pressing always, always drawing closer?"

"The Silence," Sorkt said through a yawn.

"And before The Truce there was only The Silence, and after The Truce there is only The Silence–"

"Yes," Sorkt said.

"And each time you fail The Silence must draw in and cleanse the worlds and go back again–"

"Yes."

"–until finally you succeed. Then The Silence comes and it does not go back, and there is only The Silence. The Truce is destroyed and I can return–"

"Yes."

Sorkt went to sleep. All those words and his own answers meant nothing to him then. They came, he supposed later, from the race-memory. It was too late, he said, when he understood. By that time The Silence had come.

When he awoke Luciffe had gone. He was alone in that park and everything was fresh-smelling and fine. He felt good lying there, but the minute he moved there was a twinge in his side. He put his hand over the pain, and then he sat up straight.

Still holding his side he stared through the trees. He stood up. The most beautiful woman he'd ever seen was coming toward him. She was smiling and when she saw him staring at her she laughed a little and waved.

"Hello there," she said.

Sorkt just stared. She was improperly dressed, he said. She came toward him and stood smiling and friendly looking up at him.

"Now you won't be alone," she said.

Sorkt was pretty much embarrassed and he tried not to look at her, but he couldn't just look away. That wouldn't be polite. You cannot ignore a beautiful woman, he said.

So he sat down and closed his eyes and remarked about the pain in his side.

"But of course!" she said gaily. She got some fragrant herbs and bandaged his side and he felt one hundred percent better right away. It hadn't been bad anyhow.

As soon as he thought politeness demanded it he opened his eyes to look at her again. He was much relieved. She had made herself a garment of flowers, he said, and she looked fine.

They got to talking and Sorkt got a big kick out of it. She was about the smartest girl he'd ever seen, he said, and in some ways the dumbest. Every time he asked her name she said she didn't have any yet. When he asked her radiophone wave-number she just smiled at him.

"I haven't the faintest idea what you mean," she'd say.

She didn't seem to have the faintest idea about politics or athletics or current events, either, Sorkt said. For instance she didn't even know who was chairman of the Executive Council.

She acted as though she'd never even heard of the Second Empire or the Stvatt, or who won the Inter-Pole this year.

But she was smart too, and her smartness was practical. She'd go away and come back a few minutes later with all the fruit and honey malteds she could carry. Oranges sweeter than sugar, he said. Grapes big as your fist.

It wasn't until he made a joke of naming her that he caught on, and then it was too late.

They were sitting around talking, watching the sun go down back of the trees and he said, "Well, baby, you've got to have a name. If you won't tell me, I'll give you one."

"Please do," she said. "It's about time."

They both laughed.

The sun went down. It was nice and quiet and fine. "Tell you what," Sorkt said. "We'll just call you for right now. We'll call you Evening."

"Oh, how nice!" Evening said. "And for short you can call me . . ."

And that's when it hit Sorkt that Luciffe had made a mistake. He jumped up and got out of there running, he said, like a bat. He tore through the park and out into the simultaneous region running for all he was worth. All the way he kept remembering what Luciffe and he had talked about and he remembered the dread he had felt when the old man dropped dead, and he put his head down and made tracks.

He got up the ladder. It kept hissing and twisting and it was slippery but he reached the trapdoor, stumbled across Luciffe's floor and sat down on that bench gasping for breath.

"You!" Luciffe cried and he stood spread-legged staring. Behind him the forge glowed. The Silence was bad, but it wasn't too deep in the smithy yet.

"Look, it's this way," Sorkt panted out, trying to get his breath and easing along that bench toward the front door at the same time, "I ain't him. I'm Sorkt. You got the wrong guy!"

He planned to say that, and make a run for the door. Even then he felt he might get through to Lum in time to give warning. But he didn't have a chance.

Before he could move Luciffe sprang to the door and let out a shout, Sorkt said, like a couple of planets smacking together. It knocked Sorkt out cold and the next thing he knew he was lying under the smoking wreckage of the smithy, screaming with the pain of The Silence. And the cold was coming then, too, and he began burrowing into the earth by sheer instinct.

That's how he got here, gentlemen. He burrowed right through to this cavern, more dead than alive. None of you was in this part of the Underground at the moment, gentlemen. No one but the young man from East Lum, who pulled him from the burrow and gave him artificial respiration.

While Sorkt was getting his breath the young man from East Lum told him of the coming of The Silence, how it had pushed the rivers and the mountains into the earth, dried out the seas and killed all but a few hundred people around Lum who took to the Underground in time.

When he had finished Sorkt gasped out his story. It was then he admitted he should have known what was to happen the instant he saw the old man fall dead, crying, "But you made the whistles!" Sorkt said it was shock that killed him. The shock of suddenly realizing that Luciffe had made whistles for him as a boy a hundred years or so ago, and for his father and his father's father before him. It came on the old man—seeing Luciffe away from the smithy for the first time like that—that the blacksmith should have died long ago, that no mortal could live as long as Luciffe was living. Yet here he was just as he had always been. It was too much for the old man on his one-hundred-and-tenth birthday anniversary. He just keeled over dead.

Sorkt said he should have known then, or at least it should have been clear to him when he saw that forge flaming and no bellows. He should have known then, he said, that Luciffe was no man at all but the Fallen Angel and that the fire in the forge was not earth-fire by a long shot.

But what threw him off was Luciffe himself. He was such a decent sort. Just like anyone else with an unpleasant job to do, eager to get it done and get back home, unhappy over delay.

Sorkt said he could understand a good many things now. How, for example, when men knew the world had been going on for eons there was only about seven thousand years of recorded history. He said that indicated that The Silence had come before—sometime before that seven-thousand-year mark (and he had no idea how many thousands or millions of times before that), cleansed the Earth of people, pushed in the mountains and rivers, dried up the seas, and given the race of man a fresh start in a clean new world.

Evidences of man before the historical period, he contended, being in the Earth itself, in rock strata, proved the fact, just as the future race beginning after this Silence would find evidences of the men of 1974 crushed deep into the face of the Earth.

"I see it all," Sorkt said. "Because he got too ambitious up there poor old Luciffe got exiled to Earth to ride herd on the Human Experiment, and he is having quite a time. It seems," Sorkt said sadly, shaking his head, "that our race always gets off to a flying start and then just naturally sinks down into civilization and gets so bad it has to be Silenced out and started all over again." He sighed. "And this time we might have had a chance to prepare against The Silence if I hadn't fallen down. . . . I should have known when I saw that bellowless forge!"

Or, he said, if not then, he should by any judgment have caught on when he woke up in that park with the pain in his ribs and saw the beautiful woman.

As he said that, the young man from East Lum started. His head came up and he frowned, staring hard at Sorkt. "There seems to be something mighty familiar to me about that affair," he said slowly. "Pain in the ribs, did you say?"

"Yes," Sorkt said, and pulled up his shirt to show his operation.

The young man from East Lum stared harder and his face began to change. He stepped closer to Sorkt. "And what did you say the lady's name was?" His voice had gotten low and tense.

"You mean that torrid little spark in the park?" Sorkt said with a reminiscent smile. "Why, she said she didn't have any."

"But you gave her one?"

"Well, for a joke," Sorkt said. "She wasn't handing out a name and radiophone number—you could see she'd been around—I just called her Eve—" He broke off and his face went white. He stared at the young man and took a quick step backward. "S-say—! Aren't you—?"

"You bet your socks I am," the young man said. He was very close to Sorkt then. "*You* know who I am."

"B-but it wasn't my fault!" Sorkt stuttered, backing to the wall. "Anyhow—we—we just—just talked!"

"Oh, yeah?" the young man said. He moved nearer to Sorkt.

"Now—now Mr. Adams!" Sorkt cried. "Now be reasonable—!"

But quite calmly, young Mr. Adams from East Lum reached out, grabbed Sorkt's neck and shook him to death. He shook the dead body a few times muttering to himself. He was upset.

"Just talked!" he muttered. "The devil you say!"

He dropped the corpse and stared at it a moment. "A devil of a big mistake," he gritted, "getting him for me!" A light came into his eye. "But just wait until she pulls that old apple gag *this* time!"

And with that he turned and disappeared into the burrow Sorkt had made, which closed up immediately after him.

And now, gentlemen, if you will continue your inventory of supplies brought down here at the start of The Silence. . . .

Those are the canned beans, I believe. Pulped from The Silence, of course, but edible. . . .

Jones is about to have another spell. If you will kindly crack him across the base of the skull—thank you. He can't bear The Silence even down here in the Underground, it seems. The darkness, too. . . . It's The Silence, of course, that blots out all your lamps, even down here. . . .

I? Who am I, did you ask? Pardon me while I laugh hollowly.

I? Why I am the ghost of the deceased Sorkt, waiting to represent the dead of This Silence at the Garden of Eden. I go as a serpent, you know.

What am I waiting for? Why, I must represent *all* the dead of The Silence, gentlemen. I am waiting for you.

Yes, The Silence will come even here, gentlemen. Meanwhile I choose to be helpful.

Now, how many cans did you say, of baked beans?

The Dream Quest of Unknown Kadath

BY H. P. LOVECRAFT

THREE TIMES Randolph Carter dreamed of the marvelous city, and three times was he snatched away while still he paused on the high terrace above it. All golden and lovely it blazed in the sunset, with walls, temples, colonnades, and arched bridges of veined marble, silver-basined fountains of prismatic spray in broad squares and perfumed gardens, and wide streets marching between delicate trees and blossom-laden urns and ivory statues in gleaming rows, while on steep northward slopes climbed tiers of red roofs and old peaked gables harboring little lanes of grassy cobbles. It was a fever of the gods, a fanfare of supernal trumpets and a clash of immortal cymbals. Mystery hung about it like clouds about a fabulous unvisited mountain; and as Carter stood breathless and expectant on that balustraded parapet, there swept up to him the poignancy and suspense of almost-vanished memory, the pain of lost things and the maddening need to place again what had once been an awesome and momentous place.

He knew that for him its meaning must once have been supreme, though in what cycle or incarnation he had known it, or whether in dream or waking, he could not tell. Vaguely it called up glimpses of a far-forgotten first youth, when wonder and pleasure lay in all the mystery of days, and dawn and dusk alike strode forth prophetic to the eager sound of lutes and song, unclosing fiery gates toward further and surprising marvels. But each night as he stood on that high marble terrace with the curious urns and carved rail and looked off over that hushed sunset city of beauty and unearthly immanence, he felt the bondage of dream's tyrannous gods; for in no wise could he leave that lofty spot, or descend the wide marmoreal flights flung endlessly down to where those streets of elder witchery lay outspread and beckoning.

When for the third time he awakened with those flights still undescended and those hushed sunset streets still untraversed, he prayed long and earnestly to the hidden gods of dream that brood capricious above the clouds on unknown Kadath, in the cold waste where no man treads. But the gods made no answer and showed no relenting, nor did they give any favoring sign when he prayed to them in dream and invoked them sacrificially through the bearded priests of Nasht and Kaman-Thah, whose cavern-temple with its pillar of flame lies not far from the gates of the waking world. It seemed, however, that his prayers must have been adversely heard, for after even the first of them he ceased wholly to behold the marvelous city, as if his three glimpses from afar had been mere accidents or oversights, and against some hidden plan or wish of the gods.

At length, sick with longing for those glittering sunset streets and cryptical hill lanes among ancient tiled roofs, nor able sleeping or waking to drive them from his mind, Carter resolved to go with bold entreaty whither no man had gone before, and dare the icy deserts through the dark to where unknown Kadath, veiled in cloud and crowned with unimagined stars, holds secret and nocturnal the onyx castle of the Great Ones.

In light slumber he descended the seventy steps to the cavern of flame and talked of this design to the bearded priests Nasht and Kaman-Thah. And the priests shook their pshent-bearing heads and vowed it would be the death of his soul. They pointed out that the Great Ones had already shown their wish, and that it is not agreeable to them to be harassed by insistent pleas. They reminded him, too, that not only had no man ever been to Kadath, but no man had ever suspected in what part of space it may lie; whether it be in the dreamlands around our own world or in those surrounding some unguessed companion of Fomalhaut or Aldebaran. If in our dreamland, it might conceivably be reached, but only three human souls since time began had ever crossed and recrossed the black impious gulfs to other dreamlands, and of that three, two had come back quite mad. There were, in such voyages, incalculable local dangers, as well as that shocking final peril which gibbers unmentionably outside the ordered universe, where no dreams reach; that last amorphous blight of nethermost confusion which blasphemes and bubbles at the center of all infinity—the boundless demon sultan Azathoth, whose name no lips dare speak aloud, and who gnaws hungrily in inconceivable, unlighted chambers beyond time amidst the muffled, maddening beating of vile drums and the thin, monotonous whine of accursed flutes, to which detestable pounding and piping dance slowly, awkwardly, and absurdly the gigantic Ultimate Gods, the blind, voiceless, tenebrous, mindless Other Gods whose soul and messenger is the crawling chaos Nyarlathotep.

Of these things was Carter warned by the priests Nasht and Kaman-Thah in the cavern of flame; but still he resolved to find the gods on unknown Kadath in the cold waste, wherever that might be, and to win from them the sight and remembrance and shelter of the marvelous sunset city. He knew that his journey would be strange and long, and that the Great Ones would be against it; but being old in the land of dream, he counted on many useful memories and devices to aid him. So asking a formal blessing of the priests and thinking shrewdly on his course, he boldly descended the seven hundred steps to the Gate of Deeper Slumber and set out through the Enchanted Wood.

In the tunnels of that twisted wood, whose low prodigious oaks twine groping boughs and shine dim with the phosphorescence of strange fungi, dwell the furtive and secretive Zoogs, who know many obscure secrets of the dream world and a few of the waking world, since the wood at two places touches the lands of men, though it would be disastrous to say where. Certain unexplained rumors, events, and vanishments occur among men where the Zoogs have access, and it is well that they cannot travel far outside the world of dream. But over the nearer parts of the dream world they pass freely, flitting small and brown and unseen and bearing back piquant tales to beguile the hours around their hearths in the forest they love. Most of them live in burrows, but some inhabit the trunks of the great trees; and although they live mostly on fungi, it is muttered that they also have a slight taste for meat, either physical or spiritual, for certainly many dreamers have entered that wood who have not come out. Carter, however, had no fear, for he was an old dreamer and had learned their fluttering language and made many a treaty with them, having found through their help the splendid city of Celephais in Ooth-Nargai beyond the Tanarian Hills, where reigns half the year the great King Kuranes, a man he had known by another name in life. Kuranes was the one soul who had been to the star-gulfs and returned free of madness.

Threading now the low phosphorescent aisles between those gigantic trunks, Carter made fluttering sounds in the manner of the Zoogs, and listened now and then for responses. He remembered that one particular village of the creatures was in the center of the wood, where a circle of great mossy stones in what was once a clearing tells of older and more terrible dwellers long forgotten, and toward this spot he hastened. He traced his way by the grotesque fungi, which always seem better nourished as one approaches the dread circle where elder beings danced and sacrificed. Finally the great light of those thicker fungi revealed a sinister green-and-gray vastness pushing up through the roof of the forest and out of sight. This was the nearest of the great ring of stones, and Carter knew he was close to the Zoog village. Renewing his fluttering sound, he waited patiently, and was at last rewarded by an impression of many eyes watching him. It was the Zoogs, for one sees their weird eyes long before one can discern their small, slippery brown outlines.

Out they swarmed, from hidden burrow and honeycombed tree, till the whole dim-lit region was alive with them. Some of the wilder ones brushed Carter unpleasantly, and one even nipped loathsomely at his ear; but these lawless spirits were soon restrained by their elders. The Council of Sages, recognizing the visitor, offered a gourd of fermented sap from a haunted tree unlike the others, which had grown from a seed dropped down by someone on the moon; and as Carter drank it ceremoniously, a very strange colloquy began. The Zoogs did not, unfortunately, know where the peak of Kadath lies, nor could they even say whether the cold waste is in our dream world or in another. Rumors of the Great Ones came equally from all points, and one might only say that they were likelier to be seen on high mountain peaks than in valleys, since on such peaks they dance reminiscently when the moon is above and the clouds beneath.

Then one very ancient Zoog recalled a thing unheard of by the others, and said that in Ulthar, beyond the River Skai, there still lingered the last copy of those inconceivably old Pnakotic Manuscripts made by waking men in forgotten boreal kingdoms and borne into the land of dreams when the hairy cannibal Gnophkehs overcame many-templed Olathoe and slew all the heroes of the land of Lomar. Those manuscripts, he said, told much of the gods, and besides, in Ulthar there were men who had seen the signs of the gods, and even one old priest who had scaled a great mountain to behold them dancing by moonlight. He had failed, though his companion had succeeded and had perished.

So Randolph Carter thanked the Zoogs, who fluttered amicably and gave him another gourd of moon-tree wine to take with him, and set out through the phosphorescent wood for the other side, where the rushing Skai flows down from the slopes of Lerion, and Hatheg and Nir and Ulthar dot the plain. Behind him, furtive and unseen, crept several of the curious Zoogs, for they wished to learn what might befall him and bear back the legend to their people. The vast oaks grew thicker as he pushed on beyond the village, and he looked sharply for a certain spot where they would thin somewhat, standing quite dead or dying among the unnaturally dense fungi and the rotting mold and mushy logs of their fallen brothers. There he would turn sharply aside, for at that spot a mighty slab of stone rests on the forest floor, and those who have dared approach it say that it bears an iron ring three feet wide. Remembering the archaic circle of great mossy rocks, and what it was possibly set up for, the Zoogs do not pause near that expansive slab with its huge ring; for they realize that not all which is forgotten need necessarily be dead, and they would not like to see the slab rise slowly and deliberately.

Carter detoured at the proper place, and heard behind him the frightened fluttering of some of the more timid Zoogs. He had known they would follow him, so he was not disturbed, for one grows accustomed to the anomalies of these prying creatures. It was twilight when he came to the edge of the wood, and the strengthening glow told him it was the twilight of morning. Over fertile plains rolling down to the Skai he saw the smoke of cottage chimneys, and on every hand were the hedges and plowed fields and thatched roofs of a peaceful land. Once he stopped at a farmhouse well for a cup of water, and all the dogs barked affrightedly at the inconspicuous Zoogs that crept through the grass behind. At another house, where people were stirring, he asked questions about the gods, and whether they danced often upon Lerion; but the farmer and his wife would only make the Elder Sign and tell him the way to Nir and Ulthar.

At noon he walked through the one broad high street of Nir, which he had once visited and which marked his farthest former travels in this direction; and soon afterward he came to the great stone bridge across the Skai, into whose central piece the masons had sealed a living human sacrifice when they built it thirteen hundred years before. Once he was on the other side, the frequent presence of cats (who all arched their backs at the trailing Zoogs) revealed the near neighborhood of Ulthar; for in Ulthar, according to an ancient and significant law, no man may kill a cat. Very pleasant were the suburbs of Ulthar, with their little green cottages and neatly fenced farms; and still pleasanter was the quaint town itself, with its old peaked roofs and overhanging upper stories and numberless chimney pots and narrow hill streets where one can see old cobbles whenever the graceful cats afford space enough. Carter, the cats being somewhat dispersed by the half-seen Zoogs, picked his way directly to the modest Temple of the Elder Ones, where the priests and old records were said to be; and once within that venerable circular tower of ivied stone—which crowns Ulthar's highest hill—he sought out the patriarch Atal, who had been up the forbidden peak Hatheg-Kla in the stony desert and had come down again alive.

Atal, seated on an ivory dais in a festooned shrine at the top of the temple, was fully three centuries old, but still very keen of mind and memory. From him Carter learned many things about the gods, but mainly that they are indeed only Earth's gods, feebly ruling our own dreamland and having no power or habitation elsewhere. They might, Atal said, heed a man's prayer if in good humor; but one must not think of climbing to their onyx stronghold atop Kadath in the cold waste. It was lucky that no man knew where Kadath towers, for the fruits of ascending it would be very grave. Atal's companion, Barzai the Wise, had been drawn screaming into the sky for climbing merely the known peak of Hatheg-Kla. With unknown Kadath, if ever found, matters would be much worse; for although Earth's gods may sometimes be surpassed by a wise mortal, they are protected by the Other Gods from Outside, whom it is better not to discuss. At least twice in the world's history the Other Gods set their seal upon Earth's primal granite; once in antediluvian times, as guessed from a drawing in those parts of the Pnakotic Manuscripts too ancient to be read, and once on Hatheg-Kla when Barzai the Wise tried to see Earth's gods dancing by moonlight. So, Atal said, it would be much better to let all gods alone except in tactful prayers.

Carter, though disappointed by Atal's discouraging advice and by the meager help to be found in the Pnakotic Manuscripts and the Seven Cryptical Books of Hsan, did not wholly despair. First he questioned the old priest about that marvelous sunset city seen from the railed terrace, thinking that perhaps he might find it without the gods' aid; but Atal could tell him nothing. Probably, Atal said, the place belonged to his special dream world and not to the general land of vision that many know, and conceivably it might be on another planet. In that case, Earth's gods could not guide him if they would. But this was not likely, since the stopping of the dreams showed pretty clearly that it was something the Great Ones wished to hide from him.

Then Carter did a wicked thing—offering his guileless host so many drafts of the moon-wine which the Zoogs had given him that the old man became irresponsibly talkative. Robbed of his reserve, poor Atal babbled freely of forbidden things; telling of a great image reported by travelers as carved on the solid rock of the mountain Ngranek, on the isle of Oriab in the Southern Sea, and hinting that it may be a likeness which Earth's gods once wrought of their own features in the days when they danced by moonlight on that mountain. And he hiccupped likewise that the features of that image are very strange, so that one might easily recognize them, and that they are sure signs of the authentic race of the gods.

Now, the use of all this in finding the gods became at once apparent to Carter. It is known that in disguise the younger among the Great Ones often espouse the daughters of men, so that around the borders of the cold waste wherein stands Kadath the peasants must all bear their blood. This being so, the way to find that waste must be to see the stone face on Ngranek and mark the features; then, having noted them with care, to search for such features among living men. Where they are plainest and thickest, there must the gods dwell nearest; and whatever stony waste lies back of the villages must be that place wherein stands Kadath.

Much of the Great Ones might be learned in such regions, and those with their blood might inherit little memories very useful to a seeker. They might not know their parentage, for the gods so dislike to be known among men that none can be found who has seen their faces wittingly—a thing which Carter realized even as he sought to scale Kadath. But they would have queer, lofty thoughts misunderstood by their fellows, and would sing of far places and gardens so unlike any known even in the dreamland that common folk would call them fools; and from all this one could perhaps learn old secrets of Kadath, or gain hints of the marvelous sunset city which the gods held secret. And more, one might in certain cases seize some well-loved child of a god as hostage; or even capture some young god himself, disguised and dwelling among men with a comely peasant maiden as his bride.

Atal, however, did not know how to find Ngranek on its isle of Oriab, and recommended that Carter follow the singing Skai under its bridges down to the Southern Sea, where no burgess of Ulthar has ever been, but whence the merchants come in boats or with long caravans of mules and two-wheeled carts. There is a great city there, Dylath-Leen, but in Ulthar its reputation is bad because of the black three-banked galleys that sail to it with rubies from no clearly named shore. The traders that come from those galleys to deal with the jewelers are human, or nearly so, but the rowers are never beheld; and it is not thought wholesome in Ulthar that merchants should trade with black ships from unknown places whose rowers cannot be exhibited.

By the time he had given this information Atal was very drowsy, and Carter laid him gently on a couch of inlaid ebony and gathered his long beard decorously on his chest. As he turned to go, he observed that no suppressed fluttering followed him, and wondered why the Zoogs had become so lax in their curious pursuit. Then he noticed all the sleek, complacent cats of Ulthar licking their chops with unusual gusto, and recalled the spitting and caterwauling he had faintly heard in lower parts of the temple while absorbed in the old priest's conversation. He recalled, too, the evilly hungry way in which an especially impudent young Zoog had regarded a small black kitten in the cobbled street outside. And because he loved nothing on earth more than small black kittens, he stooped and petted the sleek cats of Ulthar as they licked their chops, and did not mourn because those inquisitive Zoogs would escort him no farther.

It was sunset now, so Carter stopped at an ancient inn on a steep little street overlooking the lower town. And as he went out on the balcony of his room and gazed down at the sea of red-tiled roofs and cobbled ways and the pleasant fields beyond, all mellow and magical in the slanted light, he swore that Ulthar would be a very likely place to dwell in always, were not the memory of a greater sunset city ever goading one onward toward unknown perils. Then twilight fell, and the pink walls of the plastered gables turned violet and mystic, and little yellow lights floated up one by one from old latticed windows. And sweet bells pealed in the temple tower above, and the first star winked softly above the meadows across the Skai. With the night came song, and Carter nodded as the lutanists praised ancient days from beyond the filigreed balconies and tessellated courts of simple Ulthar. And there might have been sweetness even in the voices of Ulthar's many cats, but that they were mostly heavy and silent from strange feasting. Some of them stole off to those cryptic realms which are known only to cats and which villagers say are on the moon's dark side, whither the cats leap from tall housetops, but one small black kitten crept upstairs and sprang into Carter's lap to purr and play, and curled up near his feet when he lay down at last on the little couch, whose pillows were stuffed with fragrant, drowsy herbs.

In the morning, Carter joined a caravan of merchants bound for Dylath-Leen with the spun wool of Ulthar and the cabbages of Ulthar's busy farms. And for six days they rode with tinkling bells on the smooth road beside the Skai, stopping some nights at the inns of little quaint fishing towns, and on other nights camping under the stars while snatches of boatmen's songs came from the placid river. The country was very beautiful, with green hedges and groves and picturesque peaked cottages and octagonal windmills.

On the seventh day a blur of smoke rose on the horizon ahead, and then the tall black towers of Dylath-Leen, which is built mostly of basalt. Dylath-Leen, with its thin, angular towers, looks in the distance like a bit of the Giant's Causeway, and its streets are dark and uninviting. There are many dismal sea taverns near the myriad wharves, and all the town is thronged with the strange seamen of every land on earth and of a few which are said to be not on earth. Carter questioned the oddly robed men of that city about the peak of Ngranek, on the isle of Oriab, and found that they knew of it well. Ships came from Baharna on that island, one being due to return thither in only a month, and Ngranek is but two days' zebra ride from that port. But few had seen the stone face of the god, because it is on a very difficult side of Ngranek, which overlooks only sheer crags and a valley of sinister lava. Once the gods were angered with men on that side, and spoke of the matter to the Other Gods.

It was hard to get this information from the traders and sailors in Dylath-Leen's sea taverns, because they mostly preferred to whisper of the black galleys. One of them was due in a week with rubies from its unknown shore, and the townsfolk dreaded to see it dock. The mouths of the men who came from it to trade were too wide, and the way their turbans were humped up in two points above their foreheads was in especially bad taste. And their shoes were the shortest and queerest ever seen in the Six Kingdoms. But worst of all was the matter of the unseen rowers. Those three banks of oars moved too briskly and accurately and vigorously to be comfortable, and it was not right for a ship to stay in port for weeks while the merchants traded, yet to give no glimpse of its crew. It was not fair to the tavern keepers of Dylath-Leen, or to the grocers and butchers, either, for not a scrap of provisions was ever sent aboard. The merchants took only gold and stout black slaves from Parg, across the river. That was all they ever took, those unpleasantly featured merchants and their unseen rowers: never anything from the butchers and grocers, but only gold and the fat black men of Parg, whom they bought by the pound. And the odors from those galleys which the south wind blew in from the wharves are not to be described. Only by constantly smoking strong thagweed could even the hardiest denizen of the old sea taverns bear them. Dylath-Leen would never have tolerated the black galleys had such rubies been obtainable elsewhere, but no mine in all earth's dreamland was known to produce their like.

Of these things Dylath-Leen's cosmopolitan folk chiefly gossiped while Carter waited patiently for the ship from Baharna, which might bear him to the isle whereon carved Ngranek towers lofty and barren. Meanwhile he did not fail to seek through the haunts of far travelers for any tales they might have concerning Kadath in the cold waste, or a marvelous city of marble walls and silver fountains seen below terraces in the sunset. Of these things, however, he learned nothing, though he once thought that a certain old slant-eyed merchant looked queerly intelligent when the cold waste was spoken of. This man was reputed to trade with the horrible stone villages on the icy desert plateau of Leng, which no healthy folk visit and whose evil fires are seen at night from afar. He was even rumored to have dealt with that high priest not to be described, which wears a yellow silken mask over its face and dwells all alone in a prehistoric stone monastery. That such a person might well have had nibbling traffic with such beings as may conceivably dwell in the cold waste was not to be doubted, but Carter soon found that it was no use questioning him.

Then the black galley slipped into the harbor past the basalt wale and the tall lighthouse, silent and alien, and with a strange stench that the south wind drove into the town. Uneasiness rustled through the taverns along that waterfront, and after a while the dark, wide-mouthed merchants with humped turbans and short feet clumped stealthily ashore to seek the bazaars of the jewelers. Carter observed them closely, and disliked them more the longer he looked at them. Then he saw them drive the stout black men of Parg up the gangplank grunting and sweating into that singular galley, and wondered in what lands—or if in any lands at all—those fat pathetic creatures might be destined to serve.

And on the third evening of that galley's stay, one of the uncomfortable merchants spoke to him, smirking sinfully and hinting of what he had heard in the taverns of Carter's quest. He appeared to have knowledge too secret for public telling; and although the sound of his voice was unbearably hateful, Carter felt that the lore of so far a traveler must not be overlooked. He bade him therefore be his guest in locked chambers above, and drew out the last of the Zoogs' moon-wine to loosen his tongue. The strange merchant drank heavily, but smirked unchanged by the draft. Then he drew forth a curious bottle with wine of his own, and Carter saw that the bottle was a single hollowed ruby, grotesquely carved in patterns too fabulous to be comprehended. He offered his wine to his host, and though Carter took only the least sip, he felt the dizziness of space and the fever of unimagined jungles. All the while the guest had been smiling more and more broadly, and as Carter slipped into blankness, the last thing he saw was that dark, odious face convulsed with evil laughter and something quite unspeakable where one of the two frontal puffs of that orange turban had become disarranged with the shakings of that epileptic mirth.

Carter next had consciousness amid horrible odors beneath a tentlike awning on the deck of a ship, with the marvelous coasts of the Southern Sea flying by in unnatural swiftness. He was not chained, but three of the dark, sardonic merchants stood grinning nearby, and the sight of those humps in their turbans made him almost as faint as did the stench that filtered up through the sinister hatches. He saw slip past him the glorious lands and cities of which a fellow dreamer of earth—a lighthouse keeper in ancient Kingsport—had often discoursed in the old days, and recognized the templed terraces of Zak, abode of forgotten dreams; the spires of infamous Thalarion, that demon-city of a thousand wonders where the eidolon Lathi reigns; the charnel gardens of Zura, land of pleasures unattained; and the twin headlands of crystal, meeting above in a resplendent arch, which guard the harbor of Sona-Nyl, blessed land of fancy.

Past all these gorgeous lands the malodorous ship flew unwholesomely, urged by the abnormal strokes of those unseen rowers below. And before the day was done, Carter saw that the steersman could have no other goal than the Basalt Pillars of the West, beyond which simple folk say splendid Cathuria lies, but which wise dreamers well know are the gates of a monstrous cataract wherein the oceans of earth's dreamland drop wholly to abysmal nothingness and shoot through the empty spaces toward other worlds and other stars and the awful voids outside the ordered universe where the demon-sultan Azathoth gnaws hungrily in chaos amid pounding and piping and the hellish dancing of the Other Gods, blind, voiceless, tenebrous, and mindless, with their soul and messenger Nyarlathotep.

Meanwhile, the three sardonic merchants would give no word of their intent, though Carter well knew that they must be leagued with those who wished to hold him from his quest. It is understood in the land of dream that the Other Gods have many agents moving among men; and all these agents, whether wholly human or slightly less than human, are eager to work the will of those blind and mindless things in return for the favor of their hideous soul and messenger, the crawling chaos Nyarlathotep. So Carter inferred that the merchants of the humped turbans, hearing of his daring search for the Great Ones in their castle of Kadath, had decided to take him away and deliver him to Nyarlathotep for whatever nameless bounty might be offered for such a prize. What might be the land of those merchants, in our known universe or in the eldritch spaces outside, Carter could not guess; nor could he imagine at what hellish trysting-place they would meet the crawling chaos to give him up and claim their reward. He knew, however, that no beings as nearly human as these would dare approach the ultimate nighted throne of the demon Azathoth in the formless central void.

At the set of sun, the merchants licked their excessively wide lips and glared hungrily, and one of them went below and returned from some hidden and offensive cabin with a pot and basket of plates. Then they squatted close together beneath the awning and ate the smoking meat that was passed around. But when they gave Carter a portion, he found something very terrible in the size and shape of it, so that he turned even paler than before and cast that portion into the sea when no eye was on him. And again he thought of those unseen rowers beneath, and of the suspicious nourishment from which their far too mechanical strength was derived.

It was dark when the galley passed between the Basalt Pillars of the West and the sound of the ultimate cataract swelled portentous from ahead. And the spray of that cataract rose to obscure the stars, and the deck grew damp, and the vessel reeled in the surging current of the brink. Then, with a queer whistle and plunge, the leap was taken, and Carter felt the terrors of nightmare as earth fell away and the great boat shot silent and cometlike into planetary space. Never before had he known what shapeless black things lurk and caper and flounder all through the ether, leering and grinning at such voyagers as may pass, and sometimes feeling about with slimy paws when some moving object excites their curiosity. These are the nameless larvae of the Other Gods, and like them are blind and without mind, and possessed of singular hungers and thirsts.

But that offensive galley did not aim as far as Carter had feared, for he soon saw that the helmsman was steering a course directly for the moon. The moon was a crescent shining larger and larger as they approached it, and showing its singular craters and peaks uncomfortably. The ship made for the edge, and it soon became clear that its destination was that secret and mysterious side which is always turned away from earth, and which no fully human person, save perhaps the dreamer Snireth-Ko, has ever beheld. The close aspect of the moon as the galley drew near proved very disturbing to Carter, and he did not like the size and shape of the ruins which crumbled here and there. The dead temples on the mountains were so placed that they could have glorified no suitable or wholesome gods, and in the symmetries of the broken columns there seemed to be some dark and inner meaning which did not invite solution. And what the structure and proportions of the olden worshipers could have been Carter steadily refused to conjecture.

When the ship rounded the edge and sailed over those lands unseen by man, there appeared in the queer landscape certain signs of life, and Carter saw many low, broad, round cottages in fields of grotesque whitish fungi. He noticed that these cottages had no windows, and thought that their shape suggested the huts of Eskimos. Then he glimpsed the oily waves of a sluggish sea, and knew that the voyage was once more to be by water—or at least, through some liquid. The galley struck the surface with a peculiar sound, and the odd elastic way the waves received it was very perplexing to Carter. They now slid along at great speed, once passing and hailing another galley of kindred form, but generally seeing nothing but that curious sea and a sky that was black and star-strewn even though the sun shone scorchingly in it.

There presently rose ahead the jagged hills of a leprous-looking coast, and Carter saw the thick, unpleasant gray towers of a city. The way they leaned and bent, the manner in which they were clustered, and the fact that they had no windows at all were very disturbing to the prisoner, and he bitterly mourned the folly which had made him sip the curious wine of that merchant with the humped turban. As the coast drew nearer, and the hideous stench of that city grew stronger, he saw upon the jagged hills many forests, some of whose trees he recognized as akin to that solitary moon-tree in the enchanted wood of earth from whose sap the small brown Zoogs ferment their curious wine.

Carter could now distinguish moving figures on the noisome wharves ahead, and the better he saw them the worse he began to fear and detest them. For they were not men at all, or even approximately men, but great grayish-white slippery things which could expand and contract at will, and whose principal shape—though it often changed—was that of a sort of toad without any eyes, but with a curious vibrating mass of short pink tentacles on the end of its blunt, vague snout.

These objects were waddling busily about the wharves, moving bales and crates and boxes with preternatural strength, and now and then hopping onto or off some anchored galley with long oars in their forepaws. And now and then one would appear driving a herd of clumping slaves, which indeed were approximate human beings with wide mouths like those merchants who traded in Dylath-Leen; only these herds, being without turbans or shoes or clothing, did not seem so very human after all. Some of the slaves—the fatter ones, whom a sort of overseer would pinch experimentally—were unloaded from ships and nailed into crates, which workers pushed into the low warehouses or loaded onto great, lumbering vans.

Once a van was hitched and driven off, and the fabulous thing which drew it was such that Carter gasped, even after having seen the other monstrosities of that hateful place. Now and then a small herd of slaves dressed and turbaned like the dark merchants would be driven aboard a galley, followed by a great crew of the slippery toad-things as officers, navigators, and rowers. And Carter saw that the almost-human creatures were reserved for the more ignominious kinds of servitude which required no strength, such as steering and cooking, fetching and carrying, and bargaining with men on the earth or other planets where they traded. These creatures must have been convenient on earth, for they were truly not unlike men when dressed and carefully shod and turbaned, and could haggle in the shops of men without embarrassment or curious explanations. But most of them, unless lean or ill favored, were unclothed and packed into crates and drawn off in lumbering lorries by fabulous things. Occasionally other beings were unloaded and crated; some very like these semihumans, some not so similar, and some not similar at all. And he wondered if any of the poor stout black men of Parg were left to be unloaded and crated and shipped inland in those obnoxious drays.

When the galley landed at a greasy-looking quay of spongy rock, a nightmare horde of toad-things wriggled out of the hatches, and two of them seized Carter and dragged him ashore. The smell and aspect of that city are beyond telling, and Carter held only scattered images of the tiled streets and black doorways and endless precipices of gray vertical walls without windows. At length he was dragged within a low doorway and made to climb infinite steps in pitch blackness. It was, apparently, all one to the toad-things whether it was light or dark. The odor of the place was intolerable, and when Carter was locked into a chamber and left alone, he scarcely had strength to crawl around and ascertain its form and dimensions. It was circular, and about twenty feet across.

From then on, time ceased to exist. At intervals food was pushed in, but Carter would not touch it. What his fate would be he did not know; but he felt that he was held for the coming of that frightful soul and messenger of infinity's Other Gods, the crawling chaos Nyarlathotep. Finally, after an unguessed span of hours or days, the great stone door swung wide again, and Carter was shoved down the stairs and out into the red-lit streets of that fearsome city. It was night on the moon, and all through the town were stationed slaves bearing torches.

In a detestable square, a sort of procession was formed; ten of the toad-things and twenty-four almost-human torchbearers, eleven on either side and one each before and behind. Carter was placed in the middle of the line; five toad-things ahead and five behind, and one almost-human torchbearer on either side of him. Certain of the toad-things produced disgustingly carved flutes of ivory and made loathsome sounds. To that hellish piping, the column advanced out of the tiled streets and into nighted plains of obscene fungi, soon commencing to climb one of the lower and more gradual hills that lay behind the city. That on some frightful slope or blasphemous plateau the crawling chaos waited Carter could not doubt, and he wished that the suspense might soon be over. The whining of those impious flutes was shocking, and he would have given worlds for some even half-normal sound; but these toad-things had no voices, and the slaves did not talk.

Then through that star-specked darkness there did come a normal sound. It rolled from the higher hills, and from all the jagged peaks around it was caught up and echoed in a swelling pandemoniac chorus. It was the midnight yell of the cat, and Carter knew at last that the old village folk were right when they made low guesses about the cryptical realms which are known only to cats, and to which the elders among cats repair by stealth nocturnally, springing from high housetops. Verily, it is to the moon's dark side that they go to leap and gambol on the hills and converse with ancient shadows, and here amidst that column of fetid things Carter heard their homely, friendly cry, and thought of the steep roofs and warm hearths and little lighted windows of home.

Now, much of the speech of cats was known to Randolph Carter, and in this far, terrible place he uttered the cry that was suitable. But that he need not have done, for even as his lips opened he heard the chorus wax and draw nearer, and saw swift shadows against the stars as small, graceful shapes leaped from hill to hill in gathering legions. The call of the clan had been given, and before the foul procession had time even to be frightened, a cloud of smothering fur and a phalanx of murderous claws were tidally and tempestuously upon it. The flutes stopped, and there were shrieks in the night. Dying almost-humans screamed, and cats spat and yowled and roared, but the toad-things made never a sound as their stinking green ichor oozed fatally upon that porous earth with the obscene fungi.

It was a stupendous sight while the torches lasted, and Carter had never before seen so many cats. Black, gray, and white; yellow, tiger, and mixed; common, Persian, and Manx; Tibetan, Angora, and Egyptian: all were there in the fury of battle, and there hovered over them some trace of that profound and inviolate sanctity which made their goddess great in the temples of Bubastis. They would leap seven strong at the throat of an almost-human or the pink, tentacled snout of a toad-thing and drag it down savagely to the fungous plain, where myriads of their fellows would surge over it and into it with the frenzied claws and teeth of a divine battle-fury. Carter had seized a torch from a stricken slave, but was soon overborne by the surging waves of his loyal defenders. Then he lay in the utter blackness, hearing the clangor of war and the shouts of the victors, and feeling the soft paws of his friends as they rushed to and fro over him in the fray.

At last awe and exhaustion closed his eyes, and when he opened them again it was upon a strange scene. The great shining disk of the earth, thirteen times greater than that of the moon as we see it, had risen with floods of weird light over the lunar landscape; and across all those leagues of wild plateau and ragged crest there squatted one endless sea of cats in orderly array. Circle on circle they reached, and two or three leaders out of the ranks were licking his face and purring to him consolingly. Of the dead slaves and toad-things there were not many signs, but Carter thought he saw one bone a little way off in the open space between him and the warriors.

Carter now spoke with the leaders in the soft language of cats, and learned that his ancient friendship with the species was well known and often spoken of in the places where cats congregate. He had not been unmarked in Ulthar when he passed through, and the sleek old cats had remembered how he patted them after they had attended to the hungry Zoogs who looked evilly at a small black kitten. And they recalled, too, how he had welcomed the very little kitten who came to see him at the inn, and how he had given it a saucer of rich cream in the morning before he left. The grandfather of that very little kitten was the leader of the army now assembled, for he had seen the evil procession from a far hill and recognized the prisoner as a sworn friend of his kind on earth and in the land of dream.

A yowl now came from the farther peak, and the old leader paused abruptly in his conversation. It was one of the army's outposts, stationed on the highest of the mountains to watch the one foe which Earth's cats fear: the very large and peculiar cats from Saturn, who for some reason have not been oblivious of the charm of our moon's dark side. They are leagued by treaty with the evil toad-things, and are notoriously hostile to our earthly cats; so that at this juncture a meeting would have been a somewhat grave matter.

After a brief consultation of generals, the cats rose and assumed a closer formation, crowding protectingly around Carter and preparing to take the great leap through space back to the housetops of our earth and its dreamland. The old field marshal advised Carter to let himself be borne along smoothly and passively in the massed ranks of furry leapers, and told him how to spring when the rest sprang and land gracefully when the rest landed. He also offered to deposit him in any spot he desired, and Carter decided on the city of

Dylath-Leen whence the black galley had set out; for he wished to sail thence for Oriab and the carved crest Ngranek, and also to warn the people of the city to have no more traffic with black galleys, if indeed that traffic could be tactfully and judiciously broken off. Then, upon a signal, the cats all leaped gracefully with their friend packed securely in their midst, while in a black cave on an unhallowed summit of the moon-mountains still vainly waited the crawling chaos Nyarlathotep.

The leap of the cats through space was very swift; and being surrounded by his companions, Carter did not see this time the great black shapelessnesses that lurk and caper and flounder in the abyss. Before he fully realized what had happened, he was back in his familiar room at the inn at Dylath-Leen, and the stealthy, friendly cats were pouring out the window in streams. The old leader from Ulthar was the last to leave, and as Carter shook his paw he said he would be able to get home by cockcrow. When dawn came, Carter went downstairs and learned that a week had elapsed since his capture and leaving. There was still nearly a fortnight to wait for the ship bound toward Oriab, and during that time he said what he could against the black galleys and their infamous ways. Most of the townsfolk believed him; yet so fond were the jewelers of great rubies that none would wholly promise to cease trafficking with the wide-mouthed merchants. If aught of evil ever befalls Dylath-Leen through such traffic, it will not be his fault.

In about a week, the desiderate ship put in by the black wale and tall lighthouse, and Carter was glad to see that she was a bark of wholesome mien, with painted sides and yellow lateen sails and a gray captain in silken robes. Her cargo was the fragrant resin of Oriab's inner groves, and the delicate pottery baked by the artists of Baharna, and the strange little figures carved from Ngranek's ancient lava. For this they were paid in the wool of Ulthar and the iridescent textiles of Hatheg and the ivory that the black men carve across the river in Parg. Carter made arrangements with the captain to go to Baharna and was told that the voyage would take ten days. And during his week of waiting he talked much with that captain of Ngranek, and was told that very few had seen the carved face thereon, but that most travelers are content to learn its legends from old people and lava-gatherers and image-makers in Baharna and afterward say in their far homes that they have indeed beheld it. The captain was not even sure that any person now living had beheld that carved face, for the wrong side of Ngranek is very difficult and barren and sinister, and there are rumors of caves near the peak wherein dwell the night-gaunts. But the captain did not wish to say just what a night-gaunt might be like, since such cattle are known to haunt most persistently the dreams of those who think too often of them. Then Carter asked that captain about unknown Kadath in the cold waste, and the marvelous sunset city, but of these the good man could truly tell nothing.

Carter sailed out of Dylath-Leen one early morning when the tide turned, and saw the first rays of sunrise on the thin angular towers of that dismal basalt town. And for two days they sailed eastward in sight of green coasts, and saw often the pleasant fishing towns that climbed up steeply with their red roofs and chimney pots from old dreaming wharves and beaches where nets lay drying. But on the third day they turned sharply south where the roll of water was stronger, and soon passed from sight of any land. On the fifth day the sailors were nervous, but the captain apologized for their fears, saying that the ship was about to pass over the weedy walls and broken columns of a sunken city too old for memory, and that when the water was clear one could see so many moving shadows in that deep place that simple folk disliked it. He admitted, moreover, that many ships had been lost in that part of the sea, having been hailed when quite close to it, but never seen again.

That night the moon was very bright, and one could see a great way down in the water. There was so little wind that the ship could not move much, and the ocean was very calm. Looking over the rail, Carter saw, many fathoms deep, the dome of the great temple, and in front of it an avenue of unnatural sphinxes leading to what was once a public square. Dolphins sported merrily in and out of the ruins, and porpoises reveled clumsily here and there, sometimes coming to the surface and leaping clear out of the sea. As the ship drifted on a little, the floor of the ocean rose in hills, and one could clearly mark the lines of ancient climbing streets and the washed-down walls of myriad little houses.

Then the suburbs appeared, and finally a great lone building on a hill, of simpler architecture than the other structures and in much better repair. It was dark and low and covered four sides of a square, with a tower at each corner, a paved court in the center, and small, curious round windows all over it. Probably it was of basalt, though weeds draped the greater part; and such was its lonely and impressive place on that far hill that it may have been a temple or a monastery. Some phosphorescent fish inside it gave the small round windows an aspect of shining, and Carter did not blame the sailors much for their fears. Then by the watery moonlight he noticed an odd high monolith in the middle of that central court, and saw that something was tied to it. And when after getting a telescope from the captain's cabin he saw that that bound thing was a sailor in the silk robes of Oriab, head downward and without any eyes, he was glad that a rising breeze soon took the ship ahead to healthier parts of the sea.

The next day they spoke with a ship with violet sails bound for Zar, in the land of forgotten dreams, with bulbs of strange-colored lilies for cargo. And on the evening of the eleventh day they came in sight of the isle of Oriab, with Ngranek rising jagged and snow-crowned in the distance. Oriab is a very great isle, and its port of Baharna a mighty city. The wharves of Baharna are of porphyry, and the city rises in great stone terraces behind them, having streets of steps that are frequently arched over by buildings and the bridges between buildings. There is a great canal which goes under the whole city in a tunnel with granite gates and leads to the inland lake of Yath, on whose farther shore are the vast clay-brick ruins of a primal city whose name is not remembered. As the ship drew into the harbor at evening, the twin beacons Thon and Thal gleamed a welcome, and in all the million windows of Baharna's terraces mellow lights peeped out quietly and gradually as the stars peep out overhead in the dusk, till that steep and climbing seaport became a glittering constellation hung between the stars of heaven and the reflections of those stars in the still harbor.

The captain, after landing, made Carter a guest in his own small house on the shores of Yath where the rear of the town slopes down to it; and his wife and servants brought strange, toothsome foods for the traveler's delight. And in the days after that, Carter asked for rumors and legends of Ngranek in all the taverns and public places where lava-gatherers and image-makers meet, but could find no one who had been up the higher slopes or seen the carved face. Ngranek was a hard mountain with only an accursed valley behind it, and besides, one could never depend on the certainty that night-gaunts are altogether fabulous.

When the captain sailed back to Dylath-Leen, Carter took quarters in an ancient tavern opening on an alley of steps in the original part of the town, which is built of brick and resembles the ruins of Yath's farther shore. Here he laid his plans for the ascent of Ngranek, and correlated all that he had learned from the lava-gatherers about the roads thither. The keeper of the tavern was a very old man, and had heard so many legends that he was a great help. He even took Carter to an upper room in that ancient house and showed him a crude picture which a traveler had scratched on the clay wall in the old days when men were bolder and less reluctant to visit Ngranek's higher slopes. The old tavernkeeper's great-grandfather had heard from his great-grandfather that the traveler who scratched that picture had climbed Ngranek and seen the carved face, here drawing it for others to behold; but Carter had very great doubts, since the large, rough features on the wall were hasty and careless, and wholly overshadowed by a crowd of little companion shapes in the worst possible taste, with horns and wings and claws and curling tails.

At last, having gained all the information he was likely to gain in the taverns and public places of Baharna, Carter hired a zebra and set out one morning on the road by Yath's shore for those inland parts wherein towers stony Ngranek. On his right were rolling hills and pleasant orchards and neat little stone farmhouses, and he was much reminded of those fertile fields that flank the Skai. By evening he was near the nameless ancient ruins on Yath's farther shore, and though old lava-gatherers had warned him not to camp there at night, he tethered his zebra to a curious pillar before a crumbling wall and laid his blanket in a sheltered corner beneath some carvings whose meaning none could decipher. Around him he wrapped another blanket, for the nights are cold in Oriab; and when upon awaking once he thought he felt the wings of some insect brushing his face, he covered his head altogether and slept in peace till roused by the magah birds in distant resin groves.

The sun had just come up over the great slope whereon leagues of primal brick foundations and worn walls and occasional cracked pillars and pedestals stretched down desolate to the shore of Yath, and Carter looked about for his tethered zebra. Great was his dismay to see that docile beast stretched prostrate beside the curious pillar to which it had been tied, and still greater was he vexed on finding that the steed was quite dead, with its blood all sucked away through a singular wound in its throat. His pack had been disturbed and several shiny knickknacks taken away, and all around on the dusty soil were great webbed footprints for which he could not in any way account. The legends and warnings of lava-gatherers occurred to him, and he thought of what had brushed his face in the night. Then he shouldered his pack and strode on toward Ngranek, though not without a shiver when he saw close to him, as the highway passed through the ruins, a great gaping arch low in the wall of an old temple, with steps leading down into darkness farther than he could peer.

His course now lay uphill through wilder and partly wooded country, and he saw only the huts of charcoal-burners and the camp of those who gathered resin from the groves. The whole air was fragrant with balsam, and all the magah birds sang blithely as they flashed their seven colors in the sun. Near sunset he came on a new camp of lava-gatherers returning with laden sacks from Ngranek's lower slopes; and here he also camped, listening to the songs and tales of the men and overhearing what they whispered about a companion they had lost. He had climbed high to reach a mass of fine lava above him, and at nightfall did not return to his fellows. When they looked for him the next day they found only his turban, nor was there any sign on the crags below that he had fallen. They did not search anymore, because the old men among them said it would be of no use. No one ever found what the night-gaunts took, though those beasts themselves were so uncertain as to be almost fabulous. Carter asked them if night-gaunts sucked blood and liked shiny things and left webbed footprints, but they all shook their heads negatively and seemed frightened at his making such an inquiry. When he saw how taciturn they had become he asked them no more, but went to sleep in his blanket.

The next day he rose with the lava-gatherers and exchanged farewells as they rode west and he rode east on a zebra he bought of them. Their older men gave him blessings and warnings, and told him he had better not climb too high on Ngranek, but while he thanked them heartily, he was in no wise dissuaded. For still did he feel that he must find the gods on unknown Kadath, and win from them a way to that haunting and marvelous city in the sunset.

By noon, after a long uphill ride, he came upon some abandoned brick villages of the hill people who had once dwelt this close to Ngranek and carved images from its smooth lava. Here they had dwelt till the days of the old tavernkeeper's grandfather, but about that time they felt that their presence was disliked. Their homes had crept even up the mountain's slope, and the higher they built the more people they would miss when the sun rose. At last they decided it would be better to leave altogether, since things were sometimes glimpsed in the darkness which no one could interpret favorably; so in the end all of them went down to the sea and dwelt in Baharna, inhabiting a very old quarter and teaching their sons the old art of image-making which to this day they carry on. It was from these children of the exiled hill people that Carter had heard the best tales about Ngranek when searching through Baharna's ancient taverns.

All this time the great gaunt side of Ngranek was looming up higher and higher as Carter approached it. There were sparse trees on the lower slopes and feeble shrubs above them, and then the bare hideous rock rose spectral into the sky, to mix with frost and ice and eternal snow. Carter could see the rifts and ruggedness of that somber stone, and did not welcome the prospect of climbing it. In places there were solid streams of lava, and scoriac heaps that littered slopes and ledges. Ninety eons ago, before even the gods had danced upon its pointed peak, that mountain had spoken with fire and roared with the voices of the inner thunders. Now it towered all silent and sinister, bearing on the hidden side that secret titan image whereof rumor told. And there were caves in that mountain, which might be empty and alone with elder darkness, or might—if legend spoke truly—hold horrors of a form not to be surmised.

The ground sloped upward to the foot of Ngranek, thinly covered with scrub oaks and ash trees and strewn with bits of rock, lava, and ancient cinder. There were the charred embers of many camps, where the lava-gatherers were wont to stop, and several rude altars which they had built either to propitiate the Great Ones or to ward off what they dreamed of in Ngranek's high passes and labyrinthine caves. At evening Carter reached the farthermost pile of embers and camped for the night, tethering his zebra to a sapling and wrapping himself well in his blankets before going to sleep. And all through the night a voonith howled distantly from the shore of some hidden pool, but Carter felt no fear of that amphibious terror, since he had been told with certainty that not one of them dares even approach the slope of Ngranek.

In the clear sunshine of morning Carter began the long ascent, taking his zebra as far as that useful beast could go, but tying it to a stunted ash tree when the floor of the thin wood became too steep. Thereafter he scrambled up alone: first through the forest with its ruins of old villages in overgrown clearings, and then over the tough grass where anemic shrubs grew here and there. He regretted coming clear of the trees, since the slope was very precipitous and the whole thing rather dizzying. At length he began to discern all the countryside spread out beneath him whenever he looked about: the deserted huts of the image-makers, the groves of resin trees and the camps of those who gathered from them, the woods where prismatic magahs nest and sing, and even a hint very far away of the shores of Yath and of those forbidding ancient ruins whose name is forgotten. He found it best not to look around, and kept on climbing and climbing till the shrubs became very sparse and there was often nothing but the tough grass to cling to.

Then the soil became meager, with great patches of bare

rock cropping out, and now and then the nest of a condor in a crevice. Finally there was nothing at all but the bare rock, and had it not been very rough and weathered, he could scarcely have ascended farther. Knobs, ledges, and pinnacles, however, helped greatly; and it was cheering to see occasionally the sign of some lava-gatherer scratched clumsily in the friable stone, and know that wholesome human creatures had been there before him. After a certain height the presence of man was further shown by handholds and footholds hewn where they were needed, and by little quarries and excavations where some choice vein or stream of lava had been found. In one place a narrow ledge had been chopped artificially to an especially rich deposit far to the right of the main line of ascent. Once or twice Carter dared to look around, and was almost stunned by the spread of landscape below. All the island between him and the coast lay open to his sight, with Baharna's stone terraces and the smoke of its chimneys mystical in the distance. And beyond that the illimitable Southern Sea with all its curious secrets.

Thus far there had been much winding around the mountain, so that the farther and carved side was still hidden. Carter now saw a ledge running upward and to the left which seemed to head the way he wished, and this course he took in the hope that it might prove continuous. After ten minutes he saw that it was indeed no cul-de-sac, but led steeply on in an arc which would, unless suddenly interrupted or deflected, bring him after a few hours' climbing to that unknown southern slope overlooking the desolate crags and the accursed valley of lava. As new country came into view below him, he saw that it was bleaker and wilder than those seaward lands he had traversed. The mountain's side, too, was somewhat different, being here pierced by curious cracks and caves not found on the straighter route he had left. Some of these were above him and some beneath him, all opening on sheerly perpendicular cliffs and wholly unreachable by the feet of man. The air was very cold now, but so hard was the climbing that he did not mind it. Only the increasing rarity bothered him, and he thought that perhaps it was this which had turned the heads of other travelers and excited those absurd tales of night-gaunts whereby they explained the loss of such climbers as fell from these perilous paths. He was not much impressed by travelers' tales, but had a good curved scimitar in case of any trouble. All lesser thoughts were lost in the wish to see that carved face which might set him on the track of the gods atop unknown Kadath.

At last, in the fearsome iciness of upper space, he came around fully to the hidden side of Ngranek and saw in infinite gulfs below him the lesser crags and sterile abysses of lava which marked the olden wrath of the Great Ones. There was unfolded, too, a vast expanse of country to the south; but it was a desert land without fair fields or cottage chimneys, and seemed to have no ending. No trace of the sea was visible on this side, for Oriab is a great island. Black caverns and odd crevices were still numerous on the sheer vertical cliffs, but none of them was accessible to a climber. There now loomed aloft a great beetling mass which hampered the upward view, and Carter was for a moment shaken with doubt lest it prove impassable. Poised in windy insecurity miles above earth, with only space and death on one side and only slippery walls of rock on the other, he knew for a moment the fear that makes men shun Ngranek's hidden side. He could not turn around, yet the sun was already low. If there was no way aloft, the night would find him crouching there still, and the dawn would not find him at all.

But there was a way, and he saw it in due season. Only a very expert dreamer could have used those imperceptible footholds, yet to Carter they were sufficient. Surmounting now the outward-hanging rock, he found the slope above much easier than that below, since a great glacier's melting had left a generous space with loam and ledges. To the left a precipice dropped straight from unknown heights to unknown depths, with a cave's dark mouth just out of reach above him. Elsewhere, however, the mountain slanted back strongly, and even gave him space to lean and rest.

He felt from the chill that he must be near the snow line, and looked up to see what glittering pinnacles might be shining in that late ruddy sunlight. Sure enough, there was the snow uncounted thousands of feet above, and below it a great beetling crag like that he had just climbed, hanging there forever in bold outline. And when he saw that crag he gasped and cried out aloud, and clutched at the jagged rock in awe; for the titan bulge had not stayed as earth's dawn had shaped it, but gleamed red and stupendous in the sunset with the carved and polished features of a god.

Stern and terrible shone that face which the sunset lit with fire. How vast it was no mind can ever measure, but Carter knew at once that man could never have fashioned it. It was a god chiseled by the hands of the gods, and it looked down haughty and majestic upon the seeker. Rumor had said it was strange and not to be mistaken, and Carter saw that it was indeed so; for those long, narrow eyes and long-lobed ears, and that thin nose and pointed chin, all spoke of a race that is not of men but of gods.

He clung overawed in that lofty and perilous aerie, even though it was this which he had expected and come to find; for there is in a god's face more of marvel than prediction can tell, and when that face is vaster than a great temple and seen looking downward at sunset in the cryptic silences of that upper world from those dark lava it was divinely hewn of old, the marvel is so strong that none may escape it.

Here, too, was the added marvel of recognition; for although he had planned to search all dreamland over for those whose likeness to this face might mark them as the god's children, he now knew that he need not do so. Certainly the great face carved on that mountain was of no strange sort, but the kin of such as he had seen often in the taverns of the seaport Celephais, which lies in Ooth-Nargai, beyond the Tanarian Hills, and is ruled over by that King Kuranes whom Carter once knew in waking life. Every year sailors with such a face came in dark ships from the north to trade their onyx for the carved jade and spun gold and little red singing birds of Celephais, and it was clear that these could be no others than the half-gods he sought. Where they dwelt, there must the cold waste lie close, and within it unknown Kadath and its onyx castle for the Great Ones. So to Celephais he must go, far distant from the isle of Oriab, and in such parts as would take him back to Dylath-Leen and up the Skai to the bridge by Nir, and again into the enchanted wood of the Zoogs, whence the way would bend northward through the garden lands by Oukranos to the gilded spires of Thran, where he might find a galleon bound over the Cerenarian Sea.

But dusk was now thick, and the great carved face looked down even sterner in shadow. Perched on that ledge night found the seeker; and in the blackness he might neither go down nor go up, but only stand and cling and shiver in that narrow place till the day came, praying to keep awake lest sleep loose his hold and send him down the dizzy miles of air to the crags and sharp rocks of the accursed valley. The stars came out, but save for them there was only black nothingness in his eyes; nothingness leagued with death, against whose beckoning he might do no more than cling to the rocks and lean back away from an unseen brink. The last thing of earth that he saw in the gloaming was a condor soaring close to the westward precipice beside him, and darting screaming away when it came near the cave whose mouth yawned just out of reach.

Suddenly, without a warning sound in the dark, Carter felt his curved scimitar drawn stealthily out of his belt by some unseen hand. Then he heard it clatter down over the rocks below. And between him and the Milky Way he thought he saw a very terrible outline of something noxiously thin and horned and tailed and bat-winged. Other things, too, had begun to blot out patches of stars west of him, as if a flock of vague entities were flapping thickly and silently out of that inaccessible cave in the face of the precipice. Then a sort of cold rubbery arm seized his neck and something else seized his feet, and he was lifted inconsiderately up and swung about in space. Another minute and the stars were gone, and Carter knew that the night-gaunts had got him.

They bore him breathless into that cliffside cavern and through monstrous labyrinths beyond. When he struggled, as at first he did by instinct, they tickled him with deliberation. They made no sound at all themselves, and even their membranous wings were silent. They were frightfully cold and damp and slippery, and their paws kneaded one detestably. Soon they were plunging hideously downward through inconceivable abysses in a whirling, giddying, sickening rush of dank, tomblike air, and Carter felt they were shooting into the ultimate vortex of shrieking and demonic madness. He screamed again and again, but whenever he did so the black paws tickled him with greater subtlety. Then he saw a sort of gray phosphorescence about, and guessed they were coming even to that inner world of subterrene horror of which dim legends tell, and which is lit only by the pale death-fire wherewith reek the ghoulish air and the primal mists of the pits at earth's core.

At last, far below him, he saw faint lines of gray and ominous pinnacles which he knew must be the fabled Peaks of Throk. Awful and sinister they stand in the haunted disk of sunless and eternal depths; higher than man may reckon, and guarding terrible valleys where the Dholes crawl and burrow nastily. But Carter preferred to look at them rather than at his captors, which were indeed shocking and uncouth black things with smooth, oily, whalelike surfaces, unpleasant horns that curved inward toward each other, bat wings whose beating made no sound, ugly prehensile paws, and barbed tails that lashed needlessly and disquietingly. And worst of all, they never spoke or laughed, and never smiled, because they had no faces at all to smile with, but only a suggestive blankness where a face ought to be. All they ever did was clutch and fly and tickle; that was the way of night-gaunts.

As the band flew lower, the Peaks of Throk rose gray and towering on all sides, and one saw clearly that nothing lived on that austere and impressive granite of the endless twilight. At still lower levels the death-fires in the air gave out, and one met only the primal blackness of the void save aloft where the thin peaks stood out goblinlike. Soon the peaks were very far away, and nothing about but great rushing winds with the dankness of nethermost grottoes in them. Then in the end the night-gaunts landed on a floor of unseen things which felt like layers of bones, and left Carter all alone in that black valley. To bring him thither was the duty of the night-gaunts that guard Ngranek; and this done, they flapped away silently. When Carter tried to trace their flight he found he could not, since even the Peaks of Throk had faded out of sight. There was nothing anywhere but blackness and horror and silence and bones.

Now, Carter knew from a certain source that he was in the

vale of Pnoth, where crawl and burrow the enormous Dholes; but he did not know what to expect, because no one has ever seen a Dhole or even guessed what such a thing may be like. Dholes are known only by dim rumor, from the rustling they make among mountains of bones and the slimy touch they have when they wriggle past one. They cannot be seen, because they creep only in the dark. Carter did not wish to meet a Dhole, so he listened intently for any sound in the unknown depths of bones about him. Even in this fearsome place he had a plan and an objective, for whispers of Pnoth were not unknown to one with whom he had talked much in the old days. In brief, it seemed fairly likely that this was the spot into which all the ghouls of the waking world cast the refuse of their feastings, and that if he but had good luck he might stumble upon that mighty crag taller even than Throk's peaks which marks the edge of their domain. Showers of bones would tell him where to look, and once it was found he could call to a ghoul to let down a ladder; for strange to say, he had a very singular link with these terrible creatures.

A man he had known in Boston—a painter of strange pictures with a secret studio in an ancient and unhallowed alley near a graveyard—had actually made friends with the ghouls and had taught him to understand the simpler part of their disgusting meeping and glibbering. This man had vanished at last, and Carter was not sure but that he might find him now, and use for the first time in dreamland that far-away English of his dim waking life. In any case, he felt he could persuade a ghoul to guide him out of Pnoth; and it would be better to meet a ghoul, which one can see, than a Dhole, which one cannot see.

So Carter walked in the dark, and ran when he thought he heard something among the bones underfoot. Once he bumped into a stony slope, and knew it must be the base of one of Throk's peaks. Then at last he heard a monstrous rattling and clatter which reached far up in the air, and became sure he had come nigh the crag of the ghouls. He was not sure he could be heard from this valley miles below, but he realized that the inner world has strange laws. As he pondered, he was struck by a flying bone so heavy that it must have been a skull, and therefore realizing his nearness to the fateful crag, he sent up as best he might that meeping cry which is the call of the ghoul.

Sound travels slowly, so that it was some time before he heard an answering glibber. But it came at last, and before long he was told that a rope ladder would be lowered. The wait for this was very tense, since there was no telling what might not have been stirred up among those bones by his shouting. Indeed, it was not long before he actually did hear a vague rustling afar off. As this thoughtfully approached, he became more and more uncomfortable, for he did not wish to move away from the spot where the ladder would come. Finally the tension grew almost unbearable, and he was about to flee in panic when the thud of something on the newly heaped bones nearby drew his notice from the other sound. It was the ladder, and after a minute of groping he had it taut in his hands. But the other sound did not cease, and followed him even as he climbed. He had gone fully five feet from the ground when the rattling beneath waxed emphatic, and was a good ten feet up when something swayed the ladder from below. At a height that must have been fifteen or twenty feet, he felt his whole side brushed by a great slippery length which grew alternately convex and concave with wriggling; and thereafter he climbed desperately to escape the unendurable nuzzling of that loathsome and overfed Dhole whose form no man might see.

For hours he climbed with aching and blistered hands, seeing again the gray death-fire and Throk's uncomfortable pinnacles. At last he discerned above him the projecting edge of the great crag of the ghouls, whose vertical side he could not glimpse; and hours later he saw a curious face peering over it as a gargoyle peers over a parapet of Notre Dame. This almost made him lose his hold through faintness, but a moment later he was himself again; for his vanished friend Richard Pickman had once introduced him to a ghoul, and he knew well their canine faces and slumping forms and unmentionable idiosyncrasies. So he had himself well under control when that hideous thing pulled him out of the dizzy emptiness over the edge of the crag, and did not scream at the partly consumed refuse heaped at one side or at the squatting circles of ghouls who gnawed and watched curiously.

He was now on a dim-lit plain whose sole topographical features were great boulders and the entrances of burrows. The ghouls were in general respectful, even if one did attempt to pinch him, while several others eyed his leanness speculatively. Through patient glibbering he made inquiries regarding his vanished friend, and found he had become a ghoul of some prominence in abysses nearer the waking world. A greenish elderly ghoul offered to conduct him to Pickman's present habitation, so despite a natural loathing he followed the creature into a capacious burrow and crawled after him for hours in the blackness of rank mold. They emerged on a dim plain strewn with singular relics of earth—old gravestones, broken urns, and grotesque fragments of monuments—and Carter realized with some emotion that he was probably nearer the waking world than at any other time since he had gone down the seven hundred steps from the cavern of flame to the Gate of Deeper Slumber.

There, on a tombstone of 1768 stolen from the Granary Burying Ground in Boston, sat a ghoul which had once been the artist Richard Upton Pickman. It was naked and rubbery, and had acquired so much of the ghoulish physiognomy that its human origin was already obscure. But it still remembered a little English, and was able to converse with Carter in grunts and monosyllables, helped out now and then by the glibbering of ghouls. When it learned that Carter wished to get to the enchanted wood and from there to the city Celephais, in Ooth-Nargai, beyond the Tanarian Hills, it seemed rather doubtful; for these ghouls of the waking world do no business in the graveyards of upper dreamland (leaving that to the red-footed wamps that are spawned in dead cities), and many things intervene between their gulf and the enchanted wood, including the terrible kingdom of the Gugs.

The Gugs, hairy and gigantic, once reared stone circles in that wood and made strange sacrifices to the Other Gods and the crawling chaos Nyarlathotep, until one night an abomination of theirs reached the ears of earth's gods and they were banished to caverns below. Only a great trap door of stone with an iron ring connects the abyss of the earth-ghouls with the enchanted wood, and this the Gugs are afraid to open because of a curse. That a mortal dreamer could traverse their cavern realm and leave by that door is inconceivable, for mortal dreamers were their former food, and they have legends of the toothsomeness of such dreamers, even though banishment has restricted their diet to the ghasts, those repulsive beings which die in the light, and which live in the vaults of Zin and leap on long hind legs like kangaroos.

So the ghoul that had been Pickman advised Carter either to leave the abyss at Sarkomand, that deserted city in the valley below Leng where black nitrous stairways guarded by winged diorite lions lead down from dreamland to the lower gulfs, or to return through a churchyard to the waking world and begin the quest anew down the seventy steps of light slumber to the cavern of flame and the seven hundred steps to the Gate of Deeper Slumber and the enchanted wood. This, however, did not suit the seeker, for he knew nothing of the way from Leng to Ooth-Nargai, and was likewise reluctant to awake lest he forget all he had so far gained in this dream. It would have been disastrous to his quest to forget the august and celestial faces of those seamen from the north who traded onyx in Celephais, and who, being the sons of gods, must point the way to the cold waste and Kadath, where the Great Ones dwell.

After much persuasion, the ghoul consented to guide his guest inside the great wall of the Gugs' kingdom. There was one chance that Carter might be able to steal through that twilight realm of circular stone towers at an hour when the giants would be all gorged and snoring indoors, and reach the central tower with the sign of Koth upon it, which has the stairs leading up to that stone trap door in the enchanted wood. Pickman even consented to lend three ghouls to help with a tombstone lever in raising the stone door; for of ghouls the Gugs are somewhat afraid, and they often flee from their own colossal graveyards when they see them feasting there.

He also advised Carter to disguise as a ghoul himself—shaving the beard he had allowed to grow (for ghouls have none), wallowing naked in the mold to get the correct surface, and loping in the usual slumping way, with his clothing carried in a bundle as if it were a choice morsel from a tomb. They would reach the city of Gugs—which is conterminous with the whole kingdom—through the proper burrows, emerging in a cemetery not far from the stair-containing Tower of Koth. They must beware, however, of a large cave near the cemetery; for this is the mouth of the vaults of Zin, and the vindictive ghasts are always murderously on watch there for those denizens of the upper abyss who hunt and prey on them. The ghasts try to come out when the Gugs sleep, and they attack ghouls as readily as Gugs, for they cannot discriminate. They are very primitive, and eat one another. The Gugs have a sentry at a narrow place in the vaults of Zin, but he is often drowsy and is sometimes surprised by a party of ghasts. Though ghasts cannot live in real light, they can endure the gray twilight of the abyss for hours.

So at length Carter crawled through endless burrows with three helpful ghouls bearing the slate gravestone of Col. Nepemiah Derby, obit 1719, from the Charter Street Burying Ground in Salem. When they came again into open twilight, they were in a forest of vast, lichened monoliths reaching nearly as high as the eye could see and forming the modest gravestones of the Gugs. On the right of the hole out of which they wriggled, and seen through aisles of monoliths, was a stupendous vista of cyclopean round towers mounting up illimitable into the gray air of inner earth. This was the great city of the Gugs, whose doorways are thirty feet high. Ghouls come here often, for a buried Gug will feed a community for almost a year, and even with the added peril it is better to burrow for Gugs than to bother with the graves of men. Carter now understood the occasional titan bones he had felt beneath him in the vale of Pnoth.

Straight ahead, and just outside the cemetery, rose a perpendicular cliff at whose base an immense and forbidding cavern yawned. This the ghouls told Carter to avoid as much as possible, since it was the entrance to the unhallowed vaults of Zin where Gugs hunt ghasts in the darkness. And truly, that warning was soon well justified; for the moment a ghoul began to creep toward the towers to see if the hour of the Gugs' resting had been rightly timed, there glowed in the gloom of that great cavern's mouth first one pair of yellowish-red eyes and then another, implying that the Gugs were one sentry less, and that ghasts have indeed an excellent sharpness of smell. So the ghoul returned to the burrow and motioned to his companions to be silent. It was best to leave the ghasts to their own devices, and there was a possibility that they might soon withdraw, since they must naturally be rather tired after coping with a Gug sentry in the black vaults. After a moment, something about the size of a small horse hopped out into the gray twilight, and Carter turned sick at the aspect of that scabrous and unwholesome beast, whose face is so curiously human despite the absence of a nose, a forehead, and other important particulars.

Presently three other ghasts hopped out to join their fellow, and a ghoul glibbered softly at Carter that their absence of battle scars was a bad sign. It proved that they had not fought the Gug sentry at all, but had merely slipped past him as he slept, so that their strength and savagery were still unimpaired and would remain so till they had found and disposed of a victim. It was very unpleasant to see those filthy and disproportioned animals, which soon numbered about fifteen, grubbing about and making their kangaroo leaps in the gray twilight where titan towers and monoliths rose, but it was still more unpleasant when they spoke among themselves in the coughing gutturals of ghasts. And yet, horrible as they were, they were not so horrible as what presently came out of the cave after them with disconcerting suddenness.

It was a paw, fully two feet and a half across, and equipped with formidable talons. After it came another paw, and after that a great black-furred arm to which both of the paws were attached by short forearms. Then two pink eyes shone, and the head of the awakened Gug sentry, large as a barrel, wabbled into view. The eyes jutted two inches from each side, shaded by bony protuberances overgrown with coarse hairs. But the head was terrible chiefly because of the mouth. That mouth had great yellow fangs and ran from the top to the bottom of the head, opening vertically instead of horizontally.

But before that unfortunate Gug could emerge from the cave and rise to his full twenty feet, the vindictive ghasts were upon him. Carter feared for a moment that he would give an alarm and rouse all his kin, till a ghoul softly glibbered that Gugs have no voice, but talk by means of facial expression. The battle which then ensued was truly a frightful one. From all sides the venomous ghasts rushed feverishly at the creeping

Gug, nipping and tearing with their muzzles, and mauling murderously with their hard, pointed hoofs. All the time they coughed excitedly, screaming when the great vertical mouth of the Gug would occasionally bite into one of their number, so that the noise of the combat would surely have roused the sleeping city had not the weakening of the sentry begun to transfer the action farther and farther within the cavern. As it was, the tumult soon receded altogether from sight in the blackness, with only occasional evil echoes to mark its continuance.

Then the most alert of the ghouls gave the signal for all to advance, and Carter followed the loping three out of the forest of monoliths and into the dark, noisome streets of that awful city whose rounded towers of cyclopean stone soared up beyond the sight. Silently they shambled over that rough rock pavement, hearing with disgust the abominable muffled snortings from great black doorways which marked the slumber of the Gugs. Apprehensive of the ending of the rest hour, the ghouls set a somewhat rapid pace; but even so the journey was no brief one, for distances in that town of giants are on a great scale. At last, however, they came to a somewhat open space before a tower even vaster than the rest, above whose colossal doorway was fixed a monstrous symbol in bas-relief which made one shudder without knowing its meaning. This was the central tower with the sign of Koth, and those huge stone steps just visible through the dusk within were the beginning of the great flight leading to upper dreamland and the enchanted wood.

There now began a climb of interminable length in utter blackness, made almost impossible by the monstrous size of the steps, which were fashioned for Gugs and were therefore nearly a yard high. Of their number Carter could form no just estimate, for he soon became so worn out that the tireless and elastic ghouls were forced to aid him. All through the endless climb there lurked the peril of detection and pursuit; for though no Gug dares lift the stone door to the forest because of the Great Ones' curse, there are no such restraints concerning the tower and the steps, and escaped ghasts are often chased even to the very top. So sharp are the ears of Gugs that the bare feet and hands of the climbers might readily be heard when the city awoke; and it would of course take but little time for the striding giants, accustomed from their ghast-hunts in the vaults of Zin to seeing without light, to overtake their smaller and slower quarry on those cyclopean steps. It was very depressing to reflect that the silent pursuing Gugs would not be heard at all, but would come very suddenly and shockingly in the dark upon the climbers. Nor could the traditional fear of Gugs for ghouls be depended upon in that peculiar place where the advantages lay so heavily with the Gugs. There was also some peril from the furtive and venomous ghasts, which frequently hopped up onto the tower during the sleep hour of the Gugs. If the Gugs slept long, and the ghasts returned soon from their deed in the cavern, the scent of the climbers might easily be picked up by those loathsome and ill-disposed things; in which case it would almost be better to be eaten by a Gug.

Then, after eons of climbing, there came a cough from the darkness above, and matters assumed a very grave and unexpected turn. It was clear that a ghast, or perhaps even more, had strayed into that tower before the coming of Carter and his guides, and it was equally clear that this peril was very close. After a breathless second, the leading ghoul pushed Carter to the wall and arranged his kinfolk in the best possible way, with the old slate tombstone raised for a crushing blow whenever the enemy might come in sight. Ghouls can see in the dark, so the party was not as badly off as Carter would have been alone. In another moment the clatter of hoofs revealed the downward hopping of at least one beast, and the slab-bearing ghouls poised their weapon for a desperate blow. Presently two yellowish-red eyes flashed into view, and the panting of the ghast became audible above its clattering. As it hopped down to the step above the ghouls, they wielded the ancient gravestone with prodigious force, so that there were only a wheeze and a choking before the victim collapsed in a noxious heap. There seemed to be only this one animal, and after a moment of listening the ghouls tapped Carter as a signal to proceed again. As before, they were obliged to aid him; and he was glad to leave that place of carnage where the ghast's uncouth remains sprawled invisible in the blackness.

At last the ghouls brought their companion to a halt, and

feeling above him, Carter realized that the great stone trap door was reached at last. To open so vast a thing completely was not to be thought of, but the ghouls hoped to get it up just enough to slip the gravestone under as a prop and permit Carter to escape through the crack. They themselves planned to descend again and return through the city of the Gugs, since their elusiveness was great and they did not know the way overland to spectral Sarkomand with its lion-guarded gate to the abyss.

Mighty was the straining of those three ghouls at the stone of the door above them, and Carter helped push with as much strength as he had. They judged the edge next the top of the staircase to be the right one, and to this they bent all the force of their disreputably nourished muscles. After a few moments, a crack of light appeared, and Carter, to whom that task had been entrusted, slipped the end of the old gravestone into the aperture. There now ensued a mighty heaving; but progress was very slow, and they had of course to return to their first position every time they failed to turn the slab and prop the portal open.

Suddenly, their desperation was magnified a thousandfold by a sound on the steps below them. It was only the thumping and rattling of the slain ghast's hoofed body as it rolled down to lower levels, but of all the possible causes of that body's dislodgment and rolling, none was in the least reassuring. Therefore, knowing the ways of Gugs, the ghouls set to with something of a frenzy, and in a surprisingly short time had the door so high that they were able to hold it still while Carter turned the slab and left a generous opening. They now helped Carter through, letting him climb up to their rubbery shoulders and later guiding his feet as he clutched at the blessed soil of the upper dreamland outside. Another second and they were through themselves, knocking away the gravestone and closing the great trap door while a panting became audible beneath. Because of the Great Ones' curse, no Gug might ever emerge from that portal, so with a deep relief and sense of repose Carter lay quietly on the thick, grotesque fungi of the enchanted wood while his guides squatted near in the manner in which ghouls rest.

Weird as was that enchanted wood through which he had

fared so long ago, it was verily a haven and a delight after those gulfs he had now left behind. There was no living denizen about, for Zoogs shun the mysterious door in fear, and Carter at once consulted with his ghouls about their future course. To return through the tower they no longer dared, and the waking world did not appeal to them when they learned that they must pass the priests Nasht and Kaman-Thah in the cavern of flame. So at length they decided to return through Sarkomand and its gate of the abyss, though of how to get there they knew nothing. Carter recalled that it lies in the valley below Leng, and recalled likewise that he had seen in Dylath-Leen a sinister, slant-eyed old merchant reputed to trade on Leng, therefore he advised the ghouls to seek out Dylath-Leen, crossing the fields to Nir and the Skai and following the river to its mouth. This they at once resolved to do, and lost no time in loping off, since the thickening of the dusk promised a full night ahead for travel. And Carter shook the paws of those repulsive beasts, thanking them for their help and sending his gratitude to the beast that had once been Pickman, but could not help sighing with pleasure when they left. For a ghoul is a ghoul, and at best an unpleasant companion for man. After that Carter sought a forest pool and cleansed himself of the mud of nether earth, thereupon reassuming the clothes he had so carefully carried.

It was now night in the redoubtable wood of monstrous trees, but because of the phosphorescence one might travel as well as by day; wherefore Carter set out upon the well-known route toward Celephais, in Ooth-Nargai, beyond the Tanarian Hills. And as he went he thought of the zebra he had left tethered to an ash tree on Ngranek, in far-away Oriab, so many eons ago, and wondered if any lava-gatherers had fed and released it. And he wondered, too, if he would ever return to Baharna and pay for the zebra that had been slain by night in those ancient ruins by Yath's shore, and if the old tavern-keeper would remember him. Such were the thoughts that came to him in the air of the regained upper dreamland.

But presently his progress was halted by a sound from a very large hollow tree. He had avoided the great circle of stones, since he did not care to speak with Zoogs just now, but it appeared from the singular fluttering in that huge tree that important councils were in session elsewhere. Upon drawing nearer he made out the accents of a tense and heated discussion, and before long became conscious of matters which he viewed with the greatest concern. For a war on the cats was under debate in that sovereign assembly of Zoogs. It all came from the loss of the party which had sneaked after Carter to Ulthar, and which the cats had justly punished for unsuitable intentions. The matter had long rankled; and now, or at least within a month, the marshaled Zoogs were about to strike the whole feline tribe in a series of surprise attacks, taking individual cats or groups of cats unaware and giving not even the myriad cats of Ulthar a proper chance to drill and mobilize. This was the plan of the Zoogs, and Carter saw that he must foil it before leaving upon his mighty quest.

Very quietly, therefore, did Randolph Carter steal to the edge of the wood and send the cry of the cat over the starlit fields. And a great grimalkin in a nearby cottage took up the burden and relayed it across leagues of rolling meadow to warriors large and small, black, gray, tiger, white, yellow, and mixed; and it echoed through Nir and beyond the Skai even into Ulthar, and Ulthar's numerous cats called in chorus and fell into a line of march. It was fortunate that the moon was not up, so that all the cats were on earth. Swiftly and silently leaping, they sprang from every hearth and housetop and poured in a great furry sea across the plains to the edge of the wood. Carter was there to greet them, and the sight of shapely, wholesome cats was indeed good for his eyes after the things he had seen and walked with in the abyss. He was glad to see his venerable friend and one-time rescuer at the head of Ulthar's detachment, a collar of rank around his sleek neck and whiskers bristling at a martial angle. Better still, as a sublieutenant in that army was a brisk young fellow who proved to be none other than the very little kitten at the inn to whom Carter had given a saucer of rich cream on that long-vanished morning in Ulthar. He was a strapping and promising cat now, and purred as he shook hands with his friend. His grandfather said he was doing very well in the army, and that he might well expect a captaincy after one more campaign.

Carter now outlined the peril of the cat tribe, and was rewarded by deep-throated purrs of gratitude from all sides.

Consulting with the generals, he prepared a plan of instant action which involved marching at once upon the Zoog council and other known strongholds of Zoogs, forestalling their surprise attacks and forcing them to terms before the mobilization of their army of invasion. Thereupon, without a moment's loss, that great ocean of cats flooded the enchanted wood and surged around the council tree and the great stone circle. Flutterings rose to panic pitch as the enemy saw the newcomers, and there was very little resistance among the furtive and curious brown Zoogs. They saw that they were beaten in advance, and turned from thoughts of vengeance to thoughts of present self-preservation.

Half the cats now seated themselves in a circular formation with the captured Zoogs in the center, leaving open a lane down which were marched the additional captives rounded up by the other cats in other parts of the wood. Terms were discussed at length, Carter acting as interpreter, and it was decided that the Zoogs might remain a free tribe on condition of rendering to the cats a large tribute of grouse, quail, and pheasants from the less-fabulous parts of the forest. Twelve young Zoogs of noble family were taken as hostages, to be kept in the Temple of Cats at Ulthar, and the victors made it plain that any disappearances of cats on the borders of the Zoog domain would be followed by consequences highly disastrous to Zoogs. These matters disposed of, the assembled cats broke ranks and permitted the Zoogs to slink off one by one to their respective homes, which they hastened to do, with many a sullen backward glance.

The old cat general now offered Carter an escort through the forest to whatever border he wished to reach, deeming it likely that the Zoogs would harbor dire resentment against him for the frustration of their warlike enterprise. This offer he welcomed with gratitude, not only for the safety it afforded, but because he liked the graceful companionship of cats. So in the midst of a pleasant and playful regiment, relaxed after the successful performance of its duty, Randolph Carter walked with dignity through that enchanted and phosphorescent wood of titan trees, talking of his quest with the old general and his grandson while others of the band indulged in fantastic gambols or chased fallen leaves that the wind drove among the fungi of that primeval floor. And the old cat said that he had heard much of unknown Kadath in the cold waste, but did not know where it was. As for the marvelous sunset city, he had not even heard of that, but would gladly relay to Carter anything he might later learn.

He gave the seeker some passwords of great value among the cats of dreamland, and commended him especially to the old chief of the cats in Celephais, whither he was bound. That old cat, already slightly known to Carter, was a dignified Maltese and would prove highly influential in any transaction. It was dawn when they came to the proper edge of the wood, and Carter bade his friends a reluctant farewell. The young sublieutenant he had met as a small kitten would have followed him had not the old general forbidden it, but that austere patriarch insisted that the path of duty lay with the tribe and the army. So Carter set out alone over the golden fields that stretched mysterious beside a willow-fringed river, and the cats went back into the wood.

Well did the traveler know those garden lands that lie between the wood and the Cerenerian Sea, and blithely did he follow the singing river Oukranos which marked his course. The sun rose higher over gentle slopes of grove and lawn, and heightened the colors of the thousand flowers that starred each knoll and dingle. A blessed haze lies upon all this region, wherein is held a little more of the sunlight than other places hold, and a little more of the summer's humming music of birds and bees, so that men walk through it as through a fairy place, and feel greater joy and wonder than they ever afterward remember.

By noon Carter reached the jasper terraces of Kiran which slope down to the river's edge and bear that temple of loveliness whither the King of Ilek-Vad comes from his far realm on the twilight sea once a year in a golden palanquin to pray to the god of Oukranos, who sang to him in youth when he dwelt in a cottage by its banks. All of jasper is that temple, and covering an acre of ground with its walls and courts, its seven pinnacled towers, and its inner shrine where the river enters through hidden channels and the god sings softly in the night. Many times the moon hears strange music as it shines on those courts and terraces and pinnacles, but whether that music be the song of the god or the chant of the cryptical priests none but the King of Ilek-Vad may say, for only he had entered the temple or seen the priests. Now, in the drowsiness of day, that carved and delicate fane was silent, and Carter heard only the murmur of the great stream and the hum of the birds and bees as he walked onward under the enchanted sun.

All that afternoon the pilgrim wandered on through perfumed meadows and in the lee of gentle riverward hills bearing peaceful thatched cottages and the shrines of amiable gods carved from jasper or chrysoberyl. Sometimes he walked close to the bank of Oukranos and whistled to the sprightly and iridescent fish of that crystal stream, and at other times he paused amid the whispering rushes and gazed at the great dark wood on the farther side, whose trees came down clear to the water's edge. In former dreams he had seen quaint, lumbering buopoths come shyly out of that wood to drink, but now he could not glimpse any. Once in a while he paused to watch a carnivorous fish catch a fishing bird, which it lured to the water by showing its tempting scales in the sun, and grasped by the beak with its enormous mouth as the winged hunter sought to dart down upon it.

Toward evening he mounted a low grassy rise and saw before him flaming in the sunset the thousand gilded spires of Thran. Lofty beyond belief are the alabaster walls of that incredible city, sloping inward toward the top and wrought in one solid piece by what means no man knows, for they are more ancient than memory. Yet lofty as they are with their hundred gates and two hundred turrets, the clustered towers within, all white beneath their golden spires, are loftier still, so that men on the plain around see them soaring into the sky—sometimes shining clear, sometimes caught at the top in tangles of cloud and mist, and sometimes clouded lower down with their utmost pinnacles blazing free above the vapors. And where Thran's gates open on the river are great wharves of marble, with ornate galleons of fragrant cedar and calamander riding gently at anchor, and strange bearded sailors sitting on casks and bales with the hieroglyphs of far places. Landward beyond the walls lies the farm country, where small white cottages dream between little hills, and narrow roads with many stone bridges wind gracefully among streams and gardens.

Down through this verdant land Carter walked at evening, and saw twilight float up from the river to the marvelous golden spires of Thran. And just at the hour of dusk he came to the southern gate, and was stopped by a red-robed sentry till he had told three dreams beyond belief, and proved himself a dreamer worthy to walk up Thran's steep mysterious streets and linger in the bazaars where the wares of the ornate galleons were sold. Then into that incredible city he walked, through a wall so thick that the gate was a tunnel, and thereafter amidst curved and undulant ways winding deep and narrow between the heavenward towers. Lights shone through grated and balconied windows, and the sound of lutes and pipes stole timid from inner courts where marble fountains bubbled. Carter knew his way, and edged down through darker streets to the river, where at an old sea tavern he found the captains and seamen he had known in myriad other dreams. There he bought his passage to Celephais on a great green galleon, and there he stopped for the night, after speaking gravely to the venerable cat of that inn, who blinked dozing before an enormous hearth and dreamed of old wars and forgotten gods.

In the morning Carter boarded the galleon bound for Celephais, and sat in the prow as the ropes were cast off and the long sail down to the Cerenerian Sea begun. For many leagues the banks were much as they were above Thran, with now and then a curious temple rising on the farther hills toward the right, and a drowsy village on the shore, with steep red roofs and nets spread in the sun. Mindful of his search, Carter questioned all the mariners closely about those whom they had met in the taverns of Celephais, asking the names and ways of the strange men with long, narrow eyes, long-lobed ears, thin noses, and pointed chins who came in dark ships from the north and traded onyx for the carved jade and spun gold and little red singing birds of Celephais. Of these men the sailors knew not much, save that they talked but seldom and spread a kind of awe about them.

Their land, very far away, was called Inquanok, and not many people cared to go thither because it was cold twilight land, and said to be close to unpleasant Leng, although high, impassable mountains towered on the side where Leng was thought to lie, so that none might say whether this evil plateau with its horrible stone villages and unmentionable monastery was really there or whether the rumor was only a fear that timid people felt in the night when those formidable barrier peaks loomed black against a rising moon. Certainly, men reached Leng from very different oceans. Of other boundaries of Inquanok those sailors had no notion, nor had they heard of the cold waste and unknown Kadath save from vague, unplaced report. And of the marvelous sunset city which Carter sought they knew nothing at all. So the traveler asked no more of far things, but bided his time till he might talk with those strange men from cold and twilight Inquanok who are the seed of such gods as carved their features on Ngranek.

Late in the day the galleon reached those bends of the river which traverse the perfumed jungles of Kled. Here Carter wished he might disembark, for in those tropic tangles sleep wondrous palaces of ivory, lone and unbroken, where once dwelt fabulous monarchs of a land whose name is forgotten. Spells of the Elder Ones keep those places unharmed and undecayed, for it is written that there may one day be need of them again, and elephant caravans have glimpsed them from afar by moonlight, though none dares approach them closely because of the guardians to which their wholeness is due. But the ship swept on, and dusk hushed the hum of the day, and the first stars above blinked answers to the early fireflies on the banks as that jungle fell far behind, leaving only its fragrance as a memory that it had been. And all through the night that galleon floated on past mysteries unseen and unsuspected. Once a lookout reported fires on the hills to the east, but the sleepy captain said they had better not be looked at too much, since it was highly uncertain just who or what had lit them.

In the morning the river had broadened out greatly, and Carter saw by the houses along the banks that they were close to the vast trading city of Hlanith, on the Cerenerian Sea. Here the walls are of rugged granite, and the houses peakedly fantastic with beamed and plastered gables. The men of

Hlanith are more like those of the waking world than any others in dreamland, so that the city is not sought except for barter, but is prized for the solid work of its artisans. The wharves of Hlanith are of oak, and there the galleon made fast while the captain traded in the taverns. Carter also went ashore, and looked curiously upon the rutted streets where wooden oxcarts lumbered and feverish merchants cried their wares vacuously in the bazaars. The sea taverns were all close to the wharves, on cobbled lanes salt with the spray of high tides, and seemed exceedingly ancient with their low black-beamed ceilings and casements of greenish bull's-eye panes. Ancient sailors in those taverns talked much of distant ports, and told many stories of the curious men from twilight Inquanok, but had little to add to what the seamen of the galleon had told. Then at last, after much unloading and loading, the ship set sail once more over the sunset sea, and the high walls and gables of Hlanith grew less as the last golden light of day lent them a wonder and beauty beyond any that men had given them.

Two nights and two days the galleon sailed over the Cerenerian Sea, sighting no land and speaking with but one other vessel. Then near sunset of the second day there loomed up ahead the snowy peak of Aran with its ginkgo trees swaying on the lower slope, and Carter knew that they were come to the land of Ooth-Nargai and the marvelous city of Celephais. Swiftly there came into sight the glittering minarets of that fabulous town, and the untarnished marble walls with their bronze statues, and the great stone bridge where Naraxa joins the sea. Then rose the gentle hills behind the town, with their groves and gardens of asphodels and the small shrines and cottages upon them, and far in the background the purple ridge of the Tanarians, potent and mystical, behind which lay forbidden ways into the waking world and toward other regions of dream.

The harbor was full of painted galleys, some of which were from the marble cloud-city of Serannian, which lies in ethereal space beyond where the sea meets the sky, and some of which were from more substantial parts of dreamland. Among these the steersman threaded his way up to the spice-fragrant wharves, where the galleon made fast in the dusk as the city's million lights began to twinkle out over the water. Ever new seemed this deathless city of vision, for here time has no power to tarnish or destroy. As it has always been is still the turquoise of Nath-Horthath, and the eighty orchid-wreathed priests are the same who built it ten thousand years ago. Shining still is the bronze of the great gates, nor are the onyx pavements ever worn or broken. And the great bronze statues on the walls look down on merchants and camel drivers older than fable, yet without one gray hair in their forked beards.

Carter did not at once seek out the temple or the palace or the citadel, but stayed by the seaward wall among traders and sailors. And when it was too late for rumors and legends, he sought out an ancient tavern he knew well, and rested with dreams of the gods on unknown Kadath whom he sought.

The next day he searched all along the quays for some of the strange mariners of Inquanok, but was told that none were now in port, their galley not being due from the north for full two weeks. He found, however, one Thorabonian sailor who had been to Inquanok and had worked in the onyx quarries of that twilight place; and this sailor said there was certainly a descent to the north of the peopled region, which everybody seemed to fear and shun. The Thorabonian opined that this desert led around the utmost rim of impassable peaks into Leng's horrible plateau, and that this was why men feared it, though he admitted there were other vague tales of evil presences and nameless sentinels. Whether or not this could be the fabled waste wherein unknown Kadath stands he did not know, but it seemed unlikely that those presences and sentinels, if indeed they existed, were stationed for naught.

On the following day, Carter walked up the Street of the Pillars to the turquoise temple and talked with the high priest. Though Nath-Horthath is chiefly worshiped in Celephais, all the Great Ones are mentioned in diurnal prayers, and the priest was reasonably versed in their moods. Like Atal in distant Ulthar, he strongly advised against any attempts to see them, declaring that they are testy and capricious, and subject to strange protection from the mindless Other Gods from Outside, whose soul and messenger is the crawling chaos Nyarlathotep. Their jealous hiding of the marvelous sunset city showed clearly that they did not wish Carter to reach it, and it was doubtful how they would regard a guest whose object was to see them and plead before them. No man had ever found Kadath in the past, and it might be just as well if none ever found it in the future. Such rumors as were told about that onyx castle of the Great Ones were not by any means reassuring.

Having thanked the orchid-crowned high priest, Carter left the temple and sought out the bazaar of the sheep-butchers, where the old chief of Celephais' cats dwelt sleek and contented. That gray and dignified being was sunning himself on the onyx pavement, and extended a languid paw as his caller approached. But when Carter repeated the passwords and introductions furnished him by the old cat general of Ulthar, the furry patriarch became very cordial and communicative, and told much of the secret lore known to cats on the seaward slopes of Ooth-Nargai. Best of all, he repeated several things told him furtively by the timid waterfront cats of Celephais about the men of Inquanok, on whose dark ships no cat will go.

It seems that these men have an aura not of earth about them, though that is not the reason why no cat will sail on their ships. The reason for this is that Inquanok holds shadows which no cat can endure, so that in all that cold twilight realm there is never a cheering purr or a homely mew. Whether it be because of things wafted over the impassable peaks from hypothetical Leng or because of things filtering down from the chilly desert to the north none may say; but it remains a fact that in that far land there broods a hint of outer space which cats do not like, and to which they are more sensitive than men. Therefore they will not go on the dark ships that seek the basalt quays of Inquanok.

The old chief of the cats also told him where to find his friend King Kuranes, who in Carter's latter dreams had reigned alternately in the rose-crystal Palace of the Seventy Delights at Celephais and in the turreted cloud-castle of sky-floating Serannian. It seemed that he could no more find content in those places, but had formed a mighty longing for the English cliffs and downlands of his boyhood, where in little dreaming villages England's old songs hover at evening behind latticed windows, and where gray church towers peep lovely through the verdure of distant valleys. He could not go back to these things in the waking world because his body was dead; but he had done the next-best thing and dreamed a small tract of such countryside in the region east of the city where meadows roll gracefully up from the sea cliffs to the foot of the Tanarian Hills. There he dwelt in a gray Gothic manor house of stone looking on the sea, and tried to think it was ancient Trevor Towers, where he had been born and where thirteen generations of his forefathers had first seen the light. And on the coast nearby he had built a little Cornish fishing village with steep cobbled ways, settling therein such people as had the most English faces, and seeking ever to teach them the dear remembered accents of old Cornwall fishers. And in a valley not far off he had reared a great Norman abbey whose tower he could see from his window, placing around it in the churchyard gray stones with the names of his ancestors carved thereon, and with a moss somewhat like old England's moss. For though Kuranes was a monarch in the land of dream, with all imagined pomps and marvels, splendors and beauties, ecstasies and delights, novelties and excitements at his command, he would gladly have resigned forever the whole of his power and luxury and freedom for one blessed day as a simple boy in that pure and quiet England, that ancient, beloved England which had molded his being and of which he must always be immutably a part.

So when Carter bade that old gray chief of the cats adieu, he did not seek the terraced palace of rose crystal, but walked out the eastern gate and across the daisied fields toward a peaked gable which he glimpsed through the oaks of a park sloping up to the sea cliffs. And in time he came to a great hedge and a gate with a little brick lodge, and when he rang the bell there hobbled to admit him no robed and anointed lackey of the palace, but a small, stubby old man in a smock who spoke as best he could in the quaint tones of far Cornwall. And Carter walked up the shady path between trees as near as possible to England's trees, and climbed the terraces among gardens set out as in Queen Anne's time. At the door, flanked by stone cats in the old way, he was met by a whiskered butler in suitable livery, and was presently taken to the library, where Kuranes, Lord of Ooth-Nargai and the Sky around Serannian, sat pensive in a chair by the window looking on his little seacoast village and wishing that his old nurse would come in and scold him because he was not ready for that hateful lawn party at the vicar's, with the carriage waiting and his mother nearly out of patience.

Kuranes, clad in a dressing gown of the sort favored by London tailors in his youth, rose eagerly to meet his guest, for the sight of an Anglo-Saxon from the waking world was very dear to him, even if it was a Saxon from Boston, Massachusetts, instead of from Cornwall. And for long they talked of old times, having much to say because both were old dreamers and well versed in the wonders of incredible places. Kuranes, indeed, had been out beyond the stars in the ultimate void, and was said to be the only one who had ever returned sane from such a voyage.

At length Carter brought up the subject of his quest, and asked of his host those questions he had asked of so many others. Kuranes did not know where Kadath was, or the marvelous sunset city; but he did know that the Great Ones were very dangerous creatures to seek out, and that the Other Gods had strange ways of protecting them from impertinent curiosity. He had learned much of the Other Gods in distant parts of space, especially in that region where form does not exist and colored gases study the innermost secrets. The violet gas S'ngac had told him terrible things of the crawling chaos Nyarlathotep, and had warned him never to approach the central void where the demon sultan Azathoth gnaws hungrily in the dark. Altogether, it was not well to meddle with the Elder Ones, and if they persistently denied all access to the marvelous sunset city, it was better not to seek that city.

Kuranes furthermore doubted whether his guest would profit aught by coming to the city even were he to gain it. He himself had dreamed and yearned long years for lovely Celephais and the land of Ooth-Nargai, and for the freedom and color and high experience of life devoid of its chains and conventions and stupidities. But now that he was come into that city and that land and was the king thereof, he found the freedom and the vividness all too soon worn out, and monotonous for want of linkage with anything firm in his feelings and memories. He was a king in Ooth-Nargai, but found no meaning therein, and drooped always for the old, familiar things of England that had shaped his youth. All his kingdom would he give for the sound of Cornish church bells over the downs, and all the thousand minarets of Celephais for the steep, homely roofs of the village near his home. So he told his guest that the unknown sunset city might not hold quite that content he sought, and that perhaps it had better remain a glorious and half-remembered dream. For he had visited Carter often in the old waking days, and knew well the lovely New England slopes that had given him birth.

At the last, he was very certain, the seeker would long only for the early remembered scenes: the glow of Beacon Hill at evening, the tall steeples and winding hill streets of quaint Kingsport, the hoary gambrel roofs of ancient and witch-haunted Arkham, and the blessed meads and valleys where stone walls rambled and white farmhouse gables peeped out from bowers of verdure. These things he told Randolph Carter, but still the seeker held to his purpose. And in the end they parted each with his own conviction, and Carter went back through the bronze gate into Celephais and down the Street of Pillars to the old sea wall, where he talked more with the mariners of far ports and waited for the dark ship from cold and twilight Inquanok, whose strange-faced sailors and onyx-traders had in them the blood of the Great Ones.

One starlit evening when the Pharos shone splendid over the harbor, the longed-for ship put in, and strange-faced sailors and traders appeared one by one and group by group in the ancient taverns along the sea wall. It was very exciting to see again those living faces so like the godlike features of Ngranek, but Carter did not hasten to speak with the silent seamen. He did not know how much of pride and secrecy and dim supernal memory might fill those children of the Great Ones, and was sure it would not be wise to tell them of his quest or ask too closely of that cold desert stretching north of their twilight land. They talked little with the other folk in those ancient sea taverns, but would gather in groups in remote corners and sing among themselves the haunting airs of unknown places, or chant long tales to one another in accents alien to the rest of dreamland. And so rare and moving were those airs and tales that one might guess their wonders from the faces of those who listened, even though the words came to common ears only as strange cadence and obscure melody.

For a week the strange seamen lingered in the taverns and traded in the bazaars of Celephais, and before they sailed Carter had taken passage on their dark ship, telling them that he was an old onyx-miner and wishful to work in their quarries. That ship was very lovely and cunningly wrought, being of teakwood with ebony fittings and traceries of gold, and the cabin in which the traveler lodged had hangings of silk and velvet. One morning at the turn of the tide the sails were raised and the anchor lifted, and as Carter stood on the high stern he saw the sunrise-blazing walls and bronze statues and golden minarets of ageless Celephais sink into the distance, and the snowy peak of Mount Aran grow smaller and smaller. By noon there was nothing in sight save the gentle blue of the Cerenerian Sea, with one painted galley far off bound for that realm of Serannian where the sea meets the sky.

And the night came with gorgeous stars, and the dark ship steered for Charles's Wain and the Little Bear as they swung slowly round the pole. And the sailors sang strange songs of unknown places, and they stole off one by one to the forecastle while the wistful watchers murmured old chants and leaned over the rail to glimpse the luminous fish playing in bowers beneath the sea. Carter went to sleep at midnight and rose in the glow of a young morning, marking that the sun seemed farther south than was its wont. And all through that second day he made progress in knowing the men of the ship, getting them little by little to talk of their cold twilight land, of their exquisite onyx city, and of their fear of the high and impassable peaks beyond which Leng was said to be. They told him how sorry they were that no cats would stay in the land of Inquanok, and how they thought the hidden nearness of Leng was to blame for it. Only of the stony desert to the north they would not talk. There was something disquieting about that desert, and it was thought expedient not to admit its existence.

On later days they talked of the quarries in which Carter said he was going to work. There were many of them, for all the city of Inquanok was built of onyx, while great polished blocks of it were traded in Rinar, Ogrothan, and Celephais and at home with the merchants of Thraa, Ilarnek, and Kadatheron for the beautiful wares of those fabulous ports. And far to the north, almost in the cold desert whose existence the men of Inquanok did not care to admit, there was an unused quarry greater than all the rest, from which had been hewn in forgotten times such prodigious lumps and blocks that the sight of their chiseled vacancies struck terror to all who beheld. Who had mined those incredible blocks, and whither they had been transported, no man might say; but it was thought best not to trouble that quarry, around which such inhuman memories might conceivably cling. So it was left all alone in the twilight, with only the raven and the rumored Shantak-bird to brood on its immensities. When Carter heard of this quarry he was moved to deep thought, for he knew from old tales that the Great Ones' castle atop unknown Kadath is of onyx.

Each day the sun wheeled lower and lower in the sky, and the mists overhead grew thicker and thicker. And in two weeks there was not any sunlight at all, but only a weird gray twilight shining through a dome of eternal cloud by day, and a cold starless phosphorescence from the underside of that cloud by night. On the twentieth day, a great jagged rock in the sea was sighted from afar, the first land glimpsed since Aran's snowy peak had dwindled behind the ship. Carter asked the captain the name of that rock, but was told that it had no name and had never been sought by any vessel because of the sounds that came from it at night. And when, after dark, a dull and ceaseless howling rose from that jagged granite place, the traveler was glad that no stop had been made, and that the rock had no name. The seamen prayed and chanted till the noise was out of earshot, and Carter dreamed terrible dreams within dreams in the small hours.

Two mornings after that, there loomed far ahead and to the east a line of great gray peaks whose tops were lost in the changeless clouds of that twilight world. And at the sight of them the sailors sang glad songs, and some knelt down on the deck to pray, so that Carter knew they were come to the land of Inquanok and would soon be moored to the basalt quays of the great town bearing that land's name. Toward noon a dark coastline appeared, and before three o'clock there stood out against the north the bulbous domes and fantastic spires of the onyx city. Rare and curious did that archaic city rise above its walls and quays, all of delicate black with scrolls, flutings, and arabesques of inlaid gold. Tall and many-windowed were the houses, and carved on every side with flowers and patterns whose dark symmetries dazzled the eye with a beauty more poignant than light. Some ended in swelling domes that tapered to a point; others, in terraced pyramids whereon rose clustered minarets displaying every phase of strangeness and imagination. The walls were low, and pierced by frequent gates, each under a great arch rising high above the general level and capped by the head of a god chiseled with that same skill displayed in the monstrous face on distant Ngranek. On a hill in the center rose a sixteen-angled tower greater than all the rest and bearing a high pinnacled belfry resting on a flattened dome. This, the seamen said, was the Temple of the Elder Ones, and was ruled by an old high priest sad with inner secrets.

At intervals the clang of a strange bell shivered over the onyx city, answered each time by a peal of mystic music made up of horns, viols, and chanting voices. And from a row of tripods on a gallery around the high dome of the temple there burst flares of flame at certain moments; for the priests and people of that city were wise in the primal mysteries, and faithful in keeping the rhythms of the Great Ones as set forth in scrolls older than the Pnakotic Manuscripts. As the ship rode past the great basalt breakwater into the harbor, the lesser noises of the city grew manifest, and Carter saw the slaves, sailors, and merchants on the docks. The sailors and merchants were of the strange-faced race of the gods, but the slaves were squat, slant-eyed folk said by rumor to have drifted somehow across or around the impassable peaks from the valleys beyond Leng. The wharves reached wide outside the city wall and bore upon them all manner of merchandise from the galleys anchored there, while at one end were great piles of onyx both carved and uncarved awaiting shipment to the far markets of Rinar, Ograthan, and Celephais.

It was not yet evening when the dark ship anchored beside

a jutting quay of stone, and all the sailors and traders filed ashore and through the arched gate into the city. The streets of that city were paved with onyx, and some of them were wide and straight, while others were crooked and narrow. The houses near the water were lower than the rest, and bore above their curiously arched doorways certain signs of gold said to be in honor of the respective small gods that favored each. The captain of the ship took Carter to an old sea tavern where flocked the mariners of quaint countries, and promised that he would next day show him the wonders of the twilight city, and lead him to the taverns of the onyx-miners by the northern wall. And evening fell, and little bronze lamps were lighted, and the sailors in that tavern sang songs of remote places. But when from its high tower the great bell shivered over the city, and the peal of the horns and viols and voices rose cryptical in answer thereto, all ceased their songs or tales and bowed silent till the last echo died away. For there is a wonder and a strangeness in the twilight city of Inquanok, and men fear to be lax in its rites lest a doom and a vengeance lurk unsuspectedly close.

Far in the shadows of that tavern Carter saw a squat form he did not like, for it was unmistakably that of the old slant-eyed merchant he had seen so long before in the taverns of Dylath-Leen, who was reputed to trade with the horrible stone villages of Leng which no healthy folk visit and whose evil fires are seen at night from afar, and even to have dealt with that high priest not to be described which wears a yellow silken mask over its face and dwells all alone in a prehistoric stone monastery. This man had seemed to show a queer gleam of knowing when Carter asked the traders of Dylath-Leen about the cold waste and Kadath; and somehow his presence in dark and haunted Inquanok, so close to the wonders of the north, was not a reassuring thing. He slipped wholly out of sight before Carter could speak to him, and sailors later said that he had come with a yak caravan from some point not well determined, bearing the colossal and rich-flavored eggs of the rumored Shantak-bird to trade for the dextrous jade goblets that merchants brought from Ilarnek.

On the following morning the ship captain led Carter through the onyx streets of Inquanok, dark under their twilight sky. The inlaid doors and figured housefronts, carved balconies and crystal-paned oriels all gleamed with a somber and polished loveliness; and now and then a plaza would open out with black pillars, colonnades, and the statues of curious beings both human and fabulous. Some of the vistas down long and unbending streets, or through side alleys and over bulbous domes, spires, and arabesqued roofs, were weird and beautiful beyond words; and nothing was more splendid than the massive heights of the great central Temple of the Elder Ones with its sixteen carved sides, its flattened dome, and its lofty pinnacled belfry, overtopping all else and majestic whatever its foreground. And always to the east, far beyond the city walls and the leagues of pastureland, rose the gaunt gray sides of those topless and impassable peaks across which hideous Leng was said to lie.

The captain took Carter to the mighty temple, which is set with its walled garden in a great round plaza whence the streets go like spokes from a wheel's hub. The seven arched gates of that garden, each having over it a carved face like those on the city's gates, are always open, and the people roam reverently at will down the tiled paths and through the little lanes lined with grotesque termini and the shrines of modest gods. And there are fountains, pools, and basins there to reflect the frequent blaze of the tripods on the high balcony, all of onyx and having in them small luminous fish taken by divers from the lower bowers of ocean. When the deep clang from the temple belfry shivers over the garden and the city, and the answer of the horns and viols and voices peals out from the seven lodges by the garden gates, there issue from the seven doors of the temple long columns of masked and hooded priests in black, bearing at arms' length before them great golden bowls from which a curious steam rises. And all the seven columns strut peculiarly in single file, legs thrown far forward without bending the knees, down the walks that lead to the seven lodges, into which they disappear and whence they do not appear again. It is said that subterrane paths connect the lodges with the temple, and that the long files of priests return through them; nor is it unwhispered that deep flights of onyx steps go down to mysteries that are never told. But only a few are those who hint that the priests in the masked and hooded columns are not human beings.

Carter did not enter the temple, because none but the Veiled King is permitted to do that. But before he left the garden the hour of the bell came, and he heard the shivering clang deafeningly above him, and the wailing of the horns and viols and voices loud from the lodges by the gates. And down the seven great walks stalked the long files of bowl-bearing priests in their singular way, giving to the traveler a fear which human priests do not often give. When the last of them had vanished, he left that garden, noting as he did so a spot on the pavement over which the bowls had passed. Even the ship captain did not like that spot, and hurried him on toward the hill whereon the Veiled King's palace rises many-domed and marvelous.

The ways to the onyx palace are steep and narrow, all but the broad curving one where the king and his companions ride on yaks or in yak-drawn chariots. Carter and his guide climbed up an alley that was all steps, between inlaid walls bearing strange signs in gold, and under balconies and oriels whence sometimes floated soft strains of music or breaths of exotic fragrance. Always ahead loomed those titan walls, mighty buttresses, and clustered and bulbous domes for which the Veiled King's palace is famous; and at length they passed under a great black arch and emerged in the gardens of the monarch's pleasure. There Carter paused in faintness at so much beauty, for the onyx terraces and colonnaded walks, the gay parterres and delicate flowering trees espaliered to golden lattices, the brazen urns and tripods with cunning bas-reliefs, the pedestaled and almost-breathing statues of veined black marble, the basalt-bottomed lagoon's tiled fountains with luminous fish, the tiny temples of iridescent singing birds atop carved columns, the marvelous scrollwork of the great bronze gates, and the blossoming vines trained along every inch of the polished walls all joined to form a sight whose loveliness was beyond reality, and half fabulous even in the land of dream. There it shimmered like a vision under that gray twilight sky, with the domed and fretted magnificence of the palace ahead, and the fantastic silhouette of the distant impassable peaks on the right. And ever the small birds and the fountains sang, while the perfume of rare blossoms spread like a veil over that incredible garden. No other human presence was there, and Carter was glad it was so. Then they turned and descended again the onyx alley of steps; for the palace itself no visitor may enter, and it is not well to look too long and steadily at the great central dome, since it is said to house the archaic father of all the rumored Shantak-birds, and to send out queer dreams to the curious.

After that the captain took Carter to the north quarter of the town, near the Gate of the Caravans, where are the taverns of the yak-merchants and the onyx-miners. And there, in a low-ceiled inn of quarrymen, they said farewell, for business called the captain, while Carter was eager to talk with miners about the north. There were many men in that inn, and the traveler was not long in speaking to some of them, saying that he was an old miner of onyx and anxious to know somewhat of Inquanok's quarries. But all that he learned was not much more than he knew before, for the miners were timid and evasive about the cold desert to the north and the quarry that no man visits. They had fears of fabled emissaries from around the mountains where Leng is said to lie, and of evil presences and nameless sentinels far north among the scattered rocks. And they whispered also that the rumored Shantak-birds are no wholesome things, it being indeed for the best that no man has ever truly seen one (for that fabled father of Shantaks in the king's dome is fed in the dark).

The next day, saying that he wished to look over all the various mines for himself and to visit the scattered farms and quaint onyx villages of Inquanok, Carter hired a yak and stuffed great leather saddlebags for a journey. Beyond the Gate of the Caravans the road lay straight between tilled fields, with many odd farmhouses crowned by low domes. At some of these houses the seeker stopped to ask questions, once finding a host so austere and reticent, and so full of an unplaced majesty like to that in the huge features on Ngranek, that he felt certain he had come at last upon one of the Great Ones themselves, or upon one with full nine-tenths of their blood, dwelling among men. And to that austere and reticent cotter he was careful to speak very well of the gods, and to praise all the blessings they had ever accorded him.

That night Carter camped in a roadside meadow beneath a great lygath tree to which he tied his yak, and in the morning resumed his northward pilgrimage. At about ten o'clock he reached the small-domed village of Urg, where traders rest and miners tell their tales, and paused in its taverns till noon. It is here that the great caravan road turns west toward Selarn, but Carter kept on north by the quarry road. All the afternoon he followed that rising road, which was somewhat narrower than the great highway, and which now led through a region with more rocks than tilled fields. And by evening the low hills on his left had risen into sizable black cliffs, so that he knew he was close to the mining country. All the while the great gaunt sides of the impassable mountains towered far off at his right, and the farther he went, the worse tales he heard of them from the scattered farmers and traders and drivers of lumbering onyx-carts along the way.

On the second night he camped in the shadow of a large black crag, tethering his yak to a stake driven in the ground. He observed the greater phosphorescence of the clouds at this northerly point, and more than once thought he saw dark shapes outlined against them. And on the third morning he came in sight of the first onyx quarry, and greeted the men who there labored with picks and chisels. Before evening he had passed eleven quarries, the land being here given over altogether to onyx cliffs and boulders, with no vegetation at all but only great rocky fragments scattered about a floor of black earth, with the gray impassable peaks always rising gaunt and sinister on his right. The third night he spent in a camp of quarry men whose flickering fires cast weird reflections on the polished cliffs to the west. And they sang many songs and told many tales, showing such strange knowledge of the olden days and the habits of gods that Carter could see they held many latent memories of their sires the Great Ones. They asked him whither he went, and cautioned him not to go too far to the north; but he replied that he was seeking new cliffs of onyx, and would take no more risks than were common among prospectors. In the morning he bade them adieu and rode on into the darkening north, where they had warned him he would find the feared and unvisited quarry whence hands older than men's hands had wrenched prodigious blocks. But he did not like it when, turning back to wave a last farewell, he thought he saw approaching the camp that squat and evasive old merchant with slanting eyes whose conjectured traffic with Leng was the gossip of distant Dylath-Leen.

After two more quarries, the inhabited part of Inquanok seemed to end, and the road narrowed to a steeply rising yak path among forbidding black cliffs. Always on the right towered the gaunt and distant peaks, and as Carter climbed farther and farther into this untraversed realm he found it grew darker and colder. Soon he perceived that there were no prints of feet or hoofs on the black path beneath, and realized that he had indeed come into strange and deserted ways of elder time. Once in a while a raven would croak far overhead, and now and then a flapping behind some vast rock would make him think uncomfortably of the rumored Shantak-bird. But in the main he was alone with his shaggy steed, and it troubled him to observe that this excellent yak became more and more reluctant to advance, and more and more disposed to snort affrightedly at any small noise along the route.

The path now contracted between sable and glistening walls, and began to display an even greater steepness than before. It was a bad footing, and the yak often slipped on the stony fragments strewn thickly about. In two hours Carter saw ahead a definite crest, beyond which was nothing but dull gray sky, and blessed the prospect of a level or downward course. To reach this crest, however, was no easy task, for the way had grown nearly perpendicular, and was perilous with loose black gravel and small stones. Eventually Carter dismounted and led his dubious yak, pulling very hard when the animal balked or stumbled, and keeping his own footing as best he might. Then suddenly he came to the top and saw beyond, and gasped at what he saw.

The path indeed led straight ahead and slightly down, with the same lines of high natural walls as before; but on the left hand there opened out a monstrous space, vast acres in extent, where some archaic power had riven and rent the native cliffs of onyx in the form of a giant's quarry. Far back into the solid precipice ran that cyclopean gouge, and deep down within earth's bowels its lower delvings yawned. It was no quarry of man, and the concave sides were scarred with great squares, yards wide, which told of the size of the blocks once hewn by nameless hands and chisels. High over its jagged rim huge ravens flapped and croaked, and vague whirrings in the unseen depths told of bats or urhags or less-mentionable presences haunting the endless blackness. There Carter stood in the narrow way amid the twilight, with the rocky path sloping down before him, tall onyx cliffs on his right that led on as far as he could see, and tall cliffs on the left chopped off just ahead to make that terrible and unearthly quarry.

All at once the yak uttered a cry and burst from his control, leaping past him and darting on in a panic till it vanished down the narrow slope toward the north. Stones kicked by its flying hoofs fell over the brink of the quarry and lost themselves in the dark without any sound of striking bottom; but Carter ignored the perils of that scanty path as he raced breathlessly after the flying steed. Soon the left-hand cliffs resumed their course, making the way once more a narrow lane; and still the traveler leaped on after the yak, whose great wide prints told of its desperate flight.

Once he thought he heard the hoofbeats of the frightened beast, and doubled his speed from this encouragement. He was covering miles, and little by little the way was broadening in front till he knew he must soon emerge on the cold and dreaded desert to the north. The gaunt gray flanks of the distant impassable peaks were again visible above the right-hand crags, and ahead were the rocks and boulders of an open space which was clearly a foretaste of the dark and limitless plain. And once more those hoofbeats sounded in his ears, plainer than before, but this time giving terror instead of encouragement because he realized that they were not the frightened hoofbeats of his fleeing yak. The beats were ruthless and purposeful, and they were behind him.

Carter's pursuit of the yak now became a flight from an unseen thing, for though he dared not glance over his shoulder, he felt that the presence behind him could be nothing wholesome or mentionable. His yak must have heard or felt it first, and he did not like to ask himself whether it had followed him from the haunts of men or had floundered up out of that black quarry pit. Meanwhile the cliffs had been left behind, so that the oncoming night fell over a great waste of sand and spectral rocks wherein all paths were lost. He could not see the hoofprints of his yak, but always from behind him there came that detestable clopping, mingled now and then with what he fancied were titanic flappings and whirrings. That he was losing ground seemed unhappily clear to him, and he knew he was hopelessly lost in this broken and blasted desert of meaningless rocks and untraveled sands. Only those remote and impassable peaks on the right gave him any sense of direction, and even they were less clear as the gray twilight waned and the sickly phosphorescence of the clouds took its place.

Then, dim and misty in the darkling north before him, he glimpsed a terrible thing. He had thought it for some moments a range of black mountains, but now he saw that it was something more. The phosphorescence of the brooding clouds showed it plainly, and even silhouetted parts of it as vapors glowed behind. How distant it was he could not tell, but it must have been very far. It was thousands of feet high, stretching in a great concave arc from the gray impassable peaks to the unimagined westward spaces, and had once indeed been a ridge of mighty onyx hills. But now these hills were hills no more, for some hand greater than man's had touched them. Silent they squatted there atop the world like wolves or ghouls, crowned with clouds and mists and guarding the secrets of the north forever. All in a great half circle they squatted, those doglike mountains carved into monstrous watching statues, and their right hands were raised in menace against mankind.

It was only the flickering light of the clouds that made their mitered double heads seem to move, but as Carter stumbled on, he saw arise from their shadowy caps great forms whose motions were no delusion. Winged and whirring, those forms grew larger each moment, and the traveler knew his stumbling was at an end. They were not any birds or bats known elsewhere on earth or in dreamland, for they were larger than elephants and had heads like a horse's. Carter knew that they must be the Shantak-birds of ill rumor, and wondered no more what evil guardians and nameless sentinels made men avoid the boreal rock desert. And as he stopped in final resignation, he dared at last to look behind him, where indeed was trotting the squat slant-eyed trader of evil legend, grinning astride a lean yak and leading on a noxious horde of leering Shantaks to whose wings still clung the rime and niter of the nether pits.

Trapped though he was by fabulous and hippocephalic winged nightmares that pressed around in great unholy circles, Randolph Carter did not lose consciousness. Lofty and horrible those titan gargoyles towered above him, while the slant-eyed merchant leaped down from his yak and stood grinning before the captive. Then the man motioned to Carter to mount one of the repugnant Shantaks, helping him up as his judgment struggled with his loathing. It was hard work ascending, for the Shantak-bird has scales instead of feathers, and those scales are very slippery. Once he was seated, the slant-eyed man hopped up behind him, leaving the lean yak to be led away northward toward the ring of carved mountains by one of the incredible bird colossi.

There now followed a hideous whirl through frigid space, endlessly up and eastward toward the gaunt gray flanks of those impassable mountains beyond which Leng was said to be. Far above the clouds they flew, till at last there lay beneath them those fabled summits which the folk of Inquanok have never seen, and which lie always in high vortices of gleaming mist. Carter beheld them very plainly as they passed below, and saw upon their topmost peaks strange caves which made him think of those on Ngranek; but he did not question his captor about these things when he noticed that both the man and the horse-headed Shantak appeared oddly fearful of them, hurrying past nervously and showing great tension until they were left far in the rear.

The Shantak now flew lower, revealing beneath the canopy of cloud a gray barren plain whereon at great distances shone little feeble fires. As they descended, there appeared at intervals lone huts of granite and bleak stone villages whose tiny windows glowed with pallid light. And there came from those huts and villages a shrill droning of pipes and a nauseous rattle of crotala which proved at once that Inquanok's people are right in their geographic rumors. For travelers have heard such sounds before, and know that they float only from that cold desert plateau which healthy folk never visit, that haunted place of evil and mystery which is Leng.

Around the feeble fires dark forms were dancing, and Carter was curious as to what manner of beings they might be; for no healthy folk have ever been to Leng, and the place is known only by its fires and stone huts as seen from afar. Very slowly and awkwardly did those forms leap, and with an insane twisting and bending not good to behold, so that Carter did not wonder at the monstrous evil imputed to them by vague legend, or the fear in which all dreamland holds their abhorrent frozen plateau. As the Shantak flew lower, the repulsiveness of the dancers became tinged with a certain hellish familiarity, and the prisoner kept straining his eyes and racking his memory for clues to where he had seen such creatures before.

They leaped as though they had hoofs instead of feet, and seemed to wear a sort of wig or headpiece with small horns. Of other clothing they had none, but most of them were quite furry. Behind they had dwarfish tails, and when they glanced upward he saw the excessive width of their mouths. Then he knew what they were, and that they did not wear any wigs or headpieces after all. For the cryptic folk of Leng were of one race with the uncomfortable merchants of the black galleys that traded rubies at Dylath-Leen—those not-quite-human merchants who are the slaves of the monstrous moon-things! They were indeed the same dark folk who had shanghaied Carter on their noisome galley so long ago, and whose kith he had seen driven in herds about the unclean wharves of that accursed lunar city, with the leaner ones toiling and the fatter ones taken away in crates for other needs of their polypous and amorphous masters. Now he saw where such ambiguous creatures came from, and shuddered at the thought that Leng must be known to these formless abominations from the moon.

But the Shantak flew on past the fires and the stone huts and the less-than-human dancers, and soared over sterile hills of gray granite and dim wastes of rock and ice and snow. Day came, and the phosphorescence of low clouds gave place to the misty twilight of that northern world, and still the vile bird winged meaningly through the cold and silence. At times the slant-eyed man talked with his steed in a hateful and guttural language, and the Shantak would answer with tittering tones that rasped like the scratching of ground glass. All this while the land was getting higher, and finally they came to a windswept tableland which seemed the very roof of a blasted and tenantless world. There, all alone in the hush and the dusk and the cold, rose the uncouth stones of a squat windowless building, around which a circle of crude monoliths stood. In all this arrangement there was nothing human, and Carter surmised from old tales that he had indeed come to that most dreadful and legendary of all places, the remote and prehistoric monastery wherein dwells uncompanioned the high priest not to be described, which wears a yellow silken mask over its face and prays to the Other Gods and their crawling chaos Nyarlathotep.

The loathsome bird now settled to the ground, and the slant-eyed man hopped down and helped his captive alight. Of the purpose of his seizure Carter now felt very sure, for clearly the slant-eyed merchant was an agent of the darker powers, eager to drag before his masters a mortal whose presumption had aimed at the finding of unknown Kadath and the saying of a prayer before the faces of the Great Ones in their onyx castle. It seemed likely that this merchant had caused his former capture by the slaves of the moon-things in Dylath-Leen, and that he now meant to do what the rescuing cats had baffled: taking the victim to some dread rendezvous with monstrous Nyarlathotep and telling with what boldness the seeking of unknown Kadath had been tried. Leng and the cold waste north of Inquanok must be close to the Other Gods, and there the passes to Kadath are well guarded.

The slant-eyed man was small, but the great hippocephalic bird was there to see he was obeyed; so Carter followed where he led, and passed within the circle of standing rocks and into the low arched doorway of that windowless stone monastery. There were no lights inside, but the evil merchant lit a small clay lamp bearing morbid bas-reliefs and prodded his prisoner on through mazes of narrow winding corridors. On the walls of the corridors were printed frightful scenes older than history, and in a style unknown to the archaeologists of earth. After countless eons their pigments were brilliant still, for the cold and dryness of hideous Leng keep alive many primal things. Carter saw them fleetingly in the rays of that dim and moving lamp, and shuddered at the tale they told.

Through those archaic frescoes Leng's annals stalked, and the horned, hoofed, and wide-mouthed almost-humans danced evilly amid forgotten cities. There were scenes of old wars, wherein Leng's almost-humans fought with the bloated purple spiders of the neighboring vales; and there were scenes also of the coming of the black galleys from the moon, and of the submission of Leng's people to the polypous and amorphous blasphemies that hopped and floundered and wriggled out of them. Those slippery grayish-white blasphemies they worshiped as gods, nor ever complained when scores of their best and fatted males were taken away in the black galleys. The monstrous moon-beasts made their camp on a jagged isle in the sea, and Carter could tell from the frescoes that this was none other than the lone nameless rock he had seen when sailing to Inquanok—that gray accursed rock which Inquanok's seamen shun, and from which vile howlings reverberate all through the night.

And in those frescoes was shown the great seaport and capital of the almost-humans, proud and pillared between the cliffs and the basalt wharves, and wondrous with high fanes and carved palaces. Great gardens and columned streets led from the cliffs and from each of the six sphinx-crowned gates to a vast central plaza, and in that plaza was a pair of colossal winged lions guarding the top of a subterrane staircase. Again and again were those huge winged lions shown, their mighty flanks of diorite glistening in the gray twilight of the day and the cloudy phosphorescence of the night. And as Carter stumbled past their frequent and repeated pictures, it came to him at last what indeed they were, and what city it was that the almost-humans had ruled so anciently before the coming of the black galleys. There could be no mistake, for the legends of dreamland are generous and profuse. Indubitably, that primal city was no less a place than storied Sarkomand, whose ruins had bleached for a million years before the first true human saw the light, and whose twin titan lions guard eternally the steps that lead down from dreamland to the Great Abyss.

Other views showed the gaunt gray peaks dividing Leng from Inquanok, and the monstrous Shantak-birds that build nests on the ledges halfway up. And they showed likewise the curious caves near the very topmost pinnacles, and how even the boldest of the Shantaks fly screaming away from them. Carter had seen those caves when he passed over them, and had noticed their likeness to the caves on Ngranek. Now he knew that the likeness was more than a chance one, for in these pictures were shown their fearsome denizens, and those bat wings, curving horns, barbed tails, prehensile paws, and rubbery bodies were not strange to him. He had met those silent, flitting, and clutching creatures before: those mindless guardians of the Great Abyss whom even the Great Ones fear, and who own not Nyarlathotep but hoary Nodens as their lord. For they were the dreaded night-gaunts, who never laugh or smile because they have no faces, and who flop unendingly in the dark between the Vale of Pnath and the passes to the outer world.

The slant-eyed merchant had now prodded Carter into a great domed space whose walls were carved in shocking bas-reliefs, and whose center held a gaping circular pit surrounded by six malignly stained stone altars in a ring. There was no light in this vast evil-smelling crypt, and the small lamp of the sinister merchant shone so feebly that one could grasp details only little by little. At the farther end was a high stone daïs reached by five steps; and there on a golden throne sat a lumpish figure robed in yellow silk figured with red and having a yellow silken mask over its face. To this being the slant-eyed man made certain signs with his hands, and the lurker in the dark replied by raising a disgustingly carved flute of ivory in silk-covered paws and blowing certain loathsome sounds from beneath its flowing yellow mask. This colloquy went on for some time, and to Carter there was something sickeningly familiar in the sound of that flute and the stench of the malodorous place. It made him think of a frightful red-lit city and of the revolting procession that once filed through it; of that, and of an awful climb through lunar countryside beyond, before the rescuing rush of earth's friendly cats. He knew that the creature on the dais was without doubt the high priest not to be described, of which legend whispers such fiendish and abnormal possibilities, but he feared to think just what that abhorred high priest might be.

Then the figured silk slipped a trifle from one of the grayish-white paws, and Carter knew what the noisome high priest was. And in that hideous second, stark fear drove him to something his reason would never have dared to attempt, for in all his shaken consciousness there was room only for one frantic will to escape from what squatted on that golden throne. He knew that hopeless labyrinths of stone lay between him and the cold tableland outside, and that even on that tableland the noxious Shantaks still waited; yet in spite of all this, there was in his mind only the instant need to get away from that wriggling, silk-robed monstrosity.

The slant-eyed man had set the curious lamp upon one of the high and wickedly stained altar stones by the pit, and had moved forward somewhat to talk to the high priest with his hands. Carter, hitherto wholly passive, now gave that man a terrific push with all the wild strength of fear, so that the victim toppled at once into that gaping well which rumor holds to reach down to the hellish Vaults of Zin, where Gugs hunt ghasts in the dark. In almost the same second, he seized the lamp from the altar and darted out into the frescoed labyrinths, racing this way and that as chance determined and trying not to think of the stealthy padding of shapeless paws on the stones behind him, or of the silent wrigglings and crawlings which must be going on back there in lightless corridors.

After a few moments he regretted his thoughtless haste, and wished he had tried to follow backward the frescoes he had passed on the way in. True, they were so confused and duplicated that they could not have done him much good, but he wished nonetheless that he had made the attempt. Those he now saw were even more horrible than those he had seen then, and he knew he was not in the corridors leading outside. In time he became quite sure he was not being followed, and slackened his pace somewhat; but scarce had he breathed in half relief when a new peril beset him. His lamp was waning, and he would soon be in pitch blackness with no means of sight or guidance.

When the light was all gone, he groped slowly in the dark, and prayed to the Great Ones for such help as they might afford. At times he felt the stone floor sloping up or down, and once he stumbled over a step for which no reason seemed to exist. The farther he went the damper it seemed to be, and when he was able to feel a junction or the mouth of a side passage, he always chose the way that sloped downward less. He believed, though, that his general course was down, and the vaultlike smell and incrustations on the greasy walls and floor alike warned him he was burrowing deep in Leng's unwholesome tableland. But there was not any warning of the thing which came at last: only the thing itself, with its terror and shock and breathtaking chaos. One moment he was groping slowly over the slippery floor of an almost-level place, and the next he was shooting dizzily downward in the dark through a burrow which must have been well-nigh vertical.

Of the length of that hideous sliding he could never be sure, but it seemed to take hours of delirious nausea and ecstatic frenzy. Then he realized he was still, with the phosphorescent clouds of a northern night shining sickly above him. All around were crumbling walls and broken columns, and the pavement on which he lay was pierced by straggling grass and wrenched asunder by frequent shrubs and roots. Behind him a basalt cliff rose topless and perpendicular, its dark side sculptured into repellent scenes, and pierced by an arched and carved entrance to the inner blacknesses out of which he had come. Ahead stretched double rows of pillars, and the fragments and pedestals of pillars, which spoke of a broad and bygone street, and from the urns and basins along the way he knew it had been a great street of gardens. Far off at its end the pillars spread to mark a vast round plaza, and in that open circle there loomed gigantic under the lurid night clouds a pair of monstrous things. Huge winged lions of diorite they were, with blackness and shadow between them. Full twenty feet they reared their grotesque and unbroken heads, and snarled derisive on the ruins around them. And Carter knew right well what they must be, for legend tells of only one such twain. They were the changeless guardians of the Great Abyss, and these dark ruins were in truth primordial Sarkomand.

Carter's first act was to close and barricade the archway in the cliff with fallen blocks and odd debris that lay around. He wished no follower from Leng's hateful monastery, for along the way ahead would lurk enough of other dangers. Of how to get from Sarkomand to the peopled parts of dreamland he knew nothing at all; nor could he gain much by descending to the grottoes of the ghouls, since he knew they were no better informed than he. The three ghouls which had helped him through the city of Gugs to the outer world had not known how to reach Sarkomand in their journey back, but had planned to ask old traders in Dylath-Leen. He did not like to think of going again to the subterrane world of Gugs and risking once more that hellish tower of Koth with its cyclopean steps leading to the enchanted wood, yet he felt he might have to try this course if all else failed. Over Leng's plateau past the lone monastery he dared not go unaided, for the high priest's emissaries must be many, while at the journey's end there would no doubt be the Shantaks and perhaps other things to deal with. If he could get a boat he might sail back to Inquanok past the jagged and hideous rock in the sea, for the primal frescoes in the monastery labyrinth had shown that this frightful place lies not far from Sarkomand's basalt quays. But to find a boat in this eon-deserted city was no probable thing, and it did not appear likely that he could ever make one.

Such were the thoughts of Randolph Carter when a new impression began beating upon his mind. All this while there had stretched before him the great corpselike width of fabled Sarkomand, with its black broken pillars and crumbling sphinx-crowned gates and titan stones and monstrous winged lions against the sickly glow of those luminous night clouds. Now he saw far ahead and on the right a glow that no clouds could account for, and knew that he was not alone in the silence of that dead city. The glow rose and fell fitfully, flickering with a greenish tinge which did not reassure the watcher. And when he crept closer, down the littered street and through some narrow gaps between tumbled walls, he perceived that it was a campfire near the wharves, with many vague forms clustered darkly around it and a lethal odor hanging heavily over all. Beyond was the oily lapping of the harbor water with a great ship riding at anchor, and Carter paused in stark terror when he saw that the ship was indeed one of the dreaded black galleys from the moon.

Then, just as he was about to creep back from that detestable flame, he saw a stirring among the vague dark forms and heard a peculiar and unmistakable sound. It was the frightened meeping of a ghoul, and in a moment it had swelled to a veritable chorus of anguish. Secure as he was in the shadow of monstrous ruins, Carter allowed his curiosity to conquer his fear, and crept forward again instead of retreating. Once, in crossing an open street, he wriggled wormlike on his stomach, and in another place he had to rise to his feet to avoid making a noise among heaps of fallen marble. But always he succeeded in avoiding discovery, so that in a short time he had found a spot behind a titan pillar where he could watch the whole green-lit scene of action. There, around a hideous fire fed by the obnoxious stems of lunar fungi, there squatted a stinking circle of the toadlike moon-beasts and their almost-human slaves. Some of these slaves were heating curious iron spears in the leaping flames, and at intervals applying their white-hot points to three tightly trussed prisoners that lay writhing before the leaders of the party. From the motions of their tentacles, Carter could see that the blunt-snouted moon-beasts were enjoying the spectacle hugely, and vast was his horror when he suddenly recognized the frantic meeping and knew that the tortured ghouls were none other than the faithful trio which had guided him safely from the abyss, and had thereafter set out from the enchanted wood to find Sarkomand and the gate to their native deeps.

The number of malodorous moon-beasts about that greenish fire was very great, and Carter saw that he could do nothing now to save his former allies. How the ghouls had been captured he could not guess, but he fancied that the gray toadlike blasphemies had heard them inquire in Dylath-Leen concerning the way to Sarkomand and had not wished them to approach so closely the hateful plateau of Leng and the high priest not to be described. For a moment he pondered on what he ought to do, and recalled how near he was to the gate of the ghouls' black kingdom. Clearly it was wisest to creep east to the plaza of twin lions and descend at once to the gulf, where assuredly he would meet no horrors worse than those above, and where he might soon find ghouls eager to rescue their brethren and perhaps to wipe out the moon-beasts from the black galley. It occurred to him that the portal, like other gates to the abyss, might be guarded by flocks of night-gaunts; but he did not fear these faceless creatures now. He had learned that they are bound by solemn treaties with the ghouls, and the ghoul that had been Pickman had taught him how to glibber a password they understood.

So Carter began another silent crawl through the ruins, edging slowly toward the great central plaza and the winged lions. It was ticklish work, but the moon-beasts were pleasantly busy and did not hear the slight noises which he twice made by accident among the scattered stones. At last he reached the open space and picked his way among the stunted trees and vines that had grown up therein. The gigantic lions loomed terrible above him in the sickly glow of the phosphorescent night clouds, but he manfully persisted toward them and presently crept round to their faces, knowing it was on that side that he would find the mighty darkness which they guard. Ten feet apart crouched the mocking-faced beasts of diorite, brooding on cyclopean pedestals whose sides were chiseled in fearsome bas-reliefs. Between them was a tiled court with a central space which had once been railed with balustrades of onyx. Midway in this space a black well opened, and Carter soon saw that he had indeed reached the yawning gulf whose crusted and moldy stone steps lead down to the crypts of nightmare.

Terrible is the memory of that dark descent in which hours wore themselves away while Carter wound sightlessly round and round down a fathomless spiral of steep and slippery stairs. So worn and narrow were the steps, and so greasy with the ooze of inner earth, that the climber never knew quite when to expect a breathless fall and hurtling down to the ultimate pits; and he was likewise uncertain just when or how the guardian night-gaunts would suddenly pounce upon him, if indeed there were any stationed in this primeval passage. All about him was a stifling odor of nether gulfs, and he felt that the air of these choking depths was not made for mankind. In time he became very numb and somnolent, moving more from automatic impulse than from reasoned will; nor did he realize any change when he stopped moving altogether as something quietly seized him from behind. He was flying very rapidly through the air before a malevolent tickling told him that the rubbery night-gaunts had performed their duty.

Awakened to the fact that he was in the cold, damp clutch of the faceless flutterers, Carter remembered the password of the ghouls and glibbered it as loudly as he could amid the wind and chaos of flight. Mindless though night-gaunts are said to be, the effect was instantaneous; for all tickling stopped at once, and the creatures hastened to shift their captive to a more comfortable position. Thus encouraged, Carter ventured some explanation, telling of the seizure and torture of three ghouls by the moon-beasts, and of the need of assembling a party to rescue them. The night-gaunts, though inarticulate, seemed to understand what was said, and showed greater haste and purpose in their flight. Suddenly the dense blackness gave place to the gray twilight of inner earth, and there opened up ahead one of those flat, sterile plains on which ghouls love to squat and gnaw. Scattered tombstones and osseous fragments told of the denizens of that place; and as Carter gave a loud meep of urgent summons, a score of burrows emptied forth their leathery, doglike tenants. The night-gaunts now flew low and set their passenger upon his feet, afterward withdrawing a little and forming a hunched semicircle on the ground while the ghouls greeted the newcomer.

Carter glibbered his message rapidly and explicitly to the grotesque company, and four of them at once departed through different burrows to spread the news to others and gather such troops as might be available for a rescue. After a long wait, a ghoul of some importance appeared and made significant signs to the night-gaunts, causing two of the latter to fly off into the dark. Thereafter there were constant accessions to the hunched flock of night-gaunts on the plain, till at length the slimy soil was fairly black with them. Meanwhile, fresh ghouls crawled out of the burrows one by one, all glibbering excitedly and forming in crude battle array not far from the huddled night-gaunts. In time there appeared that proud and influential ghoul which had once been the artist Richard Pickman of Boston, and to him Carter glibbered a very full account of what had occurred. The erstwhile Pickman, pleased to greet his ancient friend again, seemed very much impressed, and held a conference with other chiefs a little apart from the growing throng.

Finally, after scanning the ranks with care, the assembled chiefs all meeped in unison and began glibbering orders to the crowds of ghouls and night-gaunts. A large detachment of the horned fliers vanished at once, while the rest grouped themselves two by two on their knees with extended forelegs, awaiting the approach of the ghouls one by one. As each ghoul reached the pair of night-gaunts to which he was assigned, he was taken up and borne away into the blackness, till at last the whole throng had vanished save for Carter, Pickman, and the other chiefs and a few pairs of night-gaunts. Pickman explained that night-gaunts are the advance guard and battle steeds of the ghouls, and that the army was issuing forth to Sarkomand to deal with the moon-beasts. Then Carter and the ghoulish chiefs approached the waiting bearers and were taken up by the damp, slippery paws. Another moment and all were whirling in wind and darkness, endlessly up, up, up to the gate of the winged lions and the spectral ruins of primal Sarkomand.

When, after a great interval, Carter saw again the sickly light of Sarkomand's nocturnal sky, it was to behold the great central plaza swarming with militant ghouls and night-gaunts. Day, he felt sure, must be almost due; but so strong was the army that no surprise of the enemy would be needed. The greenish flare near the wharves still glimmered faintly, though the absence of ghoulish meeping showed that the torture of the prisoners was over for the nonce. Softly glibbering directions to their steeds and to the flock of riderless night-gaunts ahead, the ghouls presently rose in wide whirring columns and swept on over the bleak ruins toward the evil flame. Carter was now beside Pickman in the front rank of ghouls, and saw as they approached the noisome camp that the moon-beasts were totally unprepared. The three prisoners lay bound and inert beside the fire, while their toadlike captors slumped drowsily about in no certain order. The almost-human slaves were asleep, even the sentinels shirking a duty which in this realm must have seemed to them merely perfunctory.

The final swoop of the night-gaunts and mounted ghouls

was very sudden, each of the grayish toadlike blasphemies and their almost-human slaves being seized by a group of night-gaunts before a sound was made. The moon-beasts, of course, were voiceless, and even the slaves had little chance to scream before rubbery paws choked them into silence. Horrible were the writhings of those great jellyish abnormalities as the sardonic night-gaunts clutched them, but nothing availed against the strength of those black prehensile talons. When a moon-beast writhed too violently, a night-gaunt would seize and pull its quivering pink tentacles, and this seemed to hurt so much that the victim would cease its struggles. Carter expected to see much slaughter, but found that the ghouls were far subtler in their plans. They glibbered certain simple orders to the night-gaunts which held the captives, trusting the rest to instinct; and soon the hapless creatures were borne silently away into the Great Abyss, to be distributed impartially among the Dholes, Gugs, ghasts and other dwellers in darkness whose modes of nourishment are not painless to their chosen victims. Meanwhile, the three bound ghouls had been released and consoled by their conquering kinsfolk, while various parties searched the neighborhood for possible remaining moon-beasts, and boarded the evil-smelling black galley at the wharf to make sure that nothing had escaped the general defeat. Sure enough, the capture had been thorough, for not a sign of further life could the victors detect. Carter, anxious to preserve a means of access to the rest of dreamland, urged them not to sink the anchored galley; and this request was freely granted out of gratitude for his act in reporting the plight of the captured trio. On the ship were found some very curious objects and decorations, some of which Carter cast at once into the sea.

Ghouls and night-gaunts now formed themselves into separate groups, the former questioning their rescued fellows anent past happenings. It appeared that the three had followed Carter's directions and proceeded from the enchanted wood to Dylath-Leen by way of Nir and the Skai, stealing human clothes at a lonely farmhouse and loping as closely as possible in the fashion of a man's walk. In Dylath-Leen's taverns their grotesque ways and faces had aroused much comment, but they had persisted in asking the way to Sarkomand until at last an old traveler was able to tell them. Then they knew that only a ship for Lelag-Leng would serve their purpose, and prepared to wait patiently for such a vessel.

But evil spies had doubtless reported much, for shortly a black galley put into port, and the wide-mouthed ruby merchants invited the ghouls to drink with them in a tavern. Wine was produced from one of those sinister bottles grotesquely carved from a single ruby, and after that the ghouls found themselves prisoners on the black galley as Carter had found himself. This time, however, the unseen rowers steered not for the moon but for antique Sarkomand, bent evidently on taking their captives before the high priest not to be described. They had touched at the jagged rock in the northern sea which Inquanok's mariners shun, and the ghouls had there seen for the first time the red masters of the ship, being sickened despite their own callousness by such extremes of malign shapelessness and fearsome odor. There too were witnessed the nameless pastimes of the toadlike resident garrison—such pastimes as give rise to the night-howlings which men fear. After that had come the landing at ruined Sarkomand and the beginning of the tortures, whose continuance the present rescue had prevented.

Future plans were next discussed, the three rescued ghouls suggesting a raid on the jagged rock and the extermination of the toadlike garrison there. To this, however, the night-gaunts objected, since the prospect of flying over water did not please them. Most of the ghouls favored the design, but were at a loss as to how to follow it without the help of the winged night-gaunts. Thereupon Carter, seeing that they could not navigate the anchored galley, offered to teach them the use of the great banks of oars, to which proposal they eagerly assented. Gray day had now come, and under that leaden northern sky, a picked detachment of ghouls filed into the noisome ship and took their seats on the rowers' benches. Carter found them fairly apt at learning, and before night had risked several experimental trips around the harbor. Not till three days later, however, did he deem it safe to attempt the voyage of conquest. Then, the rowers trained and the night-gaunts safely stowed in the forecastle, the party set sail at last, Pickman and the other chiefs gathering on deck and discussing modes of approach and procedure.

On the very first night the howlings from the rock were heard. Such was their timbre that all the galley's crew shook visibly, but most of all trembled the three rescued ghouls, who knew precisely what those howlings meant. It was not thought best to attempt an attack by night, so the ship lay to under the phosphorescent clouds to wait for the dawn of a grayish day. When the light was ample and the howlings still, the rowers resumed their strokes, and the galley drew closer and closer to that jagged rock whose granite pinnacles clawed fantastically at the dull sky. The sides of the rock were very steep, but on ledges here and there could be seen the bulging walls of queer windowless dwellings and the low railings guarding traveled high roads. No ship of men had ever come so near the place—or at least, had ever come so near and departed again; but Carter and the ghouls were void of fear and kept inflexibly on, rounding the eastern face of the rock and seeking the wharves which the rescued trio described as being on the southern side within a harbor formed of steep headlands.

The headlands were prolongations of the island proper, and came so close together that only one ship at a time might pass between them. There seemed to be no watchers on the outside, so the galley was steered boldly through the flumelike strait and into the stagnant, putrid harbor beyond. Here, however, all was bustle and activity, with several ships lying at anchor along a forbidding stone quay, and scores of almost-human slaves and moon-beasts by the waterfront handling crates and boxes or driving nameless and fabulous horrors hitched to lumbering lorries. There was a small stone town hewn out of the vertical cliff above the wharves, with the start of a winding road that spiraled out of sight toward higher ledges of the rock. Of what lay inside that prodigious peak of granite none might say, but the things one saw on the outside were far from encouraging.

At sight of the incoming galley the crowds on the wharves displayed much eagerness, those with eyes staring intently, and those without eyes wriggling their pink tentacles expectantly. They did not, of course, realize that the black ship had changed hands, for ghouls look much like the horned and hoofed almost-humans, and the night-gaunts were all out of sight below. By this time the leaders had fully formed a plan, which was to loose the night-gaunts as soon as the wharf was touched, and then to sail directly away, leaving matters wholly to the instincts of those almost-mindless creatures. Marooned on the rock, the horned fliers would first of all seize whatever living things they found there, and afterward, quite helpless to think except in terms of the homing instinct, would forget their fear of water and fly swiftly back to the abyss, bearing their noisome prey to appropriate destinations in the dark, from which not many would emerge alive.

The ghoul that had been Pickman now went below and gave the night-gaunts their simple instructions, while the ship drew very near to the ominous and malodorous wharves. Presently a fresh stir rose along the waterfront, and Carter saw that the motions of the galley had begun to excite suspicion. Evidently the steersman was not making for the right dock, and probably the watchers had noticed the difference between the hideous ghouls and the almost-human slaves whose places they were taking. Some silent alarm must have been given, for almost at once a horde of the mephitic moon-beasts began to pour from the little black doorways of the windowless houses and down the winding road at the right. A rain of curious javelins struck the galley as the prow hit the wharf, felling two ghouls and slightly wounding another; but at this point all the hatches were thrown open to emit a black cloud of whirring night-gaunts, which swarmed over the town like a flock of horned and cyclopean bats.

The jellyish moon-beasts had procured a great pole and were trying to push off the invading ship, but when the night-gaunts struck them they thought of such things no more. It was a very terrible spectacle to see those faceless and rubbery ticklers at their pastime, and tremendously impressive to watch the dense cloud of them spreading through the town and up the winding roadway to the reaches above. Sometimes a group of the black flutterers would drop a toadlike prisoner from aloft by mistake, and the manner in which the victim would burst was highly offensive to the sight and smell. When the last of the night-gaunts had left the galley, the ghoulish leaders glibbered an order of withdrawal, and the rowers pulled quietly out of the harbor between the gray headlands while the town was still a chaos of battle and conquest.

The Pickman ghoul allowed several hours for the night-gaunts to make up their rudimentary minds and overcome their fear of flying over the sea, and kept the galley standing about a mile off the jagged rock while he waited, and dressed the wounds of the injured men. Night fell, and the gray twilight gave place to the sickly phosphorescence of low clouds, and all the while the leaders watched the high peaks of that accursed rock for signs of the night-gaunts' flight. Toward morning a black speck was seen hovering timidly over the topmost pinnacle, and shortly afterward the speck had become a swarm. Just before daybreak the swarm seemed to scatter, and within a quarter of an hour it had vanished wholly in the distance toward the northeast. Once or twice something seemed to fall from the thinning swarm into the sea; but Carter did not worry, since he knew from observation that the toadlike moon-beasts cannot swim. At length, when the ghouls were satisfied that all the night-gaunts had left for Sarkomand and the Great Abyss with their doomed burdens, the galley put back into the harbor between the gray headlands; and all the hideous company landed and roamed curiously over the denuded rock with its towers and aeries and fortresses chiseled from the solid stone.

Frightful were the secrets uncovered in those evil and windowless crypts; for the remnants of unfinished pastimes were many, and in various stages of departure from their primal state. Carter put out of the way certain things which were after a fashion alive, and fled precipitately from a few other things about which he could not be very positive. The stench-filled houses were furnished mostly with grotesque stools and benches carved from moon-trees, and were painted inside with nameless and frantic designs. Countless weapons, implements, and ornaments lay about, including some large idols of solid ruby depicting singular beings not found on the earth. These latter did not, despite their material, invite either appropriation or long inspection, and Carter took the trouble to hammer five of them into very small pieces. The scattered spears and javelins he collected, and with Pickman's approval distributed them among the ghouls. Such devices were new to the doglike lopers, but their relative simplicity made them easy to master after a few concise hints.

The upper parts of the rock held more temples than private homes, and in numerous hewn chambers were found terrible carved altars and doubtfully stained fonts and shrines for the worship of things more monstrous than the wild gods atop Kadath. From the rear of one great temple stretched a low black passage, which Carter followed far into the rock with a torch till he came to a lightless domed hall of vast proportions, whose vaultings were covered with demoniac carvings and in whose center yawned a foul and bottomless well like that in the hideous monastery of Leng where broods alone the high priest not to be described. On the distant shadowy side, beyond the noisome well, he thought he discerned a small door of strangely wrought bronze; but for some reason he felt an unaccountable dread of opening it or even approaching it, and he hastened back through the cavern to his unlovely allies as they shambled about with an ease and abandon he could scarcely feel. The ghouls had observed the unfinished pastimes of the moon-beasts, and had profited in their fashion. They had also found a hogshead of potent moon-wine, and were rolling it down to the wharves for removal and later use in diplomatic dealings, though the rescued trio, remembering its effect on them in Dylath-Leen, had warned their company to taste none of it. Of rubies from lunar mines there was a great store, both rough and polished, in one of the vaults near the water; but when the ghouls found they were not good to eat, they lost all interest in them. Carter did not try to carry any away, since he knew too much about those which had mined them.

Suddenly there came an excited meeping from the sentries on the wharves, and all the loathsome foragers turned from their tasks to stare seaward and cluster around the waterfront. Between the gray headlands a fresh black galley was rapidly advancing, and it would be but a moment before the almost-humans on deck would perceive the invasion of the town and give the alarm to the monstrous things below. Fortunately, the ghouls still bore the spears and javelins which Carter had distributed among them; and at his command, sustained by the being that had been Pickman, they now formed a line of battle and prepared to prevent the landing of the ship. Presently a burst of excitement on the galley told of the crew's discovery of the changed state of things, and the instant stoppage of the vessel proved that the superior numbers of the ghouls had been noted and taken into account. After a moment of hesitation, the newcomers silently turned and passed out between the headlands again, but not for an instant did the ghouls imagine that the conflict had been averted. Either the dark ship would seek reinforcements or the crew would try to land elsewhere on the island; hence a party of scouts was at once sent up toward the pinnacle to see what the enemy's course would be.

In a very few minutes, the ghoul returned breathless to say that the moon-beasts and almost-humans were landing on the outside of the more easterly of the rugged gray headlands, and ascending by hidden paths and ledges which a goat could scarcely tread in safety. Almost immediately afterward the galley was sighted again through the flumelike strait, but only for a second. Then, a few moments later, a second messenger panted down from aloft to say that another party was landing on the other headland, both being much more numerous than the size of the galley would seem to allow for. The ship itself, moving slowly with only one sparsely manned tier of oars, soon hove into sight between the cliffs, and lay to in the fetid harbor as if to watch the coming fray and stand by for any possible use.

By this time Carter and Pickman had divided the ghouls into three parties, one to meet each of the two invading columns and one to remain in the town. The first two at once scrambled up the rocks in their respective directions, while the third was subdivided into a land party and a sea party. The sea party, commanded by Carter, boarded the anchored galley and rowed out to meet the undermanned galley of the newcomers; whereat the latter retreated through the strait to the open sea. Carter did not at once pursue it, for he knew he might be needed more acutely near the town.

Meanwhile, the frightful detachments of the moon-beasts and almost-humans had lumbered up to the top of the headlands and were shockingly silhouetted on either side against the gray twilight sky. The thin, hellish flutes of the invaders had begun to whine, and the general effect of those hybrid, half-amorphous processions was as nauseating as the actual odor given off by the toadlike lunar blasphemies. Then the two parties of the ghouls swarmed into sight and joined the silhouetted panorama. Javelins began to fly from both sides, and the swelling meeps of the ghouls and the bestial howls of the almost-humans gradually joined the hellish whine of the flutes to form a frantic and indescribable chaos of demon cacophony. Now and then bodies fell from the narrow ridges of the headlands into the sea outside or the harbor inside, in the latter case being sucked quickly under by certain submarine lurkers whose presence was indicated only by prodigious bubbles.

For half an hour this dual battle raged in the sky, till upon the west cliff the invaders were completely annihilated. On the east cliff, however, where the leader of the moon-beast party appeared to be present, the ghouls had not fared so well, and were slowly retreating to the slopes of the pinnacle proper. Pickman had quickly ordered reinforcements for this front from the party in the town, and these had helped greatly in the earlier stages of the combat. Then, when the western battle was over, the victorious survivors hastened across to the aid of their hard-pressed fellows, turning the tide and forcing the invaders back again along the narrow ridge of the headland. The almost-humans were by this time all slain, but the last of the toadlike horrors fought desperately with the great spears clutched in their powerful and disgusting paws. The time for javelins was now nearly past, and the fight became a hand-to-hand contest between what few spearmen could meet upon that narrow ridge.

As fury and recklessness increased, the number falling into the sea became very great. Those striking the harbor met nameless extinction from the unseen bubblers, but of those striking the open sea some were able to swim to the foot of the cliffs and land on tidal rocks, while the hovering galley of the enemy rescued several moon-beasts. The cliffs were unscalable except where the monsters had debarked, so that none of the ghouls on the rocks could rejoin their battle line.

Some were killed by javelins from the hostile galley or from the moon-beasts above, but a few survived to be rescued. When the security of the land parties seemed assured, Carter's galley sailed forth between the headlands and drove the hostile ship far out to sea, pausing to rescue such ghouls as were on the rocks or still swimming in the ocean. Several moon-beasts washed onto rocks or reefs were speedily put out of the way.

Finally, the moon-beast galley being safely in the distance and the invading land army concentrated in one place, Carter landed a considerable force on the eastern headland in the enemy's rear, after which the fight was short-lived indeed. Attacked from both sides, the noisome flounderers were rapidly cut to pieces or pushed into the sea, till by evening the ghoulish chiefs agreed that the island was again clear of them. The hostile galley, meanwhile, had disappeared, and it was decided that the evil jagged rock had better be evacuated before any overwhelming horde of lunar horrors might be assembled and brought against the victors.

So by night Pickman and Carter assembled all the ghouls and counted them with care, finding that over a fourth had been lost in the day's battles. The wounded were placed on bunks in the galley, for Pickman always discouraged the old ghoulish custom of killing and eating one's own wounded, and the able-bodied troops were assigned to the oars or to such other places as they might most usefully fill. Under the low phosphorescent clouds of night the galley sailed, and Carter was not sorry to be departing from the island of unwholesome secrets, whose lightless domed hall with its bottomless well and repellent bronze door lingered restlessly in his fancy. Dawn found the ship in sight of Sarkomand's ruined quays of basalt, where a few night-gaunt sentries still waited, squatting like black, horned gargoyles on the broken columns and crumbling sphinxes of that fearful city which lived and died before the years of man.

The ghouls made camp among the fallen stones of Sarkomand, dispatching a messenger for enough night-gaunts to serve them as steeds. Pickman and the other chiefs were effusive in their gratitude for the aid Carter had lent them. Carter now began to feel that his plans were indeed maturing well, and that he would be able to command the help of these fearsome allies not only in quitting this part of dreamland, but in pursuing his ultimate quest for the gods atop unknown Kadath and the marvelous sunset city they so strangely withheld from his slumbers. Accordingly, he spoke of these things to the ghoulish leaders, telling what he knew of the cold waste wherein Kadath stands and of the monstrous Shantaks and the mountains carved into double-headed images which guard it. He spoke of the fear of Shantaks for night-gaunts, and of how the vast hippocephalic birds fly screaming from the black burrows high up on the gaunt gray peaks that divide Inquanok from hateful Leng. He spoke, too, of the things he had learned concerning night-gaunts from the frescoes in the windowless monastery of the high priest not to be described; how even the Great Ones fear them, and how their ruler is not the crawling chaos Nyarlathotep at all, but hoary and immemorial Nodens, Lord of the Great Abyss.

All these things Carter glibbered to the assembled ghouls, and he presently outlined that request which he had in mind and which he did not think extravagant considering the services he had so lately rendered the rubbery, doglike lopers. He wished very much, he said, for the services of enough night-gaunts to bear him safely through the air past the realm of Shantaks and carved mountains, and up into the cold waste beyond the returning tracks of any other mortal. He desired to fly to the onyx castle atop unknown Kadath in the cold waste to plead with the Great Ones for the sunset city they denied him, and felt sure that the night-gaunts could take him thither without trouble, high above the perils of the plain and over the hideous double heads of those carved sentinel mountains that squat eternally in the gray dusk. For the horned and faceless creatures there could be no danger from aught of earth, since the Great Ones themselves dread them. And even were unexpected things to come from the Other Gods, who are prone to oversee the affairs of earth's milder gods, the night-gaunts need not fear; for the outer hells are indifferent matters to such silent and slippery fliers as own not Nyarlathotep for their master, but bow only to potent and archaic Nodens.

A flock of ten or fifteen night-gaunts, Carter glibbered,

would surely be enough to keep any combination of Shantaks at a distance, though perhaps it might be well to have some ghouls in the party to manage the creatures, their ways being better known to their ghoulish allies than to men. The party could land him at some convenient point within whatever walls that fabulous onyx citadel might have, waiting in the shadows for his return or his signal while he ventured inside the castle to give prayer to the gods of earth. If any ghouls chose to escort him into the throne room of the Great Ones, he would be thankful, for their presence would add weight and importance to his plea. He would not, however, insist upon this, but merely wished transportation to and from the castle atop unknown Kadath, the final journey being either to the marvelous sunset city itself, in case the gods proved favorable, or back to the earthward Gate of Deeper Slumber in the Enchanted Wood in case his prayers were fruitless.

While Carter was speaking, all the ghouls listened with great attention, and as the moments advanced, the sky became black with clouds of those night-gaunts for which messengers had been sent. The winged horrors settled in a semicircle around the ghoulish army, waiting respectfully as the doglike chieftains considered the wish of the earthly traveler. The ghoul that had been Pickman glibbered gravely with his fellows, and in the end Carter was offered far more than he had at most expected. As he had aided the ghouls in their conquest of the moon-beasts, so would they aid him in his daring voyage to realms whence none had ever returned, lending him not merely a few of their allied night-gaunts but their entire army as then encamped, veteran fighting ghouls and newly assembled night-gaunts alike, save only a small garrison for the captured black galley and such spoils as had come from the jagged rock in the sea. They would set out through the air whenever he might wish, and once they had arrived on Kadath, a suitable train of ghouls would attend him in state as he placed his petition before earth's gods in their onyx castle.

Moved by a gratitude and satisfaction beyond words, Carter made plans with the ghoulish leaders for his audacious voyage. The army would fly high, they decided, over hideous Leng with its nameless monastery and wicked stone villages, stopping only at the vast gray peaks to confer with the Shantak-frightening night-gaunts whose burrows honeycombed their summits. They would then, according to what advice they might receive from those denizens, choose their final course—approaching unknown Kadath either through the desert of carved mountains north of Inquanok or through the more northerly reaches of repulsive Leng itself. Doglike and soulless as they are, the ghouls and night-gaunts had no dread of what those untrodden deserts might reveal; nor did they feel any deterring awe at the thought of Kadath, towering lone with its onyx castle of mystery.

About midday the ghouls and night-gaunts prepared for flight, each ghoul selecting a suitable pair of horned steeds to bear him. Carter was placed well up toward the head of the column beside Pickman, and in front of the whole a double line of riderless night-gaunts was provided as a vanguard. At a brisk meep from Pickman, the whole shocking army rose in a nightmare cloud above the broken columns and crumbling sphinxes of primordial Sarkomand: higher and higher, till even the great basalt cliff behind the town was cleared and the cold, sterile tableland of Leng's outskirts laid open to sight. Still higher flew the black host, till even this tableland grew small beneath them; and as they worked northward over the windswept plateau of horror, Carter saw once again with a shudder the circle of crude monoliths and the squat windowless building which he knew held that frightful silken-masked blasphemy from whose clutches he had so narrowly escaped. This time no descent was made as the army swept batlike over the sterile landscape, passing the feeble fires of the unwholesome stone villages at a great altitude and pausing not at all to mark the morbid twistings of the hoofed, horned almost-humans that dance and pipe eternally therein. Once they saw a Shantak-bird flying low over the plain, but when it saw them it screamed noxiously and flapped off to the north in grotesque panic.

At dusk they reached the jagged gray peaks that form the barrier of Inquanok, and hovered about those strange caves near the summits which Carter recalled as so frightful to the Shantaks. At the insistent meeping of the ghoulish leaders, there issued forth from each lofty burrow a stream of horned black fliers, with which the ghouls and night-gaunts of the party conferred at length by means of ugly gestures. It soon became clear that the best course would be that over the cold waste north of Inquanok, for Leng's northward reaches are full of unseen pitfalls that even the night-gaunts dislike: abysmal influences centering in certain white hemispherical buildings on curious knolls, which common folklore associates unpleasantly with the Other Gods and their crawling chaos Nyarlathotep.

Of Kadath the flutterers of the peaks knew almost nothing, save that there must be some mighty marvel toward the north, over which the Shantaks and the carved mountains stand guard. They hinted at rumored abnormalities of proportion in those trackless leagues beyond, and recalled vague whispers of a realm where night broods eternally; but of definite data they had nothing to give. So Carter and his party thanked them kindly and, crossing the topmost granite pinnacles to the skies of Inquanok, dropped below the level of the phosphorescent night clouds and beheld in the distance those terrible squatting gargoyles which had been mountains till some titan hand carved fright into their virgin rock.

There they squatted in a hellish half circle, their legs on the desert sand and their miters piercing the luminous clouds: sinister, wolflike, and double-headed, with faces of fury and right hands raised, dully and malignly watching the rim of man's world and guarding with horror the reaches of a cold northern world that is not man's. From their hideous laps rose evil Shantaks of elephantine bulk, but these all fled with insane titters as the vanguard of night-gaunts was sighted in the misty sky. Northward above those gargoyle mountains the army flew, and over leagues of dim desert where never a landmark rose. Less and less luminous grew the clouds, till at length Carter could see only blackness around him; but never did the winged steeds falter, bred as they were in earth's blackest crypts, and seeing not with any eyes but with the whole dank surface of their slippery forms. On and on they flew, past winds of dubious scent and sounds of dubious import, ever in thickest darkness, and covering such prodigious spaces that Carter wondered whether or not they could still be within earth's dreamland.

Then suddenly the clouds thinned and the stars shone spectrally above. All below was still black, but those pallid beacons in the sky seemed alive with a meaning and directiveness they had never possessed elsewhere. It was not that the figures of the constellations were different, but that the same familiar shapes now revealed a significance they had formerly failed to make plain. Everything focused toward the north; every curve and asterism of the glittering sky became part of a vast design whose function was to hurry first the eye and then the whole observer onward to some secret and terrible goal of convergence beyond the frozen waste that stretched endlessly ahead. Carter looked toward the east, where the great ridge of barrier peaks had towered along all the length of Inquanok, and saw against the stars a jagged silhouette which told of its continued presence. It was more broken now, with yawning clefts and fantastically erratic pinnacles; and Carter studied closely the suggestive turnings and inclinations of that grotesque outline, which seemed to share with the stars some subtle northward urge.

They were flying past at a tremendous speed, so that the watcher had to strain hard to catch details, when all at once he beheld just above the line of the topmost peaks a dark and moving object against the stars, whose course exactly paralleled that of his own bizarre party. The ghouls had likewise glimpsed it, for he heard their low glibbering all about him, and for a moment he fancied the object was a gigantic Shantak, of a size vastly greater than that of the average specimen. Soon, however, he saw that this theory would not hold, for the shape of the thing above the mountains was not that of any hippocephalic bird. Its outline against the stars, necessarily vague as it was, resembled rather some huge mitered head, or pair of heads, infinitely magnified, and its rapid, bobbing flight through the sky seemed most peculiarly a wingless one. Carter could not tell which side of the mountains it was on, but soon perceived that it had parts below the parts he had first seen, since it blotted out all the stars in places where the ridge was deeply cleft.

Then came a wide gap in the range, where the hideous reaches of transmontane Leng were joined to the cold waste on this side by a low pass through which the stars shone wanly. Carter watched this gap with intense care, knowing that he might see outlined against the sky beyond it the lower parts of the vast thing that flew undulantly above the pinnacles. The object had now floated ahead a trifle, and every eye of the party was fixed on the rift where it would presently appear in full-length silhouette. Gradually the huge thing above the peaks neared the gap, slightly slackening its speed as if conscious of having outdistanced the ghoulish army. For another minute suspense was keen, and then the brief instant of full silhouette and revelation came, bringing to the lips of the ghouls an awed and half-choked meep of cosmic fear, and to the soul of the traveler a chill that has never wholly left it. For the mammoth bobbing shape that overtopped the ridge was only a head—a mitered double head—and below it in terrible vastness loped the frightful swollen body that bore it: the mountain-high monstrosity that walked in stealth and silence; the hyena-like distortion of a giant anthropoid shape that trotted blackly against the sky, its repulsive pair of cone-capped heads reaching halfway to the zenith.

Carter did not lose consciousness or even scream aloud, for he was an old dreamer; but he looked behind him in horror and shuddered when he saw that there were other monstrous heads silhouetted above the level of the peaks, bobbing along stealthily after the first one. And straight in the rear were three of the mighty mountain shapes seen full against the southern stars, tiptoeing wolflike and lumberingly, their tall miters nodding thousands of feet in the air. The carved mountains, then, had not stayed squatting in that rigid semicircle north of Inquanok, with right hands uplifted. They had duties to perform, and were not remiss. But it was horrible that they never spoke, and never even made a sound in walking.

Meanwhile, the ghoul that had been Pickman had glibbered an order to the night-gaunts, and the whole army soared higher into the air. Up toward the stars the grotesque column shot, till nothing stood out any longer against the sky—neither the gray granite ridge that was still nor the carved mitered mountains that walked. All was blackness beneath as the fluttering legion surged northward amid rushing winds and invisible laughter in the ether, and never a Shantak or less-mentionable entity rose from the haunted wastes to pursue them. The farther they went the faster they flew, till soon their dizzying speed seemed to pass that of a rifle ball and approach that of a planet in its orbit. Carter wondered how with such speed the earth could still stretch beneath them, but knew that in the land of dream, dimensions have strange properties. That they were in a realm of eternal night he felt certain, and he fancied that the constellations overhead had subtly emphasized their northward focus—gathering themselves up, as it were, to cast the flying army into the void of the boreal pole as the folds of a bag are gathered up to cast out the last bits of substance therein.

Then he noticed with terror that the wings of the night-gaunts were not flapping anymore. The horned and faceless steeds had folded their membranous appendages and were resting quite passive in the chaos of wind that whirled and chuckled as it bore them on. A force not of earth had seized on the army, and ghouls and night-gaunts alike were powerless before a current which pulled madly and relentlessly into the north whence no mortal had ever returned. At length a lone, pallid light was seen on the skyline ahead, thereafter rising steadily as they approached, and having beneath it a black mass that blotted out the stars. Carter saw that it must be some beacon on a mountain, for only a mountain could rise so vast as seen from so prodigious a height in the air.

Higher and higher rose the light and the blackness beneath it, till half the northern sky was obscured by the rugged conical mass. Lofty as the army was, that pale and sinister beacon rose above it, towering monstrous over all peaks and concernments of earth, and tasting the atomless ether where the cryptic moon and the mad planets reel. No mountain known of man was that which loomed before them. The high clouds far below were but a fringe for its foothills. The groping dizziness of topmost air was but a girdle for its loins. Scornful and spectral climbed that bridge between earth and heaven, black in eternal night, and crowned with a pshent of unknown stars whose awful and significant outline grew every moment clearer. Ghouls meeped in wonder as they saw it, and Carter shivered in fear lest all the hurtling army be dashed to pieces on the unyielding onyx of that cyclopean cliff.

Higher and higher rose the light, till it mingled with the loftiest orbs of the zenith and winked down at the fliers with lurid mockery. All the north beneath it was blackness now—dread, stony blackness from infinite depths to infinite heights—with only that pale winking beacon perched unreachably at the top of all vision. Carter studied the light more closely, and saw at last what lines its inky background made against the stars. There were towers on that titan mountaintop—horrible domed towers in noxious and incalculable tiers and clusters beyond any dreamable workmanship of man; battlements and terraces of wonder and menace, all limned tiny and black and distant against the starry pshent that glowed malevolently at the uppermost rim of sight. Capping that most measureless of mountains was a castle beyond all mortal thought, and in it glowed the demon-light. Then Randolph Carter knew that his quest was done, and that he saw above him the goal of all forbidden steps and audacious visions: the fabulous, the incredible home of the Great Ones atop unknown Kadath.

Even as he realized this thing, Carter noticed a change in the course of the helplessly wind-sucked party. They were rising abruptly now, and it was plain that the focus of their flight was the onyx castle where the pale light shone. So close was the great black mountain that its sides sped by them dizzily as they shot upward, and in the darkness they could discern nothing upon it. Vaster and vaster loomed the tenebrous towers of the nighted castle above, and Carter could see that it was well-nigh blasphemous in its immensity. Well might its stones have been quarried by nameless workmen in that horrible gulf rent out of the rock in the hill pass north of Inquanok, for such was its size that a man on its threshold stood as it were in air above the spires of earth's loftiest fortress. The pshent of unknown stars above the myriad domed turrets glowed with a sallow, sickly flare, so that a kind of twilight hung about the murky walls of slippery onyx. The pallid beacon was now seen to be a single shining window high up in one of the loftiest towers, and as the helpless army neared the top of the mountain Carter thought he detected unpleasant shadows flitting across the feebly luminous expanse. It was a strangely arched window, of a design wholly alien to earth.

The solid rock now gave place to the giant foundations of

the monstrous castle, and it seemed that the speed of the party was somewhat abated. Vast walls shot up, and there was a glimpse of a great gate, through which the voyagers were swept. All was night in the titan courtyard, and then came the deeper blackness of inmost things as a huge arched portal engulfed the column. Vortices of cold wind surged dankly through sightless labyrinths of onyx, and Carter could never tell what cyclopean stairs and corridors lay silent along the route of his endless aerial twisting. Always upward led the terrible plunge in darkness, and never a sound, touch, or glimpse broke the dense pall of mystery. Large as the army of ghouls and night-gaunts was, it was lost in the prodigious voids of that more-than-earthly castle. And when at last there suddenly dawned around him the lurid light of that single tower room whose lofty window had served as a beacon, it took Carter long to discern the far walls and high, distant ceiling, and to realize that he was indeed not again in the boundless air outside.

Randolph Carter had hoped to come into the throne room of the Great Ones with poise and dignity, flanked and followed by impressive lines of ghouls in ceremonial order, and offering his prayer as a free and potent master among dreamers. He had known that the Great Ones themselves are not beyond a mortal's power to cope with, and had trusted to luck that the Other Gods and their crawling chaos Nyarlathotep would not happen to come to their aid at the crucial moment, as they had so often done before when men sought out earth's gods in their home or on their mountains. And with his hideous escort he had half hoped to defy even the Other Gods if need were, knowing as he did that ghouls have no masters, and that night-gaunts own not Nyarlathotep but only archaic Nodens for their lord. But now he saw that supernal Kadath, in its cold waste, is indeed girt with dark wonders and nameless sentinels, and that the Other Gods are of a surety vigilant in guarding the mild, feeble gods of earth. Void as they are of lordship over ghouls and night-gaunts, the mindless, shapeless blasphemies of outer space can yet control them when they must; so that it was not in state as a free and potent master of dreamers that Randolph Carter came into the Great Ones' throne room with his ghouls. Swept and herded by nightmare tempests from the stars, and dogged by unseen horrors of the northern waste, all that army floated captive and helpless in the lurid light, dropping numbly to the onyx floor when by some voiceless order the winds of fright dissolved.

Before no golden dais had Randolph Carter come, nor was there any august circle of crowned and haloed beings with narrow eyes, long-lobed ears, thin nose, and pointed chin whose kinship to the carved face on Ngranek might stamp them as those to whom a dreamer might pray. Save for the one tower room, the onyx castle atop Kadath was dark, and the masters were not there. Carter had come to unknown Kadath in the cold waste, but he had not found the gods. Yet still the lurid light glowed in that one tower room whose size was so little less than that of all outdoors, and whose distant walls and roof were so nearly lost to sight in thin, curling mists. Earth's gods were not there, it was true, but of subtler and less visible presences there could be no lack. Where the mild gods are absent, the Other Gods are not unrepresented; and certainly the onyx castle of castles was far from tenantless. In what outrageous form or forms terror would next reveal itself Carter could by no means imagine. He felt that his visit had been expected, and wondered how close a watch had all along been kept upon him by the crawling chaos Nyarlathotep. It is Nyarlathotep, horror of infinite shapes and dread soul and messenger of the Other Gods, that the fungous moon-beasts serve; and Carter thought of the black galley that had vanished when the tide of battle turned against the toadlike abnormalities on the jagged rock in the sea.

Reflecting upon these things, he was staggering to his feet in the midst of his nightmare company when there rang without warning through that palely lit and limitless chamber the hideous blast of a demon trumpet. Three times pealed that frightful brazen scream, and when the echoes of the third blast had died chucklingly away, Randolph Carter saw that he was alone. Whither, why, and how the ghouls and night-gaunts had been snatched from sight was not for him to divine. He knew only that he was suddenly alone, and that whatever unseen powers lurked mockingly around him were no powers of earth's friendly dreamland. Presently from the chamber's uttermost reaches a new sound came. This too was a rhythmic trumpeting, but of a kind far removed from the three raucous blasts which had dissolved his goodly cohorts. In this low fanfare echoed all the wonder and melody of ethereal dream: exotic vistas of unimagined loveliness floating from each strange chord and subtly alien cadence. Odors of incense came to match the golden notes, and overhead a great light dawned, its colors changing in cycles unknown to earth's spectrum, and following the song of the trumpets in weird symphonic harmonies. Torches flared in the distance, and the beat of drums throbbed nearer amid waves of tense expectancy.

Out of the thinning mists and the cloud of strange incenses filed twin columns of giant black slaves with loincloths of iridescent silk. Upon their heads were strapped vast helmetlike torches of glittering metal, from which the fragrance of obscure balsams spread in fumous spirals. In their right hands were crystal wands whose tips were carved into leering chimeras, while their left hands grasped long, thin silver trumpets which they blew in turn. Armlets and anklets of gold they had, and between each pair of anklets stretched a golden chain which held its wearer to a sober gait. That they were true black men of earth's dreamland was at once apparent, but it seemed less likely that their rites and costumes were wholly things of our earth. Ten feet from Carter the columns stopped, and as they did so each trumpet flew abruptly to its bearer's thick lips. Wild and ecstatic was the blast that followed, and wilder still the cry that chorused just after from dark throats somehow made shrill by strange artifice.

Then down the wide lane between the two columns a lone figure strode: a tall, slim figure with the young face of an antique Pharaoh, gay with prismatic robes and crowned with a golden pshent that glowed with inherent light. Close up to Carter strode that regal figure, whose proud carriage and smart features had in them the fascination of a dark god or fallen archangel, and around whose eyes there lurked the languid sparkle of capricious humor. It spoke, and in its mellow tones there rippled the wild music of Lethean streams.

"Randolph Carter," said the voice, "you have come to see the Great Ones whom it is unlawful for men to see. Watchers have spoken of this thing, and the Other Gods have grunted as they rolled and tumbled mindlessly to the sound of thin flutes in the black ultimate void where broods the demon-sultan whose name no lips dare speak aloud.

"When Barzai the Wise climbed Hatheg-Kla to see the Great Ones dance and howl above the clouds in the moonlight, he never returned. The Other Gods were there, and they did what was expected. Zenig of Aphorat sought to reach unknown Kadath in the cold waste, and his skull is now set in a ring on the little finger of one whom I need not name.

"But you, Randolph Carter, have braved all things of earth's dreamland, and burn still with the flame of quest. You came not as one curious, but as one seeking his due, nor have you ever failed in reverence toward the mild gods of earth. Yet have these gods kept you from the marvelous sunset city of your dreams, and wholly through their own small covetousness; for verily, they craved the weird loveliness of that which your fancy had fashioned, and vowed that henceforward no other spot should be their abode.

"They are gone from their castle on unknown Kadath to dwell in your marvelous city. All through its palaces of veined marble they revel by day, and when the sun sets they go out in the perfumed gardens and watch the golden glory on temples and colonnades, arched bridges and silver-basined fountains, and wide streets with blossom-laden urns and ivory statues in gleaming rows. And when night comes they climb tall terraces in the dew, and sit on carved benches of porphyry scanning the stars, or lean over pale balustrades to gaze at the town's steep northward slopes, where one by one the little windows in old peaked gables shine softly out with the calm yellow light of homely candles.

"The gods love your marvelous city, and walk no more in the ways of the gods. They have forgotten the high places of earth, and the mountains that knew their youth. The earth has no longer any gods that are gods, and only the Other Ones from outer space hold sway on unremembered Kadath. Far away in a valley of your own childhood, Randolph Carter, play the heedless Great Ones. You have dreamed too well, O wise arch-dreamer, for you have drawn dream's gods away from the world of all men's visions to that which is wholly yours, having built out of your boyhood's small fancies a city more lovely than all the phantoms that have gone before.

"It is not well that earth's gods leave their thrones for the spider to spin on, and their realm for the Others to sway in the dark manner of Others. Fain would the powers from outside bring chaos and horror to you, Randolph Carter, who are the cause of their upsetting, but that they know it is by you alone that the gods may be sent back to their world. In that half-waking dreamland which is yours, no power of uttermost night may pursue; and only you can send the selfish Great Ones gently out of your marvelous sunset city, back through the northern twilight to their wonted place atop unknown Kadath in the cold waste.

"So, Randolph Carter, in the name of the Other Gods I spare you and charge you to seek that sunset city which is yours, and to send thence the drowsy truant gods for whom the dream world waits. Not hard to find is that roseal fever of the gods, that fanfare of supernal trumpets and clash of immortal cymbals, that mystery whose place and meaning have haunted you through the halls of waking and the gulfs of dreaming, and tormented you with hints of vanished memory and the pain of lost things awesome and momentous. Not hard to find is that symbol and relic of your days of wonder, for truly, it is but the stable and eternal gem wherein all that wonder sparkles crystallized to light your evening path. Behold! It is not over unknown seas but back over well-known years that your quest must go: back to the bright strange things of infancy and the quick sun-drenched glimpses of magic that old scenes brought to wide young eyes.

"For know you that your gold-and-marble city of wonder is only the sum of what you have seen and loved in youth. It is the glory of Boston's hillside roofs and western windows aflame with sunset; of the flower-fragrant Common and the great dome on the hill and the tangle of gables and chimneys in the violet valley where the many-bridged Charles flows drowsily. These things you saw, Randolph Carter, when your nurse first wheeled you out in the springtime, and they will be the last things you will ever see with eyes of memory and of love. And there are antique Salem, with its brooding years, and spectral Marblehead, scaling its rocky precipices into past centuries, and the glory of Salem's towers and spires seen afar from Marblehead's pastures across the harbor against the setting sun.

"There are Providence, quaint and lordly on its seven hills over the blue harbor, with terraces of green leading up to steeples and citadels of living antiquity, and Newport, climbing wraithlike from its dreaming breakwater. Arkham is there, with its moss-grown gambrel roofs and the rocky rolling meadows behind it; and antediluvian Kingsport, hoary with stacked chimneys and deserted quays and overhanging gables, and the marvel of high cliffs and the milky-misted ocean with tolling buoys beyond.

"Cool vales in Concord, cobbled lanes in Portsmouth, twilight bends of rustic New Hampshire roads where giant elms half-hide white farmhouse walls and creaking well-sweeps. Gloucester's salt wharves, and Truro's windy willows. Vistas of distant steepled towns and hills beyond hills along the North Shore, hushed stony slopes and low ivied cottages in the lee of huge boulders in Rhode Island's backcountry. Scent of the sea and fragrance of the fields; spell of the dark woods and joy of the orchards and gardens at dawn. These, Randolph Carter, are your city; for they are yourself. New England bore you, and into your soul she poured a liquid loveliness which cannot die. This loveliness, molded, crystallized, and polished by years of memory and dreaming, is your terraced wonder of elusive sunsets; and to find that marble parapet with curious urns and carved rail, and descend at last those endless balustraded steps to the city of broad squares and prismatic fountains, you need only turn back to the thoughts and visions of your wistful boyhood.

"Look! through that window shine the stars of eternal night. Even now they are shining above the scenes you have known and cherished, drinking of their charm that they may shine more lovely over the gardens of dream. There is Antares—he is winking at this moment over the roofs of Tremont Street, and you could see him from your window on Beacon Hill. Out beyond those stars yawn the gulfs whence my mindless masters have sent me. Some day you too may traverse them, but if you are wise you will beware such folly; for of those mortals who have been and returned, only one preserves a mind unshattered by the pounding, clawing horrors of the void. Terrors and blasphemies gnaw at one another for space, and there is more evil in the lesser ones than in the greater—even as you know from the deeds of those who sought to deliver you into my hands, while I myself harbored no wish to shatter you, and would indeed have helped you hither long ago had I not been busy elsewhere, and certain that you would yourself find the way. Shun, then, the outer hells, and stick to the calm, lovely things of your youth. Seek out your marvelous city and drive thence the recreant Great Ones, sending them back gently to those scenes which are of their own youth, and which wait uneasy for their return.

"Easier even than the way of dim memory is the way I will prepare for you. See! There comes hither a monstrous Shantak, led by a slave who for your peace of mind had best keep invisible. Mount and be ready—there! Yogash the black will help you onto the scaly horror. Steer for that brightest star just south of the zenith—it is Vega, and in two hours will be just above the terrace of your sunset city. Steer for it only till you hear a far-off singing in the high ether. Higher than that lurks madness, so rein your Shantak when the first note lures. Look then back to earth, and you will see shining the deathless altar flame of Ired-Naa from the sacred roof of a temple. That temple is in your desiderate sunset city, so steer for it before you heed the singing and are lost.

"When you draw nigh the city, steer for the same high parapet whence of old you scanned the outspread glory, prodding the Shantak till he cry aloud. That cry the Great Ones will hear and know as they sit on their perfumed terraces, and there will come upon them such a homesickness that all of your city's wonders will not console them for the absence of Kadath's grim castle and the pshent of eternal stars that crowns it.

"Then must you land among them with the Shantak, and let them see and touch that noisome and hippocephalic bird, meanwhile discoursing to them of unknown Kadath, which you will so lately have left, and telling them how its boundless halls are lovely and unlighted, where of old they used to leap and revel in supernal radiance. And the Shantak will talk to them in the manner of Shantaks, but it will have no powers of persuasion beyond the recalling of elder days.

"Over and over must you speak to the wandering Great Ones of their home and youth, till at last they will weep and ask to be shown the returning path they have forgotten. Thereat can you loose the waiting Shantak, sending him skyward with the homing cry of his kind; hearing which the Great Ones will prance and jump with antique mirth, and forthwith stride after the loathly bird in the fashion of gods, through the deep gulfs of heaven to Kadath's familiar towers and domes.

"Then will the marvelous sunset city be yours to cherish and inhabit forever, and once more will earth's gods rule the dreams of men from their accustomed seat. Go now—the casement is open, and the stars await outside. Already your Shantak wheezes and titters with impatience. Steer for Vega through the night, but turn when the singing sounds. Forget not this warning, lest horrors unthinkable suck you into the gulf of shrieking and ululant madness. Remember the Other Gods; they are great and mindless and terrible, and lurk in the outer voids. They are good gods to shun.

"*Hei! Aa-shanta 'nygh!* You are off! Send back earth's gods to their haunts on unknown Kadath, and pray to all space that you may never meet me in my thousand other forms. Farewell, Randolph Carter, and beware; *for I am Nyarlathotep, the Crawling Chaos.*"

And Randolph Carter, gasping and dizzy on his hideous Shantak, shot screamingly into space toward the cold blue glare of boreal Vega, looking but once behind him at the clustered and chaotic turrets of the onyx nightmare wherein still glowed the lone lurid light of that window above the air and the clouds of earth's dreamland. Great polypous horrors slid darkly past, and unseen bat wings beat multitudinous around him, but still he clung to the unwholesome mane of that loathly and hippocephalic scaled bird. The stars danced mockingly, almost shifting now and then to form pale signs of doom that one might wonder one had not seen and feared before; and ever the winds of nether howled of vague blackness and loneliness beyond the cosmos.

Then through the glittering vault ahead there fell a hush of portent, and all the winds and horrors slunk away as night-things slink away before the dawn. Trembling in waves that golden wisps of nebula made weirdly visible, there rose a timid hint of far-off melody, droning in faint chords that our own universe of stars knows not. And as that music grew, the Shantak raised its ears and plunged ahead, and Carter likewise bent to catch each lovely strain. It was a song, but not the song of any voice. Night and the spheres sang it, and it was old when space and Nyarlathotep and the Other Gods were born.

Faster flew the Shantak, and lower bent the rider, drunk with the marvel of strange gulfs and whirling in the crystal coils of outer magic. Then came too late the warning of the evil one, the sardonic caution of the demon legate who had bidden the seeker beware the madness of that song. Only to taunt had Nyarlathotep marked out the way to safety and the marvelous sunset city; only to mock had that black messenger revealed the secret of these truant gods whose steps he could so easily lead back at will. For madness and the void's wild vengeance are Nyarlathotep's only gifts to the presumptuous; and frantically though the rider strove to turn his disgusting steed, that leering, tittering Shantak coursed on impetuous and relentless, flapping its great slippery wings in malignant joy, and headed for those unhallowed pits whither no dreams reach: that last amorphous blight of nethermost confusion where bubbles and blasphemes at infinity's center the mindless demon-sultan Azathoth, whose name no lips dare speak aloud.

Unswerving and obedient to the foul legate's orders, that hellish bird plunged onward through shoals of shapeless lurkers and caperers in darkness, and vacuous herds of drifting entities that pawed and groped and groped and pawed—the nameless larvae of the Other Gods, which are like them blind and without mind, and possessed of singular hungers and thirsts.

Onward unswerving and relentless, and tittering hilariously to watch the chuckling and hysterics into which the risen song of night and the spheres had turned, that eldritch scaly monster bore its helpless rider—hurtling and shooting, cleaving the uttermost rim and spanning the outermost abysses; leaving behind the stars and the realms of matter, and darting meteorlike through stark formlessness toward those inconceivable, unlighted chambers beyond time wherein Azathoth gnaws shapeless and ravenous amid the muffled, maddening beat of vile drums and the thin, monotonous whine of accursed flutes.

Onward—onward—through the screaming, cackling, and blackly populous gulfs—and then from some dim blessed distance there came an image and a thought to Randolph Carter the doomed. Too well had Nyarlathotep planned his mocking and his tantalizing, for he had brought up that which no gusts of icy terror could quite efface. Home—New England—Beacon Hill—the waking world.

"For know you that your gold-and-marble city of wonder is only the sum of what you have seen and loved in youth . . . the glory of Boston's hillside roofs and western windows aflame with sunset; of the flower-fragrant Common and the great dome on the hill and the tangle of gables and chimneys in the violet valley where the many-bridged Charles flows drowsily . . . this loveliness, molded, crystallized, and polished by years of memory and dreaming, is your terraced wonder of elusive sunsets; and to find that marble parapet with curious urns and carved rail, and descend at last those endless balustraded steps to the city of broad squares and prismatic fountains, you need only turn back to the thoughts and visions of your wistful boyhood."

Onward—onward—dizzily onward to ultimate doom through the blackness where sightless feelers pawed and slimy snouts jostled and nameless things tittered and tittered and tittered. But the image and the thought had come, and Randolph Carter knew clearly that he was dreaming and only dreaming, and that somewhere in the background the world of waking and the city of his infancy still lay. Words came again—"You need only turn back to the thoughts and visions of your wistful boyhood." Turn—turn—blackness on every side, but Randolph Carter could turn.

Thick though the rushing nightmare that clutched his senses, Randolph Carter could turn and move. He could move, and if he chose he could leap off the evil Shantak that bore him hurtlingly doomward at the orders of Nyarlathotep. He could leap off and dare those depths of night that yawned interminably down, those depths of fear whose terrors yet could not exceed the nameless doom that lurked waiting at chaos' core. He could turn and move and leap—he could—he would—he would—he would.

Off that vast hippocephalic abomination leaped the doomed and desperate dreamer, and down through endless voids of sentient blackness he fell. Eons reeled, universes died and were born again, stars became nebulae and nebulae became stars, and still Randolph Carter fell through those endless voids of sentient blackness.

Then, in the slow, creeping course of eternity, the utmost cycle of the cosmos churned itself into another futile completion, and all things became again as they were unreckoned kalpas ago. Matter and light were born anew as space had once known them; and comets, suns, and worlds sprang flaming into life, though nothing survived to tell that they had been and gone, been and gone, always and always, back to no first beginning.

And there was a firmament again, and a wind, and a glare of purple light in the eyes of the falling dreamer. There were gods and presences and wills; beauty and evil, and the shrieking of noxious night robbed of its prey. For through the unknown ultimate cycle had lived a thought and a vision of a dreamer's boyhood, and now there were remade a waking world and an old cherished city to body and to justify these things. Out of the void S'ngac the violet gas had pointed the way, and archaic Nodens was bellowing his guidance from unhinted deeps.

Stars swelled to dawns, and dawns burst into fountains of gold, carmine, and purple, and still the dreamer fell. Cries rent the ether as ribbons of light beat back the fiends from outside. And hoary Nodens raised a howl of triumph when Nyarlathotep, close on his quarry, stopped baffled by a glare that seared his formless hunting-horrors to gray dust. Randolph Carter had indeed descended at last the wide marmoreal flights to his marvelous city, for he had come again to the fair New England world that had wrought him.

So to the organ chords of morning's myriad whistles, and dawn's blaze thrown dazzling through purple panes by the great gold dome of the State House on the hill, Randolph

Carter leaped shoutingly awake within his Boston room. Birds sang in hidden gardens, and the perfume of trellised vines came wistful from arbors his grandfather had reared. Beauty and light glowed from classic mantel and carved cornice and walls grotesquely figured, while a sleek black cat rose yawning from hearthside sleep that his master's start and shriek had disturbed. And vast infinities away, past the Gate of Deeper Slumber and the enchanted wood and the garden lands and the Cerenerian Sea and the twilight reaches of Inquanok, the crawling chaos Nyarlathotep strode brooding into the onyx castle atop unknown Kadath in the cold waste, and taunted insolently the mild gods of earth whom he had snatched abruptly from their scented revels in the marvelous sunset city.

The Weeblies

BY ALGIS BUDRYS

THE FIRST Weeblie became conscious of its existence in the middle of a deep layer of carboniferous matter. If it had possessed hands, it would have scratched its head, except that its head was so located as to be inaccessible to its hands, if it had had any. Being a more or less empirical thinker, however, and never having heard of Descartes, the first Weeblie would have spat on its hands, conditions permitting, kicked out vigorously, and proceeded to work its way upward.

It came to a layer of striated igneous rock, and paused to weeb the first weeble.

The two Weeblies continued on their journey until they reached oil-bearing shale. They weebled.

Upward and onward went the four Weeblies. They found a pocket of coral limestone and weebled.

The eight Weeblies moved upward unhesitatingly. They reached sand, and weebled.

Limestone again. Weeble.

Oil pocket. Weeble.

Coal. Weeble.

Granite. Weeble. Weeble, weeble, *weeble!*

Fifty thousand Weeblies burst out of the ground just east of Dorothy, New Jersey, and continued to weeble.

In a top-secret government laboratory, Robert Herrick stepped away from his handiwork and lit a cork-tipped cigarette on the wrong end. He frowned, coughed the smoke out of his lungs, shrugged, and philosophically continued to puff on the cigarette. He ran his ragged fingertips through his hair and regarded the apparatus with a distrustful eye.

"Hmm," he said. He cracked his knuckles and scratched his nose. "Ha," he said.

He walked over to his locker and took out a copy of *Peace of Soul.* He flipped through the pages, searching the paragraphs with bemused attentiveness. After a time he put the volume back and resumed his former inspection of the hulking jumble of tubes, wires, and bus bars that barricaded one end of the room. "Ah, the hell with it!" he said, and stamped out the cigarette.

He picked up a PBX phone and started to dial a number, then looked at his wristwatch. "Jesus! O-three hundred!" he said, and dropped the receiver back on the cutoff button. He thought for a moment, then picked up the phone again and dialed for an outside line. In due course, he was connected with a number in the small town nearest the laboratory.

"Hello?" a low and friendly voice answered.

"Uh—Miss Hunicutt, is General Southey there? This is Robert Herrick," he said with some embarrassment.

"I'll call him," the same sweet voice answered.

Herrick couldn't be blamed for sighing at the contrast as a gruff military tone superseded Miss Hunicutt's. He winced a bit as General Southey barked, "Well, Herrick, it better be good!"

"Yes, sir. It is. That is, I've got something, at last."

"What? Impossible! Why, you haven't even spent a billion dollars yet!"

"I know, General. I'm sorry. There's a lot of development ahead, anyway," he said hastily.

"All right! Now then, what have you got?" the general said, mollified. After all, completion of the project meant a new assignment, almost certainly to a job where Miss Hunicutt could not follow.

"Well, I've succeeded in manufacturing the primary effect my theories indicated, but it's not very selective. In fact," he said, "it's not selective at all."

"Is that good or bad?"

"Both, I think."

"What kind of an answer is that? You scientists are always hedging!" the General said with asperity. "Oh, double-dash it! Wait for me at the lab! I'll be right over and take a look for myself!"

"Yes, sir," Herrick said unhappily. "I hope I'm not inconveniencing you too much, sir." His only answer was a slam of the receiver as the general left Miss Hunicutt's apartment in high dudgeon.

Weeble!

Officer Czypulzinkski of Traffic A in the City of New York looked down at the asphalt of his personal intersection. The Weeblie looked back at the officer. And since a Weeblie's head is somewhat unconventionally located, the effect was rather outré.

Weeble!

Officer Czypulzinkski took his Positive out of its holster.

Weeble! Followed by many weebles.

The officer replaced his weapon and walked to his call box with deliberate, if somewhat uneven, steps. His brow was carefully unknit. It was only when he picked up the phone that he began to cry, the bitter tears rolling down his cheeks. It had been a good, satisfying twenty-eight years on the Force. It broke his heart to have to report himself unfit for further duty.

General Southey strode into Herrick's laboratory. He advanced to the wall of equipment and stood looking at it. Herrick stood beside him, casting nervous glances at the bristling figure.

"Well, Herrick?" the general said.

"Yes, sir. That is, I'll show you, sir," Herrick said.

"Well, hurry up, man!" The general swung his swagger stick against his cavalry boots.

"As you know, sir," Robert said as he crossed over to a mouse cage and removed a sleepy rodent, "I've been working on Blitzer's application of Dammermacher's Postulations. It was my theory that a wave could be produced which would inhibit the electrochemical activities of the human central nervous system."

"Of course!" the general said.

"I was wrong, however," Herrick said, dragging a model of

the full-size apparatus out from under a bench. "Apparently, I either failed to interpret Blitzer's brilliant work correctly or else the poor slob was drunk and didn't know what he was doing himself. At any rate, the results, which should have been of the coma-inducing type, are fatal instead. Like this."

He popped the mouse into a glass cage, and then slid a movable grid over the enclosure. "This grid will confine the effect to the cage," he explained. "Now I push this button, and—" The mouse rolled over on its back and entered a cat-free nirvana.

The general's eyes pushed against their lids. "It's dead? You're sure?"

Herrick regarded his expression with distaste. "Quite." He pointed at the full-size instruments. "The large model is capable of broadcasting a wave which will reflect from the Heaviside layer, and will consequently blanket this entire planet."

"Think of that!" the general said. Then he jumped, thunderstruck. "Gad, man! This solves the Russian problem! Will the big model work? Of course it will, or you wouldn't have called me. Turn it on! Turn it on, Herrick! We'll get the Medal of Honor for this!" He ran around in a small circle, swishing at the air with his swagger stick. "Medal of Honor?" he muttered. "Medal of Honor nothing! By the ethylated ghost of U. S. Grant, *this is an election year!*" he exclaimed.

Herrick shook his head sadly. "I'm sorry, General, but it wouldn't work."

"Wouldn't work! What do you mean, it wouldn't work? You controlled it when you killed that mouse, didn't you? Tune it in for Russians, and turn it on! What could be simpler?"

"It could be done, of course," Herrick said. "But the Russians might wonder why we were building a grid enclosing their country. No, I'm afraid that, as it stands, the transmitter will kill everybody on earth. With the exception of me, of course," he added.

"You! What's different about you?" the general said apoplectically.

"I'd have to operate the machine, of course. The switch and power controls are located in the center of the transmitting coils. Ergo, the wave will reach everywhere but there."

"By God, Herrick, this smacks of rank cowardice!"

"I'm sorry, sir. I should have some progress toward a beam transmitter, at least, by next year. I hope that'll be good enough."

"It damn well better be, Herrick, it damn well better be! All right! I'm going back to bed! You'd better get some sleep too, boy! You look very agitated boy, very agitated! Is something bothering you?" the general said, and strode out the door without waiting for an answer.

Burns pulled the sheet out of the teletype. He crushed a cigarette into the already well-nicotined boards of the newsroom floor and carried the bulletin over to his typewriter. He rolled in a sheet of copy paper and began to construct a lead for a new story.

"Unless some method of killing these monsters is found," the Chief Executive averred today in an unprecedented emergency session which called many legislators away from their preelection campaigns, "we will find ourselves swamped by these—uh—animals."

Burns considered this journalistic gem, shook his head and tore it up. He had a hard enough time believing that people in New York could no longer walk the streets without treading on a constantly weebling carpet of Weeblies. How was he ever going to convince his hardbitten fellow Chicagoans? He gave up in disgust and decided to let the press association bulletin go as was. He got up and went to the water cooler.

Where the hell was everybody tonight? Night editing was bad enough without the added handicap of a missing staff. As he raised the paper cup to his lips, the lights went out.

"What the hell?" he said. At the same instant, there was a sound of breaking glass that came simultaneously from each of the windows. He spun around.

The Weeblies came pouring into the room, weebling as they came.

The television mast of the Empire State Building protruded from a sea, as did the *Chicago Tribune* tower. Somewhere under this new sea the old Atlantic ran, and far to the east the gilded onions of the Kremlin broke off under the mounting pressure. The sea weebled, and increased.

New Mexico had yet to see its first Weeblie. Herrick had that much to comfort him, and little else, for he was sorely preoccupied. He threw a screwdriver to the floor with a vicious swing of his arm and listened to the bounce with some satisfaction.

General Southey looked up from his seat on a bench. "Don't tell me you're giving up, man?" he barked.

"Look, let's face it, General, I can't turn this thing into a beam transmitter in the short time we've got left, much less 'tune it to Weeblies.' I appreciate the fact that if we don't get somewhere soon, we might as well not bother, but I wouldn't depend on the transmitter to be any help," Herrick said.

"Nonsense! You're not even trying!" the general barked. "Damn it, Herrick, I'm beginning to suspect you're a Red!"

"You leave Bobbie alone!" Miss Hunicutt blazed from her corner. "He's trying his best, while the two of us are just getting in his way."

Herrick smiled at her gratefully. Miss Hunicutt was not only of such stuff as dreams are made on, she was obviously of a high order of intelligence. He sighed in silent admiration as she ignored Southey's poisonous look.

"I suppose you'd rather be back in town, where the Weeblies might start popping out of the ground at any moment?" the general said testily.

"Never mind where I'm supposed to be," she replied with asperity. "Where are *you* supposed to be, if not with the Army, trying to do something about those *things?*"

"I told you before, and you both know it anyway, that there's nothing you *can* do to Weeblies," the general replied. "If you kill some of them, the rest just—uh—weeble harder to make up for the loss. Herrick's invention is our last hope, and we're not getting anywhere with that."

"Well, if Bobbie's sure he can't change it in time, there's only one thing left to do, then," Miss Hunicutt said firmly.

"What?" said the general. Herrick raised his eyebrows.

"Bobbie'll just have to turn on the machine as it is," she said.

"Have you gone mad? That would kill *everybody,* human and Weeblie!" the general cried.

"Would you rather suffocate and be crushed to death by the

Weeblies?" Miss Hunicutt said with unassailable logic. "*I* wouldn't. As long as there's no hope, we might as well die quickly."

The general looked at her narrowly. "You know," he said, "I *thought* there was something suspicious about you turning up in town just as the project got started." He pulled his service automatic out of its holster. "You're a Communist agent!" he yelled, and drew a bead on Miss Hunicutt, who stepped back and gave a little cry of alarm.

The cry penetrated to Robert's heart. With a lithe motion, he picked up a fairly heavy hammer and threw it at the general. There was a dull *thonk,* and General Southey sank to the floor, bouncing his already contused head. Herrick stood over him, breathing deeply in satisfaction. "Now, why didn't I think of that before?" he said.

Miss Hunicutt flew into his arms. "Oh, Bobbie, you're so *forceful,*" she murmured against his chest.

"There, there, it's all right," he said, patting her head. He looked over her shoulder through a window that overlooked the plain outside. He froze.

"Weeblies!" he said. Miss Hunicutt swung around in his arms.

Out on the plain, the weebling began.

"Come on!" Robert shouted, and pulled Miss Hunicutt after him.

"What are you going to do?" she asked.

"Turn the transmitter on," he said, pushing her into the small control cubicle at the center of the machine.

"But we'll die!" Miss Hunicutt exclaimed. "There won't be any danger for a while, anyway. I don't want to die, not now," she said, plucking at his sleeve with downcast eyes.

Robert gulped, but kept his head. "We'll be all right. The field can't reach us here, as long as we stay in the control cubicle," he explained.

"Will there be enough room?" Miss Hunicutt asked.

"There will be if we stand close together."

Naturally, then, he kept his hand on the switch far longer than necessary.

The weebling had stopped. They emerged into a quiet world.

Robert took Miss Hunicutt's hand. "We are the last two people alive," he said quietly. "The new Adam and Eve," he said rapturously. "We'll build a new world," he said a little later.

"Oh yes, Robert, a new world," Miss Hunicutt said. "The old one was such a *nasty* place, all full of Weeblies and *humans*."

Robert stared at her.

Miss Hunicutt smiled. She bleebled.

Phantas

BY OLIVER ONIONS

For, barring all pother,
With this, or the other,
Still Britons are Lords of the Main.
THE CHAPTER OF ADMIRALS

I

AS Abel Keeling lay on the galleon's deck, held from rolling down it only by his own weight and the sun-blackened hand that lay outstretched upon the planks, his gaze wandered, but ever returned to the bell that hung, jammed with the dangerous heel-over of the vessel, in the small ornamental belfry immediately abaft the mainmast. The bell was of cast bronze, with half-obliterated bosses upon it that had been the heads of cherubs; but wind and salt spray had given it a thick incrustation of bright, beautiful, lichenous green. It was this color that Abel Keeling's eyes liked.

For wherever else on the galleon his eyes rested they found only whiteness—the whiteness of extreme eld. There were slightly varying degrees in her whiteness; here she was of a white that glistened like salt granules, there of a grayish chalky white, and again her whiteness had the yellowish cast of decay; but everywhere it was the mild, disquieting whiteness of materials out of which the life had departed. Her cordage was bleached as old straw is bleached, and half her ropes kept their shape little more firmly than the ash of a string keeps its shape after the fire has passed; her pallid timbers were white and clean as bones found in sand; and even the wild frankincense with which (for lack of tar, at her last touching of land) she had been pitched had dried to a pale hard gum that sparkled like quartz in her open seams. The sun was yet so pale a buckler of silver through the still white mists that not a cord or timber cast a shadow; and only Abel Keeling's face and hands were black, carked and cinder-black from exposure to his pitiless rays.

The galleon was the *Mary of the Tower,* and she had a frightful list to starboard. So canted was she that her main yard dipped one of its steel sickles into the glassy water, and, had her foremast remained, or more than the broken stump of her bonaventure mizzen, she must have turned over completely. Many days ago they had stripped the main yard of its course, and had passed the sail under the *Mary*'s bottom, in the hope that it would stop the leak. This it had partly done as long as the galleon had continued to glide one way; then, without coming about, she had begun to glide the other, the ropes had parted, and she had dragged the sail after her, leaving a broad tarnish on the silver sea.

For it was broadside that the galleon glided, almost imperceptibly, ever sucking down. She glided as if a loadstone drew her, and, at first, Abel Keeling had thought it was a loadstone, pulling at her iron, drawing her through the pearly mists that lay like facecloths to the water and hid at a short distance the tarnish left by the sail. But later he had known that it was no loadstone drawing at her iron. The motion was due—must be due—to the absolute deadness of the calm in that silent, sinister, three-mile-broad waterway. With the eye of his mind he saw that loadstone now as he lay against a gun-truck, all but toppling down the deck. Soon that would happen again which had happened for five days past. He would hear again the chattering of monkeys and the screaming of parrots, the mat of green and yellow weeds would creep in toward the *Mary* over the quicksilver sea, and once more the sheer wall of rock would rise, and the men would run. . . .

But no; the men would not run this time to drop the fenders. There were no men left to do so, unless Bligh was still alive. Perhaps Bligh was still alive. He had walked half-way down the quarter-deck steps a little before the sudden nightfall of the day before, had then fallen and lain for a minute (dead, Abel Keeling had supposed, watching him from his place by the gun-truck), and had then got up again and tottered forward to the forecastle, his tall figure swaying and his long arms waving. Abel Keeling had not see him since. Most likely, he had died in the forecastle during the night. If he had not been dead he would have come aft again for water. . . .

At the remembrance of the water Abel Keeling lifted his head. The strands of lean muscle about his emaciated mouth worked, and he made a little pressure of his sun-blackened hand on the deck, as if to verify its steepness and his own balance. The mainmast was some seven or eight yards away. He put one stiff leg under him and began, seated as he was, to make shuffling movements down the slope.

To the mainmast, near the belfry, was affixed his contrivance for catching water. It consisted of a collar of rope set lower at one side than at the other (but that had been before the mast had steeved so many degrees away from the zenith), and tallowed beneath. The mists lingered later in that gully of a strait than they did on the open ocean, and the collar of rope served as a collector for the dews that condensed on the masts. The drops fell into a small earthen pipkin placed on the deck beneath it.

Abel Keeling reached the pipkin and looked into it. It was nearly a third full of fresh water. Good. If Bligh, the mate, was dead, so much the more water for Abel Keeling, master of the *Mary of the Tower.* He dipped two fingers into the pipkin and put them into his mouth. This he did several times. He did not dare to raise the pipkin to his black and broken lips for dread of a remembered agony, he could not have told how many days ago, when a devil had whispered to him, and he had gulped down the contents of the pipkin in the morning, and for the rest of the day had gone waterless. . . . Again he moistened his fingers and sucked them; then he lay sprawling against the mast, idly watching the drops of water as they fell.

It was odd how the drops formed. Slowly they collected at the edge of the tallowed collar, trembled in their fullness for an instant, and fell, another beginning the process instantly. It amused Abel Keeling to watch them. Why (he wondered) were all the drops the same size? What cause and compulsion did they obey that they never varied, and what frail tenuity held the little globules intact? It must be due to some Cause. . . . He remembered that the aromatic gum of the wild frankincense with which they had parcelled the seams had hung on the buckets in great sluggish gouts, obedient to a different compulsion; oil was different again, and so were juices and balsams. Only quicksilver (perhaps the heavy and motionless sea put him in mind of quicksilver) seemed obedient to no law. . . . Why was it so?

Bligh, of course, would have had his explanation: it was the Hand of God. That sufficed for Bligh, who had gone forward the evening before, and whom Abel Keeling now seemed vaguely and as at a distance to remember as the deep-voiced fanatic who had sung his hymns as, man by man, he had committed the bodies of the ship's company to the deep. Bligh was that sort of man; accepted things without question; was content to take things as they were and be ready with the fenders when the wall of rock rose out of the opalescent mists. Bligh, too, like the waterdrops, had his Law, that was his and nobody else's. . . .

There floated down from some rotten rope up aloft a flake of scurf, that settled in the pipkin. Abel Keeling watched it dully as it settled toward the pipkin's rim. When presently he again dipped his fingers into the vessel the water ran into a little vortex, drawing the flake with it. The water settled again; and again the minute flake determined toward the rim and adhered there, as if the rim had power to draw it. . . .

It was exactly so that the galleon was gliding toward the wall of rock, the yellow and green weeds, and the monkeys and parrots. Put out into mid-water again (while there had been men to put her out) she had glided to the other wall. One force drew the chip in the pipkin and the ship over the tranced sea. It was the Hand of God said Bligh. . . .

Abel Keeling, his mind now noting minute things and now clouded with torpor, did not at first hear a voice that was quakingly lifted up over by the forecastle—a voice that drew nearer, to an accompaniment of swirling water.

O Thou, that Jonas in the fish
Three days didst keep from pain,
Which was a figure of Thy death
And rising up again—

It was Bligh, singing one of his hymns:

O Thou, that Noah keptst from flood
And Abram, day by day,
As he along through Egypt passed
Didst guide him in the way—

The voice ceased, leaving the pious period uncompleted. Bligh was alive, at any rate. . . . Abel Keeling resumed his fitful musing.

Yes, that was the Law of Bligh's life, to call things the Hand of God; but Abel Keeling's Law was different; no better, no worse, only different. The Hand of God, that drew chips and galleons, must work by some method; and Abel Keeling's eyes were dully on the pipkin again as if he sought the method there. . . .

Then conscious thought left him for a space, and when he resumed it was without obvious connection.

Oars, of course, were the thing. With oars, men could laugh at calms. Oars, that only pinnaces and galleasses now used, had had their advantages. But oars (which was to say a method, for you could say if you liked that the Hand of God grasped the oar-loom, as the Breath of God filled the sail)—oars were antiquated, belonged to the past, and meant a throwing-over of all that was good and new and a return to fine lines, a battle formation abreast to give effect to the shock of the ram, and a day or two at sea and then to port again for provisions. Oars . . . no. Abel Keeling was one of the new men, the men who swore by the line-ahead, the broadside fire of sakers and demi-cannon, and weeks and months without a landfall. Perhaps one day the wits of such men as he would devise a craft, not oar-driven (because oars could not penetrate into the remote seas of the world)—not sail-driven (because men who trusted to sails found themselves in an airless, three-mile strait, suspended motionless between cloud and water, ever gliding to a wall of rock)—but a ship . . . a ship . . .

To Noah and his sons with him
God spake, and thus said He:
A cov'nant set I up with you
And your posterity—

It was Bligh again, wandering somewhere in the waist. Abel Keeling's mind was once more a blank. Then slowly, slowly, as the water drops collected on the collar of rope, his thought took shape again.

A galleasse? No, not a galleasse. The galleasse made shift to be two things, and was neither. This ship, that the hand of man should one day make for the Hand of God to manage, should be a ship that should take and conserve the force of the wind, take it and store it as she stored her victuals; at rest when she wished, going ahead when she wished; turning the forces both of calm and storm against themselves. For, of course, her force must be wind—stored wind—a bag of the winds, as the children's tale had it—wind probably directed upon the water astern, driving it away and urging forward the ship, acting by reaction. She would have a wind-chamber, into which wind would be pumped with pumps. . . . Bligh would call that equally the Hand of God, this driving force of the ship of the future that Abel Keeling dimly foreshadowed as he lay between the mainmast and the belfry, turning his eyes now and then from the ashy white timbers to the vivid green bronze-rust of the bell above him. . . .

Bligh's face, liver-colored with the sun and ravaged from inward by the faith that consumed him, appeared at the head of the quarter-deck steps. His voice beat uncontrolledly out.

And in the earth here is no place
Of refuge to be found,
Nor in the deep and water-course
That passeth under ground—

II

Bligh's eyes were lidded, as if in contemplation of his inner ecstasy. His head was thrown back, and his brows worked up and down tormentedly. His wide mouth remained open as his hymn was suddenly interrupted on the long-drawn note. From somewhere in the shimmering mists the note was taken up, and there drummed and rang and reverberated through the strait a windy, hoarse, and dismal bellow, alarming and sustained. A tremor rang through Bligh. Moving like a sightless man, he stumbled forward from the head of the quarter-deck steps, and Abel Keeling was aware of his gaunt figure behind him, taller for the steepness of the deck. As that vast empty sound died away, Bligh laughed in his mania.

"Lord, hath the grave's wide mouth a tongue to praise Thee? Lo, again—"

Again the cavernous sound possessed the air, louder and nearer. Through it came another sound, a slow throb, throb—throb, throb—Again the sounds ceased.

"Even Leviathan lifted up his voice in praise!" Bligh sobbed.

Abel Keeling did not raise his head. There had returned to him the memory of that day when, before the morning mists had lifted from the strait, he had emptied the pipkin of the water that was the allowance until night should fall again. During that agony of thirst he had seen shapes and heard sounds with other than his mortal eyes and ears, and even in the moments that had alternated with his lightness, when he had known these to be hallucinations, they had come again. He had heard the bells on a Sunday in his own Kentish home, the calling of children at play, the unconcerned singing of men at their daily labor, and the laughter and gossip of the women as they had spread the linen on the hedge or distributed bread upon the platters. These voices had rung in his brain, interrupted now and then by the groans of Bligh and of two other men who had been alive then. Some of the voices he had heard had been silent on earth this many a long year, but Abel Keeling, thirst-tortured, had heard them, even as he was now hearing that vacant moaning with the intermittent throbbing that filled the strait with alarm. . . .

"Praise Him, praise Him, praise Him!" Bligh was calling deliriously.

Then a bell seemed to sound in Abel Keeling's ears, and, as if something in the mechanism of his brain had slipped, another picture rose in his fancy—the scene when the *Mary of the Tower* had put out, to a bravery of swinging bells and shrill fifes and valiant trumpets. She had not been a leper-white galleon then. The scroll-work on her prow had twinkled with gilding; her belfry and stern galleries and elaborate lanterns had flashed in the sun with gold; and her fighting-tops and the warpavesse about her waist had been gay with painted coats and scutcheons. To her sails had been stitched gaudy ramping lions of scarlet say, and from her mainyard, now dipping in the water, had hung the broad two-tailed pennant with the Virgin and Child embroidered upon it. . . .

Then suddenly a voice about him seemed to be saying, "*And a half-seven—and a half-seven—*" and in a twink the picture in Abel Keeling's brain changed again. He was at home again, instructing his son, young Abel, in the casting of the lead from the skiff they had pulled out of the harbor.

"*And a half-seven!*" the boy seemed to be calling.

Abel Keeling's blackened lips muttered: "Excellently well cast, Abel, excellently well cast!"

"*And a half-seven—and a half-seven—seven—seven—*"

"Ah," Abel Keeling murmured, "that last was not a clear cast—give me the line—thus it should go . . . ay, so. . . . Soon you shall sail the seas with me in the *Mary of the Tower*. You are already perfect in the stars and the motions of the planets; tomorrow I will instruct you in the use of the back-staff. . . ."

For a minute or two he continued to mutter; then he dozed. When again he came to semi-consciousness it was once more to the sound of bells, at first faint, then louder, and finally becoming a noisy clamor immediately above his head. It was Bligh. Bligh, in a fresh attack of delirium, had seized the bell lanyard and was ringing the bell insanely. The cord broke in his fingers, but he thrust at the bell with his hand, and again called aloud.

"Upon a harp and an instrument of ten strings . . . let Heaven and Earth praise Thy Name! . . ."

He continued to call aloud, and to beat on the bronze-rusted bell.

"Ship ahoy! What ship's that?"

One would have said that a veritable hail had come out of the mists; but Abel Keeling knew those hails that came out of mists. They came from ships which were not there. "Ay, ay, keep a good lookout, and have a care to your lodemanage," he muttered again to his son. . . .

But, as sometimes a sleeper sits up in his dream, or rises from his couch and walks, so all of a sudden Abel Keeling found himself on his hands and knees on the deck, looking back over his shoulder. In some deep-seated region of his consciousness he was dimly aware that the cant of the deck had become more perilous, but his brain received the intelligence and forgot it again. He was looking out into the bright and baffling mists. The buckler of the sun was of a more ardent silver; the sea below it was lost in brilliant evaporation; and between them, suspended in the haze, no more substantial than the vague darknesses that float before dazzled eyes, a pyramidal phantom-shape hung. Abel Keeling passed his hand over his eyes, but when he removed it the shape was still there, gliding slowly towards the *Mary*'s quarter. Its form changed as he watched it. The spirit-gray shape that had been a pyramid seemed to dissolve into four upright members, slightly graduated in tallness, that nearest the *Mary*'s stern the tallest and that to the left the lowest. It might have been the shadow of the gigantic set of reed-pipes on which that vacant mournful note had been sounded.

And as he looked, with fooled eyes, again his ears became fooled:

"Ahoy there! What ship's that? Are you a ship? . . . Here, give me that trumpet—" Then a metallic barking. *"Ahoy there! What the devil are you? Didn't you ring a bell? Ring it again, or blow a blast or something, and go dead slow!"*

All this came, as it were, indistinctly, and through a sort of high singing in Abel Keeling's own ears. Then he fancied a short bewildered laugh, followed by a colloquy from somewhere between sea and sky.

"Here, Ward, just pinch me, will you? Tell me what you see there. I want to know if I'm awake."

"See where?"

"There, on the starboard bow. (Stop that ventilating fan; I can't hear myself think.) See anything? Don't tell me it's that damned Dutchman—don't pitch me that old Vanderdecken tale—give me an easy one first, something about a sea-serpent. . . . You did hear that bell, didn't you?"

"Shut up a minute—listen—"

Again Bligh's voice was lifted up.

This is the cov'nant that I make:
From henceforth nevermore
Will I again the world destroy
With water, as before.

Bligh's voice died away again in Abel Keeling's ears.

"Oh—my—fat—Aunt—Julia!" the voice that seemed to come from between sea and sky sounded again. Then it spoke more loudly. *"I say,"* it began with careful politeness, *"if you are a ship, do you mind telling us where the masquerade is to be? Our wireless is out of order, and we hadn't heard of it. . . . Oh, you do see it, Ward, don't you? . . . Please, please tell us what the hell you are!"*

Again Abel Keeling had moved as a sleepwalker moves. He had raised himself up by the belfry timbers, and Bligh had sunk in a heap on the deck. Abel Keeling's movement overturned the pipkin, which raced the little trickle of its contents down the deck and lodged where the still and brimming sea made, as it were, a chain with the carved balustrade of the quarter-deck—one link a still gleaming edge, then a dark baluster, and then another gleaming link. For one moment only Abel Keeling found himself noticing that that which had driven Bligh aft had been the rising of the water in the waist as the galleon settled by the head—the waist was now entirely submerged; then once more he was absorbed in his dream, its voices, and its shape in the mist, which had again taken the form of a pyramid before his eyes.

"Of course," a voice seemed to be complaining anew, and still through that confused dinning in Abel Keeling's ears, *"we can't turn a four-inch on it. . . . And, of course, Ward, I don't believe in 'em. D'you, hear, Ward? I don't believe in 'em, I*

say. . . . Shall we call down to old A.B.? This might interest His Scientific Skippership. . . ."

"*Oh, lower a boat and pull out to it—into it—over it—through it—*"

"*Look at our chaps crowded on the barbette yonder. They've seen it. Better not give an order you know won't be obeyed. . . .*"

Abel Keeling, cramped against the antique belfry, had begun to find his dream interesting. For, though he did not know her build, that mirage was in the shape of a ship. No doubt it was projected from his brooding on ships of half an hour before; and that was odd. . . . But perhaps, after all, it was not very odd. He knew that she did not really exist; only the appearance of her existed; but things had to exist like that before they really existed. Before the *Mary of the Tower* had existed she had been a shape in some man's imagination; before that, some dreamer had dreamed the form of a ship with oars; and before that, far away in the dawn and infancy of the world, some seer had seen in a vision the raft before man had ventured to push out over the water on his two planks. And since this shape that rode before Abel Keeling's eyes was a shape in his, Abel Keeling's dream, he, Abel Keeling, was the master of it. His own brooding brain had contrived her, and she was launched upon the illimitable ocean of his own mind. . . .

And I will not unmindful be
Of this, My cov'nant, passed
Twixt Me and you and every flesh
Whiles that the world should last,

sang Bligh, rapt. . . .

But as a dreamer, even in his dreams, will scratch upon the wall by his couch some key or word to put him in mind of his vision on the morrow when it has left him, so Abel Keeling found himself seeking some sign to be a proof to those to whom no vision is vouchsafed. Even Bligh sought that—could not be silent in his bliss, but lay on the deck there, uttering great passionate Amens and praising his Maker, as he said, upon a harp and an instrument of ten strings. So with Abel Keeling. It would be the Amen of his life to have praised

God, not upon a harp, but upon a ship that should carry her own power, that should store wind or its equivalent as she stored her victuals, that should be something wrested from the chaos of uninvention and ordered and disciplined and subordinated to Abel Keeling's will. . . . And there she was, that ship-shaped thing of spirit-gray, with the four pipes that resembled a phantom organ now broadside and of equal length. And the ghost-crew of that ship were speaking again. . . .

The interrupted silver chain by the quarter-deck balustrade had now become continuous, and the balusters made a herringbone over their own motionless reflections. The spilt water from the pipkin had dried, and the pipkin was not to be seen. Abel Keeling stood beside the mast, erect as God made man to go. With his leathery hand he smote upon the bell. He waited for the space of a minute, and then cried:

"Ahoy! . . . Ship ahoy! . . . What ship's that?"

III

We are not conscious in a dream that we are playing a game the beginning and end of which are in ourselves. In this dream of Abel Keeling's a voice replied:

"Hallo, it's found its tongue. . . . Ahoy there! What are you?"

Loudly and in a clear voice Abel Keeling called: "Are you a ship?"

With a nervous giggle the answer came:

"We are a ship, aren't we, Ward? I hardly feel sure. . . . Yes, of course, we're a ship. No question about us. The question is what the dickens you are."

Not all the words these voices used were intelligible to Abel Keeling, and he knew not what it was in the tone of these last words that reminded him of the honor due to the *Mary of the Tower.* Blister-white and at the end of her life as she was, Abel Keeling was still jealous of her dignity; the voice had a youngish ring; and it was not fitting that young chins should be wagged about his galleon. He spoke curtly.

"You that spoke—are you the master of that ship?"

"Officer of the watch," the words floated back; *"the captain's below."*

"Then send for him. It is with masters that masters hold speech," Abel Keeling replied.

He could see the two shapes, flat and without relief, standing on a high narrow structure with rails. One of them gave a low whistle, and seemed to be fanning his face; but the other rumbled something into a sort of funnel. Presently the two shapes became three. There was a murmuring, as of a consultation, and then suddenly a new voice spoke. At its thrill and tone a sudden tremor ran through Abel Keeling's frame. He wondered what response it was that that voice found in the forgotten recesses of his memory. . . .

"Ahoy!" seemed to call this new yet faintly remembered voice. *"What's all this about? Listen. We're His Majesty's destroyer* Seapink, *out of Devonport last October, and nothing particular the matter with us. Now who are you?"*

"The *Mary of the Tower*, out of the Port of Rye on the day of Saint Anne, and only two men—"

A gasp interrupted him.

"Out of where?" that voice that so strangely moved Abel Keeling said unsteadily, while Bligh broke into groans of renewed rapture.

"Out of the Port of Rye, in the County of Sussex . . . nay, give ear, else I cannot make you hear me while this man's spirit and flesh wrestle so together! . . . Ahoy! Are you gone?" For the voices had become a low murmur, and the ship shape had faded before Abel Keeling's eyes. Again and again he called. He wished to be informed of the disposition and economy of the wind-chamber. . . .

"The wind-chamber!" he called, in an agony lest the knowledge almost within his grasp should be lost. "I would know about the wind-chamber . . ."

Like an echo, there came back the words, uncomprehendingly uttered, *"The wind-chamber? . . ."*

". . . that driveth the vessel—perchance 'tis not wind—a steel bow that is bent also conserveth force—the force you store, to move at will through calm and storm. . . ."

"Can you make out what it's driving at?"

"Oh, we shall all wake up in a minute. . . ."

"Quiet, I have it; the engines; it wants to know about our engines. It'll be wanting to see our papers presently. Rye Port! . . . Well, no harm in humoring it; let's see what it can make of this. Ahoy there!" came the voice to Abel Keeling, a little strongly, as if a shifting wind carried it, and speaking faster and faster as it went on. *"Not wind, but steam; d'you hear? Steam, steam. Steam, in eight Yarrow water-tube boilers. S-t-e-a-m, steam. Got it? And we've twin-screw triple expansion engines, indicated horsepower four thousand, and we can do 430 revolutions per minute; savvy? Is there anything your phantomhood would like to know about our armament? . . .*

Abel Keeling was muttering fretfully to himself. It annoyed him that words in his own vision should have no meaning for him. How did words come to him in a dream that he had no knowledge of when wide awake? The *Seapink*—that was the name of this ship; but a pink was long and narrow, low-cargoed and square-built aft. . . .

"And as for our armament," the voice with the tones that so profoundly troubled Abel Keeling's memory continued, *"we've two revolving Whitehead torpedo-tubes, three six-pounders on the upper deck, and that's a twelve-pounder forward there by the conning-tower. I forgot to mention that we're nickel steel, with a coal capacity of sixty tons in most damnably placed bunkers, and that thirty and a quarter knots is about our top. Care to come aboard?"*

But the voice was speaking still more rapidly and feverishly, as if to fill a silence with no matter what, and the shape that was uttering it was straining forward anxiously over the rail.

"Ugh! But I'm glad this happened in the daylight," another voice was muttering.

"I wish I was sure it was happening at all. . . . Poor old spook!"

"I suppose it would keep its feet if her deck was quite vertical. Think she'll go down, or just melt?"

"Kind of go down . . . without wash . . ."

"Listen—here's the other one now—"

For Bligh was singing again:

For, Lord, Thou know'st our nature such
If we great things obtain

And in the getting of the same
Do feel no grief or pain,

We little do esteem thereof;
But, hardly brought to pass,
A thousand times we do esteem
More than the other was.

"But oh, look—look—look at the other! . . . Oh, I say, wasn't he a grand old boy! Look!"

For, transfiguring Abel Keeling's form as a prophet's form is transfigured in the instant of his rapture, flooding his brain with the white eureka-light of perfect knowledge, that for which he and his dream had been at a standstill had come. He knew her, this ship of the future, as if God's Finger had bitten her lines into his brain. He knew her as those already sinking into the grave know things, miraculously, completely, accepting Life's impossibilities with a nodded "Of course." From the ardent mouths of her eight furnaces to the last drip from her lubricators, from her bedplates to the breeches of her quick-firers, he knew her—read her gauges, thumbed her bearings, gave the ranges from her range-finders, and lived the life he lived who was in command of her. And he would not forget on the morrow, as he had forgotten on many morrows, for at last he had seen the water about his feet, and knew that there would be no morrow for him in this world. . . .

And even in that moment, with but a sand or two to run in his glass, indomitable, insatiable, dreaming dream on dream, he could not die until he knew more. He had two questions to ask, and a master-question; and but a moment remained. Sharply his voice rang out.

"Ho, there! . . . This ancient ship, the *Mary of the Tower*, cannot steam thirty and a quarter knots, but yet she can sail the waters. What more does your ship? Can she soar above them, as the fowls of the air soar?"

"Lord, he thinks we're an aeroplane! . . . No, she can't. . . ."

"And can you dive, even as the fishes of the deep?"

"No. . . . Those are submarines . . . we aren't a submarine. . . ."

But Abel Keeling waited for no more. He gave an exulting chuckle.

"Oho, oho—thirty knots, and but on the face of the waters—no more than that? Oho! . . . Now *my* ship, the ship I see as a mother sees full-grown the child she has but conceived—*my* ship I say—oho!—*my* ship. . . . Below there—trip that gun!"

The cry came suddenly and alertly, as a muffled sound came from below and an ominous tremor shook the galleon.

"By Jove, her guns are breaking loose below—that's her finish—"

"Trip that gun, and double-breech the others!" Abel Keeling's voice rang out, as if there had been any to obey him. He had braced himself within the belfry frame; and then in the middle of the next order his voice suddenly failed him. His ship shape, that for the moment he had forgotten, rode once more before his eyes. This was the end, and his master-question, apprehension for the answer to which was now torturing his face and well nigh bursting his heart, was still unasked.

"Ho—he that spoke with me—the master," he cried in a voice that ran high, "is he there?"

"Yes, yes!" came the other voice across the water, sick with suspense. *"Oh, be quick!"*

There was a moment in which hoarse cries from many voices, a heavy thud and rumble on wood, and a crash of timbers and a gurgle and a splash were indescribably mingled; the gun under which Abel Keeling had lain had snapped her rotten breechings and plunged down the deck, carrying Bligh's unconscious form with it. The deck came up vertical, and for one instant longer Abel Keeling clung to the belfry.

"I cannot see your face," he screamed, "but meseems your voice is a voice I know. *What is your name?"*

In a torn sob the answer came across the water:

"Keeling—Abel Keeling. . . . Oh, my God!"

And Abel Keeling's cry of triumph, that mounted to a victorious "Huzza!" was lost in the downward plunge of the *Mary of the Tower,* that left the strait empty save for the sun's fiery blaze and the last smoke-like evaporation of the mists.

Not Long Before the End

BY LARRY NIVEN

A SWORDSMAN battled a sorcerer, once upon a time.

In that age such battles were frequent. A natural antipathy exists between swordsmen and sorcerers, as between cats and small birds, or between rats and men. Usually the swordsman lost, and humanity's average intelligence rose some trifling fraction. Sometimes the swordsman won, and again the species was improved; for a sorcerer who cannot kill one miserable swordsman is a poor excuse for a sorcerer.

But this battle differed from the others. On one side, the sword itself was enchanted. On the other, the sorcerer knew a great and terrible truth.

We will call him the Warlock, as his name is both forgotten and impossible to pronounce. His parents had known what they were about. He who knows your name has power over you, but he must speak your name to use it.

The Warlock had found his terrible truth in middle age.

By that time he had traveled widely. It was not from choice. It was simply that he was a powerful magician, and he used his power, and he needed friends.

He knew spells to make people love a magician. The Warlock had tried these, but he did not like the side effects. So he commonly used his great power to help those around him, that they might love him without coercion.

He found that when he had been ten to fifteen years in a

place, using his magic as whim dictated, his powers would weaken. If he moved away, they returned. Twice he had had to move, and twice he had settled in a new land, learned new customs, made new friends. It happened a third time, and he prepared to move again. But something set him to wondering.

Why should a man's powers be so unfairly drained out of him?

It happened to nations, too. Throughout history, those lands which had been richest in magic had been overrun by barbarians carrying swords and clubs. It was a sad truth, and one that did not bear thinking about, but the Warlock's curiosity was strong.

So he wondered, and he stayed to perform certain experiments.

His last experiment involved a simple kinetic sorcery set to spin a metal disc in midair. And when that magic was done, he knew a truth he could never forget.

So he departed. In succeeding decades he moved again and again. Time changed his personality, if not his body, and his magic became more dependable, if less showy. He had discovered a great and terrible truth, and if he kept it secret, it was through compassion. His truth spelled the end of civilization, yet it was of no earthly use to anyone.

So he thought. But some five decades later (the date was on the order of 12,000 B.C.) it occurred to him that all truths find a use somewhere, sometime. And so he built another disc and recited spells over it, so that (like a telephone number already dialed but for one digit) the disc would be ready if ever he needed it.

The name of the sword was Glirendree. It was several hundred years old, and quite famous.

As for the swordsman, his name is no secret. It was Belhap Sattlestone Wirldess ag Miracloat roo Cononson. His friends, who tended to be temporary, called him Hap. He was a barbarian, of course. A civilized man would have had more sense than to touch Glirendree, and better morals than to stab a sleeping woman. Which was how Hap had acquired his sword. Or vice versa.

The Warlock recognized it long before he saw it. He was

at work in the cavern he had carved beneath a hill, when an alarm went off. The hair rose up, tingling, along the back of his neck. "Visitors," he said.

"I don't hear anything," said Sharla, but there was an uneasiness to her tone. Sharla was a girl of the village who had come to live with the Warlock. That day she had persuaded the Warlock to teach her some of his simpler spells.

"Don't you feel the hair rising on the back of your neck? I set the alarm to do that. Let me just check . . ." He used a sensor like a silver hula hoop set on edge. "There's trouble coming. Sharla, we've got to get you out of here."

"But . . ." Sharla waved protestingly at the table where they had been working.

"Oh, that. We can quit in the middle. That spell isn't dangerous." It was a charm against lovespells, rather messy to work, but safe and tame and effective. The Warlock pointed at the spear of light glaring through the hoopsensor. "That's dangerous. An enormously powerful focus of mana power is moving up the west side of the hill. You go down the east side."

"Can I help? You've taught me *some* magic."

The magician laughed a little nervously. "Against that? That's Glirendree. Look at the size of the image, the color, the shape. No. You get out of here, and right now. The hill's clear on the eastern slope."

"Come with me."

"I can't. Not with Glirendree loose. Not when it's already got hold of some idiot. There are obligations."

They came out of the cavern together, into the mansion they shared. Sharla, still protesting, donned robe and started down the hill. The Warlock hastily selected an armload of paraphernalia and went outside.

The intruder was halfway up the hill: a large but apparently human being carrying something long and glittering. He was still a quarter of an hour downslope. The Warlock set up the silver hula hoop and looked through it.

The sword was a flame of mana discharge, an eyehurting needle of white light. Glirendree, right enough. He knew of other, equally powerful mana foci, but none were portable, and none would show as a sword to the unaided eye.

He should have told Sharla to inform the Brotherhood. She had that much magic. Too late now.

There was no colored borderline to the spear of light.

No green fringe effect meant no protective spells. The swordsman had not tried to guard himself against what he carried. Certainly the intruder was no magician, and he had not the intelligence to get the help of a magician. Did he know *nothing* about Glirendree?

Not that that would help the Warlock. He who carried Glirendree was invulnerable to any power save Glirendree itself. Or so it was said.

"Let's test that," said the Warlock to himself. He dipped into his armload of equipment and came up with something wooden, shaped like an ocarina. He blew the dust off it, raised it in his fist and pointed it down the mountain. But he hesitated.

The loyalty spell was simple and safe, but it did have side effects. It lowered its victim's intelligence.

"Self-defense," the Warlock reminded himself, and blew into the ocarina.

The swordsman did not break stride. Glirendree didn't even glow; it had absorbed the spell that easily.

In minutes the swordsman would be here. The Warlock hurriedly set up a simple prognostics spell. At least he could learn who would win the coming battle.

No picture formed before him. The scenery did not even waver.

"Well now," said the Warlock. "*Well,* now!" And he reached into his clutter of sorcerous tools and found a metal disc. Another instant's rummaging produced a double-edged knife, profusely inscribed in no known language, and very sharp.

At the top of the Warlock's hill was a spring, and the stream from that spring ran past the Warlock's house. The swordsman stood leaning on his sword, facing the Warlock across that stream. He breathed deeply, for it had been a hard climb.

He was powerfully muscled and profusely scarred. To the Warlock it seemed strange that so young a man should have found time to acquire so many scars. But none of his wounds had impaired motor functions. The Warlock had watched him coming up the hill. The swordsman was in top physical shape.

His eyes were deep blue and brilliant, and half an inch too close together for the Warlock's taste.

"I am Hap," he called across the stream. "Where is she?"

"You mean Sharla, of course. But why is that your concern?"

"I have come to free her from her shameful bondage, old man. Too long have you—"

"Hey, hey, hey. Sharla's my *wife*."

"Too long have you used her for your vile and lecherous purposes. Too—"

"She stays of her own free will, you nit!"

"You expect me to believe that? As lovely a woman as Sharla, could she love an old and feeble warlock?"

"Do I look feeble?"

The Warlock did not look like an old man. He seemed Hap's age, some twenty years old, and his frame and his musculature were the equal of Hap's. He had not bothered to dress as he left the cavern. In place of Hap's scars, his back bore a tattoo in red and green and gold, an elaborately curlicued pentagramic design, almost hypnotic in its extradimensional involutions.

"Everyone in the village knows your age," said Hap. "You're two hundred years old, if not more."

"Hap," said the Warlock. "Belhap Something-or-other roo Cononson. Now I remember. Sharla told me you tried to bother her last time she went to the village. I should have done something about it then."

"Old man, you lie. Sharla is under a spell. Everybody knows the power of a Warlock's loyalty spell."

"I don't use them. I don't like the side effects. Who wants to be surrounded by friendly morons?" The Warlock pointed to Glirendree. "Do you know what you carry?"

Hap nodded ominously.

"Then you ought to know better. Maybe it's not too late. See if you can transfer it to your left hand."

"I tried that. I can't let go of it." Hap cut at the air, restlessly, with his sixty pounds of sword. "I have to sleep with the damned thing clutched in my hand."

"Well, it's too late then."

"It's worth it," Hap said grimly. "For now I can kill you.

Too long has an innocent woman been subjected to your lecherous—"

"I know, I know." The Warlock changed languages suddenly, speaking high and fast. He spoke thus for almost a minute, then switched back to Rynaldese. "Do you feel any pain?"

"Not a twinge," said Hap. He had not moved. He stood with his remarkable sword at the ready, glowering at the magician across the stream.

"No sudden urge to travel? Attacks of remorse? Change of body temperature?" But Hap was grinning now, not at all nicely. "I thought not. Well, it had to be tried."

There was an instant of blinding light.

When it reached the vicinity of the hill, the meteorite had dwindled to the size of a baseball. It should have finished its journey at the back of Hap's head. Instead, it exploded a millisecond too soon. When the light had died, Hap stood within a ring of craterlets.

The swordsman's unsymmetrical jaw dropped, and then he closed his mouth and started forward. The sword hummed faintly.

The Warlock turned his back.

Hap curled his lip at the Warlock's cowardice. Then he jumped three feet backward from a standing start. A shadow had pulled itself from the Warlock's back.

In a lunar cave with the sun glaring into its mouth, a man's shadow on the wall might have looked that sharp and black. The shadow dropped to the ground and stood up, a humanoid outline that was less a shape than a window view of the ultimate blackness beyond the death of the universe. Then it leapt.

Glirendree seemed to move of its own accord. It hacked the demon once lengthwise and once across, while the demon seemed to batter against an invisible shield, trying to reach Hap even as it died.

"Clever," Hap panted. "A pentagram on your back, a demon trapped inside."

"That's clever," said the Warlock, "but it didn't work. Carrying Glirendree works, but it's not clever. I ask you again, do you know what you carry?"

"The most powerful sword ever forged." Hap raised the

weapon high. His right arm was more heavily muscled than his left, and inches longer, as if Glirendree had been at work on it. "A sword to make me the equal of any warlock or sorceress, and without the help of demons, either. I had to kill a woman who loved me to get it, but I paid that price gladly. When I have sent you to your just reward, Sharla will come to me—"

"She'll spit in your eye. Now will you listen to me? Glirendree *is* a demon. If you had an ounce of sense, you'd cut your arm off at the elbow."

Hap looked startled. "You mean there's a demon imprisoned in the metal?"

"Get it through your head. *There is no metal.* It's a demon, a bound demon, and it's a parasite. It'll age you to death in a year unless you cut it loose. A Warlock of the northlands imprisoned it in its present form, then gave it to one of his bastards, Jeery of Something-or-other. Jeery conquered half this continent before he died on the battlefield of senile decay. It was given into the charge of the Rainbow Witch a year before I was born, because there never was a woman who had less use for people, especially men."

"Probably Glirendree's doing. Started her glands up again, did it? She should have guarded against that."

"A year," said Hap. "One year."

But the sword stirred restlessly in his hand. "It will be a glorious year," said Hap, and he came forward.

The Warlock picked up a copper disc. "Four," he said, and the disc spun in midair.

By the time Hap had sloshed through the stream, the disc was a blur of motion. The Warlock moved to keep it between himself and Hap, and Hap dared not touch it, for it would have sheared through anything at all. He crossed around it, but again the Warlock had darted to the other side. In the pause he snatched up something else: a silvery knife, profusely inscribed.

"Whatever that is," said Hap, "it can't hurt me. No magic can affect me while I carry Glirendree."

"True enough," said the Warlock. "The disc will lose its force in a minute anyway. In the meantime, I know a secret that I would like to tell, one I could never tell to a friend."

Hap raised Glirendree above his head and, twohanded, swung it down on the disc. The sword stopped jarringly at the disc's rim.

"It's protecting you," said the Warlock. "If Glirendree hit the rim now, the recoil would knock you clear down to the village. Can't you hear the hum?"

Hap heard the whine as the disc cut the air. The tone was going up and up the scale.

"You're stalling," he said.

"That's true. So? Can it hurt you?"

"No. You were saying you knew a secret." Hap braced himself, sword raised, on one side of the disc, which now glowed red at the edge.

"I've wanted to tell someone for such a long time. A hundred and fifty years. Even Sharla doesn't know." The Warlock still stood ready to run if the swordsman should come after him. "I'd learned a little magic in those days, not much compared to what I know now, but big, showy stuff. Castles floating in the air. Dragons with golden scales. Armies turned to stone, or wiped out by lightning, instead of simple death spells. Stuff like that takes a lot of power, you know."

"I've heard of such things."

"I did it all the time, for myself, for friends, for whoever happened to be king, or whomever I happened to be in love with. And I found that after I'd been settled for a while, the power would leave me. I'd have to move elsewhere to get it back."

The copper disc glowed bright orange with the heat of its spin. It should have fragmented, or melted, long ago.

"Then there are the dead places, the places where a warlock dares not go. Places where magic doesn't work. They tend to be rural areas, farmlands and sheep ranges, you can find the old cities, the castles built to float which now lie tilted on their sides, the unnaturally aged bones of dragons, like huge lizards from another age.

"So I started wondering."

Hap stepped back a bit from the heat of the disc. It glowed pure white now, and it was like a sun brought to earth. Through the glare Hap had lost sight of the Warlock.

"So I built a disc like this one and set it spinning. Just a simple kinetic sorcery, but with a constant acceleration and no limit point. You know what mana is?"

"What's happening to your voice?"

"Mana is the name we give to the power behind magic." The Warlock's voice had gone weak and high.

A horrible suspicion came to Hap. The Warlock had slipped down the hill, leaving his voice behind! Hap trotted around the disc, shading his eyes from its heat.

An old man sat on the other side of the disc. His arthritic fingers, half-crippled with swollen joints, played with a rune-inscribed knife. "What I found out—oh, there you are. Well, it's too late now."

Hap raised his sword, and his sword changed.

It was a massive red demon, horned and hooved, and its teeth were in Hap's right hand. It paused, deliberately, for the few seconds it took Hap to realize what had happened and to try to jerk away. Then it bit down, and the swordsman's hand was off at the wrist.

The demon reached out, slowly enough, but Hap in his surprise was unable to move. He felt the taloned fingers close his windpipe.

He felt the strength leak out of the taloned hand, and he saw surprise and dismay spread across the demon's face.

The disc exploded. All at once and nothing first, it disintegrated into a flat cloud of metallic particles and was gone, flashing away as so much meterorite dust. The light was as lightning striking at one's feet. The sound was its thunder. The smell was vaporized copper.

The demon faded, as a chameleon fades against its background. Fading, the demon slumped to the ground in slow motion, and faded further, and was gone. When Hap reached out with his foot, he touched only dirt.

Behind Hap was a trench of burnt earth.

The spring had stopped. The rocky bottom of the stream was drying in the sun.

The Warlock's cavern had collapsed. The furnishings of the Warlock's mansion had gone crashing down into that vast pit, but the mansion itself was gone without trace.

Hap clutched his messily severed wrist, and he said, "But what happened?"

"Mana," the Warlock mumbled. He spat out a complete set of blackened teeth. "Mana. What I discovered was that the power behind magic is a natural resource, like the fertility of the soil. When you use it up, it's gone."

"But—"

"Can you see why I kept it a secret? One day all the wide world's mana will be used up. No more mana, no more magic. Do you know that Atlantis is tectonically unstable? Succeeding sorcerer-kings renew the spells each generation to keep the whole continent from sliding into the sea. What happens when the spells don't work any more? They couldn't possibly evacuate the whole continent in time. Kinder not to let them know."

"But—that disc."

The Warlock grinned with his empty mouth and ran his hands through snowy hair. All the hair came off in his fingers, leaving his scalp bare and mottled. "Senility is like being drunk. The disc? I told you. A kinetic sorcery with no upper limit. The disc keeps accelerating until all the mana in the locality has been used up."

Hap moved a step forward. Shock had drained half his strength. His foot came down jarringly, as if all the spring were out of his muscles.

"You tried to kill me."

The Warlock nodded. "I figured if the disc didn't explode and kill you while you were trying to go around it, Glirendree would strangle you when the constraint wore off. What are you complaining about? It cost you a hand, but you're free of Glirendree."

Hap took another step, and another. His hand was beginning to hurt, and the pain gave him strength. "Old man," he said thickly. "Two hundred years old. I can break your neck with the hand you left me. And I will."

The Warlock raised the inscribed knife.

"That won't work. No more magic." Hap slapped the Warlock's hand away and took the Warlock by his bony throat.

The Warlock's hand brushed his easily aside, and came back, and up. Hap wrapped his arms around his belly and backed away with his eyes and mouth wide open. He sat down hard.

"A knife always works," said the Warlock.

"Oh," said Hap.

"I worked the metal myself, with ordinary blacksmith's tools, so the knife wouldn't crumble when the magic was gone. The runes aren't magic. They only say—"

"Oh," said Hap. "Oh." He toppled sideways.

The Warlock lowered himself onto his back. He held the knife up and read the markings, in a language only the Brotherhood remembered.

AND THIS, TOO, SHALL PASS AWAY. It was a very old platitude, even then.

He dropped his arm back and lay looking at the sky.

Presently the blue was blotted by a shadow.

"I told you to get out of here," he whispered.

"You should have known better. What's *happened* to you?"

"No more youth spells. I knew I'd have to do it when the prognostics' spell showed blank." He drew a ragged breath. "It was worth it. I killed Glirendree."

"Playing hero, at your age! What can I do? How can I help?"

"Get me down the hill before my heart stops. I never told you my true age—"

"I knew. The whole village knows." She pulled him to sitting position, pulled one of his arms around her neck. It felt dead. She shuddered, but she wrapped her own arm around his waist and gathered herself for the effort. "You're so thin! Come on, love. We're going to stand up." She took most of his weight onto her, and they stood up.

"Go slow. I can hear my heart trying to take off."

"How far do we have to go?"

"Just to the foot of the hill, I think. Then the spells will work again, and we can rest." He stumbled. "I'm going blind," he said.

"It's a smooth path, and all downhill."

"That's why I picked this place. I knew I'd have to use the disc someday. You can't throw away knowledge. Always the time comes when you use it, because you have to, because it's there."

"You've changed so. So—so ugly. And you smell."

The pulse fluttered in his neck, like a hummingbird's wings. "Maybe you won't want me, after seeing me like this."

"You can change back, can't you?"

"Sure. I can change to anything you like. What color eyes do you want?"

"I'll be like this myself someday," she said. Her voice held cool horror. And it was fading; he was going deaf.

"I'll teach you the proper spells, when you're ready. They're dangerous. Blackly dangerous."

She was silent for a time. Then: "What color were *his* eyes? You know, Belhap Sattlestone whatever."

"Forget it," said the Warlock, with a touch of pique.

And suddenly his sight was back.

But not forever, thought the Warlock as they stumbled through the sudden daylight. When the mana runs out, I'll go like a blown candle flame, and civilization will follow. No more magic, no more magic-based industries. Then the whole world will be barbarian until men learn a new way to coerce nature, and the swordsmen, the damned stupid swordsmen will win after all.